The
SOUND
of
WRITING

Books by Alan Cheuse

Candace and Other Stories

The Bohemians

The Grandmothers' Club

Fall Out of Heaven

The Tennessee Waltz and Other Stories

The Light Possessed

Books by Caroline Marshall

Fugitive Grace

The
SOUND
of
WRITING

Edited by Alan Cheuse
and Caroline Marshall

with an Introduction by
Richard Bausch

Anchor Books
DOUBLEDAY
New York   London   Toronto   Sydney   Auckland

AN ANCHOR BOOK
PUBLISHED BY DOUBLEDAY
a division of Bantam Doubleday Dell Publishing Group, Inc.
666 Fifth Avenue, New York, New York 10103

ANCHOR BOOKS, DOUBLEDAY, and the portrayal of an anchor
are trademarks of Doubleday, a division of Bantam Doubleday
Dell Publishing Group, Inc.

Library of Congress Cataloging-in-Publication Data
The Sound of writing / edited by Alan Cheuse and
Caroline Marshall; with an introduction by
Richard Bausch.
p.   cm.
1. Radio stories—United States.   2. Short stories.
I. Cheuse, Alan.   II. Marshall, Caroline, 1943–
PN6120.95.R27S68   1991   90-28482
813'.0108—dc20   CIP
ISBN 0-385-41670-9

CONTENTS

PREFACE

I was standing at the bar in the Great Hall of the Folger Library trying to get the bartender's attention. After an evening of readings sponsored by the PEN Faulkner Award Foundation, my thirst for good fiction had more than been quenched, but my throat was dry. Just then a lovely woman about five foot seven approached me in the company of bearded, red-haired short story writer and novelist Richard Bausch. Bausch made a quick introduction and left.

"I love your voice," the woman told me.

I felt the cold slap of a glass in my hand as the bartender finally came through for me.

"I'll drink to that," I said, never knowing what to do about such moments.

But this wasn't the beginning of romance; it was the beginning of work. The woman was Caroline Marshall, and she had come up to ask if I would like to help produce—and host—a short story magazine for radio called *The Sound of Writing*. The PEN Syndicated Fiction Project, of which she was Director, had produced two pilot series of thirteen half-hour shows in Chapel Hill for distribution by National Public Radio, she explained. Now it was time to launch a continuous season, moving production to Washington and NPR's own studios. Was I interested?

"Why don't we both drink to that?" I said.

We met a few times in the following weeks to set up some goals and guidelines for the show before I went away for the summer. We would use the Project's annual reservoir of stories to draw from. The show would present the best short short fiction we could get the country's best writers to submit to that pool: all new work, original stories of no more than ten pages or about twenty-five hundred words. If we could get good stories of fewer words, even better. And we wanted a nationwide mix—writers from the West, Midwest, Southwest, and South, as well as the usual suspects from the East. If we could group stories by motif or theme, that was okay. Mainly we wanted to put together the best truly national magazine of new short fiction for radio that we could.

Hundreds and hundreds of writers submitted stories to the PEN call for fiction. From new graduate students in MFA programs to Pulitzer Prize winners to novices launching their first manila envelopes and SASE's, they responded. As the stories began to come in, we put the production team together, with Caroline serving as Executive Producer. Mary Lou Finnegan, our first Senior Producer at NPR, was to oversee everything at the network in addition to cutting and mixing tape, giving it all her final professional touch. Joan Bellsey, one of the creators and directors of Children's Radio Theater—an old favorite from NPR Playhouse—would work as Director, putting out the call for and managing the actors and actresses who would form the nucleus of dramatic readers for the program: our storytellers. A few writers balked when we told them that they could not read their own work, but when they realized the technical difficulties involved, some acquiesced. Quite a few even said they were eager to hear the revelations offered by another's interpretation.

This collection presents a sampling of what NPR affiliates around the country began broadcasting in April 1989. It also includes a few selections from the two earlier pilot series of shows. Together, dear reader, dear listener, they should give you the flavor of what we, I believe rightly, call "America's only short story magazine of the air."

So here are some fine new stories for your delectation, all of them having been published—or aired, to be specific—for the first time on "The Sound of Writing." Some made my heart sing, some made me laugh out loud, some chilled me. So perhaps, after all, it was romance of a sort that began the night Caroline and I met for the first time.

—Alan Cheuse

Alan Cheuse is a writer of wonderful fiction—what he just said isn't true, of course. What actually happened was this: For years I had been listening to him talk about books on NPR's *All Things Considered* and thought his voice to be the velvet in NPR's weave of sonic textures. For months I had also been after Dick Bausch, by far one of the country's best story writers and novelists and a good friend both to the Project and me, to urge some people to send in stories for our annual reading period. You should meet Alan Cheuse, he kept telling me; Alan knows everybody. This exchange went on for nine months. Finally, that night at the Folger, I realized the time had come. It was then or never. I sidled up to Bausch.

"Oh, yeah," he said. "I keep forgetting. I'll be glad to introduce you." He grinned. This, I could tell, was going to be the impish Bausch at his best. "See that guy in the sports jacket over there? That's him." He gestured across the room, then turned back to the rapt couple awaiting the next twist in his joke. I looked where he had pointed. Sure enough, there stood a man in just such a jacket, surrounded by a small, animated covey of fellow reception-goers. Clearly he had just said something humorous too; the group was still chuckling as I approached and, emboldened by the evening's Scotch, interrupted.

Alan's fiction ends there; he quoted me accurately. I do love his voice. And I love his short stories and novels too. His fiction, as witness this instance, always improves on reality. Sometimes I edit Alan simply to let the truth break through, to paraphrase Frost. Alan Cheuse is his own best character—an uncommonly humane creature, generous with his many gifts, but playful too, and that's worth knowing. It's this combination of traits, and most especially that love of quite literally toying with real-life situations and scenes, I think, that makes him the artist he is. It's also what makes the radio show.

A sense of fun, of interest in others' work—a sense of family— has been the PEN Syndicated Fiction Project's animating principle since its inception. And I'm convinced therein lies its distinction. It is a lively democracy in what it does and how it does it and in the rich diversity that results. Each year a new panel of three writers chooses what they consider to be the best short fiction they can find from the stories submitted to the Project's month-long reading period in January. The fifty or so pieces they select usually represent twenty-five to thirty states and are drawn from more than three thousand manuscripts whose writers can be found busily printing out and photocopying in all fifty states. Some even come from foreign countries where U.S. citizens are living. And, as Alan says, they represent all stages of development.

When the Project was begun in 1982 as a joint venture of the Literature Program of the National Endowment for the Arts and New York's PEN American Center, the idea was to provide this annual quota of tales to the broad familial audience served by newspapers across the country. More pointedly, the idea was to return it to the pages of Sunday magazines where it had been a staple for about a hundred years—from the 1850s, when the likes of Stephen Crane's *The Red Badge of Courage* appeared in the *San Francisco Chronicle*, to the 1950s, when you could still find the sweet purity of work by Steinbeck and Hemingway nestled among ads for bedspreads. The idea was to revive a tradition, not as a simple triumph of nostalgia but as a going back, having learned what matters. Almost 600 stories have gone out to newspaper editors since then. About 450 of that number have been published by one or more of the twenty-eight newspapers that have participated since the Project began. These stories make luminous for us the lives we live as fathers, sons, daughters, mothers, aunts, uncles—lovers.

That is a lot of voices telling what life is like a little farther down the road, where the sun will set several hours from now, or just south of here, where the weather may be better. I like to think of them as tales, whether gossipy or sonorous in tone, told between far-flung branches of family in neighborhoods so dynamic as to stimulate imaginations with real urgency. It seems altogether fitting then that they should enter homes by way of two media popular with all ages—newspapers and radio—as a kind of news of kin and kindred spirits.

There are many whose efforts have made this possible. The genius of the Project's creators in setting it up has made the day-to-day working out both a pleasure and adventure. Mary Mac-Arthur and Frank Conroy, then of the Endowment, and Karen Kennerly, Executive Director of PEN, conceived of the Project and served it as early parents. Several years later, Richard Harteis, then Project Director, got together with a couple of the Project's loyal publishers from Chapel Hill—Mark Meares and John Fredette of *The Advocate*—and dreamed up the radio show, which they launched with the invaluable assistance of Bill Hardy, Professor of Radio, TV, and Motion Pictures at the University of North Carolina, and his Playmakers' Repertory Theater. They had the infinite good fortune to hook up with Mary Lou Finnegan, late of NPR, without whom there simply would never have been a *Sound of Writing*. To all of them this volume, and Alan and I as its editors, are indebted.

—Caroline Marshall

INTRODUCTION

The Irish short story writer Frank O'Connor once spoke of what
he believed to be a kind of dilution of the quality of spoken language
in the modern short story; the master stylists Joyce, Hemingway,
and Katherine Anne Porter had refined the form so much it was
always a matter of the printed page. One no longer heard a human
voice talking. This assessment has always seemed vaguely wrong-
headed to me, since I had felt from the beginning of my own
devotion to the short story that those voices I was hearing in my
head were the voices of a truer human speech somehow, a speech
whose refinements allowed for the kind of heightened expression
one always yearned for, but rarely got, in daily discourse.

Over the years I have striven in my own work to remove any
adornments of style that I felt stood a chance of interfering with
the drama I wanted to portray, believing as I did that in the best
stories the words, the effects, disappear—the author disappears
—and one is left only with the characters in their complications
and their strife, whatever that may be. This is nothing new, of
course (I've had great fun over the years of teaching literature,
getting students to attempt to describe what they think Shakespeare's opinions might have been on any subject, including the
murder of a king's children). But I would still subscribe to the view
that any attempt to make a short story more "talkie" or more like
some imaginary spoken voice, out of whatever good motives, remains in some way an exercise in style and, in my mind, will
almost always betray itself in the act of trying to be spontaneous
and "spoken."

We have here a collection of stories submitted in the knowledge
that they were to be read aloud over the nation's airwaves, and
what I find most pleasurable in them is the stubbornness with
which all of these writers, some of them better known than others,
have maintained their own voices for the exercise: one doesn't get
very far into Charles Baxter's "Lake Stephen" before recognizing
that wonderful writer's subtle shadings; one follows Louise Erdrich's "The Immaculate Conception of Carson DuPre" with the
usual amazement at the lyrical density and beauty of the language.
The same is true of John Updike's entry, titled "The Football Factory." Like all of Updike, it is a piece full of wonderful lures and

traps, and its surface trembles with a kind of pure prose music: a language no one could merely speak; you might as well try to whistle a fugue.

What this collection provides, then, is the kind of pleasure good books always provide, and never mind the fact that radio was involved. There are strong, subtly delineated stories here by some of the country's finest artists: people of steady accomplishment like Nicholas Delbanco, Rick Bass, Joy Williams, David Michael Kaplan, Madison Smartt Bell, and T. Boyle, to name a few. And there are stories by established masters like Wright Morris, Mary Lee Settle, Reynolds Price, Ursula Le Guin, and Joyce Carol Oates. There's a story by my old schoolmate Allan Gurganus, "Nativity, Caucasian," and an engaging piece about an old woman and wild birds by Ethan Canin (with whom I played slow-pitch softball once—I think his side won). There's even a story from novelist Susan Richards Shreve, who has been known to claim that she's not comfortable working in the genre; "The Locker Room" is very much like one of those marvelous moments that accumulate so powerfully in her novels.

But apart from the satisfactions to be found in the work of these more familiar names, this extraordinary collection also contains work by new, as yet unheralded writers like Steve Amick and Jude Roy, whose talent is obvious and whose stories stand quite well alongside those of their older contemporaries.

In short, this is a deeply satisfying collection of pieces, none of them obviously or overtly intended for spoken words, yet their distinctive voices whisper to us about ourselves as convincingly as the voices of good stories always do, whether they are written or oral.

Recently, I heard a young Assistant Professor of English remark that, given the new psychologies and approaches to criticism, given the rise of deconstructionism, he couldn't understand how anyone could be interested in writing stories about people anymore. Of course, as anyone with brains knows right away, this fellow has said more about himself than he has about the writing of fiction, and while I don't want to give such extravagant stupidity more than a moment's notice, I will go on to point out that this book is not for the ideologue among us. It is far too unruly and far too playful.

Finally, the most important thing in the story as a form is the story itself, and if that sounds redundant or in some way reductive, then so be it. Without story, one has only language languaging, as it were, and while there are plenty of dull prognosticators about short fiction out there who think the function of the story is to provide a pretext, an excuse to exercise the ability to fashion gorgeous, weightless sentences, there are always the many thousands of readers subscribing to all the magazines, big and small, who could not care less about these literary matters and want merely what people have always wanted from the earliest speech: to be told a story. Style or the lack of it, refinement or no, literary pretext or simple indulgence in plain skill, the story's the thing, to paraphrase old Will.

Here then, gentle reader, under the title *The Sound of Writing*, is a volume of stories, some of which, in your travels, you may have come across in the hiss and static of the nation's radio, each of which speaks its own language and makes its own set of refinements, and all of which partake of the old delight in narrative by which the transaction between writer and reader—that most civilized form of primitive play in the world (the contradiction in the line is paradoxical and exactly true)—always takes place. "As it was in the beginning, is now, and ever shall be...."

—Richard Bausch

The
SOUND
of
WRITING

Drunk in the Afternoon

EDWARD ABBEY

I've always wanted to write a story about getting drunk in the afternoon. Getting drunk in the afternoon was something I once did on a regular weekly basis for many years. Me and my friends, such as they were. I say "were" because most of them are now dead, have disappeared, or—making a transitive verb of it as in carefree colorful romantic Latin America—have *been* disappeared.

Alan was one. Fred made two, Bob the third.

These are fictitious names. The originals might have wives, children, family still living. Of course they do.

Friday was our favorite day for the operation, since none of us had classes on Saturday. We were students at the University of New Mexico when neither that university nor that state were much known outside of little circles in Carmel, Santa Monica, Cambridge, Greenwich Village, North Beach, and Palma de Majorca.

I'm talking about 1946–50. The three of us were World War II vets, G.I. Joes loafing through school on something called the G.I. Bill. Government Issue: everything in the American world had somehow become Government Issue. And we didn't object one bit. We were anarchists. The Government had only recently tried to kill us, tried hard and seriously, shipping us overseas to Italy where people we had never met or even heard of, perfect strangers, did their best to shoot us dead with Mauser rifles, Luger pistols, burp guns, mortar fire, screaming Mimis, the Anzio Express.

We met for lunch at Okie Joe's, an all-male beer joint right off campus. We began with a pitcher of beer. Then hamburgers to help absorb the second pitcher. When the third pitcher was empty we swaggered outside into the blaze of the New Mexico sun. I mean a desert sun, unmitigated by clouds, unmediated by humidity. We were a mile above sea level and the sun only about one mile higher. You could feel the flames.

Appearance is reality, said Lucretius, taking a tip from Epicurus and Democritus, and I thought he had it about right.

I was a philosophy major. Second lieutenant anyhow. Alan was queer for economics, Fred for math, Bob for political science—politics. And we had plans. I mean plans for reshaping things a little nearer to the natural desires of the human heart.

We climbed into Alan's car, a black Lincoln convertible about twelve years old. Beaten but functional. The doors worked but we climbed in over the doors. Why not? Why the hell not? The top was down. I mean the top was always down and why not? It never rained in New Mexico anyway, and if it did we'd simply drive faster, that's all, speed forward beneath the rain. Let it rain.

Fred pulled a pint of bourbon from his inside jacket pocket, unscrewed the cap, breaking the seal, and threw the cap away. Overboard. Into the abyss of eternity. My concept, his bottle cap, Alan's terminology, Bob's perception.

We headed north along the Rio Grande River on a street called—I forget what it was called. I'm not sure I knew even then. Probably it was called Rio Grande Street. Gone now, anyhow, superseded by eight lanes of stinking asphalt, the Interstate, or by something like Calle de Valle Oro or some such land developer's poesy.

And we always called the river the Rio Grande River. Any objections? We were veterans. Me and my friends had pushed the Germans all the way from Salerno to the Alps. With forty million Italians trying to help out.

The wind roared over our heads. The sun roared down—yes, you could hear it bellowing. Like a crown fire in a forest. Like a blast furnace with the hatch open. One mile above or 93 million miles above, whatever, you could hear that sun. Bellowing, screaming, howling, the cry of the hydrogen inferno. We heard and felt it, and we raced north at 80 miles an hour in that black open speedboat of a car.

Passing the pint around. Shouting at each other. Rosy mountains on the east, the black warts of old volcanoes on the west, the brown desert and the skinny river in between.

We discussed my new model for the moral universe. Romantic naturalism, I called it. All values grounded upon the new. Only change, I argued, made life possible; therefore, all that is good is necessarily derived from—novelty.

The flaw in my scheme was that word "novelty." Somehow it

lacked the weight and dignity of, say, "L'Être" or "Zeit" or "Sein" or "Neant" or "Process" or "Reality" or even "Frijoles." Think of refried frijoles. The intractable density of matter. Think of nausea.

The pint was near empty. We stopped at the next village, Alameda, for refueling. The bar was called La Cantina Contenta. A number of locals sat on a bench in the shade by the open door, watching us climb from the car. Bob fell down but rose quickly, brushed his pants, and led the way. Nobody laughed. The sunlight, bouncing off whitewashed adobe walls, burned our eyes. The locals muttered to each other in Spanish, avoiding stares. Fred and Bob were large fellows, bulky, and carried knives strapped to their belts.

Inside it was so dark we stumbled into each other, feeling our way toward the bar. Alan ordered four long-necked bottles of Lone Star, a fair regional beer from Dallas, Texas. Fred bought another bottle of bourbon, a full quart this time. Old Crow. He checked the seal. We all had money in our pockets. This was early in the month; our G.I. checks had arrived only two days before.

Bob found the jukebox and played our cantina theme, an old ranchero song: *Adios, muchachos, compañeros de mi vida*. A Zapatista song but applicable to World War II. We liked it. We loved it. It was a big hit that year. I pulled out some greenbacks and ordered drinks for every fatherless biped in the house. A safe gesture; there seemed to be only four or five *campesinos* lounging about in the darkness. I could afford it. As soon as the bartender started pouring, however, the men outside heard the news and hurried in.

But I could afford it. I had $60 in my pocket. Saludas! we greeted one another, all ten or eleven of them, the four of us. Everybody, everybody, joined the chorus. Goodbye, boys, buddies of my life. Comrades. Pals. Brothers. Mates. Hadn't Mexico also declared war on the Axis? Yes, I think it did. Maybe it didn't, but Mexico and New Mexico, Chicano and Anglo, we were all in this cool dark stinking little barroom together, if only for the moment.

Outside, early afternoon, the white light poured down with pure, divine intensity, forced the green leaves of the cottonwoods to shake and rustle, made the street's pale dust shimmer like a carpet of crystals, gave every shadow a hard edge and a deep absolute obscurity. Alan's black car, outlined in auras of reflected heat, floated six inches above the ground. We could see it through the open doorway, baking in the sun. We could see the two little boys on the far side of the car, removing a hubcap with a big screwdriver.

The bartender ran out and drove them off, waving his arms, shouting. He set the hubcap, open side up, like a plate, on the bar before us.

Fred explained his theory of irrational numbers, binary electives, and organic equations. Would lead, he argued, when he found the key connection, to a kind of cybernetic thinking machine that could digest numerical data in such quantity and at such velocity that science itself would make a quantum leap into whole new dimensions of power over nature.

Got too much power already, Bob argued, following Alan out into the blaze of light. We blinked, we staggered, we crawled up over the gunwales of the open boat and flopped inside. Four of us in the front seat, nobody in the rear except a case of beer that Alan had acquired, somehow, as we left. Elbows and impacted ribs, shoulders jammed, we shuffled the bottle left and right as somebody, Alan perhaps, piloted the car northward under the spangled light of the trees, up the dusty street scattering chickens, pursued by yapping curs, the final passionate farewells of our new friends at La Cantina Contenta still resounding in our ears, minds, blood, *corazones. Mi corazón es su corazón, compadre*. Remember that.

Power is our destiny, Fred argued in return. We are bound for Andromeda and beyond. The earth is but a footstool to the stars. God is our goal, God is our fate, and by God if God doesn't exist we shall create the S.O.B.

The wind howled, the sun screamed, the motor sang.

Redtail hawks squinted at us from the telephone poles, one hawk per mile, regular as command posts along the Manfred Line. One black buzzard soared above, waiting. The red needle crept to 70, 80, 85.

I never saw so blue a sky. A sky so bloody blue, so deeply transparent you could see infinity through it, the fine-grained blackness of outer space, the stellar clouds of the Horsehead Nebula.

We stopped at Algodones, next town up the road, for brief refreshment. Bob's turn to stand us all a round and he knew it. Alan performed a four-wheel drift on the plaza dust. Nice old mission church there, two wooden bell towers mounted on adobe walls four feet thick. Black crosses. Golden light. Magpies screeching in the cornfields. The bar did not have a name and didn't need one. Like the other it was black as a pit inside, cool, roomy, not crowded yet, stinking of stale beer and male sweat and dried urine, the way we liked it.

We ordered tequila, salt, limes. The management had no limes. Nor lemons either. *Sí, no tenemos limones.*

Who needs fruit, explained Bob.

We poured salt on our wrists, tipped off a shot of tequila, licked the salt, drank a second, chased it with beer, licked salt, felt good, shoved each other around a bit, and rambled out into the heat and the light.

Who's driving this car? Alan? Who's that under the wheel? Nobody's driving. We're all driving. Who's in charge here? We're all in charge. This here's America, my friends, this here's democracy, and if somebody doesn't step a little harder on the gas we'll never get to Santa Fe.

Pit stop! yelled Fred.

Brake drums screamed. The car lurched from the pavement, fishtailed through a hedge of rabbitbrush, bounded down the embankment of the roadway into a ravine.

Hang on! I shouted. Or somebody shouted. Or maybe we only thought it.

The Lincoln leaped from a four-foot cutbank and crashed onto a crust of red sand. A cloud of dust engulfed us.

Don't stop! Fred shouted. Keep going!

Alan, Bob, me, whoever was driving, kept the wheels spinning as we sashayed across the sand toward the mudbank on the opposite side, a thicket of chamisa, a grove of cottonwoods. We pulled into the shade, rammed a tree trunk, halted. The engine died. We piled out, clutching beer bottles by the neck.

Chinga los cosmos! bellowed Alan, unbuttoning his fly, thrusting his fist and bottle toward the blue. He flooded the nearest anthill. The fierce red ants came spilling out, eager for a fight. He backed off, dribbling on the avant garde. Hate ants, he snarled, always hated ants, the whole formic socioeconomic order. When I get *my* tractatus finished, when *I* show the world the *true* meaning of economic science—which is, by the way, economy, *economy*, not complexity; simplicity, not perplexity—then, *maybe*, because only through simplicity can we discover true *freedom*....

He stopped.

We stared at the sky. Our little auburn-colored dust cloud floated past. Far above, black against blue, redheaded against the infinite darkness of the universe, the solitary vulture cruised in lazy spirals, contemplating life, contemplating us. Where there's life, the vulture reasons, there is also death. And where there's death there's hope.

Bob knelt in the grass and weeds, vomiting. Terrible sounds, terrible, the death rattle of a dying soldier. But he'd feel better when he was finished.

Hot water streamed from the mashed radiator of the car.

Fred opened another beer, handed it to me, opened another for himself and another for Alan. My friends, he said, my good comrades, buddies, pals, *compañeros de mi vida*, let me tell you something. I want to tell you guys something you will always remember, never forget. I want you to remember this glorious moment, this radiant goddam hour, this splendid shining immortal day, for the rest of your miserable lives.

We got home that night, some way. We graduated from that New Mexico cow college a month later. We wandered off in various directions. For a few years we exchanged letters, then postcards, then Christmas cards, then nothing. That was thirty-seven years ago. I don't know anything about any of them now.

Unnaturally Warm for October

STEVE AMICK

1962—

Teens pour from Sarasota Central in droves, ignoring President Kennedy's pleas to be calm. The world is doomed; why go to high school? Who cares about Intro Physics, Home Ec, and Shop when the bomb's about to drop?

Dora stands in the parking lot, hotrod rubber squealing in all directions. The principal gapes like Quasimodo, framed in the office window high above the American flag, which whips wildly in the wind. The principal looks helpless, resigned to the mutiny, the thundering mayhem.

Mr. Compton, Dora's hip History teacher, runs down the marble front steps, surveying the damage the missile crisis is wreaking on so many young, fragile minds. Mr. Compton, gung-ho young, doubles as the track coach. "Come on, Dora," he says. "Come back inside. Let's forget this foolishness." He speaks in the low, urgent tones of a lover, like he's pleading with her to just *try* getting pinned, just for a week. "Everything will be okay," he says. "I promise."

He no longer sounds like a teacher; he's lost all his authority. If she skips school the last hour of her life, what's he going to do, give her detention?

Dora is a sharp cookie. Like the rest of the student body, she is in hysterics. But unlike the rest, she is aware she's in hysterics. She's on the honor roll, president of the debating team, and secretary of the Sarasota Snake Club. She thought she would be attending Swarthmore next year. She's no dummy; she knows she's reacting to mass hysteria.

Just last spring she got an A in Psychology.

Tears streak her Maybelline; she just *knows* it, but so what? "I've never done anything in life. Do you know what I'm telling you? Do you know what I'm saying?"

Mr. Compton blushes slightly, glancing down at his loafers. She can tell from his discomfort that he understands exactly. "I know what you're saying, Dora. You're a good girl. But believe me, there'll be a whole lifetime for that."

Dora burns. He's just saying that because he's buddies with Richard, her boyfriend. Just looking out for his interests while he's away with the Navy.

Richard's unbroken track records still gleam in the school's show-case, though he's worlds away in the first atomic sub, spanning the ocean floor, breaking all records for self-sustaining endurance. It seems like eons since he's been gone, but they all still worship him at Sarasota Central. Especially Dora. She has vowed to be true.

One of the hoodlum auto shop boys—she thinks his name is Elwin or Elvin or something—pulls up alongside her in a patchwork Mercury. "Give you a ride," he snarls, poker-faced behind dark glasses, like this isn't fazing him one bit.

She turns, mulling it over. Mr. Compton grabs her firmly, pinning her arms to her sides, and shakes her suddenly like some new dance craze. "Dora!" he says. "Get a grip on yourself! Don't go off half cocked now. This is all going to blow over, take my word for it. This is *not* the end of the world!"

At the mention of the end of the world, she launches into further sobbing and stamps her foot; her hair cascades around her face like blinders, and she squirms from his grasp.

She gets in the car with the boy, and as they tear out of the school lot, she can't help thinking of all the time she's wasted studying, and sitting in Sarasota Central, and just *thinking*. Well, no more!

Her books lie like abandoned toys on the asphalt.

Saying goodbye to her boyfriend, so long ago, she could almost see the hermetic hatch close down on him as he descended into the depths of the U.S.S. Nautilus, *cloistering him in an underwater monastery.*

Often, on the beach, watching the tubular waves like finely rolled Havanas, she feels the guilt of being free and basking in the warmth of the sun while he's somewhere under the Arctic ice cap, sucking up canned air.

Her friends tell her to be human, to accept a date once in a while.

"Don't be a nun," they tell her. "You're gonna be
time that sub comes up for air. How long has .
kissed a boy?"
  It was so long ago.

  They worm their way through the downtown traffic. No one ʋ
the street seems to know where to go. There's a gaggle of angry
car horns. Pedestrians mill around in the street, block the flow,
squint out at the water and up at the sky. They swarm in front of
the department stores, gawking at rows of TVs behind plate glass
windows. No one seems to know where to look. They all waddle
and collide like penguins.

  As they pass the soda fountain where the Snake Club holds its
meetings, Dora turns to catch a glimpse of herself reflected in the
store window, but all she sees is a wavering blue contrail; the
Mercury rolling by.

  In front of Levitz, the traffic is worse. They're stock-still now, not
going anywhere. "Come on, come on," Dora says, unnerved by the
urgency of her own voice.

  The boy squeezes the steering wheel, tense, like he's strangling
a helpless animal. "Earth science," he mutters. Dora knows what
he says but can't understand what it means. The words, breaking
from his scaly lips, sound more like a sailor's curse or something
you call out to start a drag race.

  Or even, she imagines, something you grunt out when you're
"doing it," that slips from your lips uncontrolled.

  "What?" she asks, and instantly regrets it, knowing this means
he'll turn and look at her. She looks to her lap, straightens her
pleats.

  But he doesn't look. He turns to the mirror, picks something
from his teeth, then wipes it through his greasy hair. "Earth science," he repeats. "Last fall. I was in your class for a while."

  Dora doesn't remember. And she's usually good with names.
Her mother taught her you should remember people's names to
get ahead in life.

  "For a while?" she asks.

  "The jerk caught me stealing this rock sulfur stuff and making
stink bombs. Threw me out—the jerk."

  Dora remembers the class now. Earth science. That's where she
met Richard, and they teamed up for their final project, and they
fell in love, and they got an A.

* * *

Her eyes burn. She's been up all night, thanks to her mom. She's been punchy all day, wired, restless—even when Mr. Compton rolled in the big TV set on wheels so they could watch Adlai Stevenson hold up a blurry aerial photograph of what looked like a KOA campground. That must have been what really triggered the panic in the students, the fact that they were watching television in school. With Mr. Compton, of all people, who always chided them for doing their homework in front of the television.

Obviously, things were getting out of hand.

A big TV, too. Twenty-four inches. Full color.

And when they were herded out into the hallways to practice the "take-over drill" for the third day in a row—the teachers standing above them as they cringed below—most everybody took off in a rumbling charivari or devil's tattoo of saddle shoes and jackboots.

"Know what?" he asks, grinning. "I heard Compton and Mrs. Futelli were doing it today, in school. In the science lab."

Dora is shocked. "No way."

His head bobs like an undulating cobra. "Uh-huh. My buddy saw them. Right in the office off the science lab. Where they store all those chemicals, like rock sulfur and stuff."

Dora refuses to accept it. It can't be. Not in the science lab, anyway. It's just too . . . too unscientific.

"Right on the lab table," he says. "Right there doing it." He smirks, like *This is my kinda day!*

The night before, Dora's mom dragged her to Levitz, fighting their way through the hubbub downtown, to buy furniture. All new. "Everything must go," her mom said, numbly repeating something she'd heard on TV. Dora protested—they couldn't afford even a new ottoman, let alone all new furniture—but her mom insisted. "I'm the mom," she said. "You can make the mistakes when you're the mom."

When she saw the Swedish line, Dora's mom looked like she was going to cry. She slid one gloved hand along the blond wood backrest of a three-piece sectional, square and clean and sturdy. Her mom was a mess—they'd left home much too quickly for the proper pillbox look, mandatory for all servicemen's wives. "There was a time," her mother murmured, sinking down into the sensible cushion, "when this was going to be my life."

Dora stood back and watched as her mom negotiated with the salesman. She seemed uncharacteristically firm as she demanded, and got, not only a credit account but also a guarantee that the furniture would be delivered that very evening.

Dora imagined this was how her mother handled things once, in a time when life was going her way.

The furniture arrived that night, as promised, and the deliverymen insisted on blaring their radio in the drive, to keep updated as they lugged it all inside.

Once it was all in the front hall, her mom made her help redecorate. Dora stood by while her mother, hands on blue-jeaned hips, stared at the chaotic room, trying to decide where it should all go, then changing her mind once it was in place. Over and over, they had to move the furniture till it was *just so*.

"Mom," Dora said, "I really gotta do my homework and go to bed."

Dora's mom said "Fiddlesticks" and they stayed up till 4 A.M., trying to make it just perfect, trying to make it the way her mother had always wanted it to be.

She's got it all worked out. Richard will come home next year, amid fanfare, they'll drive up east, scattering autumnal leaves in their wake along some calendaresque covered-bridge rural road. Richard will attend school too, on the G.I. bill. They'll work together, hand in hand, in the reptile field. Then they'll get married, do it, and have children.

In that order.

With the furniture just so, her mom told her a story. Dora really didn't want to hear it; she just wanted to get some sleep so she could catch the bus to school in the morning.

The story was much more than Dora wanted to hear. It was about how Dora's mom had great dreams of doing this for a living: of going off to New York and working in interior design. It was about saying goodbye to her boyfriend, who was about to be shipped off to the Pacific and, possibly, death, and how she so wanted to do it right.

So they said goodbye. They said goodbye all night long, and the next week she got a vague, cryptic letter saying he'd been reas-

signed. He was stationed somewhere in the Southwest. Los Alamos,
she found out later, but at the time he couldn't be specific. But it
was clear that unless the Luftwaffe started strafing pueblos and
saguaro cactus, he was way, way out of the action.

"And nine months later," she told Dora, "you were born. So I
miss out on a career and you miss out on a dad that's around."

When she was done telling it, Dora asked, "Why are you telling
me all this?"

"Oh," her mom said, "I was planning to tell you sometime—
when you're a woman." She turned away suddenly, busying herself with straightening the stack of magazines on the spotless
new coffee table. Dora couldn't recognize anything in her eyes.
"Don't worry about it; I don't know why I'm telling you now."

At the boy's house, a beat-up sky-blue trailer home slouching
listlessly by the water, they park and go around back to the ski
boat he built himself. "Final project for shop class," he mutters. It
lolls impossibly low in the water, with the name *Fireball* stenciled
on the stern in flaming red.

The Gulf of Mexico shimmers like aluminum foil. The bull's-eye
sun sags low now, edging down to the waterline, and they head right
for it, cutting straight out to sea, as far away from it all as possible.

*The closest she has ever come was the night of the Science Fair.
She wins the regional trophy for her model of a nuclear reactor
and its effect on reptile life, using garden hose, hula hoops, and a
Quaker Oats box. Richard is so proud of her; he beams like she's
just given birth to twins. They stay out late, celebrating over chili
dogs as big as boas, and they talk about doing it, but then, Dora
remembers, she finally comes to her senses.*

It's simply irrational not to wait.

*Dora knows, from Health class and as her mother has told her
so many times, that if she even does it once, even with someone
she loves and plans to marry—even if she merely touches it—
poof! She will be pregnant instantly, like a sure-fire chemistry ex-
periment, complete with smoke and stench and pyrotechnics, the
kind Mrs. Futelli performs for her Intro classes, where it's supposed
to be a surprise, but you can tell from the blankness of her face
that she knows how it will turn out.*

Elvin—or whoever—cuts the engine. The Evinrude grumbles;
water laps insolently against the hull. He stands, staring out at the

sun as if she's not even there, unbuckles his crocodile belt, and drops it, dangling, to the deck like a battered water moccasin. He strips off his T-shirt, pulls out his Bronx wallet, and dives overboard in his jeans: gone. The water is as still as a desert. The sun rages, shiny and angry-red as Khrushchev's hairless head. Dora squats, huddles against her knees, cradling her head. She can hear her watch tick.

He rockets to the surface with a fiendish grin, his hair splattered across his forehead like kelp, and tells her to come on in, to live a little.

He fumbles below the murky waterline, like he's doing some underwater magic trick, then throws something up onto the deck, spraying her and landing with a cartoon *splat*. It's his jeans and underwear.

She twists and contorts her arm around to the small of her back and unzips her dress. What does it matter? Who will he tell? No one cares if you're naked at the end of the world.

Without even testing the water first, she dives right in.

The gulf is unnaturally warm for October. Dora imagines her boyfriend, many miles below the surface, churning up the water, generating heat with his subatomic voodoo and hijinks.

She imagines the conning tower, rising up through the water like a marlin's fluke. Richard to the rescue, bold as bullets, decked out in full dress whites.

But she knows full well not even an atomic sub will save the world.

She glues clippings from newspapers and magazines, everything she can find on the U.S.S. Nautilus, *to her bedroom wall: a shrine to her boyfriend. She will wait.*

On the *Fireball*, she makes no demands, preparations, or bargains.

His wet stringy hair hangs in her face, greasy and black as an overhauled cam. With his body on top of hers, blocking out the sun, she thinks of the years of useless lessons, Civil Defense drills, being brainwashed to "duck and cover." He works away earnestly, arching his back as if in pain, as if he's had a sudden realization or been struck by lightning. She tucks her knees in tight, as instructed. Duck and cover. She knows from science class that this would do nothing to protect you. It's futile. She knows now that protection would be a joke. Something has detonated inside her, an unstoppable molecular chain reaction. No matter; they will all be dead anyway. No college, no future with Richard. No motherhood, no babies, no worries.

She lies on the deck, her back rubbed raw. There is the stink of fish heads deep in the wood. There is the insect hum of his transistor radio. The deejay plays "Beyond the Sea." It was "their" song, so long ago.

There is no remorse, no panic at the prospect of facing her mom and dad, her doctor, her boyfriend Richard. Richard, unaware of the Nightly News, will go easily, placidly, not having to see it, merely sinking deeper into his cold Pacific tomb.

But the sky is as clear as pure reason; the sun, red as Castro's heart. On the radio, there are no urgent news bulletins cutting through the cheesy whine of Bobby Darin. She listens, but they're just playing music. No news reports.

She lies back, waiting for the sun to envelop them in a cold flash. Waiting for the end. Waiting for Kennedy and Khrushchev to do their thing.

The sun seems to cling to the skyline, hovering over the horizon, tenaciously. It looks exactly like it did yesterday, and the day before.

Heartwood

~~~~~~

RICK BASS

Two boys, wild boys, in my—our—valley, but it wasn't their fault. The valley itself was wild; how could they be otherwise? Victor was tall, massive, a man already—he helped his mother in the mercantile, rather than going to school. His friend, Percy, didn't do much of anything. Percy's father, whose last name was Coward, was an alcoholic, and his mother did most of the chores around the house: the wood-splitting and baby-raising, the cooking, the egg-collecting. It was funny how we had already written Percy off, even though he had just turned fifteen.

Percy was short and pale, thin, and he bruised easily. He always seemed to be wiping his nose. One eye went slightly off course, when he tried to focus on something. The cabin he lived in was back in the woods, with only propane lanterns for lighting, so it was always a little dark in his house. His hair was never combed.

When Percy's father was cognizant enough to crawl down the Yaak River Road and make it into the bar, things were okay. But usually his father just stayed at home and drank. He threw things at Percy when life wasn't going well: chunks of firewood, beer bottles, stones, cats.... Mister Coward was a large man who had lost his leg in a logging accident almost eight years ago, when Percy was seven, and even then Mister Coward had been a drinker. It just got worse, was all—after the accident.

What Percy and Victor began to do, when they turned fifteen, was to drive long steel nails deep into the trunks of all the giant larch trees in the valley. A single larch tree, a hundred and fifty or two hundred feet tall and as big around at the base as a small car, could be worth several thousand dollars to a logging crew, and the valley used to be filled with them, a sea of giant larches, trees that had already been a hundred years old back when the big fire of 1910 came through, destroying everything else, but now they were being logged out.

The way I knew the boys were doing it—spiking the big larch trees—was that they kept their spikes in my hay barn; and they painted murals of their deeds inside the barn, with cans of spray paint, on the barn's old weathered wood walls.

I never spoke to the boys, not once—words did not pass between us. When we saw each other we'd look long and hard—centuries, and forests, of words between us—but we never ever spoke. Why did they choose my barn?

Because they could read my heart, I believe. They were devils, they were cold men and wild—already. Dirt and fright and wildness were in their hearts. I'm pretty sure they wanted me to join them.

I loved those trees. I loved wildness, too, but was frightened of it.

The boys met in my barn nearly every night, with a lantern, and painted their pictures—bright red and blue and yellow hieroglyphics—two boys in the forest, pounding spikes into glowing trees—the spiked trees in the paintings had strange yellow halos—and they'd spray-paint the names of the locations beneath the paintings each night, after they'd done their work: Vinal Ridge Road, Flatiron Mountain Road, Lower Fowler Creek.

From my cabin I'd watch their lantern glow, seeping through the chinks in my barn.

The next day, in the safety of daylight, I'd go down and look at the new murals, and I'd find myself sweating. The forests are so lovely up here; they demand nothing of anyone. So safe! Why do they have to cut the biggest, oldest trees? Why can't they leave the few, very few, remaining giants?

The kickbacks began: when loggers cut into the big spiked trees, the spinning saw blade would touch the spike and snap back with the recoil of a fired cannonball, slamming right back at the sawyer's face. The men took precautions, usually testing each tree with a metal detector before felling it, but even so, they would often forget the metal detector or they would think, Surely this tree, so far off from anything, hasn't been tampered with; and then they would get hurt, sometimes badly.

One man took four hundred stitches in his shoulder, out in the field, with string and a sewing needle, and still almost died. Another had the saw hit his helmet and crack it in half, and they thought he was dead and had taken him home to get him ready for a burial, were already building the warming fires to thaw the earth, when he woke up.

He said he felt better than he had in twenty years, that he felt like a kid again, and he spoke of seeing a great white light hovering over him the whole time: a white light that wanted him but would not have him.

I kept thinking one side would give in. I kept thinking the sawyers would give up and stop cutting the giants.

Those boys—the loggers would have killed those boys.

The men were angry, I think, but also strangely *alive*—feeling the edges of life for once, is how I imagined it—and each day they went into the woods as if going off to war. It was the women whom the spikes bothered most. They'd play pinochle at the mercantile nearly every day and get drunk and talk about the things they were going to do, if they found out who it was: castrations, that sort of thing.

I'd dated—"slept with" is the better word, the more accurate term, for this valley—Victor's mother for a while, Carol, back when Victor must have been eleven or twelve. I remembered once when I'd been over there, staying the night, wide-assed naked on the bed; I remember what I was doing with Carol clearly, what she was having done, and Victor came into the room—just opened the door and walked right in—and stood there.

Carol leapt up and ushered him out of the room—didn't even put a robe on or wrap a sheet around herself—just hustled him right back out the door.

That was about three or four years ago. We got tired of one another's bodies and drifted apart.

Sometimes the women would be playing cards at the mercantile, when I went in for groceries. They played all day long, in the winter—the men out sawing, while I, the writer, the nature boy, hung around town, hung around the cabin—and the mercantile would be blue with smoke. The thing I liked about Carol, the way I remembered her, besides in bed, was how she held her cards, arranging them, and how she let her cigarette dangle from the corner of her mouth. I liked to watch all the women play, as I moved down the short aisles, selecting the day's canned goods: soup, beans.

"I'll get him," Carol said one day to the other women—deciding to lay her cards down when she realized, belatedly, that she had won. Winning always seemed to surprise her, or any of them, and they'd stare at the cards for a few moments whenever they won, even after they had laid the last card down, as if not trusting their eyes, as if unsure of what they were seeing. "Whoever it is, I'll kill him," she said, and they all nodded.

The women would start up a new hand then, playing late into the afternoon, trying not to look at the clock, I think, and trying not to wonder if one of the men was down at that very moment. It was February and hysteria seemed only a step away, as if they could walk right into it, comfortably, and settle in, with no effort at all. They spoke carefully and slowly, trying to help each other, watching for signs.

Sometimes Carol's hands would tremble as she held her cards. The man she was now sleeping with—her lover, Joe—was a logger. All the men were. It was all or nothing.

It was also in February, the year Victor and Percy were fifteen, that they began riding the horses. Davey Prouder, who ran the saloon, was keeping the horses in my pasture in exchange for my free drinks at the saloon, since I didn't drink that much, and it was one of my jobs to feed them, and to keep the ice from clogging up in their hooves, and to exercise them, if I could: Buck, a sweet line-backed dun, and Fuel, a ferocious cutting horse from Oklahoma, who was so mean they hadn't even been able to trailer him—instead, they'd had to ride Fuel all the way up here, and it had taken three months.

But when Percy turned fifteen, he somehow got it into his mind to begin riding Fuel. He'd found out that he could ride Fuel as long as it was dark and cold; and he rode after midnight, whenever he and Victor got in from spiking trees.

Percy, ugly Percy, would slip up on wild Fuel—all the cold stars at their brightest and every sound magnified, every sound a shout—and Victor would climb up on Buck, the sweet horse, the tamer horse.

The two boys would ride around the pasture at a full gallop, riding the horses through the deep drifts and up through the woods behind my cabin, clinging to the wild, startled horses' necks and shutting their eyes, trying to keep from being popped by frozen branches. I'd watch from the window, still passive, and amazed at their fury, their anger. I wanted to get back together with Carol, but she was pretty sweet on her new logger. You could see things were good between them. Why did I want to ruin that? Something about the spikes, and all the trouble in the valley that year, made me want to have sex with her again.

*   *   *

I would see Victor and Percy in the store, on weekends, and we'd exchange strange looks—glares, sometimes. Percy would be bruised and cut, from where his father had hit him with things. No one liked it; everyone wished the old man would go ahead and die or rot away, so that Percy and his mother and brothers and sisters could start over, and in April, that is what happened. Mister Coward ruptured something, some kind of bleeding started going on inside him, filling him up with his own blood, bloating him horribly, until his face was black and he was shouting, and Mrs. Coward, hysterical, called the mercantile on the truck's radio.

The pain had to be horrendous. We could hear his screams all over the valley, and one of the men finally had to pull him outside and shoot him, to put him out of his misery.

I helped bury Percy's father in the marsh, in the cemetery for loggers. It was full of tall, shady larches, centuries old, with fine filtered sunlight that came drifting down, so slowly, through the lacy fernlike leaves of the smaller trees, and the forest floor was covered with larch needles; granite headstones crept up into the woods, dating back to the early 1800s, with names like "Piss Fir Jim" and "Windy Joe Doggs." A slight breeze was always stirring in that cemetery, and that magic gold light was always there, with the sound of the river below, even at night. It was the most beautiful spot in the valley, a fine resting spot.

Mister Coward had been thirty-eight. Hardly any of the loggers made it to thirty-eight.

One day, on the mural wall inside my barn, there was a spray-painted picture of me and Carol, in her bed—me doing what I'd been doing that time three years ago. It was as if the boys were daring me, challenging me to hurt them—to turn them in.

There's a life to live. I went over to Carol's one day when Joe, her logger, was out in the woods and there wasn't a pinochle game going. Victor was gone too. Carol and I had a couple of beers. I got brave and told her I wanted to get back together again. It wasn't so hard. Carol said we should, but that she wanted to keep it a secret.

Used to be I wouldn't be much on that action—being secret, seeing her like that. But I was changing like crazy—those boys in my barn. I felt like I was on fire. I felt like burning myself up, like hurting myself. "Okay," I said. "Sure. However you want it."

I'd hike over to her house and make love to her during the day. She stopped going to all the pinochle games. I'd never known a woman with such fury, such *unquenchable* fury. It was such a strange valley, then. Just fury: *ten* men couldn't have done her, and that's a fact. Joe's benign picture—the logger—stared at us from the crowded dresser, as we rutted. Nature Boy, I thought; and then I'd think, Nature Boy, you've lived too long, you've gotten too dirty. The world has defeated you, has claimed you. It controls you.

Ten men couldn't have done her. It was better than before. It was wild.

Sometimes she almost wanted me to take her to the edge of pain, and sometimes she would try and hurt me.

Sometimes I let her. I don't know why.

In May, Victor and Percy started getting into fights. Usually Victor won, quickly blackening one of Percy's eyes or bloodying his nose; but in June, Percy got the idea of jousting rather than fist-fighting.

At first they just went at it up in the woods: chasing each other around with sawed-off poles, more swatting than any sort of jousting—the horses leaping the fallen logs in the trails, one rider taking his horse down the creek, into the mist of the great larches, into the summer morning fog; then wheeling around and riding hard back out of the ferns and mist, the sun gold in the other's eyes, blinded, just a hard-riding dark shape coming at him and then the swat of the pole, lifting one of them off the bare-backed horse to land hard on the spongy centuries-old rotting carpet of larch needles and bog; silence around them after that, and the sun so far above them, at the tops of the great trees, struggling to make it down to them.... I would run up from behind the house, into the woods, and crouch down behind logs, following them as they galloped and wheeled and chased each other through the woods on horseback.

But slowly, through the early summer, the boys' swats turned to jousts, and they would lift each other off the backs of the horses, catching the other rider under the armpit or high up in the chest, driving him backward, even lifting him up, as the horse continued forward, suddenly riderless—and then there'd be that long twisting fall, for the defeated rider, back down into the moss and the old dark soil.

It had to be a familiar feeling for Percy. He would pick himself up, never any broken bones, not at that age, and would whistle for Fuel, who, I was beginning to see, was the better fighting horse. Percy would have sugar cubes in his pocket, stolen from Victor's store, I'd bet; it was how he got Fuel to return, and he would slip them to him, when Victor wasn't looking, would whisper things in Fuel's ear.

What I saw was this: that Percy was letting Victor knock him off that horse. He was only pretending to lose.

I don't know why—even today, I can't figure it out. Perhaps losing, and pain and stupidity, is simply a thing that is in the blood.

A man on one of the logging crews was killed by the kickback from a spiked larch. Everyone had known it would happen sooner or later; they had just not known to whom it would happen. I felt immensely guilty. But they would have killed Percy, and maybe Victor: would have strung them up!

I dreamed about the dead man's face. Sometimes, when I was behind Carol and bucking on her, her back would suddenly look like a man's, in the night—*that* man's—and I'd gasp and not be able to finish, not want to finish.

Most of the men had seen the accident and the death and were starting to have nightmares. The women didn't know what to do about this. None of their men had ever had nightmares before. These were strong men. But now they were going into the woods without joking, without joy. They were gaunter, less interested in their wives, their girlfriends, in hunting and drinking, in anything. The June sun climbed high in the sky earlier and stayed up above them all day, hanging, shining white and warm, but it did not seem like spring to them, did not seem like anything.

Another man caught a kickback on the top of his helmet, two weeks later, and he lay there unconscious for two hours in the ferns by a spring creek as the men splashed water on his face, trying to revive him, and when he came to he spoke of seeing the same white light, hovering just above him, just out of reach: seeming to want him but unable to take him, seeming sad, disappointed.

The boys moved out into the meadow with their jousts. They began to use longer poles, too: heavy lodgepole, with pillows lashed to one end, like a boxing glove, and heavy steel garbage can lids for shields—but it was spring, then, the horses were rich on the green June hays and grasses, and they were running stronger, faster; that was what mattered.

The women in the valley began to watch them, bringing picnic lunches and ice chests, which they sat on as if they were chairs. They would play cards, set up umbrellas to protect themselves from the high sun in the thin mountain air, umbrellas and parasols, and they would pour each other glasses of white wine. No one had been injured, had not even seen a kickback, in almost a month. It was rumored that all the spiked trees had been cut down.

The women would place bets on the two boys, bets that increased as the afternoon lengthened and the wine bottles became empty. Some of the men had built bleachers for the wives to sit on, and out in the pasture, every half hour or so, after resting and watching the horses, the two boys would go at it.

Sometimes Victor won, but occasionally Percy would win. They kept it pretty even. I was glad to see that Percy seemed to have gotten hold of himself: he was not letting Victor win on purpose, he was no longer just giving himself over to abuse.

They were the town darlings. No one had ever seen anything like it before.

Part of the bets went to Percy and Victor. Percy bought his mother a battery-operated radio, a new dress, some perfume. Victor saved his money. Carol said he wanted to get out of the valley. I think Victor was nervous about the legacy he and Percy had already left, at fifteen, and knew there were entire forests of spiked trees that had not yet had the first tree felled in them: next year's cuttings, and the year's after that, and the next. I don't think he understood what had gotten into him. It had been Percy's idea, I think, but Victor had gone along with it. Bad luck.

Victor gave me the most murderous looks, in town and at the jousting meets, and later into the summer, as I continued to see Carol, he began to spray-paint murals of my death on my barn wall—pictures of me being dismembered by two boys with chain saws.

I'd stand there in the barn, in the daytime, and know that I should tell, that Victor was *challenging* me to tell and Percy was too—at fifteen, these two boys were simply tired of living, such was the dirt and hardness and emptiness of their lives—but I was too far into it; a man had died, and it was too late; and still, too, I held out hope for victory, hope that the spikes would save the biggest trees. I'm not saying what I did—or didn't do—was right. I'm just saying I did it, that's all. I got into a bad situation, is all, like the boys, and got swept along by it.

In August, Percy caught Victor in the neck with the pole, and

everyone who saw it agreed it was an accident, pure and simple
—everyone but me.

It was true that Percy hit Victor with the pole no differently than
he had a hundred times before—and no differently than he had
been hit by Victor a hundred times—but what I believed was that
it had been a fight to the death all along, that Percy had known
from the beginning that one of the two boys would be killed jousting, and he had determined to himself that he would ride hard
until it happened and just leave it up to luck.

Victor died before he hit the ground: bounced twice. The horse,
Buck, kept running, into the trees. I was sitting with Carol and Joe,
and she screamed and leapt up and looked out into the meadow
at her son; and then, strangely, looked off at the runaway horse
for a long time—two, three seconds—before looking back at her
son; and then, finally, she hurried down the bleachers and ran
out to the meadow to hold him, though it was too late for that.

We buried Victor where we buried everyone: always, in this valley, it seems, we're burying people.

They were just kids, but I was a grown man. The valley was
pretty, but somehow the goodness finally left it. The magic and
beauty went out of it, years ago, and that was that, the end of good
luck. We did something wrong, somewhere—I don't know what.
We might simply have held our breath wrong.

The Kootenai Indians who used to hunt up here believe that
luck is like pine sap, like tar; it's something you step into—and it
can be good or bad, but once you've stepped into it you've got to
wear all of it off your moccasin, if it's bad, say, before you can have
the chance to step into good luck, and vice versa. I have to agree.
My luck's still holding, up here in the woods. But I felt like I used
up an awful lot, being associated with those two boys. I feel like
I'm getting really close to the bottom, really wearing it out, by now.

I'm here to bear witness to luck. I fell away from Carol, once
again. Joe lost her too—she became nothing in her sorrow, a living
ghost. They've both drifted to other places on the earth—still living,
barely: passive, damned, I suppose.

Percy's still angry. Perhaps there was a way Percy's anger could
have been softened, could even have been healed, but it did not
happen; and even today, as a grown man roaming the valley, cutting trees for the Forest Service, drinking, driving wildly, and getting
in wrecks, Percy is still alive, and that anger is still in him, with
his heart wrapped around it, wrapped like wood around a deep
spike, a spike that is hidden and can never be gotten out and must

not be touched: simple fury and simple hate, at an innocence and beauty that doesn't exist, can't be found.

Those great trees are standing silent in the high forest, some of them still loaded with spikes, from the year that Percy was fifteen: still standing and still a danger, ten years later.

In the end, it all comes down to luck. Remember this and be grateful, be frightened.

We're here. We're alive.

Lake Stephen

CHARLES BAXTER

The second week of their vacation, the young man got up early to make pancakes. When his girlfriend smelled breakfast being made, she reached down to the floor and put on her nightgown. She went out to the living room in her bare feet.

"Good morning," she said. "I thought we were going to sleep late."

"Want some pancakes?" he asked, flipping them over in the skillet. "They're not great, but they do have a sort of lumberjack appeal. They taste like trees and brush."

"Doesn't this place have an exhaust fan?" she asked. "It's smoky in here."

The young man looked around. "I don't see one."

"Why did you get up? I thought we were going to laze around in bed together."

"I was restless."

"But it's vacation," she said. "It's our first vacation together. And here we are, surrounded by trees, in the Deer Park Resort. What is there to be restless about?"

"I'm not used to this," he said.

"Used to what?"

"This." He spread his hand to indicate the cabin's small living room, the door to the bedroom, the pine trees outside the picture window, and the lake, visible a few hundred feet away. "It's too much of something."

"It's too beautiful," she suggested.

"No." He walked over to the dining room table and dropped three pancakes on a plate. "There aren't any distractions. I'm used to distractions. I'm used to . . . I don't know. Craziness."

"Well, *I'm* a distraction," she said. She leaned back to let him see her in her nightgown. "I can be crazy."

"Yes," he said. "You're wonderful. That's been proved."

She nodded.

"But it all feels cooped up somehow," he said. "Even when we go canoeing or go for hikes or go swimming, it feels cooped up."

"I don't understand," she said. "How can it be cooped up when you're outside doing things?"

He looked at her for a moment. He seemed to be searching her face for some element there that was bothering him.

"I don't know," he said finally. "I think we have to get out more. Do things."

"Do what things? We've *been* doing things."

"What day is it?" he asked.

"Sunday."

"Well, if it's Sunday, we could go to church." He sat down with her after dishing out two pancakes on his own plate. He reached over for the can of maple syrup.

She laughed nervously. "Go to church? We don't go to church. We've never gone to church. We aren't Christians or anything. I don't think there's even a church around here."

"*I* saw one," he said. "About ten miles down the road, in that little crossroads village, where the grocery is, and that gas station."

"You're serious," she said. "You're really serious about this."

"Well, why not?" He smiled in her direction and laughed. "I mean, they don't keep strangers out, do they? Of course not. They *want* strangers to come in. It's a kind of show. It might be interesting. You could pretend you were an anthropologist."

"I've never been to a church," she said. "Except for weddings and funerals. My parents weren't religious."

"Same here," he said.

"They'll look at us," she said. She began eating his pancakes.

"That's all right," he said. "We'll look back at them."

The church was just inside the village of Wilford and stood next to a small shaded hill and a cemetery. It was a plain white wooden structure with a sign outside giving its name and its pastor, the Rev. Cedric Banks. Sunday worship service was scheduled to be at ten o'clock. The young man and woman drove on the dirt roads close to the church, wasting time, until five minutes before ten, when they parked their car behind a line of other cars and went inside. A few members of the small congregation, mostly middle-aged couples, turned and looked at them with what seemed to be friendly curiosity. The church smelled of white pine and cedar.

Trying to stay inconspicuous, the two young people sat in the back pew.

"I think this is wrong," she said. "This is supposed to be serious. It's not supposed to be entertainment."

"Do they kneel in this church?" he asked. He was whispering.

"How should I know?" She was looking up at the vaulted ceiling, the support beams, and the one stained-glass window at the back of the altar.

At the start of the service, a woman in a purple robe sat down at an electric organ at the front of the church and began the opening chords for a hymn. The congregation stood and began singing. Their voices were weak, except for one woman with a high, shrill soprano, and although the young woman strained to hear, she couldn't make out the words clearly. Her boyfriend was looking for the hymn in the hymnal but had still not found it by the time the music ended. When she next looked up, she saw the pastor standing in front of the altar. He had a hard-country face, she thought, a wide head and a crew cut, but somewhat tired eyes, like a boxer between rounds.

"He looks like a logger or something," the young man whispered. "Or maybe a plumber. He doesn't look very spiritual."

"How does spiritual look?" she asked, whispering back.

"Different," he said. "Like someone on television."

"Shh," she said. "Pay attention."

The minister began a series of prayers. Because of the reverberation in the church and his tendency to mumble, many of his prayers were incomprehensible to the two young people sitting in the back row. But when the young woman looked over at her boyfriend, she saw an oddly intense expression on his face.

"Do you *like* this?" she asked.

"Shh," he said. "You're just supposed to take it all in."

After several more minutes the pastor walked slowly to the right-hand side of the church, mounted a few steps, and stood behind a lectern. After a brief invocation, he began by quoting from the book of Jonah. He continued to mumble, so that his sentences went in and out of focus, but the expression on his face was earnest and direct. The subject of his sermon seemed to be surprises. The minister said that Jonah was repeatedly surprised by the persistence of God. Nothing that happened on earth was a surprise to the Almighty, he said, but then he said something that the young woman simply couldn't hear. At times he held his finger up as if to make a point. Once or twice he pounded his fist lightly on the lectern. We should contribute to the surprise of creation, the pastor said, by exercising charity, which is always outside the chain of inevitability.

"This doesn't make any sense," the young woman said in a whisper to her boyfriend. "It's all mixed up."

"He knows everyone here," the young man whispered back. "He doesn't have to explain everything to them."

"Maybe he's been drinking."

"No," the young man said. "He just mumbles."

When the service was over, the pastor stepped down the aisle and stood at the doorway to shake hands with the members of the congregation as they left. When the two young people approached him, the minister raised his eyebrows at them and smiled. Close up, he looked bulky and slightly overweight, like a man who had once played football and now drank a few beers in the evening to relax.

"I don't know you two," he said, holding out his hand toward them. "Welcome. Are you passing through?" His breath smelled of cigarettes, and the young woman found herself both pleased and slightly shocked by this.

"I *think* we're just passing through," the young man said.

"You think so?" the minister asked. "You're not sure?"

"We like it here," the young man went on. "We'd like to settle down somewhere around here, raise a family. It's such beautiful country."

"Yes, it is," the minister said, glancing down at their ring fingers. The young woman knew that she would look guilty and silly if she tried to hide the fact that she wore no wedding ring, so she looked back at the minister with a blank smile, her hand resting easily on her hip. "Well," the minister said at last, "enjoy yourselves while you're here."

Back in the car, headed in no particular direction, the young man said, "Well, what did you think of that?"

"It was all right," she said. "But why did you say we were going to settle down and raise a family here? That's a kind of weird fantasy. We don't live here. And we aren't married."

"Oh, I know," he said. "I just think about it. I play with it." He waited. She knew these pauses were awkward for him and she didn't try to interrupt. "But he was saying that surprises were good things, so I decided to surprise him and to surprise you. It was stupid, I admit it. But I agreed with him. I like surprises. I love it when things are unexpected. I *love* it."

"I don't," she said. "I don't like it much."

"I know that," he said suddenly, and the way he said it, over-enunciated so that the effort was like underlining the words, made her sit up straight. She waited inside the air pocket of silence for a moment, then put her hand on her boyfriend's thigh. She rested it there lightly. It wasn't for love or for sensuality's sake; it was to calm him.

"The trouble is," he began. Then he stopped. They both looked out through the front windshield at the pine trees on each side of the road and the occasional farm; the soil was mostly clay and rock up here, and the farming was poor. There were FOR SALE signs everywhere, on the front yards and nailed to the trees. "The trouble is," he started again, "that you anticipate every one of my moves. You anticipate everything I do. When we talk or make love or I cook or watch you or talk about the future or what I'm reading, you anticipate all of it. You nod and I can tell how predictable I'm already getting. That's why I feel cooped up. It gets to me. It's like I'm living out a script someone's written. Only the thing is, you've already gotten the script and I haven't. You know everything I'm going to do. I look into the future and you still know everything I'm going to do, for years and years, and it doesn't matter if we're married or not. You know everything I'm going to do."

"I don't understand," she said. In fact, she did understand, but she thought the rest of their vacation would go better if she pretended that she didn't.

"It's like basketball," the young man said. He laughed, a quick intake of breath, but his face became serious again quickly. "You take Kareem Abdul-Jabbar. You watch him some night. The man is a genius. You know why?" The young woman shook her head. "The reason Jabbar is a genius is that you can't anticipate his moves. It's not speed. Speed's important in basketball but it's not the most important thing. The most important thing is to do the move, the logical move, so unexpectedly and gracefully that your opponent is faked out and can't guard against it."

"Basketball isn't the world," she said. "It's not about relationships."

"Oh, yes, it is," he said. "It's a relationship between individuals on two different teams. And the more you can't be anticipated, the more effective you are." He turned off the road onto a smaller dirt road that the young woman hadn't seen, and the car took some hard bounces as they proceeded through a cluster of thick trees.

"Where does this go?" she asked. "Where are we?"

The young man smiled. "I saw a sign for a lake back there," he said. "Faked you out, didn't I?"

"Yes," she said. "You certainly did."

"Never thought I'd take you to a lake, did you?" he asked.

"Nope," she said. "You got me this time."

The road came out in a clearing for public access. The young man stopped the car and got out, walking down to the shoreline to look into the water and then across the lake to the other side. In the distance they could see one broken-down cabin, its roof fallen in. The water was very clear; they could both see minnows swimming in schools in the shallow water.

"I wonder what the name of this lake is," he said.

"*We* can name it," she said. "Let's name it after you. Let's call it Lake Stephen."

"Okay," he said. "Now that it's mine, what do I do with it?"

"You don't do anything with it."

"Yes, you do," he said. "You have to do something with it, if it's named after you." All at once he straightened up. "I'll surprise you," he said.

"How?"

"If I told you," he said, "it wouldn't be a surprise."

At exactly that moment, she knew he was going to take all his clothes off and go swimming. She knew that he was going to take off his shirt first, button by button, and hang it on the end of a tree branch, and he did; that he was going to unbuckle his belt, then slip off his shoes and socks, put the socks inside the shoes and put the shoes together neatly at the base of the tree, and he did that too; then he would lower his trousers and fold them at the knee and put the folded trousers over the shoes and socks; and then she knew, quite a bit in advance of his actually doing it, that he would grin at her, a happy smile breaking across his pleasant bearded face, and, with a yelp, lower his underwear and turn around and dash into the water, shouting as he went and making half-articulate exclamations like a man running into battle. He wanted to be dangerous and unpredictable, and so, watching him, she did her best to look amazed at what he was doing.

He swam back and forth in the water, splashing and barking like a happy seal. She watched the water passing over his pale skin.

The rest of the year, he worked indoors at a desk, and he didn't believe in getting sun, so his body was visible underwater even when he dove down, it was that white. She watched him swimming parallel to the shoreline and was pleasantly lost in his physical form, which she liked. As bodies went, his was attractive; he swam regularly and worked out. But the final effect was of frailty. Men, when you got their clothes off, looked rather simple and frail, even the strong ones. The strength was all on the outside. This was no secret, and it became more apparent as they aged.

"Come on in," he shouted. "It's great!"

"I don't know," she said, looking around. "Maybe there are people here."

"It's okay," he said. "It's my lake and my beach, and what I say goes. I'm the law here."

"Well, you sure have surprised me," she said. Then, once again, she knew that he would try to scare her and pretend to drown. She knew, before he actually did it, that he would dive down and hold his breath; that he would stay underwater for as long as he could; and that he even might try to inhale some water so that he could choke a little, not much, but just enough to give her a scare. This was just like men, to try to scare you by being dangerous and vulnerable at the same time. She took off her shoes and socks and waded out into the water, soaking her dress as she went. She waited for Stephen to come up, out of the water. She waited for what she thought was a long time. She couldn't see any bubbles; she knew he was holding his breath down there, like a boy among the minnows. He would be curled up, his feet brushing against the sandy bottom. And now he would be feeling as if his lungs were about to explode, and she went farther out into the water, so that it came up to her knees.

Then he rose to the surface, coughing and choking. She waded out to where he was and took his hand. "Stephen," she cried, "are you all right?"

He smiled. "Did I frighten you?" he asked. "Good." He spat some water out of his mouth.

"Damn it," she said, pretending to be indignant, "don't do that again."

Another large grin broke across his face. "You should come in," he said. "Come on, Jan. Come in. Take your clothes off."

"I don't want to," she said.

And then, suddenly, both of them knee deep in water, he put his bare arms around her, and she gasped. It wasn't his body. They were lovers, and she was used to that. It was that his skin was ice cold; for a moment, it didn't feel like his, or like living flesh, but something else. It was puckered with goose bumps and felt clammy, as if it had come from some other world into this one, and when he put his lips to her, she flinched.

"What's the matter?" he asked.

She could feel his wet hand soaking through the back of her blouse. He was soaking her down in small stages. Looking at him, at the water dripping off his beard and down his chest, she thought he looked a bit like a minor god or a monster, she couldn't decide which.

"Come in," he said, reaching for her.

She paused and looked at the future. She knew that he would not go on loving her if she didn't take her clothes off now; he would not, someday, propose to her; and they would not get married and have children. Unless she broke the rules now, he would not follow the rules later. He wanted her to be wild; all right, she would be wild. She grinned at him. She did a little shimmy, then unbuttoned her blouse and tossed it on the sand. She unhooked her bra, thinking, He'll still talk about this when we're old. He'll cherish this because it's our first secret. She threw her bra toward shore, then took off the rest of her clothes and dropped them on the sand. Then, knowing how beautiful she was, how physically breathtaking in sunlight, she walked toward him into the water, her back straight and her hips swaying, and, reaching him, pressed herself against him.

"You're something," he said. "I never thought you'd actually do that."

She was about to say, I know, but stopped herself.

"I take it all back," he said, his fingers playing with her hair. "I take it all, all, all back. I never expected this. You're crazy. I love you. It's wonderful."

"Are you all talk," she asked, holding hands, almost pulling him, "or are we going to swim? Come on."

They dove into the water together.

Mr. Potatohead in Love

MADISON SMARTT BELL

It isn't really *so* much like one—take the ears, for instance, they're more like cauliflower—still, they might be little embryonic potatoes that didn't quite manage to break free of the main lump: the mealy irregular oblong of his head. It's mostly bald, but sprouts of chill white rubbery hair rise up from unexpected patches of his cranium, twisting and writhing, following their own dark and secret tropisms.... Eyebrows like cracked brown knuckles, ground with dirt; the eyes pale protuberances, tipped with black. The long bumpy jaw is topologically twisted out of line from his pate, and the whole of it's thrust forward and up at eighty-odd degrees on the permanently stiff neck. Doctors can't fix it; the neck *never moves*. Mr. Potatohead!

When his hands are busy you don't notice any of this. His hands are beautiful: Flemish; van der Weyden would have been proud of them. Mr. Potatohead never has to do head fakes; his hands are so lovely they distract you from themselves. He works with his head cocked up away from them on the inflexible neck, eyes always slightly averted. A bit of juggling, a few tricks from mime, but mostly prestidigitation.

A bright clear Friday in the park, plenty of people here. It's spring—no, summer, very warm. People wear shorts; some men are bare-chested. The fountain is set in a swivel pattern that now and then throws a little burst of spray on people at the back of Mr. Potatohead's crowd. He's always looking a little up and over them. Above the arch the sky is blue, and through it Fifth Avenue goes away and away forever.

Things appear, things disappear, but Mr. Potatohead doesn't seem to even notice. People are consuming all sort of strange things while they watch him; it's a good day for spending money. A good day for buskers: Tony the Fireman's here, Charlie Barnett's here, there's a new a capella group doing Dion and the Belmonts. He hasn't seen the Dance Be-Jabbers, but then they're never quite reliable. A lot of animals are here and about; a good day for them too. Someone with a monkey, someone with a snake. Earlier the guy with three ferrets on leashes came through, all of them ferreting in three different directions.

Right in his own front row is this lovely tall woman, big-boned, big-fleshed, generously featured, who wears on one bare shoulder a parrot that matches the iridescent green ribbon wound through the strong black braid of her hair. Mr. Potatohead plays to her a little, sidling up, sidling back, rolling his eyes to the bottom of their sockets to draw her into the field of his sight. He pulls a blue bird's egg from her ear, while keeping his fingers well clear of the parrot—parrots bite. When the show's over she gives him a marvelous smile and strolls off without giving any money. Her mouth is red from kissing, not lipstick. Mr. Potatohead doesn't care.

His hat is a particolored thing with a long bill, which rides in his back pocket, never on his head. Extending the hollow crown of it he quarters his circle, magicking the money as it falls. Coins walk across the backs of his hands; great handfuls of them come corkscrewing in and out of the hat, twisted, involuted, spiraling like strands of DNA. There's some folding money, not a whole lot. When the crowd has thinned, he fades out with it, no matter if it's early. Got to knock off early today, it's imperative he be drunk before five o'clock.

He zigs across Greenwich Avenue on his long stilted legs, then zags up Seventh, forever looking only up. He sees out of the concrete canyon. Behind the blue shroud of the daylit sky the stars are still secretly plotting his course. His hands revolve in front of him like dish antennae, testing the way ahead. He never bumps into anything.

At Fourteenth Street there's a bar, and who could remember the name of it? Nobody calls it anything but Mangan's. Fixed on his high stool, Mr. Potatohead counts his coins into paper tubes, a beer glass and a shot glass before him. He's got a couple of pounds of quarters, eleven ones, and one lucky five that he folds away in the watch pocket of his breeches. The long dim interior is dried-blood red and brown-lung brown. At the rear, the sway-backed spavined booths buckle under the weight of drunks and derelicts, sleeping or comatose or maybe dead ... if they *were* dead, how long before anyone noticed? Above the front window a TV set cackles; Mangan's ancient, grizzled head grimly faces it down from the far end of the bar.

Mr. Potatohead buys Viola a drink when she comes in, changing his coin rolls for paper. Sixty-two-fifty the quarters come to, not bad for only three afternoon shows. Viola takes a cigarette; they talk awhile. She's a brassy black lady, good-looking too, excepting the one top tooth that's set in sideways at the front. When her friends get there she moves to their table. Mr. Potatohead buys a drink for himself, or maybe two, beer and a shot, beer and a shot. . . .

"Hey, Mangan," he cries, "where's the freaks?" Two doors down is a school where the *handicapped* people are brought to overcome their *deficits*; they become cobblers, things like that. They are respectable. But now and again they'll come in here, to wear a little of the new sheen of their good repute, come tapping with canes or rolling in wheelchairs, some walking in on their tongues, just about. Always a mob and no room for the merely ugly among them.

"Not their night." Mangan grunts. "They come in Thursdays now." Catching sight of his own image in the mirror, eyes turning aside from themselves, Mr. Potatohead ducks and loses it behind the rows of bottles. He goes on drinking busily, speedily, chain-smoking and watching the sunlight lower on the street outside.

"Might cut you off," Mangan allows.

"Never," says Mr. Potatohead. His cigarette laces among his five digits, the hot head of it dipping and stitching and never burning or grazing the skin. A snap of his fingers sends it end over end back into the prehensile clasp of his lips. He blows out a tidy smoke ring.

"All right, then," Mangan says, tilting the bottle to the glass. Some feckless stranger sits down and claps a hand on Mr. Potatohead's shoulder.

"Hey, there, Mr. Potatohead," he begins.

"*Dontcallmethatdontevercallmethat!*" Mr. Potatohead says, viciously slicing around on his stool. The stranger's moon face is deeply perplexed.

"But you *told* me that was your *name*," he says. "Yesterday, right here. You know, you bought me a drink, I bought you one; come on, Mr. Potatohead, don't tell me you don't rememb— aarghaarghgllhhgglllhhhh—" as Mr. Potatohead's arms strike out like twin anacondas, wrapping around the stranger's throat and thorax. One sharp elbow bats the stranger about the eyes and nose, not doing any serious damage but hurting plenty. Yes, Mr. Potatohead is surprisingly quick and strong, but Mangan can surprise you even more—

Flying out the door, Mr. Potatohead collides with all five of the Dance Be-Jabbers, who seem to have gotten off a stop too soon, possibly meaning to shoplift a late lunch or early supper at Balducci's on their way down to the park. Mangan snarls from the doorway and brandishes his big square fist, his face coronary red. It's a familiar scene. The Dance Be-Jabbers dance Mr. Potatohead back onto his feet. Each wears a T-shirt with a number. Switching around from the bar to face them, Mr. Potatohead observes that Dance Be-Jabber number 5 is rotating around on his coccyx, arms and legs tucked in, somewhat resembling a potato. Dance Be-Jabber number 4 is making power slides that take him back and back again to the self-same place, his arms winding through air in reptilian loops, his head snapping from one queer angle to another. Dance Be-Jabber number 3, his arms and legs tucked in, is rotating around on the top of his head, looking like—well, *another* potato. Dance Be-Jabber number 2 does stationary power slides, his eyes googling down at invisible workings of magic mimed between his long pale palms. Dance Be-Jabber Numero Uno keeps up an easy four-step shuffle, chanting as the others continuously bone and unbone themselves:

"Mista Potatohead, he *lean* and *mean*. He fake to the *lef'*, he fake to the *right*. And *wham! boppo! lunchmeataphobia!* Watch out fo' Mista Potatohead!"

"Gentlemen, I thank you," Mr. Potatohead says, his hat appearing expressively in his hands. "You make my poor life into poetry." Dance Be-Jabbers 2 through 5 have just become a subway train. Numero Uno slaps him a handful, then flings himself into the last car. Mr. Potatohead gathers his legs up under him, and as the Dance Be-Jabber train bumps and grinds downtown, he goes spindling off in his own directions. . . .

Before the little mirror in the Magic and Costume Shop, not too far from the Flatiron Building, Mr. Potatohead is accessorizing himself with wigs, hats, rubber ears, rubber noses, Groucho glasses, a pipe, and a trick bow tie. . . . But no, but no, nothing is right. He shucks it all off and tries the boar's-head mask again, bending from the waist to see the effect: he's all wild boar from crown to gullet.

"All right, Vic, I'll take this one." Mr. Potatohead thumbs a couple of bills up onto the counter. The mask is expensive, thirty bucks.

"How's the rats?" Victor inquires, smoothing his cue-ball hair with one hand and making change with the other.

"Beautiful, perfect," says Mr. Potatohead. "I couldn't imagine better rats. Oh, and I need the black tux too: swallowtails, dress shirt, studs, the works."

"Hundred-dollar deposit on that."

"Come on, can't you front it to me?" Butterflies flutter in Mr. Potatohead's stomach. He's *counting* on that tux.

"F'what?" Victor says. "You got a funeral?"

"Birthday party," says Mr. Potatohead, prestidigitating the notion from air. "Rich kid. You know, Upper East Side."

"Some lucky kid," Victor says moodily, peering into the boar's rubber eye sockets. "Nightmares till his *next* birthday probably. I don't know, Mister P, you smell a lot like a brewery tonight. I'm wondering are you really in a responsible frame of mind?"

"Come on, Victor," Mr. Potatohead says. "I'll let you hold the rest of my gear. Didn't I always come back before? You *know* I couldn't go too far without you. . . ."

Slightly flattened by the rush-hour subway, Mr. Potatohead re-expands himself, flowing along with the commuter stream toward the Grand Central Station main waiting room. He plucks the white handkerchief from the tux's breast pocket—with a flourish it becomes a gardenia, a bold boutonnière fixed to his lapel. Adjusting the boar's lusty throat to his high collar, he strides out under the great concrete vault, where all the light-bulb stars are gleaming down on him from the ceiling's gilt heaven. Already he sees her, near the information booth, dressed in a deep blue one-piece garment that shimmers with some constellated pattern, and she's already begun to sing, that -O-, the one note so profound and powerful it makes the whole huge hall her instrument.

The cops have already cut through to her; they never let her get any further than that. No buskers in Grand Central Station: not allowed. Before, he's seen them treat her with a kind of grudging courtesy, but tonight it looks like they might take her in. As Mr. Potatohead draws nigh, two mechanical rats descend on spider-web filaments from his palms, to scuttle and chitter across the shining shoes of all the good citizens bound for Larchmont. Screaming and scrambling ensue, and all of a sudden the cops have quite a bit to think about. Mr. Potatohead tweaks the fishlines; the rats yo-yo back into his pockets; he moves on.

She's moving out ahead of him, maybe four or five people away. She's in good shape except for a slight hunchback and one hip set higher than the other. It appears that her hands have been broken off at the wrists and reattached at right angles to her arms.

She goes up the western stairway like a crab and turns along the heavy balustrade, into a large square space that no one requires for anything except to overlook the echoing floor below. Here he catches up with her.

"Hey, lady." She turns to him. Close-cropped hair, little mouse ears, sweet and tranquil face of a dark madonna. "Hey, lady, you know? You got a nice voice."

"Thank you," she says. "Thank you so much." The lucky five appears in his hand, turns into an origami crane, and flies to her—where it disappears, for everybody has to know a little rough magic nowadays. She smiles at him, her teeth small, perfect, brilliantly white, her brown eyes bright as she looks for him down in the boar's floppy eyeholes.

"Hey, mister? You're something yourself." With a helical movement she takes his hand, and -O-, that grace note thrills down through him, searching out his loneliness, his longing, his exaltation. . . .

"He's blowing beets." His head cranked high, Mr. Potatohead watches the Staten Island ferry's ramp hydraulically lower onto the dock. Not far from him some abandoned soul is puking pale pink waves, stinking of Boone's Farm and stomach bile. "He's blowing beets," the witness remarks once more. Mr. Potatohead does not see or hear or smell a bit of it. When the crowd surges forward, he surges too.

It's a bit cold and bit windy out on the bay, so Mr. Potatohead has the prow of the boat all to himself. The sky has dropped its disguise by this time. His head is naturally in position, so as soon as he pulls off the boar's-head mask he can see all his stars to perfection, here for him again and always, as exactly as he knew they would be. Swan and Dragon, Eagle and Dolphin, Great Bear, Hercules, Asclepius, the Scorpion . . . monsters and heroes intermingled, how strangely, how wonderfully they move.

The Overcoat

GINA BERRIAULT

The overcoat was black and hung down to his ankles, the sleeves came down to his fingertips, and the weight of it was as much as two overcoats. It was given him by an old girlfriend who wasn't his lover anymore but stayed around just to be his friend. She had chosen it out of a line of Goodwill coats because, since it had already lasted almost a century, it was the most durable and so the right one for his trip to Seattle, a city she imagined as always flooded by cataclysmic rains and cold as an execution dawn.

On the Greyhound bus, the coat overlapped onto the next seat, and only when all the other seats were occupied did a passenger dare to lift it and sit down, women apologetically, men bristling at the coat's invasion of their territory. The coat was formidable. Inside it, he was frail. His friend had filled a paper bag with delicatessen items, hoping to spare him the spectacle of himself at depot counters, hands shaking, coffee spilling, a sight for passengers hungrier for objects of ridicule than for their hamburgers and french fries. So he sat alone in the bus while it cooled under the low ceilings of concrete depots and out in lots under the winter sky, around it piles of wet lumber, cars without tires, shacks, a chained dog, and the café's neon sign trembling in the mist.

On the last night the bus plowed through roaring rain. Eli sat behind the driver. Panic might take hold of him any moment and he had to be near a door, even the door of this bus crawling along the ocean floor. No one sat beside him, and the voices of the passengers in the dark bus were like the faint chirps of birds about to be swept from their nest. In the glittering tumult of the water beyond the swift arc of the windshield wiper, he was on his way to see his mother and his father, and panic over the sight of them again, and over their sight of him, could wrench him out of his seat and lay him down in the aisle. He pressed his temple against the cold glass and imagined escaping from the bus and from his parents, revived out there in the icy deluge.

For three days he lay in a hotel room in Seattle, unable to face the two he had come so far to see and whom he had not seen in sixteen years, the age he'd been when he'd seen them last. They were already old when he was a kid, at least in his eyes, and now they seemed beyond age. The room was cold and clammy, but he could have sworn a steam radiator was on, hissing and sputtering. Then he figured an old man was sitting in a corner, watching over him, sniffling and sadly whistling—until he took the noise by surprise and caught it coming from his own nose and mouth. Lying under an army blanket and his overcoat, he wished he had waited until summer. But all waiting time was dangerous. The worst you could imagine always happened to you while you waited for better times. Winter was the best time for him anyway. The overcoat was an impenetrable cover for his wasted body, for his arms lacerated by needles, scar on scar, and decorated with prison tattoos. Even if it were summer he'd wear the coat. The sun would have to get even fiercer than in that story he'd read when he was a kid, about the sun and the wind betting each other which of them could take off the man's coat, and the sun won. Then he'd take off his coat, he'd even take off his shirt, and his parents would see who had been hiding inside. They'd see Eli under the sun.

With his face bundled up in a yellow plaid muffler he'd found on the floor of the bus, he went by ferry and by more buses way out to the edge of this watery state, avoiding his mother by first visiting his father. Clumping down to the fishing boats riding on the glacial gray sea, he was thrown off course by panic, by the presence of his father in one of those boats, and he zigzagged around the little town like an immense black beetle blown across the ocean from its own fantastic region.

On the deck of his father's boat he was instantly dizzied by the lift and fall and the jolting against the wharf, and he held to the rail of the steep steps down to the cabin, afraid he was going to be thrown onto his father, entangling them in another awful mishap.

"Eli, Eli here," he said.

"Eli?"

"That's me," he said.

Granite, his father had turned to granite. The man sitting on the bunk was gray, face gray, skimpy hair gray, the red net of broken capillaries become black flecks, and he didn't move. The years had chiseled him down to nowhere near the size he'd been.

"Got arthritis," his father said. The throat, could it catch arthritis too? His voice was the high-pitched whisper of a woman struggling with a man; it was Eli's mother's voice, changed places. "Got it from the damn wet, took too many falls."

The Indian woman beside him shook tobacco from a pouch, rolled the cigarette, licked it closed, and never looked up. She must be thinking Eli was a visitor who came by every day.

"You want to sit?" his father said.

Eli sat on the bunk opposite them and his father poured him a glass of port. The storm had roughed things up, his father said, and Eli told them about the bus battling the rain all night. The woman asked Eli if anything was stolen from his boat while he was away, and he humored her; he said a watch was stolen, and his shortwave radio.

"That's a big overcoat you got there," his father said. "You prosperous?"

"Oh, yes!" he said. "I'm so prosperous I got a lot of parasites living off me."

The Indian woman laughed. "They relatives of yours?"

"Anything living off you is a relative," he said.

The woman pushed herself up in stages, her weight giving her a hard time as if it were a massive object, like a penalty. She wore two pairs of thick socks, the holes in the top pair showing the socks underneath. Her breasts hung to her waist though she had no waist, but when she lifted her arms to light a hanging kerosene lamp, he saw how gracefully she did it, her hands acting like a pretty girl's. He might fall for her himself if he were sixteen.

They did not offer him dinner. They must have eaten theirs already.

"I've got no place to sleep," he said.

They let him sleep on the bunk. They slept aft, far back in a dark space. He lay in his overcoat, drawing his legs up close against his stomach, and his feet in socks got warm. Then he thought he was a boy again, home again in the house in Seattle, under covers in his own bed while his parents drank the night away, unprotected from them but protected by them from the dreadful world they warned him about, out there.

At dawn he was waked by his shivering body. Out on the pier, the salt cold wind stiffened him, almost blinding him, so that he wound up a few times at the pier's edges. When you look back, he'd heard, you're turned to salt, and that's what was happening to him. If he fell into the sea he'd disappear faster than fate intended.

For two days he wandered around Seattle, avoiding his mother. Now that he was near to her, he wanted to go on by. He had betrayed her. *Tell me about your parents, Eli.* Strangers, creepy parole officers and boy-face psychiatrists in leather jackets and women social workers whose thighs he had hoped to open with the shining need for love in his eyes, each of them jiving with him like a cellmate and all of them urging him to tell about a woman they could never know. He had betrayed her, he had blamed her for Eli, and blamed the old man on the rocking boat. Those strangers had cut out his heart with their prying, and remorse had always rushed in to fill up the empty space where his heart had been.

They told him at the desk that his mother was ambulatory and could be anywhere. His father had called this a rest home, and he wondered why they were resting in here when all that rest was just ahead for them. The women in the rows of narrow beds he passed, and the women in their chairs between the beds, hadn't much left of womanness in them but their power over him was intact. He went along before their pale faces staring out at the last puzzling details of the world, himself a detail, a cowering man in a long black overcoat who might be old enough to be their dead father.

There she was, far down a corridor and out, and he followed her into a paved yard, walled in by brick and concrete. She put her hand to the wall to aid herself in open space, reached the bench, and sat down, and her profile assured him that he wasn't mistaken.

"Mother, it's Eli," he said.

She raised her eyes, and one eye was shrewd and the other as purely open as a child's, the blue almost as blue as ever.

"Eli," he said. "Can I sit down?"

"Room enough for everybody."

He sat, and she paid him no attention. From a pocket of her sweater she took a scrap of comb and began to comb her hair. The comb went cautiously through the limp hair, still feisty red. She was twenty years younger than his father but keeping up with him on the way out, and their son, Eli, their only child, was keeping up with them both.

"We had ourselves an earthquake," she said. "Bricks fell down. We thought the whole damn place was coming down. Did you feel it?"

"I wasn't here," he said.

"Were you scared?"

"I wasn't here."

"I bet you were scared."

"I died in it," he said.

If she wanted his company in her earthquake it was no trouble to oblige. It made no difference, afterward, when or where you died, and it was easier to tell her he was already dead than tell her he was going to be soon, even before he could get up from this bench.

"Poor boy," she said. But slowly, still combing her hair, she turned her head to take another look at him, this man who had sat down beside her to belittle her with his lies. "You never died," she said. "You're alive as me."

Off in a corner and facing the wall, he pulled up the overcoat to cover his head and in that dark tent wept over them, over them both and his father, all so baffled by what was going on and what had gone on in their lives and what was to go on. Grief for the three of them filled up the overcoat's empty space, leaving no room to spare, not even for him.

Days of Oaks, Years of Salt

LUCIENNE S. BLOCH

My grandmother walked most of the way from a little town near Graz, in Austria, to London. She was twenty, green-limbed and raw, and so was this century: both of them restless, unshackled, upheaved from an ancient order of things into a world whose recent peace was more tentative than convincing.

Of course she did not walk alone; there were, still, vestigial proprieties in operation. Her brother, senior by a couple of significant years, accompanied her: two dark-eyed travelers seeking roomier futures than the ones they stood to inherit at home. Leaving behind three younger sisters and a widowed mother, they strolled toward the possibilities that an uncle, well settled in a woolens business in London, might provide. They carried everything on their backs, food and shoes and such, the goodbyes. At night they slept in fields, in barns when the weather turned. They picked up crumbs of new languages, mouthfuls to get by on. There is no record of this legendary journey apart from the remembered and recounted one; no documentary diaries, no franked passports, no railway or steamship ticket stubs, no hotel bills, no souvenir photographs or trinkets, no many-creased maps. Did it happen, as told? I believe so. I always believed so, although I knew the reports had been altered by the time they reached me, embroidered, translated, aggrandized, I supposed. Even so, I swallowed them whole, lured and hooked like a trout by a glitteringly fabulous fly. The adventure of it!

Taking a southerly route—longer, warmer, certainly more picturesque—my grandmother and her brother climbed into Italy through the Carnic Alps where frontiers weren't as strict as they could have been. They walked across the top of Italy, each step lighter than the one before it, springier, down to Genoa, where they followed the seductive curve of the Riviera to Marseilles, then

made their way across the bottom of France to Bordeaux to board
a ship for the final leg of their leisurely journey.

Upon seeing the Mediterranean and its shores for the first time,
my grandmother was so amazed she took to singing, in the streets
particularly. She didn't sing for money; they had all the cash they
needed wrapped in handkerchiefs in their rucksacks. She sang for
the pure joy of adding her note to those that hovered, purling and
trilling, in the pellucid sea air. Making a musical offering to gods
whose existence she hadn't even suspected, she sang folk songs
in the dialect of her girlhood. Her voice, small, untrained, may have
moved a heart or two. In Antibes, singing on a boulevard planted
with flowering laurels, she was sketched by a man sitting on the
terrace of a café. It could have been Matisse, we like to think; the
dates and place are right. The man showed her the sketch but he
did not give it to her.

My grandmother arrived in London about seven months after
she commenced walking. Her cheeks were flushed, tomato-red,
despite the rough Channel crossing. Long ropy muscles snaked
down her legs to her narrow feet. Between them, she and her
brother had gone through five pairs of what they claimed were
sturdy boots, and through something less tangible, not measurable
in distance covered or time elapsed. "Why did you walk? Why
didn't you go on trains?" I asked her once when I was nine or so
and liked the mechanics of events to be fleshed out so I could
grasp them more tightly.

"I was too beauty for men in irons," she answered. "Only stars
could have my shining." She was said to be "somewhat" senile, a
vague qualifier for an already vague condition. But I could usually
catch the drift of her scattered words. She caught my more regular
ones. We understood each other.

Soon after reaching London, my grandmother made what must
be seen as a brilliant match, acquiescing to arrangements set in
motion by her uncle prior to her arrival. Was this match to her
liking? Did her likings matter? These are conjectures. The fact
appears to be that a future was perceived and undertaken by a
woman whose legs may have been stronger than her spirit and
whose song, it is possible, was silenced. I know what she told me,
repeatedly.

"I was my dream under a lock of petals," she used to say, pointing to her wedding portrait in the snapshot album we looked at
together week after week on the Saturday afternoons of my child-

hood; pictures were the safety net for what fell from her memory's difficult trapeze act. "Seven times I swanned around my stranger, then the glass broke awake to weeping. Salt in the mouth was my sadness to come."

Sadness? Was that the destination of her high adventure or only a stopping place, a marriage's way station?

There was no sadness in my grandmother when I saw her weekly. Or else I was too young to recognize what I saw, a faddedness of sorts, but one I felt was due to a lack of color rather than of cheer. The three rooms of her apartment were done in a variety of whites. Alabaster, ivory, off-white, cream-white, and egg-shell puddled into custards on the walls and upholstery, at the silk-swagged windows, on the painted tables and bureaus and kitchen cupboards. Even the rugs on the floors were pallid, washed over the years into what was no more than a thin reminder of beiges and blues. She was blanched too: snowy hair, chalky powdered face, starched white lace and linen blouses, pearly teeth she constantly took out of her soft oystery mouth to amuse me, herself also. She'd hand me the wet dentures and say something like, "Jewels to be is on the tongue. Try me on." We laughed and laughed as I tried to clamp her false teeth between my lips like Halloween vampire fangs. All that whiteness she lived in wasn't cold, wasn't bleak; it didn't chill our times together. We played cards. We baked cupcakes. We knitted wispy mohair mufflers for the entire family. We studied the single photo album she brought to this country, and she told me stories prompted by the pictures. "In the days of oaks," she'd begin; that was her habitual opening phrase.

In my own days of oaks, Granny, there were questions I might have asked you but didn't think of then. One, especially one question haunts me now, about the one photograph you kept on your bedside table to look at all the time, not just once a week when I came to visit you and we pored over the album for clues to remembering. The photograph I want to know about, the one you didn't hide between the tooled leather covers of a book that was further hidden in a drawer between layers of your silky white underwear, is of a person you seldom mentioned to me, a man I never knew because he died in the blitz before I was born.

My grandfather struts on a seaside esplanade, straw-hatted, wearing a snappy striped blazer. His stance is jaunty. He looks extremely pleased, although there isn't a smile below his mustache. His chin points toward his left shoulder, a birdlike tilt of the head.

One hand grips a silver-headed walking stick, the other is tucked into the pocket of his white flannel pants. He is a tall slim man casting a sharp pencil-slim shadow on the paved promenade. At a distance behind him, behind a wrought-iron railing, a pier stretches across the pebbled beach and stilts into the sea. There is some kind of pavilion at the end of the pier above the water, a roofed but open-sided structure. It could have been Brighton, in August perhaps. The picture must have been taken very early in the morning, given the look and angle of his shadow. There aren't any other people in the picture, no other strollers on the broad esplanade, no children squatting at the sea's curly edge. Even in the old and faded photograph, the summer morning light is so splendid and immense it fills the image and its subject with bright importance.

What I want to know is this, Granny: Where were you? Why aren't you on his arm as in all the other vacation snaps in the album, smiling at the photographer approaching and inviting you both to pose, please? What was it about this picture you're not in that made you keep it out? Did it remind you of something you wouldn't talk about even when I asked you the questions I could then? Was that your salty sadness: his self-importance? Did he shine so sharply, absolutely, right in your eyes, dazzling you into arranging for a conspicuous absence of yourself, paling your intense promising colors until they were out of season for you? Did he white you out even then?

Dying, my grandmother's determination was vivid again, her courage as fresh as young grass. I hadn't ever seen her so lofty, almost imperious; death was a dirty penny she wouldn't stoop for. I was summoned from college to her sickroom, at home, to collect what she insisted on passing to me in person, making a physical gesture that resonated far louder and clearer than any testamental paper bell could. We had already said some of our farewells a month earlier when I was home on Christmas break, but certain matters had to be postponed until the last possible minute. She was in bed dozing, waiting for me, face powdered and cheeks rouged as though for a pleasanter outing. My kiss woke her. I couldn't see the sickness below her skin, the sly cells chewing through bone, excavating an insidious one-way tunnel. She still looked intact to me; only her dark eyes were worn, sunk deep in their sockets like eight balls dropping for end shots. I plumped up her pillows, propped her to a sitting position, and sat down on the edge of her bed. My mother left the room to take a nap, make some coffee or calls, go for a walk, get away from her mother-in-law's deathbed for the short time I was there to spell her.

"Eyes, darling eyes," my grandmother greeted me, "don't water me now, I'm for drying. Don't fear such dust. I'm keeping. I'm keeping in the eyes of your time."

I wasn't afraid, but I was crying.

She opened the drawer of her night table, took out a handful of jewelry, almost flung it in my lap, dismissing it disdainfully, such absurd little things: two gold necklaces, a diamond-studded wrist-watch, a string of yellowed pearls, two rings that will never fit my thicker fingers. I thanked her. "Bauble me not!" she commanded.

Then we got down to business. She reached into the drawer for the snapshot album we passed so many afternoons with and presented it to me delicately, reverently, her thin arm floating like a ballet dancer's toward a partner, her proud head nodding up and down: yes, yes. I moved to her side, leaned back on the pillows with her, our knees bent up to form a book rest. Then we did what we'd always done, turned the pages one by one. Only this time we did it in silence because, she said, "the words cooked away before me."

Slowly, slowly, we turned the pages until she fell asleep. I sat in a chair by her bed for a.while, holding my album, listening to her breathe, listening for the small song her bones, hollowed by disease, were whistling again.

The Way Mama Tells It

ROY BLOUNT, JR.

I was telling Lylah Battle about Mary Alec Poole—you know how Mary Alec is, she makes her children all go out the door in the morning in the order of height. Well, age. And I looked over at Mama and I said, "Mama, what are you doing?"

"Nothing," she said.

And she was taking notes!

She didn't want to let me see them. I said, "Now, Mama. I have a right to see that."

And she said, "Why?"

I said, "Honestly, Mama!" I believe she would actually have run off into the next room if she could get up from a chair quick as she used to. I went over there and made her show me what she'd written down.

She had written—scribbled, you know, but I know Mama's writing, it's the first writing I ever saw. She doesn't cross her *t*'s. Never has crossed her *t*'s and never will. It's a wonder I cross mine. She had written, *I thought I was bad because I alphabetize my spices.*

I said, "Mama, I didn't say that."

"What is your problem with it then?" she said. That's the way she talks now. Either gets it from the children or television. And the *tone* she uses! She's gotten right snippy. I mean, you know Mama, she would always come out with the strangest things, but it's bad enough to talk to children the way they are, without your mother getting just as snippy, or I believe worse. And there's nothing you can do to your mother.

You know how it started. Aileen! You don't know about this? I know you know about it, you just don't want to say you know about it because you know how torn up I am that everybody in the world knows about it.

Well, you're sweet. I think you're just *being* sweet, but you're sweet to be that way. I know I can tell you things, Aileen. Because

you have got good sense about what to repeat. That is exactly what
Mama has lost every last speck of. I lie awake at night, worrying.
What has Mama told today? What is she getting ready to tell? To
an *audience*?

That's what I'm telling you. Aileen, you just don't *know*. It's . . .
I don't know. Mama is so *quiet* at home, can't get her to talk. I
wouldn't mind a little adult conversation from her. But no, she
sits there saving it up.

You know, she got down so low when Lily died. She and that
cat used to be just almost the same person. They'd rock and watch
television, rock and watch television, Mama and that cat. Lily would
not sit on anyone else to save her life, just Mama. But every now
and then she would go out and get little birds and chipmunks
and things. . . .

What? No, *Lily* would. Honestly, Aileen! And what the vet believes is that she got ahold of a mouse or a bird or something that
had got ahold of something. Mama said Lily wouldn't get ahold
of anything that wasn't moving, but the vet said, Well, it might
have been some little animal that had *just* got ahold of something.
Mama would never accept that explanation. Just would not accept it.

Anyway, Lily came in and tried to throw up—when that cat
couldn't throw up you knew she wasn't herself—and died. And
Mama was left—well, I know it *was* hard on her; she sat there on
that rocker and said, "I haven't got anything to hold."

I said, "Hold the children, Mama."

She said, "They hurt my lap."

Well, I know they do squirm.

She didn't seem to have any heart for TV anymore. She wouldn't
even want to get up in the morning. You'd have to send the children
in there right after breakfast when they've got jelly all over them.
Even that didn't get her up one morning; I had to let them go out
and play in the pouring rain and then run jump in bed with Mama
wet as little drowned rats.

So I told Vaughn to take her down to the senior center. Maybe
I was wrong. But I thought maybe they'd teach her to crochet. I
said to Mama the other day, I said, "Mama, why don't you *crochet*?"
Other people's Mamas crochet. But no, she didn't take up cro-
cheting. She didn't take up decoupage. She didn't take up arranging flowers.

Mama took a course in storytelling.

That's what I'm telling you; that's what the *problem's* been.

She goes to festivals. They have *festivals* in it. All over the state. She wears an old-timey hat. And she tells stories.

About *us*. About *everybody*. Yes.

She wins *awards*.

She was in the paper about it. You didn't see it? Well, it was the Spartanburg paper. Somebody sent it to us. Aileen, I opened that paper up and I said, "Oh, my Lord." They quoted her stories in the paper. Mama doesn't tell stories about princesses and bears. She tells stories about me. She tells stories about Vaughn. She tells stories about Lily and the children. She tells stories about nearly everybody we know. And there just doesn't seem to be any stopping her. People come by and pick her up and drive her to these festivals. She's so popular.

I guess she is. I could be popular too if I told everything I knew, but I wouldn't have any friends left.

I said to Paulette Lovejohn yesterday, I said, "Paulette, you are going to hear about this. If I don't tell you about it somebody is going to tell you about it. So I'm going to tell you about it. I'm just as embarrassed as I can be, but my mama is going all over the state telling about how that washing-machine repair man showed up to fix your washing machine in your basement with a cast on his leg and went downstairs and it was so flooded from the washing machine that you kept worrying his cast was going to melt, and then you looked down and the waters had floated up all those cat BMs around him from back behind the furnace where you didn't know the cat had been going and he didn't want to say anything about it and you didn't want to say anything about it and finally he said he believed his cast *might* melt and he thought he'd come back when the basement had had more time to drain and you were so mortified about it—only the way Mama told it, she made it even worse because—"

You didn't hear about it? Oh, Aileen, I wish you could have seen Paulette's face when she told us about it. You know how Paulette is, how just-so she is about everything, and then to have cat BMs—and it wasn't even her cat. No, she doesn't have a cat. For that reason—that she's so just-so. Oh, Paulette can't even stand to have cat *hair* in her house. But the washing-machine repair man didn't have any way of knowing that. I thought Paulette was going to *die* when she came over and told us about that repairman and the expression on his face and all. And he was so *nice* about it— that's what made it worse, and his cast had a little child's writing on it.

And of course Mama was just sitting there. But we didn't know Mama would *repeat* it. And make it *worse*. Because—

No, see, we didn't know then. We knew she was telling stories, but none of us had had time to go near her and of course she hadn't let on to us what the stories were about. And she wasn't *writing down notes* then. Now she is. She doesn't even care really if you catch her at it, she just doesn't want you to take them away from her.

But I told Paulette, I said, "Mama is not the same person she was. We do not know what to expect of her any longer." I said, "I told Mama, 'Mama, when we were children you didn't tell us stories.' She said she was too busy raising us. She said we wouldn't sit still long enough. She said she didn't realize she knew any stories back then. I just gave up trying to reason with her."

I finally felt like I had to go hear her perform. I went to the big state finals of storytelling, which Mama came in second in—which I thought she should have won against the old man who did win; he just went on and on about outhouses and snakes. But I listened to Mama hold forth up there on that stage, Aileen, and she could have just as well been somebody else entirely. And people just applauding, and laughing, and their eyes getting wide. And my face burning. And of course afterward Mama is just in a world of her own; she doesn't want to talk to *us* about it, it's as if we don't have any say over what she thinks or does.

And she talks about what people *look* like. Like, you know, how Lloyd Salley is always looking like he's just getting ready to say something? Kind of beginning to smile and lean forward and even just barely open his mouth so you keep leaning forward to hear whatever it is that he has just thought of to say, until you realize he isn't ever going to say anything, that's just Lloyd? Mama describes things like that. And if that ever gets back to Lloyd I don't know *what* he will think. 'Course I guess we'll never know, if we have to hear it from Lloyd.

Paulette of course is just as hurt as she can be. But she doesn't know what to say to Mama. I try to talk to Mama about it, and she says it's a free country. I say, "Mama, that's what we all say. But you know, and I know, that when it comes to talking about people we know—people can stand being talked about behind their backs, as long as it *is* behind their backs, but when you do it out where all they have to do to hear it *themselves* is join the general public, it's treating them like they're not right real."

She says let them sue her.

I say, "Now, Mama, you don't want to start talking like that because people *will*." And not only that—Vaughn says old ladies can get away with a lot, but they can go too far. He says it is not out of the bounds of possibility, even in this day and age, that— Vaughn says there have been *fires* in this town that haven't been investigated as hard as they might.

Because—and it's not just *telling* stories about people, it's— that's what I was telling you. Mama makes them worse.

The way she tells the story about Paulette and the washing- machine man and the cat BMs . . . it was Lily that did them behind the furnace.

Of course maybe it was, but the way Mama tells *every* story, it involves Lily. Lily being sent out by Mama. To do things.

Mama says storytelling is an art form. She says it's her art. I say, "Mama, we are *happy* for you to have an art. That is not the point."

She just looks at me like—you know how a toddler will get sometimes, all of a sudden in a crowded grocery store or some- where, just get to bucking you so hard they lay flat out on the filthy floor, wallering and actually kind of grinding themselves down into the floor, yelling when you try to pull them up? Mama looks like she is just literally about to do something like that.

Aileen, I don't know what to think. If we'd been better about going to church I'd take Mama in to counsel with the pastor, but I don't know what the new pastor's name is and I hate to ask because you know the last one was Rev. Tinkle and they've been accused of not renewing him because of his name and they're sensitive about it. And if there is anybody in First Melrose Church who has heard the story Mama tells about the last time she went to church there—

That lady was there that Sunday; you know, I've told you about her, she's not all right, poor soul. Wandering in the aisle peering under the pews like she was looking for something and muttering in the middle of the sermon and getting closer and closer to the altar, and the preacher didn't know what to say and finally he said, sort of smoothly but with a little nudge of his head so that maybe somebody would get up and lead her somewhere without his having to say right out, you know, that he wasn't so enthusiastic about suffering *her* to come unto him—he said, "We are *all* search- ing here, together, as one, that the holiness of God's word be heard." And somebody in the Board of Stewards caught his mean- ing and took her arm as she was bending over peering and she looked up, surprised, and said in that right-out-loud voice, like people who aren't all right don't know any better than to use, she said, "*Somebody's* sitting on my *dollar*. 'Cause I didn't put it in the *collection*. Cause I got that *dollar* from Mr. Lef'wich for being *sweet* to him." And everybody turned to look over at the Leftwich family. And with that Lily jumped through an open window right into Mr. Leftwich's lap. Which is all true except for the part about Lily, which just makes it a better story—to Mama.

Mama always puts such a *point* on her stories.

The Little Chill

T. CORAGHESSAN BOYLE

Hal had known Rob and Irene, Jill, Harvey, Tootle, and Pesky since elementary school. They were all forty going on sixty.

Rob and Irene had been high school sweethearts, and now, after quitting their tenured teaching jobs, they brokered babies for childless couples like themselves. They regularly flew to Calcutta, Bahrain, and Sarawak to bring back the crumpled brown-faced little sacks of bones they located for the infertile wives of dry cleaners and accountants. Though they wouldn't admit it, they'd voted for Ronald Reagan.

Jill had a certain fragile beauty about her. She'd gone into a Carmelite nunnery after the obloquy of high school and the unrequited love she bore for Harvey, who at the time was hot for Tootle. She lived just up the street from Rob and Irene, in her late mother's house, and she'd given up the nun's life twelve years earlier to have carnal relations with a Safeway butcher named Eugene who left her with a blind spot in one eye, a permanent limp, and triplets.

Harvey had been a high school lacrosse star who quit college to join the Marines, acquiring a reputation for ferocity and selfless bravery during the three weeks he fought at Da Nang before taking thirty-seven separate bayonet wounds in his legs, chest, buttocks, and feet. He was bald and bloated, a brooding semi-invalid addicted to Quaalude, Tuinal, aspirin, cocaine, and Jack Daniel's, and he lived in the basement of his parents' house, eating little and saying less. He despised Hal, Rob and Irene, Jill, Tootle, and Pesky because they hadn't taken thirty-seven bayonet wounds each and because they were Communists and sellouts.

Tootle had been a cover girl, a macrobiot, the campaign manager for a presidential candidate from Putnam Valley, New York, who promised to push through legislation to animate all TV news features; and, finally, an environmentalist who spent all her waking

hours writing broadsides for the Marshwort Preservationists'
League. She was having an off/on relationship with an Italian race
car driver named Enzo.

Pesky was assistant manager of Frampold's LiquorMart, twice
divorced and the father of a fourteen-year-old serial murderer
whose twelve adult male victims all resembled Pesky in coloring,
build, and style of dress.

And Hal? Hal was home from California. For his birthday.

Jill hosted the party. She had to. The triplets—Steve, Stevie, and
Steven, now seven, seven, and seven, respectively—were hyper-
active, antisocial, and twice as destructive as Hitler's Panzer Corps.
She hadn't been able to get a baby-sitter for them since they learned
to crawl. "All right," Hal had said to her on the phone, "your house
then. Seven o'clock. Radical. Really." And then he hung up, thinking
of the dingy cavern of her mother's house, with its stained wallpaper, battered furniture, and howling drafts, and of the mortified
silence that would fall over the gang when they swung by to pick
up Jill on a Friday night and Mrs. Morlock—that big-bottomed,
horse-toothed parody of Jill—would insist they come in for hot
chocolate. But no matter. At least the place was big.

As it turned out, Hal was two hours late. He was from California,
after all, and this was his party. He hadn't seen any of these people
in what—six years now?—and there was no way he was going to
be cheated out of his grand entrance. At seven he pulled a pair of
baggy parachute pants over his pink hightops, stuck a gold mar-
ijuana-leaf stud through the hole in his left earlobe, wriggled into
an Ozzie Osbourne Barf Tour T-shirt though it was 26 degrees out
and driving down sleet, and settled into the Barcalounger in which
his deceased dad had spent the last two thirds of his life. He sipped
Scotch, watched the TV blip rhythmically, and listened to his own
sad old failing mom dodder on about the Jell-O mold she'd bought
for Mrs. Herkowitz across the street. Then, when he was good and
ready, he got up, slicked back his thinning, two-tone, forty-year-
old hair that looked more and more like mattress stuffing every
day, shrugged into his trenchcoat, and slammed out into the storm.

There were two inches of glare ice on the road. Hal thumped
his mother's stuttering Oldsmobile from tree to tree, went into a
180-degree spin, and schussed down Jill's driveway, narrowly
avoiding the denuded azalea bush, three Flexible Flyers, and a
staved-in Renault on blocks. He licked his fingertips and smoothed
down his sideburns on the doorstep, knocked perfunctorily, and

entered, grinning, in all his exotic fair-haired California glory. Unfortunately, the effect was wasted—no one but Jill was there. Hunched in the corner of a gutted sofa, she smiled wanly from behind a mound of soggy Fritos and half a gallon of California dip. "Hi," she said in a voice of dole. "They're coming, they're coming." Then she winked her bad eye at him and limped across the room to stick her tongue in his mouth.

She was clinging to him, licking at his mustache and telling him about her bout with breast cancer, when the doorbell rang and Rob and Irene came hurtling into the room shrieking, "My God, look at you!" They were late, they screamed, because the babysitter never showed for their daughter Soukamathandravaki, whose frightened little face peered in out of the night behind them.

An instant later Harvey swung furiously up the walk on his silver crutches, Tootle and Pesky staggered in together with reddened noses and dilated pupils, and Steve, Stevie, and Steven emerged from the back of the house on their minibikes to pop wheelies in the middle of the room. The party was on.

"So," Harvey snarled, fencing Hal into the corner with the gleaming shafts of his crutches, "they tell me you're doing pretty good out there, huh, bub?"

Pesky and Tootle were standing beside him, grinning till Hal thought their lips would dry out and stick to their teeth, and Pesky had his arm around Tootle's shoulder.

"Me?" Hal said, with a modest shrug. "Well, since you ask, my agent did say that—"

Harvey cut him off, turning to Pesky with a wild leer and shouting, "So how's the kid, what's his name—Damian?"

Dead silence fell over the room.

Rob and Irene froze, clutching Dixie cups of purple passion to their chests, and Jill, who'd been opening their eyes to the infighting, petty abuses, and catastrophic outrages of the food stamp office where she worked, caught her tongue. Even Steve, Stevie, and Steven snapped to attention. They'd been playfully binding little Soukamathandravaki to one of the dining room chairs with electrical tape, but at the mention of Damian they looked around them in unison and vanished.

"You S.O.B.," Pesky said, his fingers dug so deep in Tootle's shoulder his knuckles went white. "You crippled fascist Marine Corps burnout."

Harvey jerked his big head to one side and spat on the floor.

"What'd they give him, life plus a hundred and fifty years? Or'd they send him to Matteawan?"

"Hey," Irene shouted, a desperate keening edge to her voice. "Hey, do you guys remember all those wild pranks we used to pull back in high school?" She tore across the room, waving her Dixie cup. "Like when we smeared that black stuff on our faces and burned the Jewish star on Dr. Rosenbaum's front lawn?"

Everyone ignored her.

"Harv," Hal said, reaching out to take his arm. But Harvey jerked violently away. "Get your stinking hands off me!" he roared—before he lost his balance and fell with a sad clatter of aluminum into the California dip.

"Serves you right, you bitter S.O.B.," Pesky growled, standing over him as if they'd just gone fifteen rounds. "The crippled war hero. Why don't you show us your scars, huh?"

"Pesky," Hal hissed, "leave it, will you?"

Rob and Irene were trying to help Harvey to his feet, but he fought them off, sobbing with rage. There was California dip on the collar of his campaign jacket. Hairless and pale, with his quivering jowls and splayed legs, he looked like a monstrous baby dropped there on the rug.

"Or the time Pesky ran up in front of Mrs. Gold's class in the third grade and blew on his thumb till he passed out. Remember that?" Irene was saying, when the room was rent by a violent, predatory shriek, as if someone had torn a hawk in half. It was Tootle. She twisted out from under Pesky's arm and slammed her little white fist into his kidney. "You!" she sputtered. "Who are you to talk, lording it over Harvey as if he was some kind of criminal or something? At least he fought for his country. What'd you do, huh?" Her eyes were swollen. There was a froth of saliva caught in the corner of her mouth.

Pesky swung around. He was wearing his trademark Levi's— jeans, jacket, sweatshirt, socks, and big-buckled belt. If only they made shoes, he used to say. "Yeah, yeah, tell us about it," he sneered. "You little whore. Peddling your ass just like—"

"Canada, that's what *you* did about it. Like a typical wimp."

"Hey, hold on," Hal said, lurching out of the corner in his parachute pants. "I don't believe this. We all tried to get out of it—it was a rotten war, an illegal war, Nixon and Johnson's war. What's the matter with you? Don't you remember?"

"The marches," Irene said.

"The posters," Rob joined in.

"A cheap whore, that's all. Cover girl, my ass."

"Shut up!" Tootle shrieked, turning on Hal. You're just as bad as Pesky. Worse. You're a hypocrite. At least he knows he's a piece of crap." She threw back a cup of purple passion and leveled her green-eyed glare on him. "And you think you're so high and mighty, out there in Hollywood. Well, la-de-da, that's what I say."

"He's an artist," Harvey said from the floor. "He co-wrote the immortal script for the *Life with Beanie* show."

"Screw you."

"Screw you too."

And then suddenly, as if it signaled a visitation from another realm, there was the deep-throated cough of a precision engine in the driveway, a sputter and its dying fall. As one, the seven friends turned to the door. There was a thump. A knock—*dat dat-dat-dat da*. And then: " 'Allo, 'allo, anybody is home?"

It was Enzo. Tall, noble, with the nose of an emperor and a weave of silver in his hair so rich it might have been hammered from the mother lode itself. He was dressed in a coruscating jump-suit with Pennzoil and Pirelli patches across the shoulder and chest, and he held his crash helmet in his hand. "Baby," he said, crossing the room in two strides and taking Tootle in his arms. "Ciao."

No one moved. No one said a thing.

"Beech of a road," Enzo said. "Ice, you know." Outside, through the open door, the sleek low profile of his Lazaretto 2200 Pinin Farina coupe was visible, the windshield plated with ice, sleet driving down like straight pins. "Tooka me seventeen and a half minutes from La Guardia—a beech, huh? But baby, at least I'm here."

He looked around him as if seeing the others for the first time and then, without a word, crossed the room to the stereo, ran a quick finger along the spines of the albums, and flipped a black platter from its jacket as casually as if he were flipping pizzas in Napoli. He dropped the stylus, and as the room filled with music he began to move his hips and mime the words: "Oooh-oooh, I heard it through the grapevine...."

Marvin Gaye. Delectable, smooth, icy cool, ancient.

Pesky reached down to help Harvey from the floor. Jill took Hal's arm. Rob and Irene began to snap their fingers, and Enzo swung Tootle out into the middle of the floor.

They danced till they dropped.

Angel of Mercy, Angel of Wrath

ETHAN CANIN

On Eleanor Black's seventy-first birthday a flock of birds flew into her kitchen through a window that she had opened every morning for forty years. They flew in all at once, without warning or reason, from the ginko tree at the corner of Velden Street where they had sat every day since President Roosevelt's time. They were huge and dirty and black, the size of cats practically, much larger than she had ever imagined. Birds were so small in the sky. In the air, even in the clipped ginko ten yards from the window, they were nothing more than faint dots of color. Now they were in her kitchen, though, batting against the ceiling and the yellow walls she had just washed a couple of months ago, and their stink and their cries and their frantic knocking wings made it hard for her to breathe.

She sat down and took a water pill. They were screaming like wounded animals, flapping in tight circles around the light fixture so that she got dizzy looking at them. She reached for the phone and pushed the button that automatically dialed her son, who was a doctor.

"Bernard," she said, "there's a flock of crows in the flat."

"It's five in the morning, Mom."

"It is? Excuse me, because it's seven out here. I forgot. But the crows are flying in my kitchen."

"Mother?"

"Yes?"

"Have you been taking all your medicines?"

"Yes, I have."

"Has Dr. Gluck put you on any new ones?"

"No."

"What did you say was the matter?"

"There's a whole flock of crows in the flat."

Bernard didn't say anything.

"I know what you're thinking," she said.

"I'm just making the point that sometimes new medicines can change people's perceptions."

"Do you want to hear them?"

"Yes," he said, "that would be fine. Let me hear them."

She held the receiver up toward the ceiling. The cries were so loud she knew he would pick them up, even long distance.

"Okay?" she said.

"I'll be damned."

"What am I supposed to do?"

"How many are there?"

"I don't know."

"What do you mean, you don't know?"

"They're flying like crazy around the room. How can I count them?"

"Are they attacking you?"

"No, but I want them out anyway."

"How can I get them out from Denver?"

She thought for a second. "I'm not the one who went to Denver."

He breathed out on the phone, loud, like a child. He was chief of the department at Denver General. "I'm just making the point," he said, "that I can't grab a broom in Colorado and get the birds out of your place in New York."

"Whose fault is that?"

"Mom," he said.

"Yes?"

"Call the SPCA. Tell them what happened. They have a department for things like this. They'll come out and get rid of them."

"They're big."

"I know," he said. "Don't call 911. That's for emergencies. Call the regular SPCA. Okay?"

"Okay," she said.

He paused. "You can call back later to let us know what happened."

"Okay."

"Okay?"

"Okay." She waited a moment. "Do you want to say anything else?"

"No," he said.

She hung up, and a few seconds later all the birds flew back out the window except for two of them, which flew the other way, through the swinging door that she had left open and into the living room. She followed them in there. One of them was hopping on the bookshelf, but while Eleanor watched, the other one flew straight at the window from the center of the room and collided with the glass. The pane shook and the bird fell several feet before it righted itself and did the same thing again. For a few moments Eleanor stood watching, and then she went to the kitchen, took out the bottle of cream soda, and poured herself a glass. Yesterday it had been a hundred degrees out. When she finished she put the bottle back, sat down again, and dialed 911.

"Emergency," said a woman.

Eleanor didn't say anything.

"911 Emergency."

"There's a flock of crows in my apartment."

"Birds?"

"Yes."

"You have to call the SPCA."

"They're going to break the window."

"Listen," she said, "we're not supposed to give this kind of advice, but all you have to do is move up quietly behind a bird and pick it up. They won't hurt you. I grew up on a farm."

"I grew up here."

"You can do that," the woman said, "or you can call the SPCA."

She hung up and went back to the living room. One still perched itself on the edge of her bookshelf and sat there, opening and closing its wings, while the other one, the berserk one, flew straight at the front window, smashed into it, fell to the sill, and then took to the air again. Again and again it flew straight at the window, hitting it with a sound like a walnut in a nutcracker, falling to the sill, then flapping crookedly back toward the center of the room to make another run. Already the window had small blotches of bluish feather oil on it. The bird hit it again, fell flapping to the sill, and this time stayed there, perched. Through the window Eleanor noticed that the house across the street from her had been painted green.

"Stay there," she said. "I'm going to open the window."

She took two steps toward the bird, keeping the rest of her body as still as she could, like a hunting dog, moving one leg, pausing, then moving the other. Next to her on the bookshelf the calm bird cocked its head in little jerks—down, up, sideways, down. She advanced toward the window until the berserk one suddenly flew up, smashed against the glass, fell to the sill, flew up again, smashed, and perched once more. She stopped. It stood there. To her horror Eleanor could see its grotesque pulse through its skin, beating frantically along the wings and the torso as if the whole bird were nothing but a speeding heart. She stood perfectly still for several minutes, watching.

"Hello," she said.

It lifted its wings as though it were going to fly against the window again, but then lowered them.

"My husband was a friend of Franklin Roosevelt's," she said.

The bird didn't move.

"Why can't you be like your friend?" She pointed her chin at the one on the bookshelf, which opened its beak. Inside it the throat was black. She took another step toward the window. Now she was so close to the berserk one she could see the ruffled, purplish chest feathers and the yellow ring around its black irises. Its heart still pulsated but it didn't raise its wings, just cocked its head the way the other one had. She reached her two hands halfway toward it and stopped. "It's my birthday today," she whispered. She waited like that, her hands extended, until she had counted to forty. The bird cocked and retracted its head, then stood still. When it had been still for a while she reached the rest of the way and touched her hands to both sides of its quivering body.

For a moment, for an extended odd moment in which the laws of nature didn't seem to hold, for a moment in which she herself felt just the least bit confused, the bird stood still. It was oily and cool, and its askew feathers poked her palms. What she thought about at that second, of all things, was the day her husband, Charles, had come into the living room to announce to her that President Kennedy was going to launch missiles against the Cubans. She had felt the same way when he told her that, as if something had gone slightly wrong with nature but she couldn't quite comprehend it, the way right now she couldn't quite comprehend the bird's stillness until suddenly it shrieked and twisted in her hands and flew up into the air.

She stepped back. It circled through the room and smashed into the glass again, this time on the other window next to the bookshelf. The calm bird lighted from its perch, went straight down the hall, and flew into her bedroom. The berserk one righted itself and flew into the glass again, then flapped up and down against it, pocking the wide pane with its wings like a moth. Eleanor went to the front window, but she couldn't open it because the Mexican boy who had painted the apartments last year had broken the latch. She crossed into the kitchen and looked up the number of the SPCA.

A child answered the phone. Eleanor had to think for a second. "I'd like to report two crows in my house," she said.

The child put down the phone and a moment later a woman came on the line. "I'd like to report two crows in my house," said Eleanor. The woman hung up.

Eleanor looked up the number again. This time a man answered. "Society," he said.

"There are two crows in my house," said Eleanor.

"Did they come in a window?"

"I always have that window opened," she answered. "I've had it opened for years with nothing happening."

"Then it's open now?"

"Yes."

"Have you tried getting them out?"

"Yes, I grabbed one the way the police said but it bit me."

"It bit you?"

"Yes. The police gave me that advice over the phone."

"Did it puncture the skin?"

"It's bleeding a little."

"Where are they now?"

"They're in the living room," she said. "One's in another room."

"All right," he said. "Tell me your address."

When they had finished Eleanor hung up and went into the living room. The berserk one was perched on the sill, looking into the street. She went into the bedroom and had to look around a while before she found the calm one sitting on top of her lamp.

She had lived a long enough life to know there was nothing to be lost from waiting out situations, so she turned out the light in the bedroom, went back into the living room, took the plastic seat cover off the chair President Roosevelt had sat on, and, crossing her arms, sat down on it herself. By now the berserk bird was calm. It stood on the windowsill, and every once in a while it strutted three or four jerky steps up the length of the wood, turned toward her, and bobbed its head. She nodded at it.

The last time the plastic had been off that chair was the day Richard Nixon resigned. Charles had said that Franklin Roosevelt would have liked it that way, so they took the plastic off and sat on it that day and for a few days after, until Charles let some peanuts fall between the cushion and the arm and she got worried and covered it again. After all those years the chair was still firm.

The bird eyed her. Its feet had four claws and were scaly, like the feet on a butcher's chicken. "Get out of here," she said. "Go! Go through the window you came from." She flung her hand out at it, flapped it in front of the chair, but the bird didn't move. She sat back.

When the doorbell rang she got up and answered on the building intercom. It was the SPCA, though when she opened the door to the apartment she found a young Negro woman standing there. She was fat, with short braided hair. After the woman had introduced herself and stepped into the apartment Eleanor was surprised to see that the hair on the other side of her head was long. She wore overalls and a pink T-shirt.

"Now," she said, "where are those crows you indicated?"

"In the living room," said Eleanor. "He was going to break the glass soon if you didn't get here."

"I got here as soon as I received the call."

"I didn't mean *that*."

The woman stepped into the living room, swaying slightly on her right leg, which looked partly crippled. The bird hopped from the sill to the sash, then back to the sill. The woman stood motionless with her hands together in front of her, watching it. "That's no crow," she said finally. "That's a grackle. That's a rare species here."

"I grew up in New York," said Eleanor.

"So did I." The woman stepped back, turned away from the bird, and began looking at Eleanor's living room. "A crow's a rare species here too, you know. Some of that particular species gets confused and comes in here from Long Island."

"Poor things."

"Say," said the woman. "Do you have a little soda or something? It's hot out."

"I'll look," said Eleanor. "I heard it was a hundred degrees out yesterday."

"I can believe it."

Eleanor went into the kitchen. She opened the refrigerator door, stood there, then closed it. "I'm out of everything," she called.

"That's all right."

She filled a glass with water and brought it out to the woman. "There you go," she said.

The woman drank it. "Well," she said then, "I think I'll make the capture now."

"It's my birthday today."

"Is that right?"

"Yes, it is."

"How old are you?"

"Eighty-one."

The woman reached behind her, picked up the water glass, and made the gesture of a toast. "Well, happy eighty-first," she said. She put down the glass and walked over and opened the front window, which still had smudges on it. Then she crouched and approached the bird on the other sill. She stepped slowly, her head tilted to the side and her large arms held in front of her, and when she was a few feet before the window she bent forward and took the bird into her hands. It flapped a couple of times and then sat still in her grasp while she turned and walked it to the open window, where she let it go and it flew away into the air.

When the woman had left Eleanor put the plastic back on the chair and called her son again. The hospital had to page him, and when he came on the phone he sounded annoyed.

"It was difficult," she said. "The fellow from SPCA had to come out."

"Did he do a decent job?"

"Yes."

"Good," he said. "I'm very pleased."

"It was a rare species. He had to use a metal-handled capturing device. It was a long set of tongs with hinges."

"Good. I'm very pleased."

"Are you at work?"

"Yes, I am."

"Okay, then."

"Okay."

"Is there anything else?"

"No," he said. "That's it."

A while after they hung up, the doorbell rang. It was the SPCA woman again, and when Eleanor let her upstairs she found her standing in the hall with a bunch of carnations wrapped in newspaper. "Here," she said. "Happy birthday from the SPCA."

"Oh, my," said Eleanor. For a moment she thought she was going to cry. "They're very elegant."

The woman stepped into the apartment. "I just thought you were a nice lady."

"Why, thank you very much." She took them and laid them down on the hall vanity. "Would you like a cup of tea?"

"No, thanks. I just wanted to bring them up. I've got more calls to take care of."

"Would you like some more water?"

"That's all right," said the woman. She smiled and touched Eleanor on the shoulder, then turned and went back downstairs.

Eleanor closed the door and unwrapped the flowers. She looked closely at their lengths for signs that they were a few days old, but could find none. The stalks were unswollen and cleanly clipped at an angle. She brought them into the kitchen, washed out the vase, and set them up in it. Then she poured herself a half glass of cream soda. When she was finished she went into the bedroom to the bedside table, where she took a sheet of paper from the drawer and began a letter.

> Dear President Bush,
> I am a friend of President Roosevelt's writing you on my eightieth birthday on the subject of a rare species that came into my life without warning today, and that needs help from a man such as yourself

She leaned up straight and examined the letter. The handwriting got smaller at the end of each line, so she put the paper aside and took out a new sheet. At that moment the bird flew down and perched on the end of the table. Eleanor jerked back and stood from the chair. "Oh," she said and touched her heart. "Of course."

Then she patted her hair with both hands and sat down again. The bird tilted its head to look at her. Eleanor looked back. Its coat was black but she could see an iridescent rainbow in the chest feathers. It strutted a couple of steps toward her, flicking its head left, right, forward. Its eyes were dark. She put out her hand, leaned a little bit, and, moving it steadily and slowly, touched the feathers once and withdrew. The bird hopped and opened its wings. She sat back and watched it. Sitting there, she knew it probably didn't mean anything. She was just a woman in an apartment, and it was just a bird that had wandered in. It was too bad they couldn't talk to each other. She would have liked to know how old the bird was, and what it was like to have lived in the sky.

Old Court

ELIZABETH COX

The room, even at midday, held a romantic dimness as though it were always lit by a lantern. Sunlight hit the dark wood floor and mahogany tables in a way that gave the room a yellow glow. And the optical illusion of a lantern was strong when the wind blew, changing the shadows so that light fought itself like a boxer against the walls. But even with all that sunlight, there were corners that remained unlit.

Three chairs were arranged around a rug. The larger, more comfortable chair was my mother's; so was the table beside it—her favorite, made of cherrywood. She kept her sewing on that table and would never let a glass or a bottle be set upon it. As I remember her table, and the yellow light of that room, it stands in my mind a vision that is like a dream, becoming immemorial and ancient as a court.

The Civil War had been over three years when my father died. I was nine then, too young to be the man of the house. Sometimes my uncle would come. He put his hand on my shoulder as if I were a grown man, and I liked for him to be there.

During our last summer and fall in that house, a shift of happenings began to occur. I was eleven then. Men came by on horseback. Strangers. They arrived in a flurry, as birds would, the horses jostling even as the men jumped from them. We never knew when to expect their arrival. This time, I could see from a low windowsill and count six of them, at least, all going to the back of the house to dip one by one from the well. They could just as easily have robbed us. My mother's jewelry box did not have much, but had a gold wedding band, and a watch with three diamond chips, and two pearl earrings given to her by an aunt who lived in New England.

There had been a light snow the night before, though it was

October and unusual for cold weather to come that early in Mississippi. Marigolds still bloomed in the fields. The snow came around five in the morning, but melted and was gone by ten.

"They've come back," I yelled toward the other room. My mother knew, her ears attuned to every danger. We lived in the house alone, miles from town. All we had was the house, our garden out back, my mother's job at the piece-goods store and small jobs I could take in summer months, a field lying fallow, and these men rushing to our well in bad times. The well had not filled up yet from the summer's drought. We had barely enough water for ourselves, and them taking all they could, then heading out—my mother relieved each time.

"We must go away soon," she would say, but found it hard to leave.

And when the men came, she hid herself where she could see the door, but where she wouldn't be seen. She held a shotgun loaded and ready, pointed at the door. I often wondered if she would have turned herself loose to kill or maim, if she would actually pull back the trigger.

"They've come back," I yelled again, but could see her already crouched between the large chair and table. Her hair was pulled up into a braid on the crown of her head, and she looked prettier than she had looked in months.

The men called obscenities back and forth, their talk like a thorn stuck in my mind. I hoped my mother wouldn't notice, thinking she must go out and grab them by their ears, swat each one for his remarks. In fact, I couldn't picture her failing to do this, so I wanted to warn them to hold it down, lest she hear.

I knelt by the window, my eyes barely over the sill. I thought that only my eyes were over the sill, forgetting about the top of my head. The men walked around the yard in the openness of their desires. They wore boots in summer and they wore boots now, only now they wore heavy coats and caps that fit tightly around their heads. The strong, flatland wind gave their clothes a heavy flutter, and the caps made their eyes seem wide, blank as owls.

Each man drank from a dipper beside the well, and I laughed because it was the dipper I let my dog drink from. I wondered where Buster was, since he usually barked and snapped at them. One man picked up a piece of leather. It was part of my father's belt that I had cut to make a collar for Buster. I hoped the man wouldn't take the last scrap, but as I saw him tuck it into the side pouch of his saddle, I tried to forget about it. I didn't know how many times they might come back to the house, or what else they might do. We lived halfway between two towns, and even when my father was alive men would ride by and ask for water—but they always asked.

When one of the men saw me at the windowsill, he ran and hit the screen to scare me. My mother moved in the next room. I felt the sudden queasiness one feels just before throwing up, so I lay flat against the floorboards. Upon hearing them leave, I relaxed enough to count the cracks on the wall and thought about when Uncle Josh would come.

My uncle came out on Saturdays. He was never married, though I think he had women he lived with from time to time. He was tall, like my father, and had dark hair that never looked combed. My mother's hair was straight. At bedtime when she brushed it a hundred strokes, her voice grew musical. I think it was the only time she thought of herself as pretty. She threw her hair over her face and brushed it from the nape of her neck, then pushed it back again. It was so long she could sit on it. And at those times, she talked and asked questions or listened to whatever I said, without being busy. Her expression as calm as soap.

My dad was a large man. I thought I would never be that large, and in fact I'm not. We duck hunted all winter—my dad and me and Uncle Josh—and always on Christmas Eve. Christmas Eve morning before the light, we would rise and eat the cold ham biscuits my mother left out. She said she was not getting up at any four o'clock in the morning just to fix breakfast. But she would prepare biscuits late at night and wrap them already piled with ham and butter, so that in the morning they were good, if not warm. And she always called from the bedroom anyway at four-fifteen, "You boys need anything?" so that we could tell her the biscuits were fine, maybe the best she had made, because she had been up later than we had fixing them. We thanked her in that way, so she fell asleep satisfied.

Our duck pond was not really a pond, but a slough, a natural marshland forty yards wide and good for ducks. On almost any Saturday morning in the late fall, Uncle Josh came by with hip boots and gear, and we waded the fields the way we had done with my father, breaking the ice in places. Josh broke it as he stepped, without thinking. I broke it on purpose, going whichever way I saw unbroken patches, so I could break them and hear them crack.

Sometimes Josh brought other men with him, but usually he took only me. He taught the difference between a birch and a poplar, and would tell stories of my father, how they rode together in the war. He told how they named their horses after women they loved and that my dad named his horse Ruby after my mother, saying if he was going into something he might not come back from he would go into it with Ruby. Each time Josh told me this he said it with such fervor that I wondered if that time of his life was the best and did he long for it. Once I asked him, and he stared at me for a moment as though I had shown him a truth he hadn't expected.

"Maybe," he said. He pulled me to stand close to him. "But I don't wish for it." Our hip boots touched. It was awkward to stand that close, because of our boots, but I stood, not moving. I even put my arm around his waist, not out of love, but to keep from falling. He said, "I only meant to give you an idea of it, and how we were afraid."

"You never said about that."

"I didn't?"

"No."

"It was when you saw them coming," he began, and I settled in to listen. "Saw them coming toward you with what you had, maybe more, and bent on doing to you what you would do to them." His eyes went back to remember. "It killed something in me, and in your father, too, I think. Though not as much." He looked as though he were telling something different now. "I mean," he said, "the things we had to do."

I didn't know what he meant. "Those men came back," I told him. "They kicked Buster and hurt his ribs." Josh didn't say anything, and I wondered if he knew where he was and if we would hunt anymore that day.

We did. We hunted three more hours. The sun came all the way up, but couldn't warm us because our boots and jackets were wet. Our bodies were dry, though, and warm enough, if not as warm as they would be. We walked back with greenheads hanging from the back satchels of our vests, and talked about how the house would smell like mincemeat and how the heat would hold our faces the same as the cold did, only better.

The table was set, the floor swept and slightly damp from being mopped. My mother met us at the door to prevent us from dragging in our boots. We left boots, shirts and pants on the steps, and she made us wash up. It always struck me as strange that we had to be clean for meals, but it didn't matter much if we were dressed. My mother usually wore a skirt and flowered blouse. We wore long underwear, though Josh put on pants. If company came, I put on pants, too.

"Your father is dead," my mother told me one day when I got in from school. She sat in the chair where she always sat, so that when I walked in she was what I saw first. I saw her that day, too, but she had her arms outstretched before her, leaning toward me, and I went into them as deep as I could. Then she pushed back, and I saw in her face the very root of her disbelief.

"How?" I finally asked, but she had already begun to tell me.

"He lifted lumber into a wagon. A heavy load, most likely." She sounded admonitory, if not critical. "And it fell back on him," she said. "He climbed onto the wagon, and logs rolled across him. When they lifted the load off his chest, he was already gone." She began to cry softly. I wanted to, but couldn't. Instead, I watched her tears squeeze out from those tight-closed eyelids, falling quick and soft between us. She kept her arms around me, not even attempting to cover her face as I would have done. It was as though she could not be embarrassed or ashamed, only sad. She grieved for my dad better than I did, for I refused to bear it for almost a year. And finally, when I could talk of him and show tears, my mother's tears were gone.

The men on horseback came during the summer months and on that one October day, but it was Christmas Eve when they came by at night. My mother and I attended a Christmas pageant in town and got home late, ten o'clock. The men probably had been there already and found the house empty, not wanting anything there, but wanting something to do with us, a mischief.

My mother would stay up late and put out whatever I received for Christmas, pretending still that it was brought in secret, both of us pretending, because there could be only one or two presents, and sometimes the surprise was all. So we held to this, partly because she wanted to and never mentioned doing differently, and partly because I wanted to prolong the belief. Besides, most of the time my mother thought of me as a child. It was only now and then that she stood back, even stepped back physically from me and said, "You look like your father when you do that," and she looked a little longer, not seeing him exactly, but seeing me in a different way. I always liked those times, because she wouldn't hug me to her as though she needed something I couldn't give anymore, but instead would ask me to perform some chore that she said had become too difficult for her.

We were not home fifteen minutes before we heard them, the hooves and galloping we had heard before, but always in the daytime. I had put on my pajamas, soft heavy material that kept me warmer sometimes than my clothes. My mother still had not undressed, but she had set the table for the next morning's breakfast. I hoped she might brush her hair.

When I entered the kitchen, she put out the lamp. For a moment neither of us could see, and she reached through the dark for me, whispering, "Luther, Luther."

"I'm here." But her hands had already found me.

"Get the shotgun." She went another direction as I fingered my way toward the mantel and above it to where the shotgun hung. It was always loaded.

She came toward me again, both of us now able to see each other's shadows. The moon was full and the room flooded with its light. The floor shone white as water, and I almost expected, when I stepped, to hear the crack of ice.

I handed the shotgun to her. She took it with one hand, her arm seeming longer in the moonlight, thinner than it really was. With her other hand, she pushed something toward me.

"Merry Christmas," she said.

I could not see, but knew it was a rifle, and wondered how she would pay for it. A Winchester 66. It was what I wanted, but hadn't imagined getting. I stroked it and could see the wooden stock and the silky black barrel. I felt sorry about the present I had for her. It wasn't enough.

The men had stopped their horses. They didn't go around to the well, nor did they come with the flurry of their usual visits. There were only two of them.

"Is it loaded?" I asked.

She said it was.

I readied myself in a position below the sill, and wondered if I would have to kill a man or if it would kill something in me. I didn't feel the hate I thought I would need to feel. The door was being tried—no knock, just breaking in—and I felt a rising nausea.

I squeezed the trigger, not out the door, but out the window. The breaking of glass was all I heard. I squeezed again and again and the shots came out like tears from those tight-closed eyelids. My mother called my name and at last, after what seemed an interminable wait, the noise leveled out against the night's quiet. But before full silence fell again, I could see in that holy Christmas light a horse rising up, then dropping, his legs crumpling as paper would, paper legs to hold his heavy body and head. And I heard his sound, after the sound the gun made, a whinnying too high-pitched for anything but pain. A pure calling for help, and his knees bending to that call.

"Damn." One man ran to the horse. "Damn." He looked down at it, a dark heap like coal. My mother came to the window. The man at the door yelled to his friend, and they both climbed onto the other horse. We watched as they rode off.

"They are drunk," my mother said. Her first words. But she was quiet about what I had done. And finally, when she lit the lamp, minutes after the men galloped off, her face was like chalk. And she tried to praise me, as though what I had done was well thought-out and what I planned to do.

But it wasn't. It was what I did. And she thought I had decided to shoot, but not to shoot the man. She thought my mind made the decision not to kill him.

"You decided," she said, giving me credit. "You made that decision from some old court in your mind. I am proud."

"But, Mama—"

"I am proud." She would always see me better than I was.

The next morning when I went out I knew I had to dig a hole big enough to bury the horse there where he lay. He could never be moved, not by me nor my mother, so I dug most of the day, and later in the evening my mother helped. It took two days to dig a hole big enough to shove him into. By then the flies had come and the sun had begun to bake his skin.

My mother and I wore kerchiefs on our faces to keep from breathing the odor. We were glad the air was cold and kept the flesh from rotting too quickly. I had uncinched the saddle and was able to pull it from under the horse, but I couldn't loosen the bit from his mouth. His teeth had locked shut around it. Then I remembered my father opening a horse's mouth once by squeezing the sides where the mouth began, and when I did that, the bit fell out. We threw the bridle and saddle into the hole with him, and the halter strap, but I kept the blanket that had covered his back and protected him from sores.

The day we pushed him into the hole, it was raining. My mother packed our trunk and filled the wagon with all she could. Josh and the man from the piece-goods store came to help us bring our furniture to the new house.

We did not move far, but into town where there were lawns and neighbors. A few weeks went by before I remembered that I had failed to give my mother her gift. We rode back to the house, which no one lived in now, but had been sold with the land. The mound of dirt rose fresh, and we shuddered to think what was beneath it. The door of the house had blown open, and snow or rain had ruined the front entrance. The romantic dimness had gone.

I climbed to pull a loose brick from the fireplace and removed a small, rectangular box wrapped in paper with shiny red flowers. My mother loved the paper and praised it. I watched and took the praise.

The box held a necklace, its pendant the shape of a leaf. It was yellow gold and opened like a locket. When she opened it, there was a picture inside, the only picture I could find, which was of herself when she was ten years old.

"I had forgotten," she told me. And I didn't know if she had forgotten she gave it to me, or forgotten her childhood. I had cut out the face to fit exactly inside the leaf, so that her hair and chin were leaf-shaped.

She sat down on an old crate and I stood close beside her. "Put it on me," she said. So I did. She pressed it flat against her chest. Then she turned her head to the window and fingered the leaf, opening and closing it to hear the soft click. But when she turned her gaze back to me, her eyes were so full of admiration that I felt like a small god. She put her hand on my back and the smile that came to her face was like a crescent, each corner turning upward as if it had been drawn there.

I smiled, too, but tried to pretend I had smiled at something else—outside maybe—a bush. Then I looked to see the pane still broken, and the simply rounded mound of dirt, the dark heap beneath it that would stay beneath me, like something I would have to stand on. But all around us the rest of the land lay flat, and as far as I could see, it went out straight before us.

Dying for Some Time

NICHOLAS DELBANCO

They sit in the cool of the living room, although to call it cool is just an expression, a manner of speaking; it's hot. The bedroom's worse, the kitchen unspeakable, and no one sits outside. Harriet bought an indoor-outdoor thermometer for her east-facing window last November, and when the temperature outside gets the same as inside—this morning it reached 70 by seven-forty-five— she closes the window and pulls all the blinds and turns on the fan and holds tight.

This works. She tries not to notice, tries to move slowly and drink. The radio announcer warns that very young and sick and old people particularly should stay out of the heat and avoid strenuous exercise and wear loose light clothing. So she wears her yellow nightie, the one Husband gave her forty years ago and that got too tight on her until she shrank again. She wears her white slippers to walk. Moving slowly's not a problem; it's what she can manage these years. Her younger sister, Julia, hardly moves at all. She sits in the Barcalounger, tilting up for television and for meals, then down. She lets herself be waited on as if Harriet's her servant, not the one with the sciatica, the one who pays the rent. They wait out this heat wave together—this greenhouse effect, this hottest June anybody can remember or even a madman would want.

Julia drinks iced tea. She likes pickled beans for some reason also and swears they keep her cool. She doesn't complain, doesn't admire the fan or her sister's provisions or seem to notice, even, how it's dark all afternoon. The blinds have been down since eight o'clock; the curtains with the climbing roses on the picket fence are drawn. Julia's husband, Peter, is in the hospital at Burlington; that's why she visits now. Yet how have they come to this pass? How has Harriet changed from that girl on the wall—the one with the white shirtwaist and the yellow hair?

Even now she can remember how her posy wilted while the

painter studied her, adjusting his easel, saying, There, there. She stared out the window as if she saw a sunset, trying to look soulful for three hours at a time. Then Harriet became the woman in the photograph, standing at the altar. And here it hadn't been hard to look soulful, for she could remember as if it happened yesterday, not on September 2, 1924, how her stomach had been jumping, how her mouth tasted like the bottom of a birdcage and her knees went weak. Husband had had to hold her waist not for show but for balance. Then she was the mother of one, then of three; there's a photograph of Park Street with her children on the porch. There's one of how they helped her move into this place—this pasture, as she likes to say—where they gaze for all the world the way she herself used to, staring out for all the world the way she herself used to, staring out just such a window while the photographer announced, That's it, that's fine, a little more to the left now, this way, hold it, that's wonderful, look at me, right.

"Tomorrow we'll go visiting," she says.

"What's that?" asks Julia.

"I said tomorrow we'll go up to Burlington. We'll visit Peter."

"Yes. I went to see him once."

"Four times. We saw him last Tuesday, remember?"

"When she drops her voice," Julia says to the plate, "I know I'm not supposed to hear. I know the news is bad."

The news was bad all winter. The winter this past year brought everybody down; they have been dropping like flies. Of the thirty units in the Haven Senior Citizens Retirement Community, six came up vacant since March. They filled again quickly, of course; there was never any shortage of people getting older, needing care. George Harmsworth died in May. He'd been dying for some time, but then not three weeks later his wife Ellen went along. That had been a surprise. Bill Whitely in the next apartment had cancer, and Don Harrington's liver just quit, and Lib Walters fell out of bed and broke her hip and broke her left leg in three places and then had a heart attack right in her hospital bed. Elsie Powers too was gone. It had been a bitter season, although Harriet didn't mind snow. Right after the blizzard in February, once the plows finished, she went for a walk; she bundled up and took her stick and walked around the entrance drive with snow so high-piled all around she might have been a child again, or out in the deep woods. And Frank the maintenance man came up to her and said, Mrs. Robinson, are you all right? Of course, she said, just dandy; I just want to walk in the snow.

She did not need his company. She did not want his help. She wanted to patrol the drive in circles, in the proper air. But it had been his job to watch out for tenants—the residents, they called them—and so Frank watched her, dubious, sitting in the cab of his pickup, the heater on, the motor idling, making exactly the joyless noise she thought to have escaped. She went around the circle one more time, leaning, choosing her steps. She watched her breath go visible. She couldn't hear herself think. Husband would have silenced him, would have said, Turn off the motor, man, for heaven's sake.

Peter, Julia's husband, was a different sort. He would have offered his arm. He was every inch the gentleman; he cultivated flowers. He'd say, You need some sweet peas here, something to spruce up the place. She laughed and batted her eyes at him, as she'd done for fifty years, and always to Julia's chagrin. She said, Don't fool yourself, mister, I've got a little space to plant, I've got the room for sweet peas if you say so. Right there on the patio, past what they call the pavilion. Except they don't breed sweet peas any longer with the proper smell. Never you mind, Peter promised, I'll find you the right ones, I'll find the kind that have the old perfume. And that April he had done it, brought the seeds and dug the fence posts and strung the wire in between and helped Harriet plant. When they took him to the hospital for his heart-bypass operation (the angina getting worse, the nitroglycerine no help, the pain so bad you'd never imagine he used a posthole digger only days before), he said, What I'd like from you, Sister-in-law, is a visit with blossoming peas.

"We'll go tomorrow," she offers again.

"This meat is cold," Julia says.

"Up to Burlington, I mean. I asked Seth Olson to drive."

"You wouldn't want it hot, of course. But you can't taste the flavor too cold. Room temperature's best for cold meat salad."

"Not in this room."

"What?"

"Not this room temperature, I said."

"Say it loud enough," says Julia, "and I can hear just fine."

You couldn't blame her, really. She and Peter had no children —not like Harriet's own three. Bill Jr. was in Omaha, Betty and her boys in Raleigh, little Sal across the way in Concord, so there was always family, always some birthday or other, some graduation or wedding or great-grandchild's christening or holiday to share. But Julia and Peter ate every meal alone together, went everywhere

alone together, lived in their house on East Street for sixty some-
odd years. One afternoon it stopped. One afternoon he didn't seem
able to get up out of his chair. He sat there, dropping catalogs,
holding his hand to his chest. And then they came for him and
hauled him off to Burlington and that nice young Dr. Cunningham
said the operation's a success, and Harriet was far too tactful to
remind him of the other part of the joke: operation successful,
patient dead.

So Julia comes on over every day. She just has to cross the street.
She takes up no more room than a throw pillow on the couch;
she eats like a bird, always has. She picks at her sandwich or salad
and drinks lukewarm iced tea. She turns off her hearing aid or lets
the batteries run down—just sits there, staring, lip-reading, waiting
for Peter to come.

Harriet doubted he would. When Husband went she'd had no
doubt; she knew he was going to die. She'd known it in her stomach
and her throat; she'd had no need to hear the verdict, face the
doctors, see their faces as they pulled off masks and marched
through the green swinging door. They'd had no chance to operate;
the cancer had spread everywhere they looked. At least he'd had
no pain, they said, at least you can take comfort in the fact he felt
no pain. One day, she told her sister, you simply wake up halved.
One day there's no pattering trill of his voice on the phone, no
soft bulk in blankets next to you or water in the bathtub before
you take a bath. One day a dozen eggs last twice as long, and coffee
milk, and the bananas go rotten if you buy a bunch. She's been
through that, knows how much Julia doesn't know and has to start
to learn. So Harriet tries to be patient.

"More tea?"

"Not so sweet," says Julia. "Last glass had too much sugar."

"It's a mix."

"You must have added sugar, then. This one tastes sweet, I'm
sure."

"Have it your own way," she says.

Then Julia gets weepy. "If I had it my own way," she says, "I
wouldn't be here now."

When he set the fence posts for her, Peter was meticulous. He
bought a posthole digger and raked off extra dirt. He strung the
wire tightly and crimped back the edges just so and dug a trench
beneath for her to plant sweet peas. He accepted her thanks with
his usual shy smile, and then he accepted iced coffee and a piece
of apple pie. There was no one in the county to compete with

her at apple pie, or sticky buns, or strawberry rhubarb compote. He rubbed his stomach, that morning, when she offered him ice cream. "Can't do it, Harriet," he said. "I'm bursting at the seams."

He and Husband had gotten along. The four of them played bridge on Fridays, and bingo and canasta, and they shared Sunday supper each week. Once they piled into the Oldsmobile and drove to New Orleans together, taking two weeks. It had been quite a trip. On the way they took pictures of the Washington monument, the Lincoln Memorial festooned with cherry blossoms like a picture postcard, the picnic they had in Roanoke where Husband's people came from, and Colonial Williamsburg too. They bought souvenirs of Mt. Vernon and Monticello and Charleston and the Okefenokee Swamp, though in truth they didn't visit the Okefenokee because it was a hot day, far away, and Julia so terrified of alligators she swore she wouldn't leave the car; they bought a dozen 3-D views of it instead.

Julia was jealous. She accused her sister—never quite saying it, coming right out—of trying to put Peter in Husband's empty place. And it would have been the most natural thing, the very simplest procedure. He mooned about the kitchen or insisted they come over in a storm; he'd call her on the phone to say, Harriet, don't miss the moon. He praised her needlework and wanted her for his partner, always, in bridge. He said the roses on her patio were the most perfect roses, and the hollyhocks, and her famous oyster stew. He studied the oil portrait of Harriet at eight years old and said, I'd know you anywhere, you haven't changed a bit. Well, perhaps just the tiniest bit, he said—smiling that infectious grin, taking her good right hand—but all that's happened is improvement; you've gotten more lovely, is all. "Why, you old coot," she said. "I mean it, Harriet," he said. She knew he didn't mean it but it pleased her all the same. That's called chivalry, she said to Julia; chivalry's not dead.

"I never remember such heat," Julia complains. "It must be the Russians."

"It's what they're calling the Greenhouse Effect."

"Nonsense. It's a plot."

"Well, according to the paper we've as much to do with it as anybody else. All those cars of ours, those factories. That acid rain."

"You've been brainwashed," Julia says. "There's nothing wrong with Vermont."

Harriet puts down her scarf. She has twelve to make for Christmas, and twelve sets of mittens and matching caps for grandchildren.

"There's not anything wrong with this part of the world." Julia continues her long litany of praise. "There's no tornadoes, no hurricanes, no tidal waves. No blizzards to speak of, or earthquakes. No poisonous snakes."

"What will you do when Peter comes home?" she inquires. "How are you planning to manage?"

"This tea is too sweet," Julia says.

Seth Olson showed up now and then, living down there with *his* sister, but it wasn't any better for poor Seth. She asked him how he liked it, and he said, Not much. He smoked like a chimney and complained that Betsy didn't allow him to smoke in the house; he looked like an ashtray, she insisted, and smelled like the back of a bus. Seth had been a handsome man, with that devil-may-care strut to him, but when he came back from the war in the Pacific he'd had the shakes so bad you'd hardly be able to watch. And though he did get over it he never quite got together again; it was like Humpty Dumpty, Harriet thought: he'd shattered into so many pieces you couldn't help noticing the glue.

Seth drove. He had kept up his license and enjoyed a drive. He came to visit, often, to help her with the groceries or maybe to touch up the paint. He wanted nothing in exchange, just companionable presence, just the chance to smoke in peace. But last month he and Betsy had moved out to that trailer on the edge of the state line, the one behind their nephew's, and helped young Brian with the kennel and saved a second rent. When you're thrown together nightly like that things get worse; a person needs space, Seth maintained. A person needs some privacy and the one you shared your high chair with isn't about to provide it. Grow old along with me, he said, ain't the same as saying (though they told us that in high school—remember, Harriet, remember we used to recite it?) the best is yet to be. The answer is, Grow old because you can't help it, because there's no choice, but not because it's best. In my opinion, Harriet said, if you can't beat 'em, join 'em; I've got *my* sister here."

So tomorrow they will travel up to Burlington, where Peter waits. They will visit his hospital room. Younger men do fine with such an operation, she tells Julia; it's like a tonsillectomy when you and I were young. Like an appendectomy, adds Seth. They will enter. He will see them; he will hold out both his hands. He has a pencil-thin mustache, and fresh-scrubbed fingertips always, a meticulous look about him, a patient, cleanly man. He will keep his eyes closed, probably, and they'll talk about the weather and how fortunate he is to be here where it's cool. He will ask them how they're doing down there in heaven without him, and Julia will say I'm fine and Harriet will say, We miss you, come on back, old shoe. He will ask her how her flower bed is doing in this heat. He will have clipped his nails. She will tell him, Well, we're managing, and offer what she collected: the sweet peas in profusion, and the roses and the lilacs and the cherry blossoms blown, the memory of flower beds, the sweet hovering smell of them gone.

The River Song

ROBERT DUNN

The call that changed everything came from New York and rang
the back-room phone at the studio out Route 28, the same phone
that had jangled during the release take of "Poor Beggar in Love,"
when after the song's been rocking rough as stones in a can, it
gets eerily quiet, the bass just tumping the A string and the drums
patiently brushing, and LeRoy cups his ear and listens, nobody
knowing what he's hearing until, *brring, brring* the phone goes,
and then LeRoy's stingy strum kicks in and the bass and drum
come up pounding and the song whoops home with all three of
them crying, "On my knees, I'm on my knees for your love," over
and over, then laughing down the fade. Everybody always thought
it was the ringing phone that kicked LeRoy into the song (the
engineer remastering the CD even boosted the volume on it), but
in a late interview, after he started giving concerts again, LeRoy
admitted that he'd never even heard the phone, instead had hung
his ears on the Mississippi River, running half a mile away from
Saturn Studios, and was counting off its near-silent beat until it
told him when to snap back into the song.

When the phone rang this time the only one around was Jim
White, who was trying to divine a hit from Baby Joey's *Hootie
Patootie* session the week before, so he took the call, and though
his heart dropped because he knew what it meant to cut in the
New York money boys, he promised to have LeRoy get back to
them as soon as he could be found. But White and Bates Mandell
and Win Frees spent the next three days drinking Cokes and
powwowing in the back room about how to hold on to LeRoy's
contract, until Snake Peters at WHJK, who had broken the first
single, "How High," heard something from the boy from the drugstore running the cherry and vanilla Cokes and whispered rumors
into his heavy aluminum microphone, and Mrs. Hohannis, who
kept the radio on all day so she wouldn't miss one of her boy's

records, understood the insinuations and ran out to the pasture where LeRoy lay flat on his back, pitching meaty clods of dirt into a rippling blue sky and dreaming of that furious impending success that at this moment was more vivid than his life.

What happened next was near enough to the legend to make LeRoy's walking dreams look like prophecy. Mrs. Hohannis roused her slope-shouldered boy and had him drive her into town in the black Chevy he'd bought with the first Saturn Records money, and they went to the crank phone in the post office and tried to ring New York, their thick, callow accents making trouble getting through, and it was at that moment that the red-haired kid the nervous money boys had sent down by car pulled into Tyler and stopped at the post office for directions on how to find LeRoy Hohannis's place. The postmistress said, "Well, aren't you lucky! There's LeRoy and his mother right over there," and the red-haired kid smiled his huge smile and said, just as he'd rehearsed it all the way down, "Madam, we're going to make your boy a star." Mrs. Hohannis gasped, her fingers scraping at her well-powdered chin, but LeRoy just shrugged his shoulders and rolled his eyes, saying, "What took you so long?"

Then everything speeded up: LeRoy's first airplane trip, stewardesses giggling at his long, lanky black hair, still just a shy boy-face pressed against the window glass, then a ride in an unearthly yellow taxicab, huge skyscrapers, elevators, bursting flashbulbs, men wearing boxy suits and snakeskin boots, girls like out of movies, dry-faced hovering yea-sayers, a pale fluorescent-lit corridor, pinholed acoustic tiles, three big black cameras pointing thick muzzles at him, and a skinny guy in a lemon-colored sweater saying, "LeRoy, a little more to the left, smile now, that's good," and LeRoy holding the half smile, half sneer on his face, joyful with it because now he was skimming, lifted farther than ever by the river current he'd first felt as a kid when he went lolling his feet in the mud-sucky water, thinking absolutely nothing at all, and this pulsing rhythm seemed to rise off the center of the river, long and clear and powerful, making him feel for the first time like he was some real person rather than the ghost he'd always half believed himself to be. The cameras were like that too, making him feel real, and so it was no problem calling up with perfect control that clear river stream and staring down those TV cameras and letting just enough of the river's rocking and rolling rhythm flow out of him and through the cameras to go flooding over the wide plain of America so within days he was known in more places than even the President.

When he was a boy LeRoy would go down to the river, to sail stick boats, skim rocks, watch the morning vapors twist and turn over the humpy swells of the current, and he would think of the river as his special friend, more comforting than anyone but his mother, in whose thick chambray skirts he could hide when the whole crazy non-river world became too much. As a boy he didn't really understand the world, its alarums and hard and confusing rules, and trusted only the river as it pulled him away from the cowlicked boys and spindly cotton-dressed girls who jammed their hands in the air every time his teacher, Miss Stone, asked for adding and subtracting at the blackboard and LeRoy slunk down in his back-row seat, drawling a thick, sardonic, and only stupid-sounding "Yes, ma'am" out of the side of his mouth when Miss Stone brought her flustered, carping words down on him; and pulled him farther from his grubby, whiskey-breath father, who couldn't restrain his anger and his belt strop and whose red-stained face grew horns and vicious teeth in the nightmares that sent LeRoy bounding up hysterical in his bed, calling out for "Mother, Mother," and Mrs. Hohannis would press him to her bosom and say soothingly, "There, there, LeRoy, quiet yourself. You're not listening, LeRoy. Quiet, listen. Do you hear it?" And he would soon enough, that intense, rustling, pulsing rhythm off the river, and he could collapse back into sleep like it was a mountain of feathers.

He was also pulled closer to the church, where, in his clean-pressed Sears, Roebuck shirt and baggy serge trousers, the tips of his hair still beaded from the weekly washing, LeRoy would stand tall and sing "Holy, Holy, Holy," in the choir right between bald-headed Mr. James and the postmistress, Miss Reilly, both of whom would drop a hand and pat his hair after his bell-bright tenor lifted away from the rest of the singers like a sleek, brassy bird. (True, like the biographers wrote: One day their hands found each other's and they decided to get married.) But LeRoy heard the river clearest when he was alone in his room after supper, and he'd stand up on his rickety straw chair and twist the bare light bulb into its socket and then slide the cloth-covered guitar case (with the big *L* and *H* his momma had painted with her fire-engine-red fingernail polish) from under his cot, take out the once-pawned black guitar with the ripply overstrummed scratches below the sounding hole, and perch himself on the edge of his bed, wrapping his left hand around the upper fret board and stretching and pressing until his fingers found E and A chords and his right-hand strums would make sounds only a little better than barn doors screaking and chickens shrieking around. But he always heard the river in his ear, and after six months he could play it, his fingers molded into chord shapes without thinking and the guitar dangling off his neck and swinging back and forth as free as a balloon tied to a string, and he would stand and face the warping mirror his mother had bought him at the Woolworth's as a special present, then throw his torso to the right and to the left, making awkward, self-conscious twitches that at first seemed nasty and forbidden even to his don't-care-nothing-'bout-nothing eyes, until, with more practice, he smoothed down to the same rhythm that made him so famous later, the rhythm he could snap out just as far as he wanted, then ease back slow and cool, Mr. Control, Mr. Artful Motion, looking like he was winking at and mocking everything, though all he was doing was moving along the crest of something ancient and unrelenting and just trying to keep up with it.

So that was the miracle: that the river stayed with him to New York and then everywhere he played, reaching through the television and leaping off the record grooves, so when any audience heard him, at least half of them would scream and cry and faint with delight. Anything was possible, and everywhere you turned there was his picture, the pale yellow-fire skin, pure as cherubim, the meaty lips, curling and taunting, and there were the girls, hanging over LeRoy, slumming at his feet, flaunting their nice-girl smiles, and daring him to do something about it. We would see LeRoy canted at unimaginable angles in front of a microphone pole and looking the empyrean hood in front of the three sallow-faced sweater boys singing backup, and though he might get shy and crumbly just when we wanted him brash and assertive, the next time we heard him he'd show up every mealy-mouthed adult in the country just when we were sure he was going to brown-nose their exhausted morality again. We all were sending prayers to LeRoy so bold there was no faith anyone could answer them, and there, on his next record, he hit a note and struck a pose that were the very lineaments of our desire.

Even so, we weren't ready for his picture turning up fifty feet tall outside Rialtos and Strands all across the country, his hair

oiled back, black leather jacket flying open, legs and torso twisted
in a hallelujah rave-up pose, and there, inside the theater, big as
the screen, was LeRoy, and those who had only known him from
the radio and already scratchy 45's and the flickering appearances
on TV now saw a LeRoy big as their dreams, and fans lined up
over and over and plunked down their sixty cents and cried and
pulled at their hair and screamed themselves shrill. The first movie
was the best, though it was almost a fluke; the hired-cheap screen-
writers sitting around cooking up a script that had Leroy playing
a brash New York ad executive who falls in love with Sandra Dee
were interrupted by the continuity girl, who said, "Hey, you guys
have never even heard his music, have you?" and proceeded to
tell them the whole LeRoy Hohannis story; and they jumped up
and said, "Keep talking, get this down, it's great," so *On the Way
Up* became *Jambalaya*, and LeRoy got to play himself, fresh and
awed to be living his life over again before a camera. "Disturbingly
authentic," said the *L.A. Times*, and "a near magical invocation of
what is already a myth," wrote the *New Orleans Register*, and they
mentioned specifically the moment early on in the movie when
LeRoy's on the prowl in a Memphis roadhouse, and he's just struck
out with a flip-haired bar tease when someone drops a quarter
into the jukebox and the song he didn't even know had been
released yet comes on, and right there on the screen his callow
boy-face changes and his eyes come alive, his lips start softly singing and his feet can't help falling into the beat, and the bubble-
cute pickup says, "Hey, mister, is that you there singing?" and
everyone in the bar stops dead because the song is "Dark Swamp,"
and it's at that moment that the whole world saw LeRoy as he was
back beside the river, truly hearing himself for the first time, and
his discovery is so quiet and powerful that the girl screams hushed,
and the publicists, who had promised unmodulated hysteria to
the press boys, ran out of the theater and demanded the scene
be cut. It was too late to take it out, but they made sure nothing
like that moment ever came in another LeRoy Hohannis movie,
though one after another followed the success of the first, and
though the directors and publicists thought they should make a
sort of *Jambalaya* over again, they learned they didn't even have
to do that: it was enough to have Leroy walk around, sing a few
songs, and smile the white smile no longer corrupted by his am-
biguous half sneer. So the directors didn't try and, worse, LeRoy
learned he didn't have to try either; he could just stand there and
beam, the only acting being the way he had to pretend he wasn't

embarrassed, and then he no longer was embarrassed, and that
was when the river that lifted him lost its jumpy, rock-leaping,
spray-showering urgency and went flat and wide, less like a river
than a damned-up lake.

That's when LeRoy slowed down; granted the sultan's prerog-
ative of getting anything he wanted at any time, making no distinction between knuckle-big aquamarines and jujubes, between
beluga caviar and Heinz pickle relish, between his girl bride and
any teen queen whose pert, soignée face had shone off the cover
of *16* magazine, he butterballed up on yard-long hot dogs and
mush piles of grits and gallons of peppermint-stick ice cream, and
fleshy fat soon spilled over the alligator belts he used to wear
just to keep his leather pants up. Those were the days everything
got tired, repetitive, slow: dozy sprawls on the back seat of his
white limousine, glancing with only muted curiosity at the still-
idolatrous faces pressed against the glass, late nights spent with
the guys, where they were docked ten bucks' pay for every joke
that didn't make LeRoy hoot, the halfhearted whimsical detour on
his private jet to Kansas City to eat barbecued ribs, the private
screenings of Rock Hudson movies, the powdery Thai sticks, other
nights spent gazing at the wall-size TV that burned endlessly, like
a picture window into some better world. Something was lost, and
instead of going after it, LeRoy hid behind the cakey pancake and
rouge he painted over his still untraced face, the double-knit For-
mula One racing suits bedizened with Tex Ritter rhinestone em-
broidery (butterflies, tigers, wrestling women), and the flurry of
Vegas dance steps, choreographed and memorized, but never the
eruption of that startling energy that seemed to whip him out of
nowhere; and then he even lost the beat and went looking for his
truth in the endless static takes of Good News hymns, LeRoy not
even listening for the river but instead calling straight to God (and
stunned to hear nothing back).

What's remarkable is how LeRoy kept the faith of his fans, could
still make blushy and flustered the women who no longer stayed
up all night rocking their hips and sipping Cokes spiked with
bourbon but who now arrived at his concerts after tucking the
kids in and checking the stove's pilot light at least twice, in strained
temporary alliance with their exes, celebrating now almost fully
desiccated memories of when their own river was leaping and
sloshing over the narrow banks of their lives, when they were dead
sure they would ride it to something more glorious than the daily
wearing ignominy and inner dust. What's remarkable is how LeRoy

still believed (and made all who loved him believe) that if he had
to he could bend the broad timeless stream back through him
(and back through them) until it lifted all their lives again.

And maybe he could. Although during his last tour he was mostly
all awkward lurches, forgotten lyrics, and mysterious tears, and
more than once he dropped his guitar and stood there mute and
bemused in front of the twenty-foot-high flashing blue *L* and *H*,
while the three leggy soul girls and the six-man cowboy-hatted
band choogled indifferently on to the end of the song, and for the
audience he was so swollen and transparent that they didn't seem
to see him, remembering only the baby-innocent seraphic face of
what had become the great myth of their lives, a myth kept frozen
on the picture posters, scratched records, and paintings on souvenir plates they kept like a shrine at home, and in the semiannual
concert at the civic center (for no matter what they tell you now,
only the diehards went; to everyone else LeRoy was an almost
embarrassing piece of history); still there was one amazing moment
in Portland, Oregon, where two thirds into the show a plaintive,
desperate voice shrieked through the slack audience, "Oh, come
on, LeRoy, do it *dirty*," and LeRoy stopped the band in the middle
of "How Long the Road to Jesus" and peered out from the stage
with eyes fighting to get focus, and said, "What's that?" and the
same voice came back, "Dirty, LeRoy, dirty like you used to," and
everyone stopped and watched LeRoy think it over for a minute,
the band vamping, until he waved them down and said, "Yeah,
fellows, kill this. Let's try 'Poor Beggar in Love,' " and the bass slid
down into its funky figure and the drummer rolled his tom-tom,
and suddenly there LeRoy was, the old angles teasing beneath his
puffy cheeks, the sweat shaking off his brow, and then the drums
got brushy and the bass low, and he cupped his hand over his
ear and listened, stood there for a minute just listening, then came
up growling notes so pure and nasty that they slammed the rau-
cous crowd into silence, because there it was, the real thing, and
that couldn't be taken away from him, even though three months
later he would lie bloated and naked on the yellow tiles his boys
pulled him onto after he'd dived so deep into his huge travertine
pool that he never came up for air.

What happened in Portland? Did he suddenly see where all
those years of going the easy way had brought him, that what he
had taken to be the pulse of inspiration had become just the
shifting of thick sludge? Did he finally understand that though the
audience was happy to let him make it once, he needed to keep

making it that hard for himself every day? Or had he simply heard a dark pulmonary rattle or some shuffly steps coming after him? And what would have happened if he'd been able to stay with the river and ride its current to the other side, up into what was always to him only a blur of sand and weepy trees? Does myth always have a shape more bending than our will? What is the price for changing the world?

The Immaculate Conception
of Carson DuPre

LOUISE ERDRICH

Carson was named after Johnny Carson. That much he knew. Things he did not know were whether his conception had been planned, if Flobert was his real father, if it had hurt Otalie very much to give birth to him, and why he was the only child. He had not wondered about these things until he left Havana, North Dakota, for the university where young men occasionally discussed their origins. In Havana nobody asked their parents much of a personal nature.

Otalie DuPre was nearly seventy years old. Flo was slightly older. How had Carson managed to slip beneath the wire?

"Was I adopted?" he asked the backs of their heads, "or did you really ...?" Even then he could not bring himself to utter the possibility. "Were you watching *The Late Show* when it happened? Did you notice what was going on?"

This was cruel, but they wouldn't hear him. The car traveled in a loud rush of air, and in the front seat the radio was blaring.

"Silent night, holy night."

Otalie turned the dial. She and Flobert were big healthy pink people with dimples and two chins, while Carson was fragile and intensely pale with staring brown eyes. He didn't even seem left-over from the stuff that made Otalie and Flo. He was different altogether. That was why he sometimes thought he might have been dropped off on their doorstep, hidden in their quonset hut, shoved into their big rural-route mailbox.

He closed his eyes and leaned back into the warm plush. "I don't know why I bothered to come home," he said. "You're not even going to pretend to listen."

"No," said Otalie, "the stores were closed."

The radio gave a strange shrill chuckle.

"Gift items," Flobert said.

Carson was dressed in shabby secondhand woolens. His coat

sported the moth-eaten pile collar of the college intellectual. Otalie had sewed a complete college wardrobe for him the summer before he matriculated, but in the second week of classes Carson had carried his suitcase into the local Salvation Army store and asked to exchange the bright-patterned checked, striped garments for a more suitable wardrobe. He was now elegantly drab.

"Bringing you an inspirational message," the radio said.

Otalie turned up the volume. A man's deep voice filled the car.

"The Christmas heart is the most beautiful heart that ever beat ... perhaps it is better this way. Those who mean so much to us ... let's push up the shades of their window so light may fall into the sick world of the healing medicine of love. Let us light all the candles so the glow may light up the world for others. And make this a permanent thing. Let's do it. And Merry Christmas to your Christmas heart."

"Amen," said Otalie.

"I'd like to shoot that radio," said Carson. He was filling with rage.

A woman's voice came on. "We have other outstanding specials! Take for instance the console with Mediterranean styling and re-mote control so you can sit there in your easy chair and never move."

"I wouldn't mind remote control," Flobert said.

"You are on remote control," said Carson. The weight of their stupidity was overwhelming him. He was losing control. "Oh, God, oh, God," he groaned. "Why did I ever come back?"

"You sleeping back there, Carson?" Flobert shouted. "You're sure quiet."

"I'd like to shoot your damn radio," Carson said.

It began to snow in large, lazy wet flakes that stuck to the wind-shield and hood. The sky turned dark gray and puffy. An odd green light came from behind the clouds. The flakes condensed, fell faster, and wisps of snow began to slither across the highway.

"A White Christmas," said Otalie in her loudest voice.

"Hazardous driving conditions," said the radio. "High winds and heavy snowfall can be expected throughout the tri-state area."

In the back seat, Carson made himself drift off over his book, so he didn't know it when Flobert made the wrong turn and lost the road. He woke to the first argument he'd ever heard between his parents. He listened with intense interest, not to what they said but to the undercurrent of strain in their voices.

"We should have hit Hennessey by now," Flobert said.

"We did."

"Well, where the hell was it? I never seen it."

"Overpass."

"You mean to say they remodeled this road again?"

"No, they never remodeled it. That long curve was always an overpass."

"It wasn't. Next chance I'm gonna turn around."

"No, you don't."

But Flo had already slammed on the brakes as Otalie said this, not because he'd found a place to turn but because, Carson saw, lifting his head, they were completely enveloped in whiteness. Then they were sliding and then, suddenly, they were falling for a long minute. They landed still moving, fishtailed, and then they fell again. The car smacked into something and stopped.

Carson had flown, light as a bird, into the front seat between his parents. Everything was perfectly still for a moment. Then the radio went on.

"It's cheaper, I'll grant you that," the voice said.

"Turn that thing off!" Flobert reached for the dial. It was jammed on, however, and only spluttered cheerfully and jabbered louder when he tried to disconnect the wires beneath the dash.

"Oh, Flobert, leave it on," said Otalie. "It's connected to the heater. Let's see where we are."

Flobert worked his way out of the driver's door and disappeared. After a few moments he opened the door and got back inside.

"We fell into one of those deep storm ditches, Otalie. Even if I had a bucket of sand, besides my shovel, we couldn't get it out of here. Our best hope is to put a flag up on our antenna, and maybe one out by the road. Then there's nothing to do but wait it out."

"You have some red flags in the trunk, Flo?"

But he didn't, and Carson's suitcase held only simple grays and browns.

"What did you do with the clothes I made you? *You threw them out?*"

Carson thought that Otalie seemed more shocked and frightened by this than at their plight or the dropping temperature. But then, of course, it meant she would have to give up her brilliantly colored coat. She took it off. Then she and Carson put on everything they could find. Otalie tied Carson's shirts and slacks around her legs and wrapped herself in another blanket they kept in back. Flo got back into the car and lit a candle out of the emergency kit. He stuck this in a pie tin and gave it to Carson, still between them, to hold. The aluminum pie tin was supposed to catch and reflect the heat from the candle. Flobert turned the heater on for a few minutes and warmed up their feet. It was getting colder. As soon as the heater went off Carson felt the coldness seeping up through the rubber mats and metal floor, flowing into his legs like a weak electric current.

Carson drew his feet up under his coat and crouched between his parents. The three leaned together, a bit self-consciously at first. Flobert made a little joke about conserving warmth. After a while, though, they hugged out of real need because Flobert didn't dare turn the engine on too long. They were low on gas. He could hardly afford to recharge the battery, which the radio was wearing down.

Flobert managed to turn the volume low but still it blabbed constantly, giving them useless warnings about the storm system, playing "Have a Holly Jolly Christmas," and "O Little Town of Bethlehem." The candle flickered in the pie tin, and Carson felt the warmth of it ebb and flow in his lap. Vaguely, he considered something he'd never known before—he could get so cold that he could feel warmth itself moving in molecules. His parents were no longer people to him but parcels of warmth-generating flesh. Once, when they kissed over his head, he felt a small burst of warmth from their touching lips. For the first time he reacted to their touching not with disgust but outright pleasure and wished they would kiss again.

As the hours went on with no change except to become darker and colder, the three went deep into themselves. Flobert and Otalie hunched into their clothing and seemed to sleep. Carson stayed awake with the last candle in the pie tin, watching it burn lower. The radio was still on. At one point the man's voice came back on the air.

"The Christmas heart. It defies contradiction in the human world. It is a guiding thought and magnet of peace that supports us through each day. We must never let it down, for it will renew us with its endless consolation. Let it be yours from this moment on. Let's make it part of us. And Merry Christmas to your Christmas heart."

The candle burned completely down to a pool of wax on the tin, and warmth began to flood quickly away. Carson knew that the mindless voice would go on until it ate up the battery and the heater and the gas and they were dead. He fell asleep with the pie tin on his legs. Much later, he woke to silence. The radio had gone out, and with it the battery. Flobert tried to turn the engine over, but all he got was a sluggish whir.

He believed at first, when his parents bent over him, that they were going to keep him warm in the human cave of their bodies. He thought they truly were going to give him life this time, that he was going to be conceived again and born of them as he never had before. Then later, when he grew cold, he knew the opposite was happening. They bent over him the way they would huddle over a small flame, to absorb what warmth they could. Helplessly, they were taking back the life they had given him. He knew, but by then it was too late. He felt them growing heavy, bearing down on him with their cold unconscious bodies, while he contracted around the bit of warmth he had left. It grew smaller. Then he was shrinking into the dark, trying to capture and nurture that little flame before it vanished.

He put his mind to the point of light and pursued it, reaching deeper and deeper until he thought he had it. He stretched and brought it toward him, huffed until the light widened, grew, and still kept widening.

When the light flared he thought he had never seen anything so beautiful. The light gripped him with wonder. He breathed it still brighter, determined to use his last breath on it. Breathing, breathing, he used everything he was as fuel and kept burning, so that the last thing he knew of himself was when he was caught in a great surge of forgiving radiance that flowed out of him and wrapped his parents over and over in its raveling fire.

The Dreamer's Portrait

ROSARIO FERRÉ

The man is still dreaming, amid the mournful buzzing of the drones, scratched from time to time by the wrath of bees as by a sharpened feather's quill on a steel plate. Try as he may, this man will never reach inmortality in his dreams, the impersonal hatred of dry point on iron, the mathematical calculations of white space on black. Be they etched by steel edges or drawn by felt tips, be they drawn or dreamt, his efforts are doomed to failure. He'll never get to live forever except smoothly, softly, caressed by my brush as it strokes his hair, his hands joined peacefully over his chest; by the delicate mantle of dust that has settled over him in the course of the afternoon. The sun is going down and the tile floor has begun to cool under my hands as I go on painting silently, the canvas spread out on the floor. The man is still dreaming. I'm in no hurry to finish my portrait.

Every afternoon we follow the same ritual. I come and sit next to him on the floor, spread my canvas quietly on the tiles, and begin to paint. From my vantage point I can spy on his breathing as its slows into parched regularity. I always sit patiently in the same place, waiting for him to wake up, ready for our daily struggle. Eventually he wakes, looks at me with irate eyes, and begins to tear up my canvas. He crushes it and throws it furiously out the window. Then he leaves the room and I'm alone again. Feeling strangely relieved, I sit in the midst of my torn painting and listen to the wail of our neighbor's clarinet split clean through the heavy fog that has begun to settle on the nearby mountainside.

I've never understood what life is all about. I smear it, rub it, smooth it over with my brush, but it always manages to escape me. The speed of its flight, as it squirms out of my hands, is all I can ever remember about it. I must be getting tired of always going through the same struggle, because lately I've begun to feel a

Translated by the author in collaboration with Nancy Bentel

strange pity for the dreamer stirring in me. I've been a professional portrait painter now for many years and have earned the respect of the critics. This morning I've begun to paint his portrait once again. I've tried unsuccessfully to paint many times, but it's the most difficult piece I've ever attempted and will probably again be doomed to failure.

I've painted hundreds of portraits since my father threw me out of the house because I wanted to be a painter, and I last saw our orchard of carefully grafted orange trees and our ivy-covered staircase. During all these years, before I've started on each new canvas, I've conjured up the picture of the dreamer, of his irate waking and our ensuing struggle. Lately, however, I've noticed he sleeps more soundly. It's becoming more difficult to wake him before I begin each new piece. It's as though, after all this time, his anger were abating and he no longer assaults me with his customary rage, accusing me of living off the fat of the land while he works himself to death at the farm for my sake. His eyes no longer flash forth from a bottomless pit as they used to, and now he shakes the brittle latticework of his bones before my face to no avail. Little by little, dust has begun to settle on his shoulders and cobwebs have lodged on his face; at night he curls up and sighs to himself in the dark. He knows that now I'm the only one who can prevent him from dying. I consider it my duty to make him go down fighting, to urge him to struggle for his immortality. It's the least I can do, in gratitude for the loyalty of his daily combat all these years.

I stand before him now, brush in hand. He's sound asleep on the living room couch, his head propped on his elbow. The philodendrons have reached out to him through the open window; the bromeliads have begun to crack open the parched linen of his suit, piercing it with their bloody swords. The scene begins to come out vividly, swathed generously in oil paint. I feel as though the years hadn't gone by as I whisper to him to wake up. I can tell he still loves me because, after a brief struggle, he responds to my call. He sits up slowly, looks at me once more with his terrible eyes, and joins me in combat. He is pitiless, as usual, but this time I'm the stronger one. His anguished eyes, his wrought-up features, his flying fists, all come rushing out of my brush as I manage to overwhelm him. A woman, her hair heavy with water, has come into the room and kneels next to him on the canvas, cradling him in her arms.

That Boy

LAURA FURMAN

We'd been trying in a lazy way to get hay for days, my husband and I. When Bob drove into the city to work, he noticed signs along the road, HOGS & PIGS FOR SALE SOON; HAY; COASTAL HAY, BALES AND ROUNDS, but he never stopped. He didn't mind the ride into the city but he didn't like to stop. In the morning when I watched our old dog do her business out on the front lawn, checking her to be sure she didn't wander off the way she did sometimes, I'd pick up the giveaway paper from the sidewalk and look in the classified ads. I guess if one of the ads had said, "I'll bring the hay to your garden, clip the wire, and spread your mulch for you," I might have called. As it was, I strolled to the trash can at the curb and dropped in the paper. My husband called it as close to nothing as you'd want to read.

We lived in Garland for five years, and each year it was like we were starting the garden all over again. One year it was tomato blight, another the drought stunted everything. One year I went up to Colorado to visit with my sister, and it was a storm of tomatoes; my husband's busy time, and he'd come home to an evening of picking tomatoes and making sauce. When I got back the garden was full of weeds, purple native morning glories twining tight around each tomato cage, Johnsongrass into everything I'd worked so hard to clear in the spring. But the tomatoes were there if you looked, starting to be too much for the two of us, even with sauce.

I made a practice of not saying things like that much—just the two of us, the two of us in that big house. There were kids all over town from morning to night, walking or riding their bikes to the school a few blocks from where we lived on Guadalupe Street, dragging their jackets behind them in the winter, running past in their little shorts in the hot days toward summer. After school there were more of them—two boys on a bike, one riding the handlebars—and when I went to the high school track to jog my two miles there were the cheerleaders, and every time I went to the Wal-Mart there were babies grabbing for candy at the checkout. At night, driving through town, I'd turn a corner and my lights would catch a child on a bicycle riding silent through the dark streets. There were kids and mothers everywhere, and at first when we moved to the town it was a continual reminder of what I didn't have in a way that it wasn't in the city where there's plenty of kids but more grown-ups, it seemed to me. I didn't plan to be childless. I didn't ever think of myself that way. I tried, and I let the doctors have their day, but there it was. We didn't plan to live in a small town either, but most of the time it was fine. Sometimes in the evenings when I had supper cooking and I was cleaned up from the day in the garden or working on the house, I'd go back out to see how the garden was doing after it had time alone to settle down, and as I stood looking at Marie Pavie, my favorite little rose, or the Louisiana hibiscus, tropical and almost gaudy, I heard the Mr. Softee ice-cream truck on the next street, playing an old tune to gather in the children.

Bob and I were doing square-foot gardening, and that meant laying out pieces of wood and measuring where to plant. It was a fussy way to garden but it looked like it would work. It gave order, though I liked the twenty-foot rows we used to have. This way it was like little rooms in a house, and I was moving furniture around inside each room.

We were pretty desperate for hay when my friend Margaret, who was more industrious than I, called to say she'd found us three bales each.

"Is two dollars too much?" she asked. "I don't know from Shinola about hay, so when my neighbor said two dollars, I said fine."

"It's fine," I said. "I've seen it for one-fifty, but it doesn't matter."

"Oh, hell," she said. "I knew I should have asked you. I just figured it would be okay and it didn't seem like—"

"It isn't much, Margaret. For pity's sake, it's only fifty cents."

"I just figured—oh, well. I'll bring it by this morning, after the kids wake up from their nap."

Margaret had two girls, little terrors both of them, though the younger, Tracy, was worse. Sugar had some manners. When she went to school the next year she got even better.

"What time's their nap?" I asked. I never remembered and felt like I should.

"I usually get them down by ten."

"I'll be by at ten-thirty," I said.

"It's no trouble for me to do it."

"Margaret," I said. "You're the one who went to the trouble of getting the hay. There's no call for you to haul it, and anyway it'll take two of us to get it up in the car."

"I hope it's all right," she said. "He's my neighbor, you know, right next door, and he was mowing his yard and I asked him to dump his grass into my compost heap. So when he did that we got to talking, and I asked if he knew where I could get some hay. Turned out he has a farm out somewhere and he said he'd bring some by, and he had no idea when, but then he showed up Saturday when we were having supper. I didn't have a penny to pay him but he said that was fine."

"I can pay him," I said.

"Oh, Teddy paid."

"Well, I'll give you my money and you can do what you like with it."

"I'll give it to Teddy," she said. "There's no need to piss him off."

I was gardening pretty hard because there were two guys working on the upstairs bathroom, a two-day job (they said) in its second week. It wasn't really their fault. This old pipe or that wouldn't come out or broke or gave them some kind of time-eating trouble. Twenty dollars an hour for Donnie and his helper, a sweet flat-faced Mexican kid named Ricky. I liked them fine but I was used to being in the house all day by myself. It improved the garden no end, though there was always more to do than I ended up doing.

I pulled into Margaret's driveway and she was standing there with the two little girls. I wouldn't stay for coffee, I decided.

"Hi," Sugar said, and she gave me a big smile. Tracy came from behind her sister and looked up at me. Her dark eyes were deep-set, and it was hard to tell what color they were unless you were nose to nose.

"Hi, girls," I said. "I thought you were napping."

"No way," Tracy said. "No way, José."

"Some days you win, some days you lose," Margaret said.

She was a large, skinny woman, full of energy for everyone in the world besides herself. Margaret was voted Volunteer of the Year at her church and delivered Meals on Wheels and did a lot of things I didn't know about, though I'd admire her for them if I did.

"That hay looks good," I said. It looked a little fresh for my purposes. It was better to mulch with spoiled hay, but this was a gift horse if ever there was one. I opened the back of the station wagon and was fooling around, trying to fold down the back seat.

"The boy across the street hung himself this morning," Margaret said. "There was an ambulance there real early, and I wondered what it was."

I turned and climbed out of the station wagon. "Which boy?"

"The Harvey boy," she said. "There were police cars too." Sugar was hanging onto Margaret's baggy jeans, and Tracy was getting ready to stop being shy.

"Which house is it?" I'd never noticed that side of the street much before. The houses were alike, bungalows, not the grand kind but the humble variety. One was a kind of medium green, a color of paint that might have been bought on sale, and the other was peeling and gray, like Margaret's house. The green house had a bunch of cars in the driveway and in front, and an old pickup. Margaret and Teddy didn't lift a finger on their house because it was a rent house. She would have, but he wouldn't let her.

"I called my other neighbor," she said, pointing to the new brick fourplex right next to her house. "He works on the paper so he knew."

"Which house is it?"

"He said the boy must have hung himself last night or early this morning."

I looked at Sugar, who'd heard the story before and was starting to look antsy, tugging more at her mother and sticking her thumb in her mouth.

"Is it the green house?" I asked.

"The Harvey house," Margaret said, gesturing at the green one. The color looked sad to me now, and I could imagine what was going on inside: the phone ringing, the calls to relatives, people arriving, hesitating at the door, and looking scared to enter, then the bursts of sobbing and embraces.

"I saw him in the driveway the other day," Margaret said, "just hanging around with his girlfriend. He had his arm over her shoulders and was kind of leaning on her. I thought, What a cutie. My God, I was in love from the time I was ten years old and every time I got my heart broken, but I never ever thought of killing myself."

I looked down quickly at Sugar, who was frowning and starting to droop, and I wondered what she was making of all this. Tracy was hunkered down on the driveway, gathering stones, looking up at my hubcaps, as if to measure the distance. I'd never known Margaret to lower her voice, and I hoped the people in the green house couldn't hear her.

"It's different now," I said, just to have something to say. "There are lots of kids doing it."

Sugar broke away and headed into the backyard, which was fenced in, and when Tracy saw her sister moving along, she got up and toddled after her, leaving her stones behind.

"All I can think," Margaret said, looking after the little girls, "all I've thought about all morning is that our kids are growing up in this mess."

I watched the girls too, until they'd disappeared around the corner of the house. It always amazed me first of all that mothers let their children out of sight and second of all that they can stand watching them so long.

"Let's load this hay," I said, "and I'll give you your money. I have it in quarters so you can wash your car."

Margaret said, "I'll buy us some ice cream. Or dinner."

I got home and drove the car out to the back. Donnie and Ricky followed me and unloaded the bales for me, putting one by the garden, the others in the shed. Ricky went back to the house to finish touching up a wall where he'd left a big handprint the day before.

"So you spread that stuff around," Donnie said. "Now why would you do that?"

"To keep the weeds down," I said. "And it breaks down and lightens up this clay soil."

"I just went to the lumberyard," Donnie said.

He went to the lumberyard three or four times a day, to pick up some little notion, and always came back with news that he and Ricky mulled over together.

"They're taking up a collection for that boy who hung himself."

"Word gets around fast," I said.

"His father's a roofing contractor," Donnie said, "so the father knew everyone at the lumberyard."

"How come there's a collection?"

"They don't have the money to bury that boy," Donnie said. "Don't ask me why, they just don't."

"That's terrible," I said. I looked around at the scrawny little tomatoes in their big cages. The week before we'd had a hard freeze and I'd lost half of them, and the other half still looked pretty shook up.

"Ricky knew the boy. It was drugs. He was in trouble with the cops for drugs and he told on his friends. They don't like him so much anymore."

So it wasn't love.

"He was a friend of Ricky's? How old is Ricky?" I had never thought about Ricky's age, or whether he lived on his own or with his family.

"I don't know. Eighteen or nineteen. Same as that boy. Maybe he's younger."

Donnie wandered back to the house as soon as I started to work, and it was an hour before I finished out in the garden, or until I got hungry. I was in the kitchen, making myself an apple stuffed with peanut butter for lunch, when Ricky knocked at the kitchen door and came in, holding a dry brush.

"You got a bigger brush?" he asked. "I'm starting on the floor."

"Somewhere," I said, and we went into the toolroom to look in the mess for the brush I knew we had. "Did you know that boy?" I asked. "The one who hung himself."

"I knew him," Ricky said.

"What was going on?"

"He was in trouble," Ricky said. "He got picked up for drugs and told on some friends. The other kids wouldn't talk to him."

"What kind of drugs?" I asked. I handed the brush to Ricky and saw his face close over.

"Just some kind," he said, and I knew he wouldn't say anything more about it. "This won't work. It's too messed up."

I looked some more and came up with another brush, in better shape, and two sponge brushes that I offered to him and he refused.

"Did he graduate?" I asked. "That boy?"

"Yeah," Ricky said. "I think he did. Last year maybe."

After lunch, I stayed in the kitchen. I thought I might go out to the garden once more, to see if the mulch was shading the tomatoes excessively, but I didn't have the heart to do it. With Donnie and Ricky upstairs working, I didn't feel right taking a nap, which I liked to do sometimes after lunch. I thought of going over to the lumberyard to make my contribution, but instead I took out a bunch of cookbooks and when I settled on my old favorite, I began to make the cake that I made for all occasions. It was a six-egg cake and called for real butter, which I had to thaw, and I had to add some heavy cream to the skim milk and hope it would do. When the batter was done and the layers in the oven, I started grinding up pecans for the sugar icing. It had been a good fall for pecans and I had a gallon shelled and frozen in the freezer. I'd made the same cake for our anniversary the month before, and it stayed in the refrigerator on the good cake stand for a week while we nibbled away at it, telling ourselves not to.

Donnie and Ricky came downstairs a few times, saying how good the cake smelled, but I didn't offer them any, nor did I say what the cake was for. I just smiled and looked mysterious in the way my own mother did when we kids were begging something from her.

They left as I was icing the cake. At first the silence when they were gone was heavenly; then the house felt too big and empty without them. I finished the cake and carried it into the dining room. It was the only room in the house not suffering from the work going on upstairs. It was the way it always was, summer and winter—dark and clean and cool, waiting for people to fill it up, our family room. I set the cake in the center of the round oak table beneath the big ceiling fan. The stained-glass window was full of the evening light. It was the time I let a cake settle, just after the icing, before the cutting, let it become itself before it was given away, sliced up, and gone forever. I took a seat at the table to admire the cake. I almost put out a finger to touch it. It would be a wonderful cake, I could tell, light and sweet to taste, but not too sweet.

I thought of carrying the cake over to people I'd never laid eyes on, especially at such a time. I would appear at their door, the cake on a plastic plate that I wouldn't expect them to return. Why burden them with returning a plate at that moment? I knew I could get Margaret to give it to them for me, but that was the coward's way out, and still they'd know it was from me and they'd feel obliged to find out who I was and to thank me, a stranger— and why add to all they needed to do? I would bring the cake myself. I would knock at their door as if they expected me, as if they knew me now, and knew that we were all alike. I would stand at their door, a nice woman holding a better-looking cake, someone who looked like nothing bad had ever happened to her, and I'd be the sign that trouble was in their home for good.

The Right Thing to Do
at the Time

GEORGE GARRETT

This is a true story about my father, a true story with the shape of a piece of fiction. Well, why not? Where do you suppose all the shapes and forms of fiction came from in the first place? And what's the purpose of fiction anyway, whether it's carved out of the knotty hardwood of personal experience or spun out of the slick thin air like soap bubbles? "What's the purpose of the bayonet?" they used to yell when I was a soldier years ago. The correct answer was: "To kill, *to kill*, TO KILL!"

The purpose of fiction is simply to tell the truth.

My father was a small-town southern lawyer, not a writer, but he was a truth-teller. And he would tell the truth, come what may, hell or high water. And since he loved the truth and would gladly risk his life (and ours, the whole family's) for the sake of it, he would fight without stint, withholding nothing, offering no pity or quarter against what he took to be wrong—that is, against the untruth. He would go to any length he had to. And that is what this story is all about—how far one man would go to fight for the truth and against what was and is wrong.

We were living in the cow town of Kissimmee, Florida, in the early years of the Great Depression. Disney World is near there now, and it looks pretty much like everyplace else. But it was a hard, tough place then, a place where life was hard for many decent people, black and white. And it was a place where some not-so-decent people had managed to seize power and to hold power and were extremely unlikely to be dislodged from power. Among the people in power in those days were the Ku Klux Klan, not a sad little bunch of ignorant racists in bedsheets but a real clan, a native-grown kind of organized crime family.

My father and his law partner were fighting against the Klan in court and in public with the promise that they would (as they, in fact, did) represent free of charge any person at all who chose to resist the Klan and wanted a lawyer.

This exposed position led to a whole lot of trouble, believe me. And in the end it led to the demise of the Klan as a power of any kind in central Florida. But the big trouble came later. This happened early on as the lines were being drawn and the fight was just getting under way.

Sometimes in the early evening we would go together, my mother and father and the other children, into town for an ice-cream cone: a great treat in those days. One evening we piled into our old car and drove into the center of town and parked in front of the drugstore. Went inside and sat on tall swivel chairs at the counter eating our ice-cream cones. We were all sitting there in a row when a young policeman walked in. Try as I will, I can't remember his name anymore. Just that he was very young and that my mother, who was a teacher then, had taught him in high school. He greeted her politely at first. He seemed a little awkward and embarrassed.

"Mr. Garrett," he said to my father, "I'm afraid I'm going to have to give you a red ticket."

"Oh, really?" my father said, still licking his ice-cream cone. "What for?"

"Well, sir, your taillights don't work."

"They did when I came down here."

"Well, sir, they sure don't now."

"Let's us have a look."

So we all trooped outside and looked at the taillights. They didn't work, all right, because they were broken and there was shattered red glass all over the street right behind the back bumper.

"I wonder who would do a thing like that," my father said, giving the young cop a hard look.

"Well, I wouldn't know, sir," he said. "I just work for the city and I do what I'm told. And I have to write you a ticket."

"Fine," my father said. "I understand that."

Then he surprised the cop and us too by asking if he could pay for the ticket right then and there. And the cop said yes, that was his legal right, and he said it would cost five dollars.

Now that was considerable money in those days when grown men with some skills were earning eight or ten dollars a week. Nobody had any money in those days, nobody we knew or knew of. Most of my father's clients, those who could pay at all, paid him in produce and fresh eggs, things like that.

My father peeled off five one-dollar bills. The cop wrote him a receipt. Then my father told my mother to drive us on home when we had finished our ice cream. He had to go somewhere right away.

He whistled loudly and waved his arm for a taxi. One came right over from the Atlantic Coastline depot directly across the way. He kissed my mother on the cheek and said he would be back just as soon as he could. Gave her the keys to our car and hopped into the cab.

None of us heard what he told the driver: "Let's go to Tallahassee."

Tallahassee was and is the state capital, a good three hundred or so miles away by bad, narrow roads in those days.

Much later we learned what happened. They arrived very late. Slept in the cab. First thing in the morning he got himself a shave in the barbershop. Then went to the legislature. Where, exercising a constitutional right to speak on this kind of matter, he quickly established that the town charter for Kissimmee, Florida, was completely illegal and unconstitutional. In a technical, legal sense that town did not exist and never had. It would require a special action of the state legislature to give the town a new charter and a legal existence. Having made his point, he thanked the legislators kindly and left the capitol. Woke the snoring taxi driver and said, "Let's go back home."

It probably cost him a hundred dollars for that ride. Maybe more. He never told us, and nobody, not even my mother, ever dared ask him.

By the time he arrived home there was a delegation waiting to see him at our house: the mayor, the chief of police, the judge, pretty much the whole gang. Legislators had been on the phone all day to them, and they were deeply worried. Because, you see, everything they had ever done, in the absence of a valid town charter, including collecting taxes, had been illegal. You can imagine what that could mean if people got it in mind to be litigious about things.

Everybody came into our living room. And the whole family, too, because, he said, we saw the beginning of it and deserved to see the end.

Before the mayor or any of them said a word, he explained to them exactly what he had done. And he told them that, under the state constitution, establishing a town was a very tricky legal business. He said the chances were a hundred to one that they would mess it up again. He wished them good luck, promising that if they ever bothered him or us anymore, he would go to Tallahassee again and close them down for keeps.

There was a lot of silence. Finally the mayor spoke.

"What do you want from us, Garrett?"

"Ah," said my father. "I knew it would come down to that. And I'm glad it did, because there is something I do want from you all."

They were all looking and waiting. I reckon they were ready to do or pay most anything. That's how things were handled.

"Damn it!" he said. "I want my five dollars back from that phony traffic ticket."

Long pause.

"That's all?"

"That's all. You give me my five dollars back and I'll give you back your receipt."

So they paid him the five dollars and he tore the receipt in two and they filed out of our house.

"You beat them, Daddy," I said. "You won!"

"That's right, boy," he told me. "And I taught them a very important lesson."

"What's that?" my mother asked, nervously.

"If they want to stop me now," he said, "they're going to have to kill me. And I don't think they've got the guts for it."

Then he laughed out loud. And so did I, not because it was funny, but because it seemed like the right thing to do at the time.

Nativity, Caucasian

ALLAN GURGANUS

("What's *wrong* with you?" my wife sometimes asks. She already knows. I tell her anyway.)

I was born at a bridge party. This explains certain frills and soft spots in my character. I sometimes picture my own genes as crustless multicolored canapés spread upon a silver oval tray. Mother'd just turned twenty-six and was eight and one half months gone. A colonel's daughter, she could boast a laudable IQ plus a smallish independent income. She loved gardening but, pregnant, couldn't stoop or weed. She loved swimming but felt too modest to go out in a suit. "I walk like a duck," she told her husband, laughing. "Like six ducks trying to keep in line. I *hate* ducks."

Her best friend, Cloe, local Grand Master, tournament organizer, a perfect whiz at stuffing compatible women into borrowed seaside cottages for marathon contract bridge, phoned.

"Bianca? I know you're incommoded but listen, dear. We're short a person over at my house. Saundra Harper Briggs finally checked into Duke for that radical diet? And not one minute too soon. They say her husband had to drive the poor thing up there in the station wagon, in the *back* of the station wagon. I refuse to discriminate against you because of your condition. We keep talking about you, still ga-ga over that grand slam of yours in Hilton Head. I could send somebody over to fetch you in, say, fifteen minutes? No? Yes? Will that be time enough to throw something on? Unless, of course, you feel too shaky. . . ."

Hobbyists often leap at compliments with an eagerness unknown to pros. And Bianca Larkin Everett was the classic amateur, product of a Richmond that, deftly and early on, topiaries, espaliers, and bonsais its young ladies, pruning this and that, preparing them for decorative root-bound existences either in or very near the home. Bianca, a white girl, a post-deb, was most accustomed to kind comments concerning clothes or looks or her special ability to fox-trot. And any talk about the mind itself, even mention of her well-known flare for cards, delighted her. So, dodging natural duty, bored with being treated as if pregnancy were some debilitating terminal disease, she said, "Yes, I'd adore to come. See you shortly, Cloe. And God bless you for thinking of me."

The other women applauded when she strolled in wearing a loose-cut frock of unbleached linen, hands thrust into front patch pockets piped with chocolate brown. (All this I have on hearsay from my godmother, a fashion-conscious former nurse and some-time movie critic for the local paper: Irma.)

With much hoopla, two velvet pillows were placed on a folding chair, the new guest settled. They dealt her in. Young Bianca Everett. Phrases floated into the smoky air: Darling girl. Somewhat birdlike. Miscarried her first two, you know? Oh, yes. Wonderful organizer—good with a garden. School up north but it hadn't spoiled her outlook or even her accent: pure Richmond. Good bones. Fine little game player. Looking fresh as a bride.

These women liked each other, mostly. At least they *knew* each other—which maybe mattered more. Their children carried family secrets, cross-pollinating, house to house. Their husbands owned shares of the same things, they golfed in groups. If the women knew all about each other first, then either liked one another or not—husbands liked each other (till proven wrong) but didn't always *know* each other deeply—in short, community. Shelter, assured Christmas cards, to be known by name on the street.

One yard above the carpets and Persian rugs, temporary table-tops paved a whole new level. Surfaces nestled along halls and on the second-story landing. Women huddled from four edges toward each other. That season's mandatory pastels, shoulder padding. Handbags propped on every level ledge. Mantels, banisters. Cloisonné ashtrays glutted with half-smoked cigarettes. Refreshments, aspics, watercress, cucumber, all waiting in the kitchen. The serving lady late, Cloe, a plumpish blonde, discreetly glancing at her watch. Such nice chatting. Exclamations over bad hands and good. Forty belles and semi-belles. Junior guilded. All rooms musical with voices, the great gift of southern women, knowing how to coax out sounds, all ringing like this. Queen Anne furniture, ancestral portraits, Moroccan-bound books, maroon and gilt, Williamsburgy knickknacks. Beiges. Muted olive greens. A charming house chock full of lovely noise, and smokers not inhaling but hooked anyway.

Cloe's prize Pekingese, Mikado, snorted under card tables as through a tunnel ridged with nyloned columns. He edged, grimly interested, toward this new arrival's scent. An ancient wheezy male animal, Mikado took the liberty en route of sniffing up as high on women's limbs as he could reach, of rubbing languidly against the swishy silk and hazy shins of every woman there. Cloe had tied a yellow bow around his topknot; he tolerated this on bridge days, a fair trade for the cozy sense of being underneath a long playhouse of gaming tables, cards fatly snapping overhead. His path lay strewn with kicked-off shoes. Dainty aromatic feet to nudge. Mikado, the Blankenships' cranky one-time ribbon winner, is only mentioned here because he suspected before any other living creature in this murmurous house that something was about to give.

He sauntered to a halt, stood under the table, stared, proprietory and enraptured, up at the area (dare I go through with this grisly sequence and its raunchy aftermath, my life?) between the young Bianca's barely opened knees.

Mikado's flat face was mostly nose, very wet, chill as the jellyish aspic now gleaming on a kitchen counter. Cataracts had silvered over both his popping goldfish eyes. Smell, swollen to exciting new dimensions, remained the one great jolt and consolation left him. He nuzzled near enough and quite almost against the silk to get a better sample scent of something rich and decidedly awry here. The placing of his wide cool snout upon her shinbone made Bianca, who'd just spread her cards, shudder with a little flinch. The subtlest sort of pelvic twist, then a serene smile of recognition. "Oh, Mikado," she whispered to her geisha fan of cards. For this was a society where ladies knew the names of other ladies' gardeners and maids and lapdogs.

Next ... into this party cubicle of china shop small talk and play-it-safe decor, nature lunged fairly bullishly. Intent on clobbering mere taste, it went right for a trigger spot and let loose one deep-seated wallop. It happened Now.

The Peke got hit by falling waters, about a bucket's worth. He yelped and scrambled down the hallway through a grove of table legs and female feet, skidding to safety under a favorite sideboard's shadow. Once there, Mikado collapsed and was panting when Bianca, mouth a perfect O, bellowed forth in some voice totally unladylike and three full octaves deeper than her usual musical lilt, "Oh, my Gawd, I've stawrted!"

Cards scattered atop the table, some teetered onto her steep lap, fell to dampened carpet. Her three tablemates stood, overturned the Samsonite. With it went a coaster full of lipsticked butts.

Table to table, downstairs, then up, news darted at the speed of sound. Three women moved to help Bianca stand but she'd stretched out all her limbs, was less seated on the chair than propped against it, semi-rigid as a starfish, muttering some Latin from her convent days.

First they dragged her toward the velvet chaise. But Cloe, who'd just spent a fortune having that piece reupholstered, dissuaded them by backing, beckoning, through the kitchen's swinging portholed door. The cluster veered in there and, for want of a better spot, laid Bianca on the central counter, under a panel of humming fluorescent tubes. Her shoulder bumped a wooden salad bowl filled with party mix (pretzel sticks, nuts, cereals, sprinkled salts, and Worcestershire sauce) and sent this scattering across linoleum's fake brick. Other dishes toppled, too. Pink and green mints rattled dicelike everywhere, the silver compote clanging toward a corner. One red aspic fell, splitting to shiny smithereens before the Spicer twins took charge and set the other party foods along shelves or on the floor around the waist-high counter where Bianca lay, distended.

Friends bustled to hold her hands, daub her skirt with paper toweling. Ruth Smiley quickly phoned the hospital for advice, forgetting to request an ambulance. Others listened in on two upstairs extensions, scolding her when she hung up. Then someone just as flustered dialed the fire department. Irma, my godmother, the movie reviewer, a short sensible woman who'd seen more films more times than practically anyone, now did what they would do in movies at such moments, on sea voyages, at Western way stations: she put water on to boil and fetched some string plus a bottle of Jack Daniel's (still in last year's Christmas gift box). She spread what seemed to be a sheet under my poor mother, rocking her from side to side. Bianca, chewing her knuckles, apologized to Cloe, "Really ruined your party. If I'd only guessed. . . . Richard will be absolutely peeved. Oh, this is so *unlike* me."

"Hush," Cloe said. "You couldn't know. It's nature's doing, darling. Keep calm. Help's coming. We all love you, Bea."

Others, timing her contractions by the kitchen's sunburst wall clock, mumbled yes, they did. They patted her wrist, pressed cool terry cloth scented with wintergreen across her forehead. Irma said, "Forgive me, dear, I hate to do this," but she boldly flapped Bea's dress back, took a look, mumbled, "Uh-oh. Somebody did call someone, an ambulance or something, right?" Others gathered behind Irma, stooped, shook their heads, held on to one another. Mavis DeWitt gave an empathetic moan, recalling her twins' six-hour delivery. She whispered, "I think I'm going home. I feel ... I feel ... goodbye."

At the corner of Elm Avenue and Country Club Drive, the ambulance, ignoring a stoplight, overcome by the power of its siren and right-of-way, bisected the route of a northbound fire truck headed to the same address, and each vehicle, similarly entranced and headstrong with mission-of-mercy noise, mistook the other for its own potent echo. They collided. Nobody was hurt but the vehicles got pretty well smashed up. A medic shunted about applying first aid to firemen, all in black rubber raincoats and seated on someone's lawn. The assistant fire chief lifted the ambulance's hood and sniffed for smoldering.

Women fought to peek through the door's porthole. Bianca was thrashing now, and Irma Stythe, a war nurse and squat level-headed person, ordered all potential fainters to the living room. Then Ruth Smiley barged in with news that sirens had been heard from an upstairs window and, grinning at her own alertness, saw my mother laid upon the work counter, legs apart, surrounded on the floor by platters of party foods like offerings around some sacrificial altar—my demure mother spread-eagled where the light refreshments should be, now writhing, gasping rhythmically, some heady severance already evident—and Ruth, usually so stalwart, tottered toward the sink, blacking out en route, grabbing a hanging split-leaf philodendron, taking this down and falling in a rich dark blur of store-bought dirt and looping greenery. Irma promptly shooed the others out, all but the hostess and the reliable Spicer twins, who for twenty years had locally team-taught Home Ec. The lanky sisters hoisted Ruth from either end and crunched toward the living room, shuffling through broken crockery, vines, aspic scattered here and there like wobbly carnage. They'd revived her when Mikado waddled in, having licked himself clean of perfectly respectable waters. He sniffed at the damp towels blotting Cloe's rug. A beast, wet to half his normal size, white in the eyes, still licking his dark chops, sent Ruth Smiley out again with one sleepy shriek. The Spicers simply lifted her legs back onto the furniture.

"Where *are* those ambulances?" Cloe got out ice tongs, any tool that looked silvery and surgical. "Sirens have been going for ten minutes." Mother's wails now filled the entire house. Thirty acquaintances took up handbags, met at the front door, faces waxy as if Bianca's fate had befallen each and all of them. They told one another in lowered voices, "We'll only be underfoot," and—once assured of their basic good sense—fled.

Bianca pleaded, between quickening seizures, to be gagged for decency's sake. She kept screeching personal charges against her husband, saying this mess was all his fault, his fault, his fault. Irma cradled Mother's head, lifted a water tumbler of Jack Daniel's, tried to tip some between the victim's lips. But she kept choking. So instead they doubled over a tulip-shaped potholder and simply stuffed this between chattery teeth. "Bite down," Irma told her, "It's risky to move you, dear, and we hear them, hold on tight."

At the phone, Cloe was barking orders to the manager of the Country Club two blocks away. "Smytheson, listen up. You get into a cart right now. You ride out and you grab any doctor on the course. A dentist, a vet, anybody. But, Smytheson, hurry. The poor little thing's head is out already."

A fringe-topped golf cart wobbled into the driveway. Two young doctors, an eye-ear-nose-and-throat man plus a dermatologist, wearing three-toned golf shoes and flashy shirts, lunged in without knocking, found a fainted woman sprawled on the living room's chaise, hurried over, peeled back her skirt, yanked down panties. Elmyra Spicer, unmarried and long aware of men's baser drives, flew enraged across the room, slapped Dr. Kenilworth's head and sports cap, shrilling, "Not her. Not her, you. In there."

The kitchen was an epic mess. Cereal, pretzels, soil, shards of aspic, stepped-on mints both pink and green. All this litter split and crackled under their spiked shoes, which sent Cloe swooping through the kitchen door to check on her inherited Orientals. But the kitchen did smell wonderful: good bourbon. Someone with nothing better to do perked coffee.

A wet Pekingese sat on hind legs in the pantry doorway, panting, a soggy yellow ribbon draped across its head. The doctor's caddy, a handsome black kid of fourteen, now jangled in from the cart, heaving forward two golf bags. In his excitement, he stood braced, as if expecting the players to choose a proper putter for this situation.

The doctors studied the event with an old amazement, some wonder missing at the hospital, studied the committee of busy improvising women, studied a red rabbit-sized and wholly uninvited little wriggler aim out toward fluorescent light, looped to a pink cord that spiraled downward. Irma Stythe (God bless her sane and civil heart) guided the creature, eased it—still trailing slick

residues and varnishes—up into general view. Just now, Irma recognized the doctors, grinned wanly over at them, said, "You want
to slap it?" proffering the ankles.

"No." Kenilworth shook his head, took his cap off, modest at the
sight of women in such complete control. "No. Please. You." He
lifted one hand as if offering her the option of a waltz.

So Irma hauled off and slapped it smartly. She did this again.
And once more, until it squalled into Me. They all smiled to hear
a new human voice in the room. In recognition, the caddy clapped.
Applause. But just a smattering.

The ambulance driver, nose bloodied, rushed in to explain the
delay, chatted with a doctor who dabbed at his upper lip. Ruth
Smiley, coming to, hearing the cries, insisted on getting up. The
door swung open just long enough for the company to see Ruth
grin, glimpse the coral-colored cord, blanch of human coloration
and drop backward to the carpet as the door fell closed. They
wrapped the baby in monogrammed towels and laid him in his
mother's arms. Her face was puffed, glossy with tears. Her bun had
come undone some time ago, brown hair a woolly pagan mess.
She gazed down at the purplish child, still bawling, fists already
pounding air in spastic if determined blows and—as if the sight
of him were the final indignity in a series of such, Bianca sobbed,
disconsolate. Elmira Spicer tugged the potholder from my mother's
mouth but she groaned, "You put that back." A new siren; then
the fire chief lumbered in, wearing full regalia. Bianca and the
infant, both wailing in different registers, were carried past the
card tables, borne over the prone Ruth Smiley and her attendant,
Elvyra, who bent across her, pressing down the hem, sure the men
had come back for a second try.

Irma phoned Richard's insurance office to make sure he knew.
Somehow, no one had thought to call him. His best business voice,
"Yes, Irma? Actually I'm in the middle of a Group Life conference.
But what can I do for you?"

She gave one croupy giggle and leaned against the wall, fatigued,
cackling. Irma clamped a hand over the receiver as if to smother
him and, pointing at the phone, told Cloe, "Richard's asking what
he can do for *me*."

Cloe was wandering around, palms pressed to her cheeks, surveying the remains of her model kitchen.

"You heard right. Go to her, Richard. Take flowers. She was so
brave. The baby has real lung power. No, have your *secretary* send
the flowers. You get going."

Cloe stumbled into the front room and collapsed on the belea-
guered chaise. Irma followed, stood looking down at the hostess,
Grand Master, rubbing her neck and shoulders, eyes pressed shut.

The twins dragged Ruth Smiley home a few doors down. Abandoned handbags lay scattered under chairs. Cards and party favors,
a set of keys, one ashtray smoldering.

"Irma," Cloe lifted her head, "You're still standing? Could I ask
for one more thing? That damask tablecloth on the counter, the
one that was under her. Could you just toss it into the washer?
Pour in about a pound of Oxydol. I can clean up the rest later. I'll
just call Fatima and her sister, and their whole neighborhood, to
come over here and work for a solid week. But I don't think I can
handle the sight of that cloth."

"You mean the sheet?"

"Yes, it was a tablecloth, actually. Damask. You couldn't have
known, Irma. It was Grandmother Halsey's, 1870 or so. No problem."

Irma leaned back in. Its pattern of wheat sheaves, bounty, harvest
home, was now spread with urgent gloss and gore. Mikado trotted
after her toward the laundry room. Upstaged all afternoon, antsy
for attention, he now rolled over, played dead dog, sat on his
haunches, then, tentatively, pranced.

Irma held the tumbler full of bourbon above the chaise. Cloe
sniffed once, opened her eyes. The house was oddly silent. A few
yards away, some lawn mower hissed and yammered, reassuring.
Cloe sat up, took the glass in both hands as a child might, and
tossed back three adult swallows. Mikado circled the heaped towels, smelling them. "No," Cloe called, halfhearted. "Bad dog." But
the animal climbed onto the pile, gave a huffy sigh, and, head
resting on crossed paws, closed his eyes.

"How about a toast?" Irma retrieved the glass. "Here's to it, to
the baby. To the neighborhood's new baby. Some start, huh? And
to the neighborhood. God help us all."

Both of them glanced at the closed kitchen door. They'd just
decided, without words, to go back in and start the cleaning job
themselves. It would be wrong to burden the maid and her sister.
Those two women had lives and troubles of their own. Besides,
this was probably some sort of tribal duty, a task too ludicrous
and personal to inflict on anybody else.

Cloe stood and stretched. "Well, my dear, are you ready?"

Irma nodded, then punched open the swinging door and lightly
draped one arm around Cloe's shoulder. They lingered there on

the threshold for a moment, two well-meaning white women, old friends, studying the whole mess realistically.

"You know, it's not nearly so bad as I remembered," Irma said.

Then they scuffed straight into ankle-deep debris, waded toward the broom closet, got boldly back to it, got on with it, with life as it is practiced on this particular side street in this particular country; they got on with business as usual. World without end, Amen.

Piano Lessons

DAVID MICHAEL KAPLAN

When I was seven years old, my mother decided I should have piano lessons—why, I don't know. We had an upright piano inherited from an uncle of hers on the side porch, and I think she felt it should be used. My father didn't like the idea at all. I'd never shown any interest in music, he said; it was a waste of time and money. Most of all, he didn't like the idea of the nuns. Except for Mrs. Kresky, who lived thirty miles away in Schuylerville, the nuns at St. Stanislaus were the only piano teachers in the county, let alone Tyler, the little town in western Pennsylvania where we lived. "I don't like him being over there with them," my father said, but my mother was insistent.

"For God's sake," she told him, "what do you think they're going to do? Convert him?"

So on Wednesday afternoons that December, my father waited after school to take me to my piano lesson. As our Packard coughed and spluttered like an old, tired beast, we'd drive across the bridge to the Third Ward, the side of town where St. Stanislaus was. I'd crane my neck and look down at the frozen French River, its ice mottled and dirty. Once I asked my father where it went. "Nowhere," he said, and I thought, *The river is going nowhere*. We'd pass tired houses, their yards littered with broken toys, empty doghouses, rusted iceboxes and washers, cars slowly being stripped to skeletons. In one yard, a gutted deer carcass hung by chains from a child's swing set. Often their lights weren't yet on, and I wondered if anybody really lived there, and did they have children like me who also took piano lessons.

"Mind now," my father told me as he handed me a dollar for the lesson, "if those nuns try and teach you anything besides piano, you let me know."

I didn't know what he meant. I knew nothing about nuns, had

never even been close to one until I started taking piano lessons, and his words frightened me.

"You just tell me," he said, "and we'll put an end to that. I don't care what your mother says." Then he'd leave me to go wait somewhere—I never knew where—while I had my lesson.

I'd knock on the priory door and be ushered into the music room to wait for Sister Benedict. The room had a stale, waxy smell and was always too warm, the radiator sporadically hissing like a cornered cat. The drapes were kept closed, and shadows seemed everywhere. Above the piano a wooden Christ gazed down on me in agony. Sometimes I'd hear doors softly opening and closing in the hallway, but I never saw any people pass by, nor did I hear voices, or the sound of pianos being played by any other children taking lessons. What I did hear was the rustle of Sister Benedict's habit in the hall, and then she'd be there, hands folded, lips thin and unsmiling, smelling like old sweaters and my mother's laundry starch. She'd nod and sit beside me on the piano bench and uncover the keys. "Let's begin," she'd say.

I always played badly. Meter was a mystery to me. I was either going too fast or too slow or losing the count altogether. "Do it again," Sister Benedict would murmur, and I would try, but still I couldn't get it right. Sometimes when I played particularly badly, she would pinch the bridge of her nose between her fingers and rub. "Again," she'd tell me, tapping her pencil on my music book in an attempt to mark the beat. I would blink with frustration as I struggled to find the proper rhythm. I rarely finished an exercise. "No, no—like this"—Sister Benedict would interrupt—and then demonstrate. "Do you understand now?" I'd nod, even though it was still a mystery and a secret, and I didn't understand at all.

Afterward, my father would be waiting for me in the car; after the first lesson, he'd never gone back inside the priory. "Did those nuns try and tell you anything?" he'd ask. I would shake my head.

And then one afternoon everything changed. Snow was falling thickly when my father dropped me off for my lesson. "I have something for you," Sister Benedict said when she entered the music room, and she was smiling, something she'd never done before. She went to the closet and came back with something I'd never seen, a wooden box with a metal shaft and scale. "I got this for you," she said, putting the metronome on top of the piano. "Maybe it will help." She wound it and pressed a button on the side. The shaft clicked back and forth like an admonishing finger.

"Play," she told me. "Try keeping up." I tried, but the metronome only made things worse. Like a shaming, clucking tongue, it seemed to mock me. I stopped playing.

Sister Benedict stopped the metronome. "What's the matter?" she asked.

"I—I can't keep up."

"Let's try it slower," she said, and adjusted the metronome. But still I couldn't find the proper beat. I felt myself sweating underneath my shirt.

Once more she reset it. "Try again," she urged.

But it was always gaining on me, pushing furiously onward with a pace and a will of its own. My fingers missed more and more notes, the page became a blur, and still the metronome marched on, and with every tick it seemed to say, *You will do this again and again and again; you will never get it right; you will be in this music room forever*.

My fingers froze. I began to cry.

"What's the matter?" Sister Benedict asked anxiously. "Why are you crying?" I couldn't reply. I sat with my hands rigidly by my side, chest heaving, my face hot with tears.

"Jonathon," she said, using my name for the first time, "please." Her hand fluttered, as if she would touch me, then fell into her lap. "I don't understand," she said. "Please stop crying." But I couldn't—I couldn't stop at all.

"Stay here," she murmured and, as much to herself as to me, "I'll get Mother Superior." She left and soon was back with an older nun, who wore a white shawl over her black habit.

"He just started bawling," Sister Benedict told her. "He won't stop."

"What's wrong, child?" the other nun asked gently. I shook my head. I couldn't say what was wrong.

"He has trouble," Sister Benedict said. "He gets frustrated."

The older nun put her hand on my forehead. "He feels hot," she said. She stroked my hair. "He should go home today."

"His father should be coming for him shortly," Sister Benedict said.

"Would you like to rest until your father comes?" the older nun asked me. I nodded. She took my hand and led me down the hallway to a narrow room with mullioned windows that looked out onto a courtyard lit by a single lamp on a post. The snow was still falling fast and had already covered the bushes, the ground, the benches. I'd stopped crying now but was still sniffling hard.

"You can lie down over there until your father comes," the nun told me, pointing to a settee by the window. I went over and lay down. She softly closed the door.

I heard a high-pitched yell in the courtyard. I rose to my knees and looked out. Four nuns were standing in the falling snow. I couldn't see their faces clearly because of the thick flakes, the poor illumination, and my breath, which kept misting the pane. One nun had thrown a snowball at another, who was laughing and pointing her finger accusatorially. She bent over and made her own snowball and threw it back at her assailant, who shrieked and dodged. And then they were all making snowballs and tossing them awkwardly at one another, laughing and running about like excited children. One tall nun scooped up a lapful of snow in her skirt. Making a chugging sound, she chased the one who'd started it all, who squealed and tried to escape, only to slip and fall in the snow. Her attacker flipped up her habit, dumping snow on her. Then they were all upon her, furiously shoveling snow with their hands. "No, no," she screamed, and laughed, and they were all laughing, until one by one they collapsed, panting, their black habits powdered white with snow. For one moment, no one and nothing moved in the courtyard except the snow falling from far above and far away, and all of it—courtyard and snow and nuns —looked like a miniature scene in the snow globes I'd seen at the five-and-dime. *If I breathe*, I thought, *they will vanish.*

And then they rose, and brushed themselves off, and quietly walked across the courtyard and into the dark.

I heard voices in the hall, the loudest my father's. The door opened, and there he was. "Let's go," he said, his lips tight. We saw no one as we left.

We got into the car and drove away from St. Stanislaus. The streets were silent except for the crunch of our tires.

My father gripped the wheel tightly with both hands. "Goddam snow," he muttered. A muscle in his jaw twitched.

Everything looked different, I thought. The houses in the Third Ward seemed transformed, the cluttered yards now soft undulating hillocks of snow, the stripped cars fantastic caverns, the gutted deer on the swing magically rimed and glistening and frosted. Lights were on in the houses; people lived there after all.

"What happened?" my father asked. "What did those damn nuns say to you?"

"Nothing," I murmured, as I stared at the houses. Through one window I could see a man brushing his wife's hair with slow, gentle strokes; in another, a young couple danced languidly while a little boy drove a toy car around their legs. I thought, *I have never seen any of this before*. We crossed the bridge. It was too dark to see the river, but I knew it was there and that below its ice it was flowing, away from Tyler, and even though I didn't yet know its destination, still—it was flowing somewhere.

"They must have said *something*," my father said, looking at me hard. "They told me you were crying."

I thought of the nuns playing in the snow. The car seemed hot and close, and I rolled down my window a crack. The sliver of cold air felt bracing. And I wondered, Could Sister Benedict have been one of the nuns in the courtyard? And I just hadn't seen, hadn't known? I thought and thought but couldn't decide.

"Well, that's it," my father said, making a cutting motion with his hand. "No more piano lessons! You're through with that." He slapped the steering wheel. "I'll just have to have it out with your mother."

But I wasn't listening anymore at all. I laid my head against the window and closed my eyes and felt the rest of my life come rushing toward me, like the French River flowing back on itself, and I knew with a shiver approaching wonder that all of it would be both more terrible and more wondrous than anything I'd ever been told before.

The Shirt

JANET KAUFFMAN

The navy blue shirt is the one I want to talk about. I've looked at it for a good many years, on a man's chest, and it would satisfy me to keep looking, accumulating the least noticeable and most pointless facts, so that when I began talking about it, I'd be freer to pick out or discard from that hoard of material—maybe pinpointing the pinpoints where the shirt was basted in Manila, or recounting the numbers and sorts of washings.

Does it matter whose arms are inside the arms?

It's the work shirt of a uniform, but that doesn't mean a man on a yacht would not be comfortable in such a shirt, and pleased to own it—a solid weave, with worn cuffs and one or two loose threads on the top fold of the collar. I've counted the buttons on the shirt, seven down the front, navy blue buttons, each with four drilled holes and crisscrossed navy blue thread.

When I picture the shirt hung on the back of a chair—and I've seen it there, its shoulders hiked and squared off by the wooden back of the chair—I can picture it with the white linen trousers that men wear on the *Lisa-Marie* and the *Vel-Delana*, at Port Huron. But it's really the shirt of a uniform, and paired with matching navy blue pants, the luxury look disappears: the marina, the sun, the clear bottles of gin, one lime on the table—all of that disappears. And so I've learned to collapse this marina scene around the edge of the shirt, into the fine line that separates the shirt from the wall behind it or from the carpet. The marina, after all, fits in there.

But for a fact, I have seen only two sorts of walls behind the shirt: first, the reinforced concrete wall of my office; and second, the papered wall, willows and footbridges on it, of the Ranchero Motel two miles east.

The man whose shirt it is is named Wilson, a middle-of-the-road name—I know it—a name so old it doesn't mean anything anymore. Over the years we have made love four times and had dinner together once.

Those facts tell nothing. Not as much as the shirt the man wears when we talk, when we sit together and do nothing.

Against regulations, he takes his breaks in my office, where we drink tea and sometimes hold on to each other's hands. His wife knows to call him there, and even when he talks on the phone to her, he touches my hand. His wrist slips forward away from the cuff of the shirt and pauses over my hand and then presses down there.

We are not like children holding hands. More like the aged, who love without hindrance, without the future offering up entice- ments. There's not much more to say on the subject of love, is there?

When name tags listed the full name, he wore his ID all the time, hooked onto the shirt pocket. But with the new administration, and new tags listing the last name and initial only—WILSON, H.— he found ways to forget about wearing it. He's been cited four times, but he usually has the ID on him somewhere. On reports, he writes in the blank for comments, *faulty clip* or *dislodged during exercise*. He prefers to be called by his first name. When somebody new comes along and yells out, "Hey, you!" he turns around, nods his head just barely, and says, "Harley, the name is Harley."

He likes the idea of work in a uniform, so that people know what his job is and he doesn't have to fool anybody. That's how honest he'd like to be.

But who hasn't seen men with closets of money, with stupefying power, who claim to be ordinary men and who dress like ordinary men?

Harley says no, in the end those men cannot resist modifications, noticeable ones: brass buttons, a gold-plated pin, a slightly more flattering cut to the collar, tipped and lengthened, for better place- ment of the pin.

Nobody talks advancement with Harley. The morning the office is only one number off in the lottery pool, somebody asks him if he had a million dollars what would he do? He can't say. He walks to the chair at my desk. People resume their talk.

"What I'd do," he says carefully, and he pulls at the shirtfront with his fist, "is give you the shirt off my back." I know what that means, and what it doesn't.

Since what he said could count as an offer, million or no, I believe I'll ask for the shirt someday.

I wouldn't think of it as a relic—it's a work shirt. I'd wear it. In fact, in the open air—where we have nothing to do with each other, where the sky looks flat in its blue colors and the wind does to cloth what it does to trees—I'd be happy to wear it out.

Doom

JAMES HOWARD KUNSTLER

On a spring day that could not have been more perfect, Tim Howland came to the dreadful realization that his life would someday
end. The effect was shattering. One might think that a sixteen-
year-old boy would have already encountered at least the idea of
mortality. In fact, the previous fall the family's beloved bluetick
hound, Jupiter, had been run over by a Buick, and Uncle Randy
had succumbed to a wasting illness before his fortieth birthday.
Despite these tragic examples, death remained an abstraction to
Tim, as remote from his own existence as the earthquakes and
typhoons that regularly destroy the faceless natives of Asia by the
tens of thousands. It was something that happened to others.

A normal boy, not given to metaphysics, who loved baseball and
trout fishing and liked to read American history and listen to old
jazz, and who had a profound crush on a girl named Bridget Gruen,
Tim came to the terrible knowledge of his own inevitable demise
in a seemingly haphazard way.

There he was, standing in left field in the seventh inning of a
varsity game. His team, the Hanover Catamounts, were way out in
front of the Albion Yeomen by a score of 12 to 0. The first batter
whiffed. A momentary vision of Bridget Gruen played across his
mind like a gust of abnormally warm wind in the weeds beyond
the third base line. The truth was, he barely knew her and certainly
had never seen her in the buff. Just then he heard a buzzing and
looked down into the grass. A bumblebee was grazing in new
clover. He stepped on the bee in his cleats, then lifted his foot and
stooped down to peer closer. In the distance, the umpire cried,
"Strike three!" and the second batter skulked back to the visitors'
dugout.

The plump, furry bee was motionless down in the clover, its
head neatly crushed by a plastic spike. A pang of regret rose in
Tim's throat as he considered his sole and total responsibility in

ending the harmless creature's life. And what was its life? A tiny glimmer amid the fantastic fathomless ethers of eternity? He alone had stamped out its existence, like a great, hulking, merciless, capricious God. Where there had been a speck of light, now there was a little blot of darkness. What if a correspondingly huge, merciless, and indifferent force looked down upon himself and took a sudden notion to crush him, to end his existence? Tim dropped from a crouch to one knee as the idea rocked him. If the life was squashed out of him, he thought, the world as he knew it would vanish. For that matter, the entire universe would end! Even if he wasn't squashed at this exact moment on the ball field, someday, he realized, the universe as perceived by himself would cease to exist. What did it matter that it might go on for others? In time, their worlds would end too, and in a bit more time the earth would burn up like a cinder, the stars and planets would be sucked into an awesome vortex, and the whole thing would disappear. And if, perhaps, something came along and replaced it, he, Tim, would not be a part of it, ever, forever and ever, and evermore. . . .

Tim did not hear the crack of the bat as he gazed up openmouthed in nausea. He did not hear the yells of his teammates and the sprinkling of hometown fans, did not see the white arc of the ball as it rose high above the shortstop's head and then descended into left field, ultimately bouncing off the center of his cap where the letter *H* was superimposed over the silhouette of a leaping mountain lion.

He regained consciousness moments later—though it might as well have been days, years, eons. A ring of faces gazed down at him around a central dome of empty blue sky. The faces seemed miles away.

"Are you all right, son?" Coach LeRoy Bottomly asked.

"No," Tim said. "The universe is coming to an end."

His teammates chortled and poked each other in the ribs.

"Guess we're gonna have to get that old squash X-rayed," the coach said.

Down at the hospital emergency room Tim was surrounded by victims of mayhem, misfortune, and reckless motoring. He sat quietly in a plastic chair with his baseball glove in his lap while the gurneys wheeled by with their groaning passengers. A fat woman in stretch garments and her brood of three children occupied the chairs closest to him. One of her offspring, a boy of nine, stood squarely before Tim and said, "Can I see your mitt, mister?"

"Here," Tim said. "You can keep it."

"I can?" the boy replied in amazement. "Like forever?"

"Sure, forever," Tim told him, savoring the piquant irony of his knowledge that sooner or later the freckle-faced boy would be reduced by the centuries to an inert pile of dust. He thought for a while about all the time he had put into breaking in the glove, kneading it with neat's-foot oil hour after hour, sleeping on it tucked under his mattress with a hardball inside. What a waste it had all been.

"Our dad fell into the web press down to the printing plant and squooshed his hand," the boy said, almost proudly, as though it were a heroic distinction. "Why are you here?"

"I got hit in the head with a ball."

"Is that how come you gave me your mitt?"

"No," Tim said.

"You look all right."

"It doesn't matter. I'm going to die."

"I don't see no blood."

"I mean someday in the future. You will too."

At this point, the boy's mother glanced sideways across her plump shoulder and squinted disapprovingly at Tim. "You sit down before I slap you," she growled at her offspring, who giggled behind a screen of his own wiggling grublike fingers.

By and by, an X-ray technician took Tim down the hall for his pictures. When they were done a young physician of Asian demeanor came in to examine him, peering into his eyeballs with an ophthalmoscope.

"You are going to live," the doctor pronounced jokingly in the clipped English of the great subcontinent.

"Only for a while," Tim said. "Then I'll be dead."

"But you shall return," the doctor said, pointing to the cat silhouette on Tim's uniform. "Perhaps as a tiger."

"And then I'll be dead again."

"And then you shall come back again, perhaps as an elephant."

"Until all the animals are extinct—and then what happens?"

"Beats me," the doctor said, erupting in high-pitched laughter.

Tim left the hospital and walked home across town, down streets lined with dignified old houses. He couldn't escape dwelling on the idea that the people who had originally built the houses were now dead and gone, moldering in one of the town cemeteries, a fate inevitably awaiting the present occupants. When he reached his own house on Academy Street, violet spring dusk was gathering softly on the wide porch while birds newly arrived from the tropics twittered sweetly in the fresh-leaved maples. To Tim, it might as well have been eventide in Antarctica.

The house was redolent of his mother's homemade spaghetti sauce.

"Is that you?" she called musically from the kitchen.

"No, it's only me," Tim said, feeling wholly insignificant in the face of eternity. Yet, despite the weight of the centuries, he was drawn into the kitchen by the tantalizing aroma.

"It *is* you," his mother insisted. "How did your game go?"

"My game?" Tim laughed bitterly at the suggestion that a baseball game had any meaning in the immense scheme of things. "I have no idea."

"You played, didn't you?"

"We were ahead. Then I lost track."

Tim's mother glanced warily at him from the range, where she stood poised over a big enamel pot with a wooden spoon.

"Hungry?"

He was, but he couldn't bear to acknowledge it. Why prolong the absurd process of consumption, digestion, and elimination?

"Here, taste," she said, holding up the spoon, now filled with steaming red sauce, including a chunk of ground beef that had simmered slowly and succulently all afternoon. Like Quasimodo shrinking away from Esmeralda's gift of life-giving water, Tim at first regarded the spoon with fear. Then, giving in to pure instinct, he opened his mouth and accepted it. "Good?" his mother asked.

Tim nodded gravely. "Mom, do you ever think about us all being dead someday?"

"You mean in an accident of some kind?" she said, a little horrified, but less at the idea specifically than at the morbidness of teenagers in general.

"Let's say just from natural causes," Tim said.

"But why would I think about that?"

"Because it's inevitable."

"I'm too busy thinking about a million and one other things," she said.

"But how can you ignore it? When we're gone, we'll be gone forever."

She paused a moment to consider, twiddling the wooden spoon as though it were the baton she once wielded on the sidelines of Catamount football games. "Whenever I think about not being here anymore, I try to imagine all the eons that went by *before* I was born. Eternity is a two-way street, you know?"

"Hunh?" Tim croaked, shocked as much by this new wrinkle on the dreaded subject as by his mother's enunciation of it. She, like her son, was not a person normally given to metaphysics.

"Anyway," she went on, "I figure I didn't mind all those millions of years that ticked away *before* I was born, so I won't be bothered by the millions of years that come *after* I'm gone." By this time, Tim had fairly reeled out of the kitchen and was trudging upstairs to his room as though he were climbing the steps of a gallows.

There, among the posters of exalted guitar pluckers and major-league sluggers, the hanging plastic models of aircraft and space-craft, the pictorial history books, the skates, skis, barbells, and racquets, the albums of Cootie Williams and Blind Willie McTell, and other miscellaneous playthings he had outgrown, Tim flung himself onto his bed as though he were falling into his grave.

With his eyes closed, the interstellar spaces seemed as close as the dark of night. This is what it would be like to be dead, he thought: a trillion years of loneliness, without even any supper waiting at the end to make it worthwhile. His stomach growled. The little morsel of beef had roused the sleeping behemoth that was his appetite. The spaghetti sauce smelled *so* good. He wondered if his mother would make garlic bread and Caesar salad too, as she often did those nights she cooked Italian. His thoughts of the dining room table groaning with victuals dissolved into an image of Bridget Gruen. The very syllables of her name were chewy, he thought, as though she were a kind of beautiful food. And in a way, he hungered for her the same way that he hungered for a meal after a ball game. Her creamy curves and golden hair gave her the appearance of a rich dessert. He hardly knew her. She was in his chem class, and one day they were assigned to be lab partners. He spilled sulfuric acid on her looseleaf binder and dissolved all her notes from the preceding week's classes. Now, as he fell down the slippery slope of dreams, he found himself back in that chem lab with Bridget. Except it was night. They were, mysteriously, the only ones there. Bridget wore a black shimmery strapless cocktail dress that made her look enchantingly grown-up. The two of them were lounging on the black marble lab counter drinking champagne out of beakers and nibbling dainty little hunks of garlic bread. . . .

"Wake up, son." It was his father. The overhead light was brutal. Tim wanted to slip back to the zone of dreams, but his father wouldn't let him alone. "I hear you're all bent out of shape about something."

"Nothing," Tim mumbled, too embarrassed to say.

"Your hormones are probably in an uproar," said his father, who was an attorney and often stated his opinion as though he were giving expert testimony. "A few molecules get loose in the old brain pan, and all of a sudden it seems like the end of the world. Come on down. It's suppertime."

There was garlic bread and Caesar salad, and afterward there was fresh pineapple with home-made chocolate chip cookies. Tim's sister, Ruthie, who was thirteen, monopolized the table talk with an elaborate recounting of the status rivalries in junior high school.

"And so I go, 'Jodie, that is absolutely the *stupidest* reason to like a boy,' and she goes, 'Well, it's not only his hair. . . .' "

Tim took it in, feeling sorry for all of them, thinking that in a relatively short time his family's lives and all their heroic and pathetic strivings for happiness would be reduced to naught as the atoms of their beings dispersed through the heavenly vapors.

The beast of his appetite was appeased and he asked to be excused from the table. Wishing now to avoid his room, with its scary intimations of the grave, Tim retreated to his father's study. Though it too seemed to have some sepulchral qualities—the dark walnut-paneled walls, the draperied and louvered windows—it had always been Tim's favorite room in the house. He sat in a luxurious leather chair behind the large desk, gazing at a Winslow Homer print on the far wall—thinking how the artist was no longer among the living. Idly he reached down for the telephone directory in a bottom drawer and leafed through it until he found the name of one Herman Gruen, a music teacher over at the college. This, he knew from previous explorations, was Bridget's dad, and hence this was her home number.

Tentatively he reached for the phone, hesitated, then snatched it out of its cradle and punched in the seven numbers without leaving himself the time to chicken out. Bridget herself answered.

"Yes, hello," he said. "This is Tim Howland and I don't have very long to live, so I thought maybe we could go out or something."

There was a pause that you could have hummed the first several bars of Beethoven's Ninth through.

"Tim? From school?"

"That's right. Chem class," he said, sounding slightly annoyed, though in fact he was breathlessly nervous. "Don't you remember me?"

"Oh, yes. Of course. But are you very sick?"

"No. I'm not sick at all."

"I thought you said you didn't have long to live."

"I meant life is short." Tim struggled to explain himself. "Too short. For all of us."

"You make it sound so tragic."

"Are you making fun of me?"

"Not at all. I had no idea you were so . . . deep."

"I think about stuff," he admitted. "Will you come to the movies with me on Saturday night?"

Another pause, like the interval between movements in a symphony, fraught with emotion.

"Yes, I think I'd like that," Bridget finally said.

"Seven o'clock?"

"Okay."

"Great. See you then, then," Tim said and hung up. The room took on a weird rosy glow. A warm sensation rose in his chest, and suddenly the world and all its ancillary cosmic outlands seemed not such a bad place after all. In fact, as he rose from the desk, Tim was seized by a feeling of ineffable rightness about the universe and his place in it. Upstairs, his sister Ruthie turned up a record album by a quartet of sniveling British punks and Tim thought he heard the voices of the angels.

Texts

URSULA K. LE GUIN

Messages came, Johanna thought, usually years too late, or years before one could crack their code or had even learned the language they were in. Yet they came increasingly often and were so urgent, so compelling in their demand that she read them, that she do something, as to force her at last to take refuge from them. She rented, for the month of January, a little house with no telephone in a seaside town that had no mail delivery. She had stayed there several times in summer; winter, as she had hoped, was even quieter. A whole day would go by without her hearing or speaking a word. She did not buy the paper or turn on the television, and the one morning she thought she ought to find some news on the radio she got a program in Finnish from Astoria. But the messages still came. Words were everywhere.

Literate clothing was no real problem. She remembered the first print dress she had ever seen, years ago, a genuine *print* dress with typography involved in the design—green on white, suitcases and hibiscus and the names *Riviera* and *Capri* and *Paris* occurring rather blobbily from shoulder seam to hem, sometimes right side up, sometimes upside down. Then it had been, as the saleswoman said, very unusual. Now it was hard to find a T-shirt that did not urge political action, or quote lengthily from a dead physicist, or at least mention the town it was for sale in. All this she had coped with, she had even worn. But too many things were becoming legible.

She had noticed in earlier years that the lines of foam left by waves on the sand after stormy weather lay sometimes in curves that looked like handwriting, cursive lines broken by spaces, as if in words; but it was not until she had been alone for over a fortnight and had walked many times down to Wreck Point and back that she found she could read the writing. It was a mild day, nearly windless, so that she did not have to march briskly but could mosey along between the foam lines and the water's edge where the sand reflected the sky. Every now and then a quiet winter breaker driving up and up the beach would drive her and a few gulls ahead of it onto the drier sand; then as the wave receded she and the gulls would follow it back. There was not another soul on the long beach. The sand lay as firm and even as a pad of pale brown paper, and on it a recent wave at its high mark had left a complicated series of curves and bits of foam. The ribbons and loops and lengths of white looked so much like handwriting in chalk that she stopped, the way she would stop, half willingly, to read what people scratched in the sand in summer. Usually it was JASON + KAREN or paired initials in a heart; once, mysteriously and memorably, three initials and the dates 1973–1984, the only such inscription that spoke of a promise not made but broken. Whatever those eleven years had been—the length of a marriage? a child's life?—they were gone, and the letters and numbers also were gone when she came back where they had been, with the tide rising. She had wondered then if the person who wrote them had written them to be erased. But these foam words lying on the brown sand now had been written by the erasing sea itself. If she could read them they might tell her a wisdom a good deal deeper and bitterer than she could possibly swallow. Do I want to know what the sea writes? she thought, but at the same time she was already reading the foam, which though in vaguely cuneiform blobs rather than letters of any alphabet was perfectly legible as she walked along beside it. "Yes," it read, "esse hes hetu tokye to' ossusess ekyes. Seham hute' u." (When she wrote it down later she used the apostrophe to represent a kind of stop or click like the last sound in "Yep!") As she read it over, backing up some yards to do so, it continued to say the same thing, so she walked up and down it several times and memorized it. Presently, as bubbles burst and the blobs began to shrink, it changed here and there to read, "Yes, e hes etu kye to' ossusess kye. ham te u." She felt this was not significant change but mere loss and kept the original text in mind. The water of the foam sank into the sand and the bubbles dried away till the marks and lines lessened into a faint lacework of dots and scraps, half legible. It looked enough like delicate bits of fancywork that she wondered if one could also read lace or crochet.

When she got home she wrote down the foam words so that she would not have to keep repeating them to remember them, and then she looked at the machine-made Quaker lace tablecloth on the little round dining table. It was not hard to read but was, as one might expect, rather dull. She made out the first line inside the border as "pith wot pith wot pith wot" interminably, with a "dub" every thirty stitches where the border pattern interrupted.

But the lace collar she had picked up at a secondhand clothes store in Portland was a different matter entirely. It was handmade, handwritten. The script was small and very even. Like the Spenserian hand she had been taught fifty years ago in the first grade, it was ornate but surprisingly easy to read. "My soul must go," was the border, repeated many times—"my soul must go, my soul must go,"—and the fragile webs leading inward read, "sister, sister, sister, light the light." And she did not know what she was to do, or how she was to do it.

Remembering Orchards

BARRY LOPEZ

In the years I lived with my stepfather I didn't understand his life at all. He and my mother married when I was twelve, and by the time I was seventeen I had gone away to college. I had little contact with him after that until, oddly, just before he died, when I was twenty-six. Now, years later, my heart grows silent, thinking of what I gave up by maintaining my differences with him.

He was a farmer and an orchardist, and in these skills a man of the first rank. By the time we met, my head was full of a desire to travel, to find work like my friends in a place far from the farming country where I was raised. My father and mother had divorced violently; this second marriage, I now realize, was not just calm but serene. Rich. Another part of my shame is that I forfeited this knowledge too. Conceivably, it was something I could have spoken to him about in my early twenties, during my first marriage.

It is filbert orchards that have brought him back to me. I am a printer. I live in a valley in western Oregon, along a river where there are filbert orchards. Just on the other side of the mountains, not so far away, are apple and pear orchards of great renown. I have taken from these trees, from their arrangement over the ground and from my curiosity about them in the different seasons, a peace I cannot readily understand. It has, I know, to do with him, with the way his hands went fearlessly to the bark of the trees as he pruned late in the fall. Even I, who held him vaguely in contempt, could not miss the kindness, the sensuousness of these gestures.

Our home was in Granada Hills in California, a little more than forty acres of trees and gardens which my stepfather tended with the help of a man from Ensenada I regarded as more sophisticated at the time. Ramon Castillo was in his twenties, always with a new girlfriend clinging passionately to him, and able to make anything grow voluptuously in the garden, working with an aplomb that bordered on disdain.

The orchards—perhaps this is too strong an image, but it is nevertheless exactly how I felt—represented in my mind primitive creatures in servitude. The orchards were like penal colonies to me. I saw nothing but the rigid order of the plat, the harvesting, the pruning, the mechanics of it ultimately. I missed my stepfather's affection, understood it only as pride or gratification, missed entirely his humility.

Where I live now I have been observing orchards along the river, and over these months, or perhaps years, of watching, it has occurred to me that my stepfather responded most deeply not to the orchard's neat and systematic regimentation, to the tasks of maintenance associated with that, but to a chaos beneath. What I saw as productive order he saw as a vivid surface of exquisite tension. The trees were like sparrows frozen in flight, their single identities overshadowed by the insistent precision of the whole. Internal heresy—errant limbs, minor inconsistencies in spacing or height—was masked by stillness.

I have, within my boyhood memories, many images of these orchards, and of neighboring groves and orchards on other farms at the foot of the Santa Susanas. But I had a point of view that was common, uninspired. I could imagine the trees as prisoners, but I could not imagine them as transcendent, living in a time and on a plane inaccessible to me.

When I left the farm I missed the trees no more than my chores.

The insipid dimension of my thoughts became apparent years later, on two successive days after two very mundane observations. The first day, a still winter afternoon—I remember I had just finished setting type for an installment of Olsen's *Maximus Poems*, an arduous task, and was driving to town—I looked beneath the hanging shower of light-green catkins, just a glance under the roof crown of a thousand filbert trees, to see one branch fallen from a jet-black trunk onto fresh snow. It was just a moment, as the road swooped away and I with it.

The second day I drove more slowly past the same spot and saw a large flock of black crows walking over the snow, all spread out, their graceless strides. I thought not of death, the usual flat images in that cold silence, but of Ramon Castillo. One night I saw him twenty rows deep in the almond orchard, my eye drawn in by moonlight brilliant on his white shorts. He stood gazing at the stars. A woman lay on her side at his feet, turned away, perhaps asleep. The trees in that moment seem not to exist, to be a field of indifferent posts. As the crows strode diagonally through the orchard rows I thought of the single broken branch hanging down, and of Ramon's ineffable solitude, and I saw the trees like all life —incandescent, pervasive.

In that moment I felt like an animal suddenly given its head.

My stepfather seemed to me, when I was young, too polite a man to admire. There was nothing forceful about him at a time when I admired obsession. He was lithe, his movements very physical but gentle, distinct and hard to forget. The Chinese say of the contrast in such strength and fluidity, "movement like silk that hits like iron"; his was a spring-steel movement that arrived like a rose and braced like iron. He was a pilot in the Pacific in the Second World War. Afterward he stayed on with Claire Chennault, setting up the Flying Tigers in western China. He was inclined toward Chinese culture, respectful of it, but this did not show in our home beyond a dozen or so books, a few paintings in his office, and two guardian dogs at the entrance to the farm. In later years, when I went to China and when I began printing the work of Lao-tzu and Li Po, I began to understand, in a painful way, that I had never really known him.

And, of course, my sorrow was too that he had never insisted that I should. My brothers, who died in the same accident with him, were younger, more disposed toward his ways, not as ambitious as I. He shared with them what I had been too proud to ask for.

What drew me to reflect on the orchards where I now live was the stupendous play of light in them, which I began to notice after a while. In winter the trunks and limbs are often wet with rain and their color blends with the dark earth; but blue or pewter skies overhead remain visible through wild, ramulose branches. Sometimes, after a snow, the light in the orchards at dusk is amethyst. In spring a gauze of buds and catkins, a toile of pale greens, closes off the sky. By summer the dark ground is laid with shadow, haunted by odd shafts of light. With fall an elision of browns, the branches now hobbled with nuts, gives way to yellowing leaves. And light again fills the understory.

The colors are not the colors of flowers but of stones. The filtered light underneath the limbs, spilling onto a surface of earth as

immaculate as a swept floor beneath the greens, the winter tracery
of blacks, under a long expanse of gray or milk or Tyrian sky, gave
me, finally, an inkling of what I had seen but never marked at
home.

I do not know where this unhurried reconciliation will lead. I
recognize the error I made in trying to separate myself from my
father, but I am not in anguish over what I did. I do not live with
remorse. I feel the error only with a little tenderness now, in these
months when I find myself staring at these orchards I imagine are
identical to the orchards that held my stepfather—and this is the
word. They held the work of his hands, his desire and aspiration,
just above the surface of the earth, in the light embayed in their
branches. It was an elevation that followed on his courtesies toward them.

An image as yet unresolved for me—it uncoils slowly, as if no
longer afraid—is how easily as boys we ran from adults who
chased us into orchards. They could not race away as we could
through that understory. But if we had been in a pasture, had
stolen rides bareback on a neighbor's horses, and had tried to run
away across the plowed fields, our short legs foundered in the
furrows, and we were caught.

Beneath the first branching, in that grotto of light, was our sanc-
tuary.

When my stepfather died he had been preparing to spray the
filbert orchard. He would not, I think, have treated the trees in this
manner on his own, but a type of nut-boring larvae had become
epidemic in southern California that year and my brother argued
convincingly for the treatment. Together they made a gross mistake
in mixing the chemicals. They wore no protective masks or clothing. In a single day they poisoned themselves fatally. My younger
brother and a half-brother died in convulsions in the hospital. My
stepfather returned home and died three days later, contorted in
his bed like a root mass.

My mother sued the manufacturer of the chemical and the sup-
plier, but legal maneuvers prolonged the case and in the end my
mother settled, degraded by the legal process and unwilling to
sacrifice more years of her life to it. The money she received was
sufficient to support her for the remainder of her life and to keep
the farm intact and working. We buried my brothers in a cemetery
alongside my mother's parents, who had come to California in

1923. My stepfather had not expressed his wishes about burial, and I left my mother to do as she wished, which was to work it through carefully in her mind until she felt she understood him in that moment. She buried him, wrapped in bright blue linen, one row into the filbert orchard, at a spot where he habitually entered the plot of trees. By his grave she put a stone upended with these lines of Robinson Jeffers:

> It is not good to forget over what gulfs the spirit
> Of the beauty of humanity, the petal of a lost flower
> blown seaward by the night-wind, floats to its quietness.

I have asked permission of the owners of several orchards along the river to allow me to walk down the rows of these plots, which I do but rarely and harmlessly. I recall, as if recovering clothing from a backwater after a flood, how my stepfather walked in our orchards, how he pruned, raked, and mulched, how his hands ran the contours of his face as he harvested, the steadiness of his passion.

I have these memories now. I know when I set type, space line to follow line, that he sleeps in my hands.

What's New, Love?

WRIGHT MORRIS

Sometimes, months running, Molly saw him like clockwork, two, three times a week, before the day shift took over, coming in to take his usual seat at the counter, away from the door and the draft. A little whoosh of the night air came along with him, freshening things up. When she turned to face him with the pot of coffee he would be reaching for one of the ashtrays—she saw to it he always had an ashtray. "What's new, love?" he would say, as if she knew, but even if she knew it would have slipped her mind. Molly was a big girl, as Doc called her, not the sort of waitress the men kidded around with. People could sit right beside him and not recognize him, or see anything of interest about him, but when he spoke to her they would glance up just to see if he meant it, which he didn't. He smoked too much, but anyone who knew anything knew his voice.

She first saw him in *Picnic* with Kim Novak. Her friend Adele, who saw the movie with her, didn't think he was the man for Kim Novak, which spoiled so much of the movie for Molly she had to go alone and see it over. Long before all the men were taking off their clothes he didn't have to do more than unbutton his shirt and let the tails hang out. Kim Novak knew that, the moment she saw him, but neither was she the right person for him, and knowing that it wasn't going to work out saddened Molly every time she saw the movie.

The truth was, but it took her years to see it, they never really found the right woman for him, or realized he made a better loser than a winner. When she saw him at the counter, his eyes bloodshot, the swallow of hot coffee making him squint and grimace, he looked like one of the LA cops after a long night in the patrol car. "You get some sleep," she would tell him, and she was the one who filled and refilled his cup of coffee.

"Just a half cup more, love," he would say, pushing his cup toward her. "Make it the bottom half."

From the time Molly could open the refrigerator, along with a bottle of Coke, and carry it through the house to the bathroom, her mother had spent most of the day floating in a tub of almost hot water. It pained her to walk, make a fist with her hands, move her head from side to side, or ride on buses. As a child Molly felt her mother's soft swollen body had soaked up most of the water she soaked in. All her flesh was a puffy, off-white color, like bread dough, but she painted her lips and put rouge on her cheeks while Molly held her father's shaving mirror. Her bobbed hair was black. With the water in the tub up to her neck her head looked like a clown's mask. She had come to Hollywood to be a dancer, where she met and fell in love with a big studio chauffeur. Her mother's pain began soon after Molly was born, beginning at the tips of her toes and fingers, then moving slowly up her veins to grip the joints of her body. Only in a tub of water, her body in suspension, her breasts floating like collapsed balloons, was she free of the pain she could sometimes see like glowing hot coals around her joints. During the day she listened in the bathroom, to the religious pro- grams over the radio, but at night, propped up in bed, she watched the late movies.

That house had been large and airy, with a fenced yard at the back where two small dogs barked and yapped at her, but she never came to know where the water heater was, or where her husband kept the extra fuses. A big black woman cleaned it, and cooked for Molly and her mother, but her father took his meals elsewhere. Molly thought he was a soldier and went off to the army, because he wore a uniform and leather puttees, but he worked for the studio and drove people to Malibu, Palm Springs, and such places. When Gloria Swanson did *Sunset Boulevard*, it was her father who drove her around. After Molly and her mother moved from that house she thought her father just went on living in it. That's how dumb she was.

The house on Kansas Street, in Santa Monica, had green shingles on the sides and a chain swing on the porch. Sometimes a neighbor parked his car in their front yard. Out in front, in the curb walk, were two palm trees with tops she could see from the swings in the schoolyard, when she was swung really high. The tops were so high they cast shadows on the next block, but never on their own house. In the new house, however, her mother felt much better and only spent part of the morning in the bathroom. Molly remembers the two of them, sitting on the bed, eating the take-out food she brought home from Doc's Place as they watched Shirley Booth in *Come Back, Little Sheba*. Her mother had said to her, Now you know what your mother's life was like.

Molly was a sunny, friendly, cheerful Irish girl with a face so broad she seemed to have no features. Everything but her wide smiling mouth was too small. At school she was well liked by the sisters for the way she cleaned the erasers and the blackboards. She liked to be helpful, but she didn't much care for school. Her first job in Doc's Place, behind the deli counter, was to help make up the coleslaw and the cream cheese. She was the sort of strong, willing worker that customers got to know and ask for. "Where's she at?" they would say, meaning her. From there she went to a part-time waitress with three tables of her own during the rush hour. "How are you, Mr. Altman?" she would say, since she found it natural to be respectful. They were Jewish people, mostly, from New York, used to Irish waitresses and good pastrami.

She usually knew, before most people, if he was away somewhere making a movie. What the movie was he never mentioned: she got the feeling he didn't care much for movies. How much better she got to know him than he did her! She knew him in all the roles he had played, but he only knew her as a waitress. What took the longest time in coming to her was that being a waitress was all she was. She had once started a movie she hadn't finished about a poor, battered woman by the name of Wanda, her whole life so terrible that Molly couldn't bear to watch it. What she saw of her, little as it was, was like seeing herself.

It was a fact she looked better at night, her hair almost copper-colored in the food warmer, but for all the way she worked, and spent time on her feet, she got heavier instead of lighter. The flesh of her arms hung loose as pouches when she reached for her orders at the service counter. She didn't take it personal, but she wanted him to know that when he said, "What's new, love?" she heard him.

Because she was the waitress most of the good tippers wanted, the younger ones felt a resentment toward her, complaining about the way she blocked the aisles during the rush hours. For every-body's sake, including her own, Doc moved her to the night shift behind the counter. It surprised her to find how much better everything looked at night, as she stood listening to the background

music. Through the wide front windows she could see down Wilshire, farther than she had ever been, except to see a doctor or a
dentist. If the fog was in, or it rained, she might take a cab back
to her house, the TV glowing in her mother's bedroom. Leaving
the TV on seemed to help her to sleep. All around her on the bed
would be the coupons she had cut from the supermarket circulars,
a decent Irish-Catholic woman resigned to what it was she couldn't
help. What Molly tried to do, at times, was share the worst of it
with her, such as what might become of Molly if she wasn't around
to keep an eye on her.

If Molly was tireder than usual and couldn't sleep, she would
lie awake thinking of this fight he had with John Wayne in a Civil
War movie. They fought like two bloodthirsty kids, in a gully where
they couldn't get away from each other, a fight to the death. If it
was a John Wayne movie she knew who would lose. The fact that
he made a better loser than a winner should have tipped her off,
but it didn't. She was a sucker for a loser, and it was harder for
her to cope with the roles he played than it was with him.

On this drizzly, humid morning she stopped to glance at the
headlines on the corner rack of newspapers. There he was, smiling
up at her, as if he had just pushed his empty cup toward her. It
said he had died of natural causes in this building she could
see from where she stood at the counter, with a view all the
way to Catalina. Joggers were passing by under the palm trees,
their leafy tops lost in the mist. By some trick of the light they
all seemed to be running on a cushion of air, detached from the
earth. It was her deep longing to be one of them that relieved her
despair. She took steps toward them, her belt buckle dangling,
until the meaning of what she read came to her. He had been
alone. At the very moment he had needed her the most, she had
not been there.

All day long, on the hour and the half hour, she heard it repeated,
but on the late news she heard the worst of it. He had been dead,
his poor dear head bleeding, for almost a week. Nobody had come
to see him or called to ask why he didn't answer. He had been
drinking; he had tripped and fallen. When he cried out nobody
had answered. In the rest room she had locked herself in a booth
and sobbed like a child.

Was it possible for a person, for a woman, to feel worse than
she felt? She stole time to sit with her head in her hands, a burden she would like to be free of. Doc put her back on the day shift
so she would have more than herself to think of. What would that

be? The way her tips fell off. She was no longer the person she had been, and the people who knew that didn't like it. Some of the early delivery trucks made their stops at different places or picked up coffee-to-go in the deli. When that was pointed out to her, and it was, Doc said what she needed was a "break." "You take a break, Molly," he said, and paid Lennie Tyler, one of the older cabbies, to keep an eye on her. "You're special, Molly," Doc said to her, and slipped a bill into her apron pocket. One of the things she had done was change the daily menus, but he let one of his own fat girls do it, on her way to school, smearing the purple ink with her sticky fingers. Molly had her pride. She had her uses. Who else would ever know when the new cashiers took in more money than they rang up? In the mirror at the back of the pie case Molly could tell by the way they flicked their hair, cracked their gum, or avoided her eyes what they were up to. In all her years Molly had never once cheated until her tips fell off, and she made up the difference with her own money.

On stormy nights Doc arranged for Lennie Tyler to see her to her door. The TV light was flickering in her mother's bedroom. "It's company," he said. "A lot of people do it. There's women who can't sleep without it."

Molly might not have noticed, by herself, the way water was seeping beneath the front door. "You got a dog?" he cracked, as he let her in, the light shining on the film of water in the hallway, all the way down to the bathroom. He went ahead of Molly, sloshing the water, to push in the door. Steam filmed Molly's glasses. "You need a plumber," he said, as they stood watching the water spill over the rim of the tub, to splash on the floor. Her mother's hands, like rubber gloves full of air, were floating on the surface with her yellow wig.

"Where's your phone, kid," Lennie said, as if he had just heard it ringing. And that was all Molly remembered before she passed out.

Whatever there was left for her to feel, she felt, but it wasn't much after the funeral, or the questions nobody could answer. How had she got herself, weak as she was, into water so hot it almost cooked her, and why was the phone in her bedroom off the hook? Molly had this dream about a wake so lifelike she actually confused it with a silent movie, a long line of people filing past a coffin in a hall with posters advertising *his* movies. When her turn came to look into the coffin it was *him* she saw, not her mother, looking the way he did with Gloria Swanson.

Doc and the others advised her to sell the house and live in one of the places with people to wait on her. "If you want to be waited on," Lennie said, "I'm waiting." In his time off, on the weekends, he repainted the kitchen and put screens on the sleeping porch her mother had never slept on. Under the bed she found green food in the saucers she had put out for stray cats. Lennie fixed it all up so Molly could lie there and see the palms sway, way up where the rats lived. It worried her to think what they did when it rained, what they did when it swayed.

Lennie took her to the movies, when one of *his* was showing, then came by to pick her up in the lobby later. He put in a space heater, and moved the TV so she could lie in bed and watch the night baseball. Molly hadn't even known that they could play baseball at night. As they were watching *Sunset Boulevard* on the TV, he leaned over to whisper "You were sweet on him once, weren't you?"—which startled her more than it should have. What business was it of his who she was sweet on? "You know what you need?" he went on, sticking her with his elbow, "You need a new boy friend!"

All this time he had been such a fool he didn't know that she had one, and would never give him up. In the movie Gloria Swanson had said it was the pictures that had got small, not her, and that's how it had been with Molly. When it was time for him to say—and one day it would be—"What's new, love?" she would tell him. Not that he didn't know, but the time hadn't come for her to say.

Owls

LEWIS NORDAN

Once when I was a small boy of ten or eleven I was traveling late at night with my father on a narrow country road. I had been counting the number of beers he drank that night, nine or ten of them, and I was anxious about his driving.

Neither of us had spoken for a long time. What was there to say: the beers, the narrow road, the stubble fields, a bare bulb shining out in the darkness from a porch far back from the road, the yellow headlights? What was there to talk about? The car held the road on the curves; the heater was making its familiar sound.

Then I saw a road sign, bright yellow and diamond-shaped, and on it I read the word SLOW. My father kept on driving at the same speed and did not slow down, though I knew he had seen the sign.

So I was bold. I said, "Did you see that sign?"

Immediately my father let up on the gas and the car began to slow down. He said, "You're right. We should go back."

He pulled his car onto the berm and stopped and looked back over his left shoulder for safety and then pulled out onto the road again and made a U-turn.

I was frightened. I said, "Why are we going back?"

My father shifted the gears, and we began driving back in the direction we had come. "The sign," he said. "I'm going back to see the sign."

I said, "Why? Why are we doing that?"

He said, "Isn't that what you meant? Didn't you want to go back?"

I said, "I wanted you to slow down. I was afraid."

We drove on in the darkness for a minute. My father said, "The sign didn't say SLOW."

I said, "It didn't? I thought it said SLOW."

My father said, "It said OWLS."

So we kept driving and I didn't argue. I listened to the quiet sound of the heater fan. I saw the red eyes of a rabbit on the roadside. I saw the stubble fields. For one second I believed I had lived a very long hard life and that I was all alone in the world.

Then the sign came into view again: the back of the sign, of course. My father slowed the car and pulled over far to the right, and when he had come to a complete stop he checked over his shoulder for safety and made another U-turn so that we might face the sign again and read its message. The headlights made the sign huge and bright.

My father had been right. The sign said OWLS.

We kept sitting there for a long time. The engine was running; there was a small vibration.

Then my father turned off the engine. The early spring night air was cold, but he rolled down the windows.

I knew my father wanted me to be quiet. I'm not sure how I knew this. I knew he wanted us to listen. I scarcely breathed, I was listening so hard. I did not move at all.

Then I heard the owls overhead. I heard the soft centrifugal buffeting of their feathers on the night air. I heard a sound from their owl throats so soft I believed it was their breathing. In my mind I counted them and thought that they were many. The owls were circling and circling and circling in the air above us.

I don't know what I believed would happen. I think I believed I would feel the fingers of my father's hand touch my arm, the sleeve of my shirt. I believed I would turn to him and for the first time in my life I would know what to say. I would tell him all my secrets. I believed my father would say, "I love you." This was what it meant to sit in a car with your father in the middle of the night and listen to a flock of owls while looking at a diamond-shaped sign that said OWLS.

Then he rolled up his window, and so I rolled up mine. In the darkness he said, "You know, your mother is a terrible house-keeper."

We only sat there looking at the OWLS sign. I knew things would not go well after this.

And so then he started up the car and we drove away, back along the dark road, and we did not say anything else to each other that night, and he drank a few more beers.

All I mean to say is this: Many years later I fell in love with a woman, and she was beautiful and strange. One afternoon, after we had made our love, we lay in a band of sunlight that fell across our bed and I told her the story of my father and the dark road and the sign that said OWLS.

I said, "You don't believe me, do you."

The woman said, "Have you ever told this story to anyone before?"

I said, "I told my mother. That same night, after my father and I got home and my mother came upstairs to tuck me in."

The woman said, "Tell me again about your room, then, with the fake stars on the ceiling."

I told her what she already knew. I said, "It was an attic room, with a slanted ceiling. A desk and even my clothes drawers were built into the wall to save space. There was a crawl space in the back of my closet, where I sat sometimes, in the rafters. On the ceiling above my bed were pasted luminous decals of stars and the planets and the moon. Saturn had rings. A comet had a funny tail."

She said, "Tell me again about the real moon."

I said, "The moon outside my window."

She said, "How large was it?"

I said what I had said to her many times. I said, "It was a peach-basket-sized moon."

She said, "And you were lying in your bed, with the fake stars shining down on you and the peach-basket moon outside your window, and then—"

I said, "I heard my mother coming up the stairs to tuck me in."

She said, "Your mother had been worried about you, out in the car with your father when he had been drinking."

I said, "Yes, she had been worried. She would never say this."

She said, "What did she say?"

I said, "She said, 'Did you have a nice time with Daddy tonight?' "

She said, "What did you say?"

I said, "I told her the story about seeing the sign. About stopping and listening to the owls in the air."

She said, "What did your mother say then?"

I said, "She said, 'That's about like your daddy.' "

She said, "Your mother didn't believe you?"

I said, "She was right. There was no OWLS sign. It's ridiculous. There is no way to hear owls in the air. And anyway, think about the coincidence of a drunk man and his oversensitive kid stopping at just the moment the owls happen to be flying above a sign."

She said, "Hm."

I said, "And you know that thing my father said. That thing about 'Your mother is a terrible housekeeper'?"

She said, "Mm-hm."

I said, "That's a part of an old joke we used to hear in the South when I was a boy. The punch line is, 'My wife is a terrible house-keeper; every time I go to piss in the sink it's full of dirty dishes.'" I said, "I think I made the whole thing up."

She said, "Where did the owls come from?"

I said, "I'm not sure. Do you remember in *Winnie-the-Pooh*, the character named Owl?"

She said, "Yes."

I said, "Remember, somewhere, in one of those books, we learn that Owl's name is misspelled on a sign as WOL. Maybe that's where I got the idea. I just happened to think of that book. Jesus. It's possible I made this whole thing up."

She said, "Are rabbits' eyes really red?"

I said, "I don't know. I saw a blind dog in my headlights one time, and its eyes looked red. Christ."

The way the sunlight fell across this bed was ... well, I was so much in love.

She said, "Was your father magic?"

I said, "I wanted him to be."

She said, "He might have been."

Now she looked at me, and it was the night of the owls all over again. The car's heater, the vibration of the engine, the red eyes of the rabbit, the stubble fields, the music of the odd birds in flight, the OWLS sign before me. And also the feeling that there was some-one beside me to whom I could tell my most terrible secret and the secret would be heard and received as a gift. I believed my clumsy drunken inexpert father, or my invention of him, had pre-pared me for this magic. The woman beside me said, "I love you."

In that moment every good thing I had expected, longed to feel with my father, I felt with her. And I also felt it with my father, and I heard his voice speak those words of love, though he was already a long time dead. He was with me in a way he could not be in life.

For one second the woman and I seemed to become twins, or closer than twins, the same person together. Maybe we said noth-ing. Maybe we only lay in the band of sunlight that fell across our bed. Or maybe together we said, "There is great pain in all love, but we don't care, it's worth it."

—for C.C.

Where *Is* Here?

JOYCE CAROL OATES

For years they had lived without incident in their house in a quiet residential neighborhood when, one November evening at dusk, the doorbell rang, and the father went to answer it, and there on his doorstep stood a man he had never seen before. The stranger apologized for disturbing him at what was probably the dinner hour and explained that he'd once lived in the house—"I mean, I was a child in this house"—and since he was in the city on business he thought he would drop by. He had not seen the house since January 1949 when he'd been eleven years old and his widowed mother had sold it and moved away, but, he said, he thought of it often, dreamt of it often, and never more powerfully than in recent months.

The father said, "Would you like to come inside for a few minutes and look around?"

The stranger hesitated, then said shakily, "I think I'll just poke around outside for a while, if you don't mind. That might be sufficient." He was in his late forties, the father's approximate age. He wore a dark suit, conservatively cut; he was hatless, with thin silver-tipped neatly combed hair: a plain, sober, intelligent face and frowning eyes. The father, reserved by nature, but genial and even gregarious when taken unawares, said amiably, "Of course we don't mind. But I'm afraid many things have changed since 1949."

So, in the chill, damp, deepening dusk, the stranger wandered around the property while the mother set the dining room table and the father peered covertly out the window. The children were upstairs in their rooms. "Where is he now?" the mother asked. "He just went into the garage," the father said. "The garage! What does he want in there?" the mother said uneasily. "Maybe you'd better go out there with him." "He wouldn't want anyone with him," the father said. He moved stealthily to another window, peering through the curtains. A moment passed in silence. The mother,

pausing in the act of setting down plates, neatly folded paper
napkins, and stainless steel cutlery, said impatiently, "And where
is he now? I don't like this." The father said, "Now he's coming
out of the garage," and stepped back hastily from the window. "Is
he going now?" the mother asked. "I wish I'd answered the door."
The father watched for a moment in silence, then said, "He's
headed into the backyard." "Doing what?" the mother asked. "Not
doing anything, just walking," the father said. "He seems to have
a slight limp." "Is he an older man?" the mother asked. "I didn't
notice," the father confessed. "Isn't that just like you!" the mother
said.

She went on worriedly, "He could be anyone, after all. Any kind
of thief, or mentally disturbed person, or even murderer. Ringing
our doorbell like that with no warning, and you don't even know
what he looks like!"

The father had moved to another window and stood quietly
watching, his cheek pressed against the glass. "He's gone down to
the old swings. I hope he won't sit in one of them, for memory's
sake, and try to swing—the posts are rotted almost through." The
mother drew breath to speak but sighed instead, as if a powerful
current of feeling had surged through her. The father was saying,
"Is it possible he remembers those swings from his childhood? I
can't believe they're actually that old." The mother said vaguely,
"They were old when we bought the house." The father said, "But
we're talking about forty years or more, and that's a long time."
The mother sighed again, involuntarily. "Poor man!" she murmured. She was standing before her table but no longer seeing it.
In her hand were objects—forks, knives, spoons—she could not
have named. She said, "We can't bar the door against him. That
would be cruel." The father said, "What? No one has barred any
door against anyone." "Put yourself in his place," the mother said.
"He told me he didn't *want* to come inside," the father said. "Oh,
isn't that just like you!" the mother said in exasperation.

Without a further word she went to the back door and called
out for the stranger to come inside, if he wanted, when he was
through with looking around outside.

They introduced themselves rather shyly, giving names, and forgetting names, in the confusion of the moment. The stranger's
handshake was cool and damp and tentative. He was smiling hard,
blinking moisture from his eyes; it was clear that entering his
childhood home was enormously exciting yet intimidating to him.

Repeatedly he said, "It's so nice of you to invite me in—I truly hate to disturb you—I'm really so grateful, and so—" But the perfect word eluded him. As he spoke his eyes darted about the kitchen almost like eyes out of control. He stood in an odd stiff posture, hands gripping the lapels of his suit as if he meant to crush them. The mother, meaning to break the awkward silence, spoke warmly of their satisfaction with the house and with the neighborhood, and the father concurred, but the stranger listened only politely and continued to stare, and stare hard. Finally he said that the kitchen had been so changed—"so modernized"— he almost didn't recognize it. The floor tile, the size of the windows, something about the position of the cupboards—all were different. But the sink was in the same place, of course; and the refrigerator and stove; and the door leading down to the basement—"That *is* the door leading down to the basement, isn't it?" He spoke strangely, staring at the door. For a moment it appeared he might ask to be shown the basement, but the moment passed, fortunately —this was not a part of their house the father and mother would have been comfortable showing to a stranger.

Finally, making an effort to smile, the stranger said, "Your kitchen is so—pleasant." He paused. For a moment it seemed he had nothing further to say. Then, "A—controlled sort of place. My mother ... when we lived here ..." His words trailed off into a dreamy silence, and the mother and father glanced at each other with carefully neutral expressions.

On the windowsill above the sink were several lushly blooming African violet plants in ceramic pots, and these the stranger made a show of admiring. Impulsively he leaned over to sniff the flowers—"Lovely!"—though African violets have no smell. As if embarrassed, he said, "Mother too had plants on this windowsill, but I don't recall them ever blooming."

The mother said tactfully, "Oh, they were probably the kind that don't bloom—like ivy."

In the next room, the dining room, the stranger appeared to be even more deeply moved. For some time he stood staring, wordless. With fastidious slowness he turned on his heel, blinking and frowning and tugging at his lower lip in a rough gesture that must have hurt. Finally, as if remembering the presence of his hosts and the necessity for some display of civility, the stranger expressed his admiration for the attractiveness of the room, and its coziness. He'd remembered it as cavernous, with a ceiling twice as high. "And dark most of the time," he said wonderingly. "Dark by day,

dark by night." The mother turned the lights of the little brass
chandelier to their fullest: shadows were dispersed like ragged
ghosts and the cut-glass fruit bowl at the center of the table glowed
like an exquisite multifaceted jewel. The stranger exclaimed in
surprise. He'd extracted a handkerchief from his pocket and was
dabbing carefully at his face, where beads of perspiration shone.
He said, as if thinking aloud, still wonderingly, "My father was a
unique man. Everyone who knew him admired him. He sat *here*,"
he said, gingerly touching the chair that was in fact the father's
chair, at one end of the table. "And Mother sat *there*," he said,
merely pointing. "I don't recall my own place or my sister's but I
suppose it doesn't matter.... I see you have four place settings,
Mrs.—? Two children, I suppose?" "A boy eleven, and a girl thirteen," the mother said. The stranger stared not at her but at the
table, smiling. "And so too *we* were—I mean, there were two of
us: my sister and me."

The mother said, as if not knowing what else to say, "Are you
—close?"

The stranger shrugged, distractedly rather than rudely, and
moved on to the living room.

This room, cozily lit as well, was the most carefully furnished
room in the house. Deep-piled wall-to-wall carpeting in hunter
green, cheerful chintz drapes, a sofa and matching chairs in nubby
heather green, framed reproductions of classic works of art, a
gleaming gilt-framed mirror over the fireplace: wasn't the living
room impressive as a display in a furniture store? But the stranger
said nothing at first. Indeed, his eyes narrowed sharply as if he
were confronted with a disagreeable spectacle. He whispered,
"Here too! Here too!"

He went to the fireplace, walking now with a decided limp; he
drew his fingers with excruciating slowness along the mantel as
if testing its materiality. For some time he merely stood, and stared,
and listened. He tapped a section of wall with his knuckles. "There
used to be a large water stain here, like a shadow."

"Was there?" murmured the father out of politeness, and "Was
there!" murmured the mother. Of course, neither had ever seen a
water stain there.

Then, noticing the window seat, the stranger uttered a soft,
surprised cry and went to sit in it. He appeared delighted: hugging
his knees like a child trying to make himself smaller. "This was
one of my happy places—at least when Father wasn't home. I'd
hide away here for hours, reading, daydreaming, staring out the

window! Sometimes Mother would join me, if she was in the mood, and we'd plot together—oh, all sorts of fantastical things!" The stranger remained sitting in the window seat for so long, tears shining in his eyes, that the father and mother almost feared he'd forgotten them. He was stroking the velvet fabric of the cushioned seat, gropingly touching the leaded windowpanes. Wordlessly, the father and mother exchanged a glance: who was this man, and how could they tactfully get rid of him? The father made a face signaling impatience and the mother shook her head without seeming to move it. For they couldn't be rude to a guest in their house.

The stranger was saying in a slow, dazed voice, "It all comes back to me now. How could I have forgotten! Mother used to read to me, and tell me stories, and ask me riddles I couldn't answer. 'What creature walks on four legs in the morning, two legs at midday, three legs in the evening?' 'What is round and flat, mea- suring mere inches in one direction and infinity in the other?' 'Out of what does our life arise? Out of what does our consciousness arise? Why are we here? Where *is* here?' "

The father and mother were perplexed by these strange words and hardly knew how to respond. The mother said uncertainly, "Our daughter used to like to sit there too, when she was younger. It *is* a lovely place." The father said with surprising passion, "I hate riddles—they're moronic some of the time and obscure the rest of the time." He spoke with such uncharacteristic rudeness, the mother looked at him in surprise.

Hurriedly she said, "Is your mother still living, Mr.—?" "Oh, no. Not at all," the stranger said, rising abruptly from the window seat and looking at the mother as if she had said something mildly preposterous. "I'm sorry," the mother said. "Please don't be," the stranger said. "We've all been dead—*they've* all been dead—a long time."

The stranger's cheeks were deeply flushed as if with anger, and his breath was quickened and audible.

The visit might have ended at this point, but so clearly did the stranger expect to continue on upstairs, so purposefully—indeed, almost defiantly—did he limp his way to the stairs, neither the father nor the mother knew how to dissuade him. It was as if a force of nature, benign at the outset, now uncontrollable, had swept its way into their house. The mother followed after him, saying nervously, "I'm not sure what condition the rooms are in, upstairs. The children's rooms especially." The stranger muttered that he did not care in the slightest about the condition of the household and continued on up without a backward glance.

The father, his face burning with resentment and his heart accelerating as if in preparation for combat, had no choice but to follow the stranger and the mother up the stairs. He was flexing and unflexing his fingers as if to rid them of stiffness.

On the landing, the stranger halted abruptly to examine a stained glass fanlight. "My God, I haven't thought of this in years!" He spoke excitedly of how, on tiptoe, he used to stand and peek out through the diamonds of colored glass, red, blue, green, golden yellow: seeing with amazement the world outside so *altered.* "After such a lesson it's hard to take the world on its own terms, isn't it?" he asked. The father asked, annoyed, "On what terms should it be taken, then?" The stranger replied, regarding him levelly, with a just perceptible degree of disdain, "Why, none at all."

It was the son's room—by coincidence, the stranger's old room—the stranger most wanted to see. Other rooms on the second floor, the "master" bedroom in particular, he decidedly did not want to see. Speaking of it, his mouth twitched as if he had been offered something repulsive to eat.

The mother hurried on ahead to warn the boy and to straighten up his room a bit. No one had expected a visitor this evening! "So you have two children," the stranger murmured, looking at the father with a small quizzical smile. "Why?" The father stared at him as if he hadn't heard correctly. " 'Why'?" he asked. "Yes, *why?*" the stranger repeated. They looked at each other for a long strained moment. Then the stranger said quickly, "But you love them—of course." The father controlled his temper and said, biting off his words, "Of course."

"Of course, of course," the stranger murmured, tugging at his necktie and loosening his collar. "Otherwise it would all come to an end." The two men were of approximately the same height but the father was heavier in the shoulders and torso; his hair had thinned more severely so that the scalp of the crown was exposed, flushed, damp with perspiration, sullenly alight.

With a stiff avuncular formality the stranger shook the son's hand. "So this is your room, now! So you live here, now!" he murmured, as if the fact were an astonishment. Not used to shaking hands, the boy was stricken with shyness and cast his eyes down. The stranger limped past him, staring. "The same! The same! Walls, ceiling, floor, window—" He drew his fingers slowly along the windowsill, around the frame; rapped the glass, as if, again, testing materiality; stooped to look outside—but it was night, and nothing but his reflection bobbed in the glass, ghostly and insubstantial. He groped against the walls; he opened the closet door before the mother could protest; he sat heavily on the boy's bed, the springs creaking beneath him. He was panting, red-faced, dazed. "And the ceiling overhead," he whispered. He nodded slowly and repeatedly, smiling. "And the floor beneath. That is what *is*."

He took out his handkerchief again and fastidiously wiped his face. He made a visible effort to compose himself.

The father, in the doorway, cleared his throat and said, "I'm afraid it's getting late; it's almost six."

The mother said, "Oh, yes, I'm afraid—I'm afraid it *is* getting late. There's dinner, and the children have their homework—"

The stranger got to his feet. At his full height he stood for a precarious moment swaying, as if the blood had drained from his head and he was in danger of fainting. But he steadied himself with a hand against the slanted dormer ceiling. He said, "Oh, yes, I know! I've disturbed you terribly! You've been so *kind*." It seemed, surely, as if the stranger *must* leave now, but, as chance had it, he happened to spy, on the boy's desk, an opened mathematics textbook and several smudged sheets of paper and impulsively offered to show the boy a mathematical riddle. "You can take it to school tomorrow and surprise your teacher!"

So, out of dutiful politeness, the son sat down at his desk and the stranger leaned familiarly over him, demonstrating adroitly with a ruler and a pencil how "what we call 'infinity' " can be contained within a small geometrical figure on a sheet of paper. "First you draw a square; then you draw a triangle to fit inside the square; then you draw a second triangle, and a third, and a fourth, each to fit inside the square, but without their points coinciding, and as you continue—here, son, I'll show you; give me your hand, and I'll show you—the border of the triangles' common outline gets more complex and measures larger and larger and larger— and soon you'll need a magnifying glass to see the details, and then you'll need a microscope, and so on and so forth, forever, laying triangles neatly down to fit inside the original square *without their points coinciding!*" The stranger spoke with increasing fervor; spittle gleamed in the corners of his mouth. The son stared at the geometrical shapes rapidly materializing on the sheet of paper before him with no seeming comprehension but with a rapt fascination as if he dared not look away.

After several minutes of this the father came abruptly forward and dropped his hand on the stranger's shoulder. "The visit is over," he said calmly. It was the first time since they'd shaken hands that the two men had touched, and the touch had a galvanic effect upon the stranger: he dropped ruler and pencil at once, froze in his stooped posture, burst into frightened tears.

Now the visit truly was over; the stranger, at last, *was* leaving, having wiped away his tears and made a stoical effort to compose himself; but on the doorstep, to the father's astonishment, he made a final, preposterous appeal—he wanted to see the basement. "Just to sit on the stairs? In the dark? For a few quiet minutes? And you could close the door and forget me, you and your family could have your dinner and—"

The stranger was begging but the father was resolute. Without raising his voice he said, "No. *The visit is over.*"

He shut the door and locked it.

Locked it! His hands were shaking and his heart beat angrily.

He watched the stranger walk away—out to the sidewalk, out to the street, disappearing in the darkness. Had the streetlights gone out?

Behind the father, the mother stood apologetic and defensive, wringing her hands in a classic stance. "Wasn't that sad! Wasn't that—*sad*! But we had no choice but to let him in; it was the only decent thing to do." The father pushed past her without comment. In the living room he saw that the lights were flickering as if on the brink of going out; the patterned wallpaper seemed drained of color; a shadow lay upon it shaped like a bulbous cloud or growth. Even the robust green of the carpeting looked faded. Or was it an optical illusion? Everywhere the father looked, a pulse beat mute with rage. "*I* wasn't the one who opened the door to that man in the first place," the mother said, coming up behind the father and touching his arm. Without seeming to know what he did, the father violently jerked his arm and thrust her away.

"Shut up. We'll forget it," he said.

"But—"

"We'll forget it."

The mother entered the kitchen, walking slowly as if she'd been struck a blow. In fact, a bruise the size of a pear would have materialized on her forearm by morning. When she reached out to steady herself she misjudged the distance of the doorframe—

or did the doorframe recede an inch or two?—and nearly lost her balance.

In the kitchen the lights were dim and an odor of sourish smoke, subtle but unmistakable, made her nostrils pinch.

She slammed open the oven door. Grabbed a pair of potholders with insulated linings. "*I* wasn't the one, God damn you," she said, panting, "and you know it."

Something to Do with Baseball

RICHARD PANEK

On the way home from work, the dads would detour past the field where their sons played ball. They slowed their cars, coughing machines with payment plans that always outlived the engines, and pulled to the curb. No matter how their work had gone, the dads knew that at the end of the day they could count on their sons.

It didn't matter if the boy at bat was their own. The dads didn't come here to see how well their sons played ball. Later, the dads would care about the days of their children and wives. During dinner or in front of the TV, they could hear about the failing grade or flooding sink that had made this day different from all the others. And if anyone bothered to ask, the dads would say that their day had gone okay, the usual, the same as always, and in a way it was. Every day brought another new worry, something wrong to remind them where they were. Their grandfathers, refugees from another continent who had crossed an ocean with nothing to their names, had managed to provide their families with a home. And their fathers, by the time they'd reached this age, already had found a new promised land, the blocks of bungalows that were then crowding across the outskirts of the city. But these dads hadn't even made it out of the neighborhood. They'd gotten only as far as the complex of apartment buildings that rose one year to replace the few remaining empty lots. To their children the dads could offer no lawns, no basements or attics, nothing permanent, none of the places that had brought to light the pioneering spirit of their own boyhoods. Instead, the legacy of these dads would be two and a half rented bedrooms of temporary furnishings, temporary memories, temporary security. And if, by some stroke of good fortune that always seemed to happen to the other guy, one of the dads did make the move to the suburbs, all the families in the unit would gather for a farewell barbecue in the parking lot out back,

where there should have been a yard. There the dads would re-
assure one another that they'd done what they could. They'd given
their children a fine education, in a safe neighborhood, with one
good ball field. Every month, when the dads would sit down with
their wives to pay the bills, they'd go over the figures again, checking their expenditures and adjusting their estimates, based on their
joint incomes as well as current interest rates, and the result was
always the same. The day they could get their families out of here
was still far away. Then they'd help with the homework or fix a
faucet. But in the late afternoons, when the day was still their own,
what the dads did was only for themselves. They watched their
sons, boys who were worried by nothing but the distance they
could bat a ball.

A home run was a fly ball onto the blacktop beyond the patch
of grass that the boys called left field. The boys understood there
were strategies on the base path, fundamentals of fielding, subtle-
ties to the batting stance they were ignoring. But that was the stuff
of the major leagues. This was sandlot ball, with only four or five
guys to a side. Almost everyone got to bat at least once an inning.
It was hardly baseball at all. It was more like batting practice, except
that they kept score. Base hits were okay, and trying to stretch a
single into a double got the adrenaline going, but the aim of the
game, really, was to hit the ball long enough to land on the tar for
a home run.

The boys played every day. The neighborhood was mostly old
people now, so the boys didn't have competition for their field. In
summer, they started playing so early that the sun was in the
batter's eyes. The grass was wet enough to soak through sneakers,
but by noon their feet were dry, and in the late afternoon the sweat
percolated off their bronze skin. They stayed until the shadows
from the row of bungalows across the street covered the infield
and the sun was in the eyes of the left fielder. In spring, they had
to wait until school was over, but then they ran here as fast as
they could, in a race against the setting sun. No matter what the
calendar said, no matter how many times their teachers explained
about the orbit of the earth in relation to the sun, the boys knew
that spring didn't really start until the first pitch.

One spring, they had to wait clear into May. First there was a
freak April snowstorm. Then there was rain, and then more rain.
Even after the rain stopped, the boys had to wait while overcast
skies and damp winds kept their field from drying. Every day they
brought their bats and gloves to school in case today was the day.

Baseball was what had gotten them through winter, and now it was what pulled them through school. They daydreamed about the weight of the wood in their hands, that moment when anything might happen, then the whack of bat upon ball. And even if nothing happened, there was always next time, another inning, tomorrow. The only time there was no tomorrow was at the end of the season, when their heavy coats forced them into football. But at the start of the season, summer still lay ahead, and summer always lasted forever, almost. It would be another few years before the boys had to worry about jobs.

Finally they got their chance. One day during recess, the air was so hot and the sky so blue that they said nothing. They simply stood still and breathed the heat and scanned the horizon for clouds. At the final bell they burst from the school running, and they didn't slow until they reached the ball field, picking sides along the way. One team took the field, the other team chose a batting order, and with a squint into the sun and a kick at the dirt to make sure it all was real, they played ball.

The first batter hit the first pitch of the new season for a home run. The ball rose, a shrinking circle of white against a blinding sky, and they all knew it was gone. Even the team on the field cheered when it bounced on the blacktop. Then they pounded their fists in their mitts to let the other team know that now they meant business.

But the next batter hit a home run too. The team on the field didn't yell. The left fielder just turned his back when he saw the ball leap off the bat, and he trotted off to shag it. But the team at bat howled, slamming their hands against their new hero's back even before he crossed home plate.

Then the third batter hit a home run. This time his teammates gave a nervous giggle, but before he reached first base they were whooping again. When the fourth batter also hit a home run, they waited until he crossed second base before calling to the team on the field that it was going to be a long, long day.

It was this day that all the dads came to watch their sons play ball. They too had been outwaiting the weather. Every afternoon for the past week, one or two dads had driven past the field, only to find puddles and mud. This afternoon, though, with a cloudless sky and a warm breeze that made them think of green, the dads knew their sons would be there. They drove like teenagers showing off their first cars. They squealed around corners, windows down, radios up, speakers crackling, fingers snapping in time with the tunes.

The first dad to arrive saw six consecutive home runs. Afraid to break the spell, he stayed in his car until one of the boys made an out, a long fly ball undercut just enough that the left fielder caught it a couple of steps from the tar. Then the dad shut off the ignition, waited for the engine to quit clattering, and approached the field.

When the next dad found the first dad outside his car, he knew something was up. It took him three home runs in a row to figure out what it was. Then he too climbed from his car. As other dads arrived, they took their places along the third-base foul line, their hands in their back pockets, their bodies swaying forward and backward on the bottoms of their feet. At first they stared only at their sons and their home runs. Before now, when a dad had seen another dad at the ball field, he would pretend to check his watch, wave politely to the neighboring dad, and then head for home. Until now, it had not occurred to any of the dads that they each came here often.

Now, as the home runs rocketed overhead, they stole glances at the other dads. They allowed themselves smiles, then grins. Soon they were elbowing one another in the ribs. With each home run they exchanged high-fives. They pointed to one another's hair-lines high above their foreheads, and they poked themselves in the flab at their waists. They swung their own imaginary bats.

The dads found it hysterical that none of them had any idea of the score. They wished aloud that they'd had a day like this when they were their sons' age. They agreed, leaning on each other's shoulders, that they didn't see one another often enough. Then they planned a barbecue in the parking lot that weekend, for no reason except to have a barbecue.

They also studied their sons. Something out there was different. The field was the same, the creeping shadows were the same, so it had to be their boys. Sometime over the winter their sons had acquired the power to make it to the tar. The dads hadn't noticed the changes day by day, but now, conjuring in their minds the image of these boys from last summer, they could see the difference.

It was in their arms, and it was in their legs, and it was in their chests. All their limbs had thinned into muscle, while their torsos had swollen. The wrists had lost their baby fat. The fingers were nimbler. Angles had entered their cheekbones, jawlines, brow ridges. Their eyes flicked with each pitch, straining to pick out the weakness that would send the ball onto the tar. Their backs arched in anticipation. They shifted their hips. As the shadows of the houses across the street stretched over the batter's box, and past the pitcher's mound, and onto the outfield grass, the dads grew quiet.

One by one they called to their sons that it was time to go home.

But the boys didn't budge. The team on the field held their positions, shading their eyes. The team at bat stayed along the first-base line and stared back at the dads. The dads looked at the ground, then back at the line of cars at the curb, then at the shadows on the infield. Soon it would be too dark to play. Soon it would be the end of another day. Besides, isn't this magic what they wanted most for their sons?

Someone ran to get a couple of six-packs. The other dads took turns walking to the corner phone booth and calling their wives and trying to explain. But they couldn't explain. The words wouldn't come. It had something to do with baseball, something to do with their sons outgrowing this field, something to do with having something to do. They couldn't say for sure. They took turns squinting through the scratched glass of the phone booth at the other dads in the dusk and wishing they were back there.

The ball continued to career onto the tar. The boys were whooping again. They raised their fists in the air as they rounded the bases, pounced upon home plate with yowls, pounded one another on the shoulders, the rump, the back. The score climbed into the dozens and dozens for each side, and still the game was many innings away from a regulation finish. Between two innings, the boys met on the pitching mound. The dads strained to hear. When they broke their huddle, the boys called to the dads that they would no longer keep track of the score. The game would end when they had tired of hitting homers. The dads did not argue. Someone ran for another couple of six-packs.

The ball was white against the dark blue, then purple, then blackening sky. Still it sailed. This could go on all night, the dads told one another, this could go on forever. They chuckled. They congratulated each other. These boys, they said, then corrected themselves: these men. These men will make us proud. These men have got what it takes. And do you know why? They knew why. Because of us, they told one another, because of you and me.

When the shadows on the field finally merged with the night, nobody noticed, not the dads and not their sons. But the boys started to miss swings. Their grunts and curses reassured the dads that a game was still going on out there in the dark. After a quick inning of three straight strikeouts on each side, the boys didn't take the field.

They gathered instead by home plate. They shook hands all around. If the dads hadn't broken this up, the game would have ended then. But the dads charged in there and demanded to know what their sons thought they were doing. Darkness, they told their sons, is for cowards.

The sons gaped up at their dads. But, they protested, it's really dark.

The dads strummed their stubble. They thought hard about driving back from this black to the brightness of their apartments. They thought about a baseball game without a score. Then they told their sons that necessity is the mother of invention; give them a minute to think of something.

The sons said they didn't care. They said they were tired and hungry.

Tired and hungry, the dads said, is for now. Did they really want this day, when they could do nothing but hit home runs, to end? If they ever wanted to grow up, the dads said, they'd better start thinking about for keeps.

The boys wanted to grow up. They waited while their dads gathered in a circle around third base and whispered. Soon the dads marched to their cars, and the boys started to follow, but their dads told them to wait, just wait.

The cars started like a single long machine. Piece by piece the machine climbed the curb, bounced over the sidewalk, flattened the grass to the foul line. The cars lined up, side by side, with their headlights illuminating the outfield and the infield and the batter's box. When the dads emerged from the machine, they'd turned off the engines but left the lights aglow.

The sons cheered. They slapped their dads on the back and swore they were the best dads in the world. The dads laughed. They squeezed their sons' shoulders, feeling through the flimsy fabric of the school uniform their sons' firm muscles. Go on, the dads said, get out there now and make your old man proud.

The sons attacked the ball with new fierceness. The homers returned, flying from the bat faster than ever. They rose higher, landed farther out on the tar. But now the sons were silent. In time, they came to set their jaws for each new home run, as if it were their duty, and the dads came to nod their heads, as if it were their due. None of the dads dared to look at his wristwatch.

Instead, they stood side by side along the foul line, their hands in their back pockets, their bodies swaying forward and backward, and they tried to commit this day to memory. They tried to take what they found on this field now and, between sips of beer, put it together with what they remembered of the game during daylight.

What the dads conjured was a cloudless blue sky that carried a breeze with the promise of summer to the biceps of boys who homered back into the cloudless blue.

The headlights dimmed. None of the dads made a move to save a car. Everyone, dads and sons alike, understood that the game would end when the field again was dark. Two by two the lights winked out. The sons cracked baseballs onto the blacktop until the last of the batteries was dead.

The sons didn't return to the field the next day, or the day after, and neither did the dads. When the sons eventually went back, it was to play soccer. They never mentioned that day to each other, and they never discussed it with their dads, and the dads never mentioned it to the other dads. The day of all the homers was never spoken of again. Still, the following weekend, each of the dads did pace inside his apartment, back and forth past the one window that overlooked the parking lot, watching for the first sign of a barbecue.

Salt Water Jews

ROBERT PINSKY

Grandpa Abe was a profane, skeptical, violent sort of Jew with an immense head, like the ugly wrestler known as the Swedish Angel, and hairy hands too big for his body. This is a common type on the Jersey shore. Grandpa Abe himself called them salt water Jews—he had a theory that being near the ocean and the racetrack, just close enough to the flash and pressure of New York, just far enough from the oppressive weight of its neighborhoods, brought certain traits to the surface.

He drove a gray Packard and wore the sporty clothes of a retired bootlegger: black and white wingtip shoes in the summer, half boots with elastic gores and pigskin gloves in the fall, an alpaca muffler and cabled vest under his sheepskin coat in the winter. When he was young he was a professional boxer for a time. Then during Prohibition he went into the liquor trade. In the course of a business discussion, he once broke the kneecap of a man who was pointing a gun at his colleague and protégé Frank Sweeney, later chief of the Long Branch Police. Abe struck the man, who went on to a successful career in the asphalt paving business, with a chair leg.

Abe's first wife, Rose Lateiner, was said to be a famous beauty. She died in childbirth when she was twenty-six, leaving Abe with three small children. The eldest, my mother, was seven when Rose died. The Lateiner clan found him a replacement wife, a strapping thirty-year-old cousin called Bessie. Abe rapidly gave her two more babies and moved out. Now he lived over his bar, the Paddock Lounge, with the Irish barmaid—the relatives stressed that word, barmaid—Daisy Quinn. The five children were left with my grandma Bessie. The oldest, my mother, never forgave him.

Without warning, he would show up in the Packard as I was leaving the house and take me away, after a few terse exchanges.

"He's supposed to go to school, Abe."

"Write him a note. 'We thought it best to keep him home, he had a little touch of the grippe.' Put on your coat, Michael, we need to go to the city."

"You write it, Abe."

"Don't worry about it, Rozzy. 'Upset stomach, we thought it best.' I need to look at some fixtures in the city. Michael can keep me company."

"Goodbye, Abe." She looked at him with a grim, knowing smile, nodding to herself a little, as if she was piling up evidence to use against him later. "Goodbye, Michael. Take your good coat."

The elephant-colored Packard spun a silky calm. The throb through the gray nap of its upholstery made me sleepy, like a sip of brandy. Abe and I spoke little, but I was grateful for the day off, content to watch his furry paws on the ivory wheel, his pigskin gloves on the seat between us. He wore brown gabardine slacks and a tweed jacket with panels of suede sewn into it.

We always stopped at Steinbach's Department Store to buy me a pair of shoes for wearing into New York, sharkskin tips and immaculate welts befitting the city and the subdued plush of the Packard. My scuffed old pair, swathed solemnly in tissue paper, went into the box. Abe knew the salesman, who let us out through a tunnel of shoe boxes to an employee's exit, convenient to the parking lot.

Knowing somebody, the pattern of small privilege accorded insiders, mattered to him. Also, large and small angles: getting in free, paying wholesale, a better table—all part of an ethics of loyalty and corners cut in the name of friendship, with mistrust for legal arrangements and official policies. Even a child could sense that this was a code at least as demanding as the opposite standard of playing by the rules. In the world of who you know, acknowledgment is all. Like the shoe salesman, everybody in Long Branch seemed to know my grandfather, from the Paddock Lounge or from the misty gangster days of Prohibition.

He introduced me to Jack Dempsey, who seemed also to know him. Or maybe Jack was simply greeting lunchtime customers at his restaurant. But in any case, Abe knew how to murmur the words that commanded his attention. The great champ gave me his immense hand and asked me how I was making out. I had him confused with Toots Shor, to whom Abe had introduced me on the Long Branch boardwalk the previous summer.

Over our steaks, I asked Abe about his business. I had waited in the car for twenty minutes while he went into a building downtown to see a man about the fixtures.

"What's fixtures mean, Grandpa?"

"It could mean lights, counters, chairs. Fixtures is display cases, or it could be a cash register, coat rack, anything you keep in a business. It could be anything but the merchandise. Like if you said the furnishings."

This was innocent, I'm pretty sure—something like secondhand chandeliers for the bar, or a shuffleboard. But I knew that not everything Abe did was legal. I had heard my mother's stories of Grandpa Abe's gangster days, and his answer sounded evasive. When she told me about those capers and escapes and payoffs— the time he threw three hoods off a dock, the time he and Lou Cioffi sold the borrowed truck along with the whiskey—her sneaking admiration got mixed up with her disapproval, just as her anger at him as a father got mixed up with his criminal life.

Since I often saw Abe with Daisy Quinn but never with Grandma Bessie, who was legally his wife, it was easy to imagine him breaking the laws of society. He had a Christmas tree, he had a Smith & Wesson police revolver. Drinking my second Coke with a cherry in it while Abe had his second old-fashioned, I pictured him negotiating with hoodlums for tommy guns or nitro when we stopped on the way to Dempsey's. "Fixtures" was just a code word.

"So. How you like school?"

I shrugged and grunted. Abe seemed amused.

"But you like the piano?"

"Yes."

"Longhair music, right?"

I shrugged.

"Could you play 'Lay That Pistol Down, Babe'?"

"Yes." My piano teacher, Mrs. Reznikoff, approved of me picking up tunes I liked from the radio. She used them to teach the rudiments of musical theory. The song reminded me of Daisy Quinn, her cigarettes and rouge and the authoritative way she presided over the Paddock Lounge. Sometimes Abe called her "Babe." I wanted to ask him if he had a pistol with him. It might come in handy when looking at fixtures. Abe studied me awhile, unsmiling.

"That's good. That's a good song, 'St. Louis Blues.' I heard you play once. How about 'Night and Day'?"

"I don't think so." I had never heard of it.

"Okay," said Abe, looking relieved. We dropped the subject.

We had apple pie and ice cream for dessert. He bought two cigars, the Berings that come in a silver tube. The angle when you're buying a cigar, he explained to me, was to choose a good seller, because if they turn over a lot of them then you're going to get a fresh one.

He lit one of the Berings on the way back to Long Branch, puffing it considerately out his window of the Packard, though I got a little sick anyway, watching dull stretches of Newark, Rahway, Perth Amboy roll past, exposed by the clear October sunlight. I studied the fine print on the tube of the unopened cigar that Abe had nested on the pigskin gloves. The nap of the upholstery seemed to exhale numbing smoke under my cheek.

As we came into Long Branch, he pulled up in front of De Luca's Florists. Inside, the cool ferny smell of peat moss woke me up. Abe had the De Luca daughter at the counter wrap up two dozen pink roses in two separate green paper cones.

"So, where's Rocky?"

"Rocky's out with the truck at the moment, Mr. Duboff," she said, smiling at me. "I'll tell him you fellows was in."

Grandpa Abe turned the Packard up Long Branch Avenue, toward the Jewish cemetery, halfway to the Inlet and Pleasure Bay. He guided the car through the iron gates and up the gravel drive. I knew my grandmother's grave well, having walked here from time to time with my mother since I was small. This was the only time I visited it with Abe.

He led the way with his rolling, springy gait, the dapper clothes adding to the apelike vitality. He carried his bundle of roses at a careless downward angle that I copied with mine. A rainstorm the day before had thrown down a damp yellow carpet of maple leaves lit by the slanting sun. I imagined an ambush of Mob enemies, Abe and me dodging among headstones. A brilliant freckled leaf clung to the tip of one new shoe. On our way down the familiar path we passed the concrete caretaker's shed, open but empty. Through the doorway I could see an oilcloth-covered table with a teapot, a carton of milk, a copy of the *Jewish Daily Forward*.

The caretaker, Mr. Sokol, was usually around, chanting prayers softly into his mustache in a high, autistic murmur. Sometimes when he saw me he would begin to belt them out, beaming and adding little decorative trills and cantorial minor triads.

"Abramowitz!" he would announce and then perform, in recognition of my great-great-grandfather Yechiel Abramowitz, who on a legendary occasion muffed his chance for the cantor's job at the Great Central Synagogue of Bucharest.

At his audition, my ancestor sang like an angel, they say, dazzling the board of directors with his vocal riffs and ornaments. But the chairman of the synagogue board was a Romanian banker whose hobby was Kabbalah. To a Kabbalist, counting the number of words or syllables in a prayer is important, and Yechiel was wailing out sixteenths and thirty-secondths where the book had whole notes. In short, my great-great-grandfather lost a major gig because he was prone to scat singing. That is part of what amused Mr. Sokol with his shiny brown head and his Akim Tamiroff mustache.

This anecdote used to be told in Yiddish all over the world by people like Mr. Sokol. Sometimes there's a tag at the end where the banker says, "If a man says to me, 'Mr. Sylber, I need a loan,' I may give him a loan. Even if a man says to me, 'A loan I need, Mr. Sylber,' I may give him a loan. But when somebody says, 'Mr. Sylber, I need a loan a loan a loan a loan a loan a loan'—I turn him down."

They tell me it's a riot in Yiddish.

My grandmother Rose Duboff's gravestone is taller than the stones around it and shaped like the base of a tree sawed off at the top, with truncated branches, to symbolize the fact that she died young in childbirth. High up, on three scrolls carved onto the tree trunk, are the English phrases *Adored Wife*, *Beloved Mother*, and *Precious Daughter*, in that order. Near the ground, the dates and above them her name in Hebrew and English—*Rose Lateiner Duboff, Born 20 October 1897—Died 16 April 1924*—and above that, at eye level, her portrait: an oval photograph sealed under thick protective glass. It shows a mischievous, dark face, with thick black eyelashes like Buster Keaton's girlfriend in *The General*.

I watched Abe to follow his lead. Bringing flowers to a grave seemed to me daring and unconventional. When I went to the graveyard with my mother we gathered pebbles from the driveway to put on the stone curbing at the foot of Rose's grave, according to the Jewish custom. The pink roses swathed in fern that Abe unwrapped and laid at the base of the stone tree trunk looked elegantly pagan and out of place. Clumsily I unwrapped my bunch of flowers and put them next to his. I studied the stone again.

"Hey, look: twenty October, that's today. It's her birthday."

"Right."

Abe took the waxy green tissue from me and bunched it in his hand with a brisk unsentimental motion. He meditated the grave at his feet. The ivy had been cut back severely, laying bare a network of twisted runners. A few spurts of pale new growth competed for sunlight with clumps of brownish plantain and crabgrass. Abe murmured, more to the network of brown stems than to me, "That ain't good. I'll be back in a minute." He walked back down the path.

I made my way farther up the row of graves while he was gone, trying to sound out the carved Hebrew characters. I had had a few weeks of Hebrew school, and Grandma Bessie's brother Solly had begun testing me with headlines in his Yiddish *Forward*. Some of the names of the dead—Greenberg, Schwartz, Weinstein—seemed so American to me that shaping their sounds in the backward-facing flame-shaped letters had the quality of a secret joke. And in men's names I thought of as Jewish—Sidney, Herbert, Milton —I didn't recognize great English families or poets, any more than my own mother's name—Rosalind—had any taste of Shakespeare and the greenwood for me, though it may have had for the pretty face on my grandmother's headstone.

Abe came back a few paces ahead of Mr. Sokol, who was wearing a long canvas apron over his Orthodox suit and necktie. On his shiny brown head was a cheap satin yarmulke—his work yarmulke, I suppose—and in the pouches of his apron were gardening tools. He was crooning to himself and carrying the green tissue paper from De Luca's, working it in a ball between both hands. Abe waited for him at Rose's grave. Mr. Sokol stopped courteously next to him. Abe pointed to the ivy and took his billfold from the inside pocket of his Norfolk jacket, handing a bill to Mr. Sokol, who bobbed his head and accepted it without quite looking at Abe or at the grave.

"Tomorrow morning," Mr. Sokol was saying as I came up to them. "Tomorrow morning we do this row and I make everything extra special. All trimmed nice." He began humming to himself again, still not looking at my grandfather.

"Do me a favor," said Abe. "Do it now."

Mr. Sokol nodded, to Abe or to the music, but began walking back up the row toward his cement shed. For a few seconds my grandfather seemed lost in thought, standing at the grave like an illustration in a book. Then he walked after the caretaker, who was chanting louder. They looked like figures in a ritual procession. Abe gained on him and, as he came up behind him, very gently put his arms around the other man's waist and lifted him off the ground, rotating him back in the air so that Mr. Sokol was turned

toward me with Abe almost invisible behind him, the caretaker's
face perfectly calm, his feet dangling and the yarmulke still centered on his head, as in a dream or a customary stage of the ritual
they were performing. Then in seven or eight deliberate steps Abe
carried him back to Rose's grave and lowered him to the ground.
Neither man moved. They were about the same height, possibly
the same age, though to me ageless in their two different ways.

Mr. Sokol crooned a few grieving bars of his endless, beginning-
less psalm, nodding to himself like a jazz man taking in the sweet-
ness of a tune or as if he were agreeing with a profound argument
Abe had just presented. Still singing he took from the deepest
pocket of his apron a soiled sponge-rubber kneeling pad. He un-
rolled it and spread it in front of the stonework where my two
pebbles sat at Rose's feet. Then he took a trowel and shears from
the apron and, dropping them next to him, sank easily to his knees.

As if that ended the religious observance, Grandpa Abe signaled
to me that it was time to go.

"Take it easy," he said to Mr. Sokol, who waved his head in his
same agreeing way without interrupting his crooning or turning
his head to watch us walk back to the Packard. Inside the car, Abe
picked up the tube of the second Bering, as if about to open it
and light up. He tapped the package on his lip, looking at me, and
returned it to its nest on the yellowish perforated gloves.

A couple of days later, on Grandma Bessie's porch, I tried to tell
this story to her brother, who sometimes showed an interest in
my outings with Abe. Solly had been testing me on words in the
Forward, sounding out from the bold vowel-less consonants of
headlines unlikely syllables like "Truman," "Wisconsin," or "Frank
Sinatra." Solly responded with a question.

"You think it was smart, what your grandpa done to Sokol?
Maybe that's how you want to do?"

I was thinking about my grandfather's key chain. He had left it
in the Packard's ignition while he looked at the fixtures. Hanging
along with his keys were a tiny pearl-handled knife and an inch-
long plastic telescope. Leaning along the seat, without taking the
key from the ignition, I had opened and closed the blade of the
knife and peered into the telescope. When you tilted it to the light
you saw a picture of a naked red-haired woman smiling and holding a kitten on her lap.

Solly looked at me quizzically. I shrugged. It was hard to say.

A New Stretch of Woods

REYNOLDS PRICE

My mother was down for her afternoon nap, so I was taking my second aimless walk of the winter day. We lived way out in the country, then. Three sides of our house were flanked by woods— deep stands of pine, oak, poplar, and hickory that you could walk beelines in for hours and meet nobody, no human being. But the ground teemed with foxes, raccoons, possums, squirrels, snakes, occasional skittish but kingly deer, and frogs, salamanders, and minnows in the narrow creek, not to speak of the birds, who'd learned to trust me as if I could also fly and worry, which were their main gifts.

I was sure I'd formed an intricate union with each and all, even the snakes. I'd managed to touch one live wild bird. I'd handled three nonpoisonous snakes. But even when they hid, I could sit by their haunts and talk my sorrows out by the minute; and child-hood sorrow is bitterer than most, being bare of hope. As often as not, my mournful words would charm them. They'd edge into sight, then cock their heads and fevered eyes and wait till I finished. Often they'd stay on for a long last moment, in silence that I could read as their answer, before disappearing. They generally managed to vanish like fog. Since I never scared them, they at least never ran.

But the strangest time began with the dog. My Boston bull terrier had died that fall; and with Mother pregnant, Father had told me to wait till the baby was settled in. As a man, I can see his practical wisdom—Mother didn't need one more job now, a messy pup; and once a rival child arrived, I'd need a tangible private possession to share the trials of learning that I was no longer the fulcrum of household love. We had two housefuls of neighbors on the road and they had dogs, but the dog that found me that afternoon was not one of theirs.

It was an odd pale shade of gray with solid gray eyes that seemed to lack pupils, as if it saw without using light. Those traits today would make me think of a weimaraner, but that dog then was half the size. It was also sleek as a grayhound or whippet; and though it never actually spoke, of the animals I was to meet that day, the dog came nearest and triggered the others. Those eyes alone plainly yearned to say what it knew so well but could not deliver.

And I know it was real, an actual thing with hair and bone, weight and heat. When it broke in on me at the Indian Round, I thought at once that it meant me well. I stooped to stroke it, then hefted it onto my lap for a moment. It bore those attentions with quiet ease; but it gave me none of the wild affection small dogs mostly give, the desperate kisses that put all human lovers to shame. So I set it back on the ground and watched. (I call the dog *it* since, that day, I never thought to look for its sex. For years I told myself it was male—it came at a time when female friends mean little to a boy—but now I feel the need for precision.)

The Indian Round was a secret name I'd given to a natural cleared ring in the woods where, for whatever reason, no trees or weeds grew. At once I felt that the Indians made it or found it countless ages before me. In any case I knew on sight that it had sacred power. I'd given very little close attention to God, but I knew when the ground gave off a force no human could name or overcome. And through the years we'd lived nearby, I brought any fine or mystic object I found back here and set it in the midst: a big white rock, three real arrowheads, and the skull of what I guessed was a wolf, with a crest of bone to which the mighty jaw and throat muscles had once been attached.

What I made, and was making, was more a museum than an altar or temple. I never prayed here or enacted rites. I recognized a fact. This spot on Earth was clearly magic; it gave off invisible force like a god and therefore deserved my childish tributes of care and beauty. The only private thing I did was sometimes to strip and lie on my back, staring at the hole of distant blue sky and telling myself all others were dead now, the whole world empty of all but me and the beasts I knew were watching me from secret lairs in reach of my voice and the smells of my body. I'd only begun to love my body late that summer, when I turned ten. So I already knew how dangerous my own loving hands could be, even then when I'd touched no body but mine and, rarely, the public parts of my parents.

But that first day, when I set the dog down, I suddenly knew that it came as a guide. And next it walked to the far north edge of the Indian Round, where the woods began again, thicker still. At every few steps, it would look back toward me and give a hook of its avid head, calling me on. Then it entered the thicket.

In my mind, from then on, I called it Scout and thought of it as male. And I followed him close as the woods would let me, the briars and vines, the stinging limbs against my eyes. Scout stayed in sight, just glimpses and sounds, till we came to the stream. At first I thought it was my old creek, the one I explored in all kinds of weather, wading and probing under rocks with sticks or lying on the bank and going silent to watch its surface and deeps for long minutes, as one by one the ghostly transparent crawfish or toads the size of your little fingernail offered their private acts to my eyes, their brute and merciful transactions, grander and surer to last than ours.

But I quickly understood I was elsewhere. This was not the same creek I'd known before, no part I had seen. It was twice as wide and way too deep to see into. With a running start I just might jump it, but how would I get a running start in such dense undergrowth? And was that Scout's intention for me?

He was gone anyhow. I stood entirely still to listen. Even in winter no live stretch of woods is thoroughly silent. If nothing else, the drying hearts of the trees themselves will groan and crack. But now I was sunk in a well of stillness that was not only new to me but scary, though my favorite virtue was bravery. The trees and bushes were normal species, the water was wet and cold to the touch; only the air between us had changed. I doubt I'd heard of a vacuum, but I knew I was in peculiar space and that, all around me, the air was thinning in a quiet rush to leave me entirely unimpeded, more naked than ever, though I wore my leather jacket and aviator's cap.

Scout never returned. But in the new thin air around me, in my bald fear, his message sounded plainer than words: *Cross this water*. I retreated the few available steps, turned my fear into reckless strength, and tried the leap—which I made, and to spare. I landed an easy yard past the water on ground I could feel was new to my feet. And before I was firmly upright on my pins, I called myself brave.

Then came the bird, a perfectly normal golden eagle. The strangeness dawned only two days later when I learned that golden eagles were unheard of in the coastal plain where we lived. It stood on a pine limb, four yards above me, and kept its head in rigid profile like something Egyptian but fixed on me, the way nothing can but meat-eating birds with the talons and beaks to do their will. For the better part of two or three minutes, it never so much as shut an eye.

I tried to freeze my body in respect, but after a while I needed to prove it was still alive, the ferocious bird. So I bent right over and touched the ground, just to make a move—I didn't plan to pick up a rock to throw.

Before I was back upright, it raised off its limb on wings the size of a black four-door new roadster.

If I'd been thinking clear and fast, I might have feared it was aimed at me and covered my eyes. But it went skyward so straight and fast, with so much perfect power to burn, that I know I actually laughed a high note and followed with some such word as "Lord!"—I hadn't yet got to the harsher cries. Only when it had also vanished did I understand the words it left me, silent as the dog: *Stay still right here.*

I stayed till the sun was nearly gone and an evening chill was taking my feet. I hadn't interpreted the eagle strictly. A few minutes after it disappeared, I went to sit on a bent tree trunk near the stream and waited there but facing the woods, the strange territory, not the way back home. Something had let me know, all along, that I wasn't lost, that home lay behind me the way I'd come. All I had to do was leap that stream a second time, while I still had daylight, and wind my old trail back up beneath me like a thread I'd laid behind me or crumbs.

The only question was, What would come next? And would it come before night fell and Father got home and started calling my name to the dark and scaring Mother, tender as she was these last weeks? For all I knew, Scout might come back and guide me in or onward to some whole other new life, elsewhere than here. I turned that last thought over awhile and knew I would go, wherever he led, whoever wound up with a broken heart if I too vanished and no trace of me was found on Earth, no thread of my clothes. Most honest men will own to similar vengeful thoughts in late childhood.

Then the black snake streamed on out of the woods, crossed the narrow bank six feet beyond me, poured itself down the slope, swam most of the stream in a straight line across, then sank a few inches short of land and never surfaced, nowhere I could see. Like the eagle, it had all the normal traits of its kind. Only it was thick as a plump young python; and where I lived then, all snakes are deep asleep in winter and would no more enter an ice-cold stream than a raging fire.

But when I'd thought my way through that, I got the final news of the day. It stuck up mean in the quick of my mind like the snake itself, that strong and rank: *The baby your mother wants to make is a boy. It would be your brother, but it will not live.*

The news itself didn't hurt at first, but I wanted to stay for amplification. Had I caused the promise? Was it good or bad? Would I be blessed or punished next? Did it mean I must act thus or so, from here on? And I did linger there on the tree till I knew I had only five more minutes of light, then freezing dark with its own business that I couldn't yet face. I thought if anything, good or evil, was using me, it could follow me home and tell me there. I thought I'd say at least a short prayer for strength to make the leap again and bravery to see me back through the woods. But I found my mind would simply not pray; all I heard was the last news again: *It will not live.*

So I leaped and made it, though with no ground to spare. And each hedged step of the backward way was hard and cowardly. I somehow still couldn't pray for help, for me or for my brother, who had been so lively this afternoon when Mother told me to press her belly and feel his foot. Worse, I couldn't even pray for her—that whether he came out well or dead, she be spared pain, not to mention bloody death. She was three fourths of all I'd known or loved, and she'd earned every calorie of all my heat.

But my arms and legs worked on as before; and by the time it was actual night, my hands alone could guess I was almost home by the touch of familiar trees, especially pines, with the scaly bark I knew as well as my favorite skin. The last few yards took what seemed years, but the hands were right. At last home was there, bright before me in its own safe clearing.

Inside, in Mother and Father's room, my mother's face was hid in their pillows. She was fully dressed but the tan wool skirt she'd worn all day was dark with blood, and I could count the wrenching cries that tore her heart. Around us three, the air had the hot iron smell of blood. It was so much my strongest sight till then that I can call it up whole this minute and be there again. I wanted of course to flee to the woods and learn a way to reverse the spell my trip had cast. But bravery showed me my kind-eyed father standing beside her, hands at his sides, unable to help. When he saw my face, he said, "She lost your brother, son."

I saw his words had calmed her cries, for the moment at least, which was all it took to brace myself for the sight of the eyes she turned on me next, her mouth like a razor wound in her face. I told her the only thing I knew. "I will be him too. You can love us more than ever."

Father shook his head and touched his lips for silence.

But slowly my mother rigged a smile and pressed it toward me before her head sank back to sleep.

Le Traiteur

JUDE ROY

My father was a traiteur, a healer.

"That's a fact," he said when I asked him about it. "It's an old, old tradition passed on to me by Jacob Patout while he was on his deathbed. Someday, before I die, I'll pass it on to you. It's an honor to be chosen, son. It's got little to do with me or you, though. It's in His hands. And theirs, them that come to be healed. You got to be a believer to be healed. And a believer ain't scared what'll happen. He knows in his heart. It's in his eyes. The eyes'll always tell you."

Mr. Theophilus Jogneaux was a believer. When he visited our house with his son, I sat at the kitchen table eating cookies and milk. My father asked them in and poured Mr. Theo a cup of coffee. The boy stood next to his father and eyed my cookies with large dark eyes. I offered him one, but Mr. Theo shook his head when the boy looked up at him. My father waited until Mr. Theo was seated at the table and had sipped his coffee before asking him what was wrong with his son.

"My boy got a nasty sore throat, Monsieur Leclerc. You think you could treat him?" Mr. Theo spoke in Cajun. His voice was soft and respectful.

My father asked the boy to come closer. He did as he was told and stood before him, arms at his side, his body rigid and straight. My father had gentle hands. He ran them along the boy's throat and neck, poking gently here and there. Whenever he hit a sore spot, the boy flinched. But he did not make a sound.

"Get my lantern," my father told me, and I ran and grabbed the lantern hanging next to the front door. I lit it and handed it to him. He adjusted it and told the boy to open his mouth. The boy did as he was told, and my father shined the light in his face. I could see the lantern light reflected from his eyes. They were wide and fearful.

"Get me a spoon, son," he told me, and I brought him one from the kitchen drawer. He used it as a tongue depressor. He said nothing. After a few moments of staring into the boy's mouth, he pulled back and traced a cross over the boy's lips with his thumb and forefinger. Like magic the fear disappeared from his eyes.

"Stand right where you are, son. Don't move," my father said and walked into the bedroom. I watched from the kitchen table. He cut a section of string about a foot long. He tied thirteen knots in the string and said a silent prayer over each knot. His lips moved, but no sound came through them. The prayers were secret.

I checked to see if Mr. Theo and his son watched too, but Mr. Theo gazed into his coffee cup. The boy looked up at the ceiling. My father returned.

"Son," he said to the boy, "this string has the power to heal your sore throat. I believe that with all my might. But it won't work unless you believe it too." My father let a few moments of silence pass. "Do you?" The boy said, "Yessir," and my father tied the string around his neck. He opened the boy's mouth and blew three times into it. Then he traced another cross over his lips when he was done.

"You got to keep that string around your neck until it comes off by itself. If you do that, then you'll never have a sore throat again." After another cup of coffee, Mr. Theo and his son left.

My father never charged for his service.

But it was Mr. Theo who drove my father to the charity hospital in New Orleans when he became sick. The doctors told him he had cancer and it was too late for him to expect miracles. They didn't exactly say that, but he saw it in their eyes. He told me so when he came back. There was one chance, he said, and that was to visit Mr. Elcid Thibodeaux, a broom maker and healer who lived five miles away in the woods off the Isaacton Road.

We had made the trip many times before. My father liked to hunt squirrel in the woods behind Mr. Elcid's shack. But this time it took longer than usual. He had to stop and rest often. He did not talk much, and when he did, his words came out in gasps as if he were struggling to talk and breathe at the same time.

Mr. Elcid sat in his rocker on his front porch whittling on an oak sapling, a handle for one of his brooms, when we walked up his dirt lane. Several finished brooms stood together, leaning against one corner of the porch next to a few old cypress boards. Job, Mr. Elcid's Catahoula, barked and growled when he saw us but stopped when Mr. Elcid slammed his foot on the porch. He put his knife and the sapling aside and stood up slowly.

"Seth Leclerc, you old dog, you. Ain't seen you since squirrel season two years ago. What brings you to my front porch?" My father shook hands with him and sat next to the steps. He struggled to breathe and his face looked haggard and drawn.

"Give me a chance to catch my breath, Cid." Mr. Elcid nodded and sat back down in his rocker. It was impossible to tell how old Mr. Elcid was. He had gray hair the color of moss and a sharp little chin that jutted out from his toothless mouth. Two milky brown eyes, almost the same color as Job's, watched my father from behind the mass of wrinkles that was his face. He turned them on me, and I saw the worry in them.

"How you doing, boy? How's school?" he asked after a while.

"Fine, Mr. Elcid. I start the seventh grade next month."

"The seventh grade, eh? Boy, ain't you the smart one. You going to be a doctor or something?"

"Nosir," I answered. Job rubbed against my leg, and I bent over and petted him. Mr. Elcid turned his eyes on my father again.

"Ready to talk yet, Seth?" My father took a deep breath and looked up at Mr. Elcid. His blue eyes looked pale and troubled.

"Hello, Cid. I'm afraid I come on some business," he said.

"What business can you have with me? You need a broom?" Mr. Elcid grinned, exposing his gums. My father did not grin back.

"No, Cid. I need you to treat me."

Mr. Elcid lowered his eyes and let them travel up the length of my father's body, stopping at his eyes.

"Well, you sure don't look too well. What's the matter with you?" He sat up in his rocker.

"The doctors in New Orleans tell me I got cancer. I don't know too much about it, but they tell me it eats up your insides until there ain't nothing left. They said I had a chance, but they didn't believe none of that. They said one thing, but their eyes said I was as good as dead."

Mr. Elcid stood. "Stand up there in front of me, Seth. Let me have a look at you." My father stood. Mr. Elcid ran his hands over my father's chest. He looked into his eyes. He sat and waited until my father was seated before speaking.

"It pains me to say it, Seth. Me and you go back a ways. But there ain't nothing I can do for you."

I looked at my father. I saw the fear in his eyes. He looked down at his feet. When he spoke, his voice was soft, almost a whisper, almost pleading. I reached out and touched his pants leg. He never noticed.

"I was kind of hoping, Cid. Kind of hoping."

"Seth, things change. People know more nowadays. Them doc-teurs from New Orleans, they know about this cancer. They got pills and medicine and Lord knows what-not to fight it. You know what I mean?"

"I know," my father whispered. "But none of that stuff is going to work. They so much as told me."

"Me and you, what we got, Seth?"

"Faith."

Mr. Elcid said nothing. He picked up his knife and sapling and began whittling again. My father stared off into the dark woods. He picked nervously at a splinter in the porch. Job scratched at a flea.

"Seth," Mr. Elcid said after a long silence, "a few prayers and a string ain't going to work on this."

"It was never them that worked anyway, Cid."

Mr. Elcid stood up and walked to the edge of the porch.

"How can I treat something I don't understand, Seth?" He looked up into the sky. His pointy chin bobbed up and down as he spoke. "My papa taught me how to make brooms. 'People'll always need brooms,' he told me. He was wrong. People use vacuum cleaners now and all kinds of things I ain't got no idea about. Oh, a few old-timers still come by to buy one of my brooms, but that's mostly because they want to chat with me." Mr. Elcid turned his eyes on my father. They were shiny and moist. "Seth, me and you, the things we do and believe, people don't need them anymore. The vacuum cleaners do a better job. And if they can't do the job, then my old brooms sure won't. Tu comprend, Seth? You understand what I'm saying?"

"Je comprend, Cid."

"We're like old Job." At the mention of his name, Job stood, stretched, and slowly made his way to Mr. Elcid's side. "I trained him to hunt wild boar, but there ain't none left around these parts." He ran a hand along the dog's back. "Soon there won't be no Catahoulas, not Job's kind, leastways. What'll people want with a dog bred to hunt wild boar when there ain't none left?" Job walked over to my father, who scratched behind the dog's ear. Job curled up next to him. "Do you understand what I'm saying, Seth? Tu comprend?"

"Je comprend, Cid." My father looked at the dog for a long time in the silence that followed, as if he were trying to decide something.

Mr. Elcid did something very strange. He cried. No sound came out, just tears, two of them that slowly trickled down from each eye and disappeared in the furrows of his face. My father stood and placed a hand on Mr. Elcid's shoulder.

"Je comprend, Cid," he said softly.

"I got the power to heal, Seth. But how can I heal something I don't understand? Something like this cancer—something that eats up your insides. How can I fight that, Seth? How?"

"Je comprend, Cid."

Mr. Elcid raised his hand to the sky, palm upward, and brought it down and laid it gently on my father. He took his thumb and forefinger and traced a cross over his chest that ran from his forehead to his belt buckle and from the left shoulder to the right shoulder. Then he disappeared into his shack and returned with a string which he tied around my father's neck. There were seven knots in the string.

"It's all I can do, Seth."

My father caught my hand in his. "It's time to go, son." His eyes were shiny and moist, but there was no fear in them anymore.

"Yessir," I said. "Are you going to die, Daddy?"

"Not really, son." He squeezed my hand.

I looked back once. Mr. Elcid snatched a cypress board from against the wall and laid it across his lap. Job curled up at his feet.

My father died in his sleep a few weeks later, Mr. Elcid's string still tied around his neck. He never did make me a traiteur. I never asked. I saw the pain in his eyes and never asked.

The funeral was a small one. A few people followed the hearse to the cemetery outside the town. I looked around for Mr. Elcid at the burial, but I didn't see him. At the head of my father's grave, though, stood a cross made of cypress. And inscribed on it:

SETH LECLERC

1909–1961

LE TRAITEUR QUI VIVE TOUJOURS

Mr. Theo and his son were at the burial, too. They stood outside the small circle of mourners. As we were leaving, they walked up to the gravesite. I stopped and watched as Mr. Theo removed his hat. His son stood next to him, head bowed. Mr. Theo said something and the boy looked up. I noticed the string, still tied around his neck. I tried to see his eyes, but he never faced me. I wondered what was in them as he gazed at my father's coffin.

Someone tugged on my arm and I left. I never did see the boy's eyes but I imagined they mirrored my own—shiny, moist, and filled with sadness because we were believers.

The Movie Murders,
or the Killer in the Cast

LORE SEGAL

Call me Dick. I'm hard-boiled. Turned fifty my last birthday. Time's wingèd chariot, they say. Anyways. That producer, Peter Popper, calls. I go round to the set near Wilshire. Dead young lady lays on the altar, in like this chapel. Out comes my notebook. Peter Popper says, "Name was Sadie, our social worker for Joel, our juvenile. Had to send Joel home till we get her replaced. That's your child labor laws—and I'm three days into the shoot," cries Popper, "and two days behind schedule!"

I'm looking at this Sadie's angle of her head. Out comes my tape measure. I'm measuring; somebody hollers. Fellow with a clipboard charges in, says, "You won't believe this! Curtis, the caterer? Dead on the kitchen floor!"

"You are kidding me!" says Popper. Over we trot, Popper, me, this fellow Stan with the clipboard, and there's a sure-enough dead young fellow with his pot holder in his hand. Cookies all over. Chocolate chip. I observe the angle of his head and I measure.

Popper is distraught, says, "You don't need Stan, do you? Stan's our stage manager, supposed to be setting up the scene with the sword."

"Carry on," I tell them, "and when I'm finished here, I'll want to talk to everybody in the cast."

Popper says, "We got sixty-plus people working on this set!"

"One at a time," I tell him.

Movies is mostly everybody stands and waits around. The lady director, Desiree Deyer, says, "Mike, try it kneeling down." Mike is the midget that stands in for Joel, the juvenile lead, and is holding the sword in his right hand. Out comes my notebook. "Gregor," Desiree tells the grip, "gimme an archway on the right. Roy," she yells to the gaffer's best boy, way up in the catwalk, "I could do with a spot on the sword."

Everybody waits. Everybody watches Roy forty foot up under the roof rolling this real heavy spot. Light bounces right off of the sword the midget hands Belinda Barr. Belinda is the star.

"I'm ready to shoot Belinda," says Desiree Deyer.

Stan, the stage manager, says, "Everybody not in this scene, would you get the hell out of the way, please. Bernie," he tells the bozo with the boom, "we need the mike over Belinda's head."

Bernie brings the boom about. He cries, "Kenneth, watch out!" but the mike conks the tall blond kid in the head. Kid goes down and everybody laughs. The kid colors.

"Two murders and one accident-prone college kid!" groans Peter Popper. "Kenneth, you are okay?"

"I'm okay, I'm fine," the kid says. Got his arm in plaster way to the shoulder, but will he take the hand the stage manager holds out to help him up? Not this kid Kenneth!

"His dad is our main money man," moans Peter Popper in my ear. "*Says* the kid wants to work in movies. If you ask me, Daddy got himself hitched to a cutie the kid's age. Comes vacation he wants him out the way."

The bell buzzes. Stan says, "Ready? Roll it!" The sound man says, "Speed." Camera says, "Mark it." Man with the marker says, "Scene ten, take one," and claps the clapper. Desiree Deyer says, "Action." Everyone freezes. Mike the midget kneels and hands Belinda Barr the sword. Desiree says "Cut." The bell buzzes. Desiree says, "Freddy, frizz me Belinda's hair."

Hairdresser walks over. Everybody stands around. Everybody waits. Desiree says to me, "You the detective?"

I say, "Yes, ma'am."

Says, "Somebody's murdering my movie, and what are you going to do about it?"

"Ma'am," I said, "what I'm going to do is I'm going to get my notebook out and going to put a line down the middle of this page. Left side I'm putting what I don't know, which is who has done it, how, and why. On the right I'm going to put down what I do know."

"Which is?" asks Desiree.

"One," I said, "is we're looking for that old blunt instrument. Two, the first victim, which is Sadie the social worker, had her head bashed sacking out on the altar, maybe having herself a little snooze. Three, her head was the same distance off of the floor as the head of victim number two, which is Curtis, the caterer, squatting down to check the batch of cookies he was baking in his oven—"

"Promised me chocolate chips," pipes up Belinda Barr.

Freddy the hairdresser says, "Curtis—he was a cute fellow. Very friendly."

"Medical evidence," I tell them, "shows both death blows to have been delivered thusly"—I demonstrate a short left-to-right downward stroke, starting by my left ear—"from which point," I say, "the killer would have had to hold a blunt instrument with a bent arm, which you can't do and get your leverage."

"Could have been kneeling down," says Desiree.

"Could have," I agree, "but would you, if you were going to batter somebody to kingdom come, kneel yourself down to do it? So what we're looking for's a murderer size of a midget, and don't you get yourself het up," I say to Mike, whose mouth has opened up to holler. "The murderer must be a *left*-handed midget, and I mean a left-handed midget who knows the neatest way to kill a body is a well-delivered blow back of the neck."

"Everybody on this set knows that!" says Stan. "It's in the script. Scene one, bad guy teaches little Joel how to whack Belinda on the back of her neck!"

"Ready to shoot," says Desiree.

Camera cries, "Kenneth, duck!"

The crane comes about. Down goes the kid. Everybody laughs. Poor kid is one of your chronic blushers. Remember—you were nineteen! You don't start out hard-boiled. So I say, "Can I take Kenneth? He can start and answer me some questions."

Popper says, "Take Kenneth! Take Kenneth far, far away!"

Kid colors crimson.

This old sound stage is like walking inside a giant cube with quilted walls with ladders, lots of bits of scenery. The kid and I cross—I guess this is a moat with real water. We walk through a cobbled courtyard under a tower, battlements, the works. I like all the sixty-plus people doing their job or reading or sacked out and waiting till their job needs doing. "Not a left-handed midget in the lot," I say to the kid. "You have to wonder who will be our next body."

"There doesn't need to *be* a next!" the kid cries, and now I see he is upset: one of those blond types, eyes so close they look like they're going to cross over. This is one kid meant to be clean-cut, but he's ripped his new blue jeans seam to seam—stupid kid don't know enough to know the knees would go first. You got to be sorry for kids nowadays with all the crap coming down the pike. I want to always tell them, Go away! Come back in twenty years, I'll buy you a drink. And this kid, Kenneth: sounds like his daddy is a louse.

I ask him, "So what is this movie all about?" but the bell buzzes. We stop. We listen: "Ready." "Roll it." "Speed." "Scene ten, take two." The clapper. "Action."

Kenneth obediently freezes till the bell buzzes. Then he says, "This is a medieval mystery set in the anti-future."

"Say no more," I tell him.

"The sword's electronic which the bad guy operates long distance. Let's go and sit inside the dungeon that is all high-tech torture."

I said, "Bet there's not a single old-fashioned blunt instrument!"

Kid says, "It's really just black Styrofoam." He ducks under the archway; all hell breaks! Gregor—I told you Gregor is the grip but sixty people plus, I know, is hard to keep apart. Anyways, Gregor is the grip. "Get out of my dungeon, pronto please," he hollers. "That is a hot set!"

Kenneth calls back, "It's okay. It's just fine!"

A lot of laughter, with Gregor saying, "*Hot* means I got it ready for the shoot and nobody, but nobody, goes in there."

Kid has turned a color like tomato.

I ask Gregor, "Can we go sit up in the tower?"

Gregor says, "Sure, so long as he don't put his elbow through my battlements," meaning Kenneth's plaster cast.

The kid and I climb this ladder. "How did it happen?" I ask him.

"I fell over those!" Kenneth points down at the black cables on the studio floor like some congress of young snakes. "On my first day."

"I got good news for you," I tell the kid.

"What?" he asks, suspicious. We walk out on these wood and papier-mâché ramparts.

"You'll get to be middle-aged, like everybody else, and won't give a red-hot hoot how much of an ass you make of yourself."

"I don't know what you mean," the kid says, and his eyes cross. Anyways.

I ask him if he ever met this Sadie.

"Yes," says the kid. "She was a really nice person. She really talked with me." Looks like the kid is starting to cry. He says, "She was really beautiful!"

"She was so really beautiful," says Bernie—Bernie, remember, is the bozo with the boom. Bernie is standing grinning on the top step, says, "You thought she was the star!"

"Did not!" says the kid.

"Did too," says the bozo, and with like the kid's little uptight voice he says, " 'I've seen you in the movies, lots of times!' "

Kid says, "I didn't say that!"

"I heard you!" says Bernie. "And Sadie says, 'I never in my life was in a movie.' "

The kid says, "How do you know I said what you said I said when you weren't even there?"

This bastard Bernie says, "Maybe not, but my ears were!" and he makes the mike jump on the boom up and down under the kid's nose. "And Curtis was there, bringing round a batch of fudge, and he said, 'This is Sadie the social worker,' and *you* got excited and said, 'Yeah yeah yeah yeah yeah! That was the movie I saw you in, where you were the social worker!' and Sadie says, 'You must mean Belinda Barr!' "

Kid keeps saying, "She did not say it! I did not!"

Bernie says, "Look at him bluuu-shing!"

So then I said, "Cut it out. Kenneth, go down and find me Peter Popper. Tell him after lunch I want to talk to him." To Bernie, I said, "Kindly take your boom out of my face and mind somebody don't murder *you*."

Which somebody did! Everybody's sitting, having our lunch, when Roy, the fellow in the roof I told you was the gaffer's best boy, barges in, says, "Bernie got it in the neck."

"Dead, you mean?" hollers Peter Popper.

"Yep," Roy says. "In the men's john. Must have been bending down to take a drink at the sink. The water was still running."

"What's the power play," cries Peter Popper, "wasting Sadie, the social worker?" He and I are leaning on the battlements, watching director Desiree, in the cobbled courtyard, setting up the scene in which two guys are going to have a duel. "Who," howls Peter Popper, "is going to get rich knocking off the man making the chocolate chips? Was somebody insanely jealous of Bernie's boom?"

"The heart has other reasons," I tell him.

"Like what?" Popper wants to know.

"Well, like for instance, why did folks used to fight duels?"

"Because they were nuts," says producer Popper.

"True," I tell him, "except imagine some fellow offends another fellow so this other fellow feels the world's not wide enough to hold the both of them. One or the other of the two has got to go."

"Nuts!" Peter Popper shouts.

"Or imagine some young fellow makes a public booboo and is so embarrassed he cannot live till he wipes every witness, and everyone who heard anything about it, off the face of the earth?"

"You," says Peter Popper, "are one detective out of your ever-loving mind while some nonexistent left-handed midget keeps on murdering one person at a time!"

I says, "Nope. Now there is only one other person he has got to murder."

He says, "How do you know that?"

I said, "Because I know why."

Popper says, "So why don't you tell me?"

I says, "I just did."

He says, "So you know who done it?"

I says, "Facts say a left-handed midget."

Poor Peter Popper says a dirty word.

"I will tell you what I'm going to do," I tell him. "What I'm going to do is go and lie myself down in that hot dungeon where nobody is going to bother me till I have figured how the how fits the facts if it kills me."

I go in the dungeon. I lie down on the rack, my back to the archway. Outside the people are doing their sixty-plus jobs. I hear hammering, Desiree saying, "Bring the baffle right another inch and a bit. That'll do it!" Stan says, "Belinda, please, on the set." The bell buzzes. "Ready?" "Roll it!" "Speed." It's not a sound behind my back, but the feel of a body where there had been air. "Mark it." The last scene, take one. A clap. The body bends above me. "Action." I shoot my right hand out and catch the blunt plaster elbow about to send me to you know where. The bell buzzes. The kid and I freeze, looking each other in the eye. "Cut!" says Desiree. The bell buzzes, and I snap the handcuffs on the kid's right wrist and on my left feeling a regular fool not having figured from the first how a cast can kill.

"Come!" I tell the kid. "Mind the cables now." We walk around the moat. Sixty-plus pairs of eyes follow us out the door.

Kid's face is the color of boiled lobster.

Pineville

MARY LEE SETTLE

All the way north across Tennessee it rained, not the simple down-rain of cities and valleys, but the brute roar of the mountains. The coal trucks passed me, and heaved spumes of dirty water against the windshield of my rented car, as if they were trying to hide the road from strangers.

But when I got as far as Middlesboro, across the Kentucky border, it stopped, and the mist rose higher and higher slowly, revealing the slopes of Pine Mountain. I sang, as Bobby Low had taught me when I was four, "Cumberland Gap, ain't very fer, just three miles from Middlesburr."

I sang all the way through the gap, on a road I didn't recognize, a new road to run strip-mine coal out of Harlan County, but the sign I looked for was there, and finally, I saw it—Pineville, Kentucky, population 2,500.

This was where I spent the first six years of my life. Towns, like people, are benign or are cold. Hoboes know this. They mark towns, and houses, with witch signs on fences. I had, for myself, marked Pineville, Kentucky, with secret signs within my memory. It was my small lost Eden—before I was untimely ripped from the place when I was six.

It lies in a cup below Pine Mountain on the banks of the Cumberland River. There had been, then, a doctor, a lawyer, a druggist, several coal operators, and a county courthouse set solid in the middle of the town, where once, when I had gone to the end of our street to the post office for my mother, I saw a man being carried out on a stretcher. He was wearing highly polished button shoes. I didn't know then that I was seeing a dead man. He had been shot with a sawed-off shotgun from the courthouse window while he was being tried for the murder of somebody his family was feuding with. I never quite knew who he was, because the grown-ups stopped talking about it when

I came out on the porch, as if I hadn't already seen the whole thing.

We lived in a one-story wooden cottage with a porch wrapped around it. Sometimes I see cottages like it at the springs in the mountains, where the cool porch protects the rooms, and people still sit on swings and rock back and forth, and I know the swings creak where the chain connects to the metal rings in the porch ceiling. It had a garden beside it where my mother planted flowers with names I liked to say, cosmos, delphinium, Mary Gold.

Until I was four years old, I was certain of two things. I knew that the word *ice cream* and the word *Flocoe* meant the same thing, and I thought, and told anyone who asked me, that Bobby Low was my father. This embarrassed not only my mother, but her best friend, Genevieve, who was Bobby Low's wife. The Flocoe had a marble floor made out of colored bits in a pattern that looked like a quilt. There was a marble counter, and little round marble tables. I sat on a chair made of wire lace. My chin reached the table. All ice cream was chocolate.

Bobby Low lived up a steep road on Pine Mountain at the edge of the town, in a brown house with the town on one side downhill, and a whole mountain where he worked his bird dogs on the other. From the swing you could see the town when there weren't too many leaves. When there were, you were in a bower and nobody could bother you or find you, at least for a little while.

About once a month I ran away. I put all my belongings in a red wagon, and I pulled it up the hill to Bobby Low's and sat in the swing on his porch until he found me. He taught me not to be afraid in the woods, how to scratch a dog on its belly, how to love silence more than speech, how to carry a gun broken over my elbow with the barrel toward the ground, the different songs of birds, the loud whir of the grouse, the scream of the panther, all of this before I was six years old.

I turned the car off the new road that ran in a high ramp over Pineville, splitting the town apart as if it no longer mattered. Below the high dam the ramp made, down on courthouse square, the road might as well not have existed. It was quiet. Nothing moved, not a car, except my own, not a person. There seemed to be more green grass, long and dark. The trees were bigger, their shade wide and dark, too. I had forgotten, or never had known, that the high steps I remembered of the courthouse were the same at both ends, and that the porches with high columns, now brackish with age, were the same on both sides.

I was, for a minute, disoriented. I drove around the square several times, slowly, trying to find a landmark. The post office I remembered had been moved. Some of the stores around the square where we used to buy ribbon and thread and summer cotton in fruit colors were boarded up, long empty. The hotel was gone where I had tried on Pearl White's wigs when she came there to make a picture show. At first I thought the wigs on their stands were severed heads. Theodore Dreiser had been run out of town from there for speaking for the Wobblies, only they said at The Flocoe he got fresh with a Pineville girl. I was finding out as I drove that I had missed little of grown-up whispers.

Then I saw the sign, on the corner where it had always been— THE FLOCOE, across from the courthouse, where during the sessions the lawyers had gathered and talked about coal leases, and how the United Mine Workers were making the bottom drop out of the coal business.

The door was still catty-cornered to the sidewalk. It was cool inside, the way I remembered it. There were two white-haired men sitting at a small round table. The marble counter and the fine marble floor were still there. I said aloud, and to myself, "Thank God, they haven't changed it."

One of the men, in a white coat, got up to introduce himself. "I'm the druggist," he said, "Mason Combs."

"You're not Buster's little brother?"

"Yes I am. Who are you?"

"I'm Mary Lee Settle. I used to live here."

"Why, you're Joe Ed's little sister!" The other man got up and came over to shake hands.

It had been sixty-four years.

We stood there together, pointing out places that no longer existed—where the post office had been, Miss Mabel Osborne's shop, the old hospital—and the town we remembered became the town we were seeing from the catty-cornered door of The Flocoe.

I asked about Bobby Low, and what had happened to him. I had not been wrong about him. Mason Combs said he was sorely missed. He had been a judge for years, and he had died when he was sixty-nine, twenty-five years before, one of the most beloved men in the county, and I remembered that you didn't live in towns in the mountains, you lived in counties, and this was Bell County.

But the Bobby Low I had brought back with me was thirty, a

tall russet man, walking ahead of me through the long grass, watching the dogs work.

I drove my car to where our house had been, to go from there,
as I had when I was so small. It was a concrete parking lot and
service station. Then I drove slowly down the street, seeing and
remembering all of it, the whole area of my life then to its borders.
I passed the house where I got a front tooth knocked out in a fight
at a birthday party. I saw the Reeses' house, where when they
made beaten biscuits on a machine on the back porch, you could
hear the thunk all through the house. There was Mr. Marting's,
where I played chess. They were Quakers and said thee and thou
to each other.

Then I came to the turn toward the hill.

I drove straight uphill to Bobby Low's house, over the same
corrugated asphalt road. It had been a quarter of a mile, a long
way for a little girl to pull her belongings uphill to find her father.
The swing was there, or another. The house had been painted
white. It didn't matter. No one knows when they make grown-up
decisions that in the backseat of a Chandler sedan may be a child
who is learning too quickly about the end of things. No one asked,
or imagined it, but Bobby Low, and his last words to me were,
"Don't worry, little onion, you'll be back in no time."

I sat there in my rented car. Bobby Low was right. It was no
time, sixty-four years later.

I went to say goodbye, to the cemetery that was on the next hill
at the foot of the mountain. It lay with a horseshoe of a road, going
all the way up the hill, turning at the top, and coming down again
to the road below. It had been built so long ago that it was too
narrow for any modern car, and the coffins had to be carried by
hand, as they always had been so long ago. I walked slowly up
the left-hand side.

Over and over, in the grass and under the trees, there were
marble stones with the names of people remembered, and I saw
the way they had looked, and heard the way they had spoken. I
passed playmates and enemies and their parents and their grand-
parents.

I searched the little graveyard for nearly an hour, but I could
not find Bobby Low. I went on up the hill, and I told myself not
to give up, that he wouldn't let himself be buried down at the
bottom with a bunch of bankers and coal operators. He didn't like
people like that anyway.

At the top of the horseshoe road, I turned to the right to follow it back down the hill again. Up above me among the last graves two little dogs were playing, a feist dog and a little country beagle. I spoke aloud again, "Please God, help me find Bobby Low." I didn't know until then that it was a prayer that had echoed faintly all through my life.

Within two seconds the little beagle had jumped up on my leg, his tail wagging hard. I petted him and walked on along the right-hand road. He followed me and jumped up again, then ran back to the left and looked back, waiting for me. I followed him. He kept checking back, every ten feet or so, to see that I was still following.

At the end of a small footpath, where I could just glimpse Bobby Low's house through the trees across the ravine, the dog stopped, turned to a catty-cornered eleven o'clock from the path, and froze on point, like a bird dog. There, directly between his ears, I read the words carved on the stone—ROBERT GIBSON LOW.

I said a prayer for both of us, and said goodbye at last. Then I went back down the hill. When I last saw the beagle, he was standing against the sky with a mountain *immortelle*, a plastic wreath, in his mouth. His other job at the graveyard seemed to be to move plastic wreaths from one grave to another so that nobody would be forgotten.

The Locker Room

SUSAN RICHARDS SHREVE

In the morning early, I swim in the Olympic-size pool underneath the basketball court of a boys' Episcopal school. Back and forth in the turquoise dawn, keeping to the left of the black line, careful not to crash into the wall. Half a mile, predictably, and then the locker room. This morning is no different.

The locker room is like a men's locker room, without privacy—a tile room with showers lined up against one wall. You will rub against the flesh of the woman next to you unless you are centered neatly under the spray from your own nozzle. That's how familial and democratic this locker room is, with women I have seen every day for ten years first off in the morning before coffee and the newspaper, more regular than my husband or my mother.

I don't know their names. I probably wouldn't recognize them on the street. Many of them are older than I am and have been swimming much longer than this sport has been popular. They swim for survival because they have lost a breast or have had back surgery or arthritis. One has a pin in her hip and walks with a walker. Another has had heart attacks.

What is striking about older women, I have noticed, is that the flesh on the torso remains supple in spite of the assaults of age on the face, the slackening of the skin on the arms and legs. I did not know this about women until I started to swim here. In fact I knew very little about nakedness.

When I was a girl, especially in junior high school, I never dressed in the locker room. I stood on the toilet behind the locked cubicle door and only exposed my breasts to the empty space for half a minute between changing from school clothes to gym clothes and back.

So this locker room has been a liberation for me. To stand naked, one in a line of naked women, to know them intimately without knowing their names, has made me feel a kind of membership I never knew before.

This morning, the very tall woman with white hair to her waist is back. "Rapunzel," I call her to my husband. She is fair and freckled, with one small breast, a long incision crosswise on her belly, and high hips. She comes into the shower just after me, takes off her suit slow motion, lets her hair fall out of the white old-fashioned rubber cap. Everyone is glad to see her.

"Hello," I say. "We missed you."

"Thank you," she says. She has a certain dignity that commands a room in spite of the lopsided oddness of her figure.

"Were you on holiday?" the sweet-faced round woman who keeps her walker just in front of her while she showers asks.

"No," the Rapunzel woman says. "There was of course no way for you to know." She turns the shower to hot and stands facing out, underneath the nozzle, her eyes closed, her head tilted back. "My younger child died."

We are stunned. The soft round woman takes hold of her walker, forgetting to rinse the shampoo out of her hair. Weak-kneed, as though this news is personal, I sit on the wooden bench next to Abigail, the one woman whose name we all know because she is southern and gregarious and insists we know her name.

"Oh, my God," Abigail says. "How awful. This is such terrible news." She seems to be the only one among us to whom language comes as easily as living.

"She was ill for a very long time," the Rapunzel woman says. "I didn't tell you because I didn't want to believe it was true."

She pours Flex shampoo into the palm of her hand, lathers it quickly, washing and rinsing her hair simultaneously so her whole body is sudsy.

"I don't know what to say, dear," the woman with the walker says. "I am so sorry."

"Thank you," Rapunzel says. She turns off the shower and steps out.

I embrace her wet and slippery body. I am weeping. The woman with the walker takes her hand and kisses the fingers. Abigail steps into the room where the lockers are and tells the other women, half dressed, drying their hair, putting on stockings, tieing their shoes.

"Thank you," Rapunzel says as she embraces one after another of the women. "It was only bad in the last weeks." She combs out her long white hair, puts on gray wool slacks and a turtleneck. I notice that she doesn't once look in the mirror at herself.

"Suddenly she got much worse." She puts on a wool cap over her wet hair and a down ski jacket.

"Thank you all very much." Shyly, she blows a kiss toward the rest of us dressing. Just as she is about to leave, she says, as if in answer to a question, "Her name was Caroline Marie."

After the door closes, the woman with the walker, bundled for winter, shakes her head.

"I would send her flowers if I knew where." She touches my cheek. "Goodbye, dear."

"Goodbye," I say.

"Goodbye," she says to the others.

I put my hood up, tie the laces of my heavy boots.

"Goodbye," I call, opening the door to the cold. "See you tomorrow," I say, flooded unaccountably with gratitude. "See you tomorrow."

Outside, it has begun to snow—a thin gray city snow, falling in sheets at an angle to the earth, obscuring the people on the sidewalk hurrying to work. But I am suddenly lifted out of the darkness of a winter dawn.

My Father's Girlfriends

DARCEY STEINKE

It was April. My mother and I sat under a willow near my dorm. In the caved branches she folded a leaf into angles and told me she suspected my father would leave. Her dark hair was parted jaggedly and her face had a pale blue cast, I guessed from the combination of willow shadow and sleeplessness. What I remember best, beside her troubled features, was the drone of the mower as it stripped the lawn and how, after trying to shout above the whir, we were forced to move. As she stood, I saw that grass had made a mass of hectic indentations on the backs of her legs and realized for the first time how young her legs looked, how much they resembled my own.

Within that same week my father showed up to take me to lunch. He seemed overly formal, almost datelike. We both had herbal iced tea with mint in tall beveled glasses. And at the table next to us sat six little girls in smocked dresses eating lemon sherbet from silver bowls. He didn't tell me he was leaving, just that he liked the big Victorian house I'd taken a room in and the sprawling lawns and important-looking brick buildings of my university. I wanted to ask him about his girlfriends, but seeing him made me think my mother was mistaken, and besides he seemed so relieved to see me, like I was one thing he didn't have to worry about. To his mind I was in order, and for a brief moment he gratefully covered my hand with his own. One of the little girls blew loudly into her party horn, a boomerang-shaped helicopter swirled to our table, and I felt ferns of blush edge into my cheeks as I realized everyone around us thought my father and I were in love.

When I got home late in June he was gone and my mother was Xeroxing copies of his love letters and placing them in the pages of the bathroom magazines and by the telephone. There were long passages on conventions, seminars, banquets, and a charter bus tour out to some Indian burial ground. One letter described a ride in a glass elevator, a beer tab on her finger to prove marriage, how they rode to the top looking over Baltimore's Inner Harbor. "The lights were blinking just for us," my father's girlfriend wrote in a big sweeping hand.

After reading the first letter, I slipped it back where I found it on the coffee table and went to my room. There I lay on my bed all day, thinking about him with strange women. I felt weighted as I had about certain difficult love affairs, but this seemed worse because it was my father and I'd been in love with him for years. It wasn't that he'd ever touched me, just that there were times I thought if I wasn't his daughter I might be his girlfriend. For a while we were both secret smokers, and we'd sit together in lawn chairs in a blind spot in the backyard while Mom busied herself in the kitchen or read one of her self-help books. His voice would be different then, like the lights of the house were far away, already just a picture in his head.

Those letters seemed to set off a chain of discoveries, one while I was visiting an old friend. Sarah had a shivering way about her even in summer and she wore octagonal glasses that made her eyes look huge. We stood with our wineglasses on her deck at dusk, watching lights go off all over the neighborhood, and I told her some of the subtler repercussions of the separation. She listened for a while, then turned her head to the tangled slope of the backyard. "I guess I can tell you now," she said, once I trailed off, "that your father use to come over and ask my mother if he should get divorced." I tried to imagine my dad with her mother, a dance teacher: a tight muscle of a woman, short hair brushed wispy toward her face, red lipstick. I pushed him into Sarah's mother's bed with the poster over it of worn toe shoes and dove wings fluttering around them.

I found another girlfriend at a dinner party in a fieldstone house. Three of us stood near a low brass lamp: Jill, a recent divorcée who wrote short stories about angels floating up in the corners of rooms, a Lutheran poet from the Midwest, and myself. The poet was talking in a creepy séance voice about journals of Holocaust survivors. After a prolonged silence, Jill said, "I was just looking over *my* old journals and I saw your father's name. He was in that life drawing class." Smoke mixed with her dark hair and she smiled. "A nice man and so blond all over." I stared at her; she had slept with my father, maybe even in the studio, the canvas tarp underneath them and a forest of easels ahead. I wanted to say something flippant and rude but I knew I'd feel badly about it later. The thought of them together, his long hair falling from his bald spot and brushing her chin, was pitiful and embarrassing and I changed the subject as quickly as I could.

There were other girlfriends: our dental hygienist, a woman in my ballet class—the way they spoke of him with a combination of reverence and familiarity seemed strange, like they were talking about someone I didn't know, and I began to see that he'd always been false and phantomish in our house. I called him then to ask if I could come to New York.

I told my mother the plan to take the morning train and handed her the letters. Her breakfast since he left lasted hours. She was still in her bathrobe, though it was late afternoon, drinking tea.

She answered me languidly, looking up from her paper. "You tell me where you think these should go," she said. There was something damaged even in the measured way she spoke now. At times it seemed like she'd had a minor stroke or been bruised badly in a car accident. She moved around the house delicately, careful to have nothing touch her. Most days were these sluggish kind but there were also the occasional hysterical ones, when she bustled around with tears in her eyes.

"It makes me feel bad to have them around everywhere," I said.

Her hand tightened on her teacup and the worry lines around her mouth narrowed. "You're just mad because you thought your father was something great."

"He's taking me to see the Yankees," I said, as if that might be proof of his worth.

"That is just wonderful," she said. "I hope you get what you're looking for up there."

She faded then into her own thoughts. It had happened before; she would catch herself sounding strange or desperate and her tone showed her the extremities of her heartache, which then embarrassed her and made her silent.

The Southern Crescent swayed along and the morning light fell in a pale and pleasant line across the love letters on my lap. Mom had driven me to the station this morning; she was still brooding and dangerous, and we hardly spoke at all. I'd been reading the letters and composing a list of his girlfriends, half hoping I might feel less hysterical if I had the names in my hands. But I couldn't shake the sensation that his women were everywhere, and I threw the copies onto the seat near me and watched speed turn the Pennsylvania countryside into a long ragged green line.

The trip was uneventful and I slept until just before Newark. There a woman in a cream-colored linen suit got on and settled herself in the window seat across from me. She had a look set into her face that reminded me of some of the girlfriends, an expression I've noticed lately on a lot of women. It somehow says that there are certain rules that do not apply to them. I wondered, as the train lugged forward, if my father would like her.

Outside the window lay the sprawl of hinterlands around the city: gray metal fences, smokestacks, skin-colored buildings, that particular kind of clutter which is somehow so oddly empty.

Over all that I saw the tip of Manhattan. Dad's had two girlfriends since he moved there. The first was a personal essayist. He sent me a copy of one piece, "Love Weekends," with her photo: short black hair, serious face, big bronze earrings. At first he told me he liked it that she was a Catholic convert and member of a civilian police patrol, but later he confided that she was as rigid as my mother and that their affair had ended badly. Mary is the current one. All I know is that she wanders somewhere in her twenties and that he met her in the botanical gardens in front of an oasis of white orchids and palms.

The train stopped dead in Penn Station. Right away out the window I saw him in a seersucker suit, up against a *Cats* billboard. Green eyes leered up at me over his shoulder. He pitched away a long thin cigarette and took a step forward. He'd lost weight and his fringe of hair was slightly longer than I'd ever seen it. I gathered the list and the letters into my bag and bumbled up the aisle behind the woman. He never seemed to merge completely with his sur-roundings. Even on the platform now, his good-natured, ruffable expression made him look different, more radiant and human, than the others waiting. He watched her legs as the woman in linen walked briskly toward the station. I was right next to him by the time he turned his head. He didn't say anything, just held my arms out as if checking the parameters of my body. "You look great," he said and kissed my forehead. My plan had been to show him the letters right away. But I had forgotten how disarming he could be, and I decided instead to watch him and wait.

Saying we'd take the subway to the game, he turned toward the station. He seemed more preoccupied, but less self-consciously so than I remembered, and though I could never say he was a hand-some man, age continued to pleasantly shift his features.

I took big steps to keep up. "A lot of people have asked about you," I said. "Some I didn't even think you knew."

"So they miss me?" he said.

I was surprised by his careless tone and didn't answer right away.

He looked at me; his face, which had been sunny and animated, now showed dread. "What are you talking about, Rachel?" he said.

We were in the main room, under the big domed ceiling with the stars and zodiacs traced among them.

I pulled out the letters. There were ten or so, and several fell to the mottled floor. He gathered these up and began to read one. At first I could tell he presumed they had to do with me or they were a plea from my mother, but in another moment his face reddened. "Why did you bring these?" he said.

I shrugged. I had thought he'd be defensive or dismissively confident about the girlfriends, but instead he seemed shaken.

"Look," he said, "this whole mess is between me and your mother. It has nothing to do with you."

"You don't know what it's like to live in that house."

He stared at me. "Of course I do."

People swayed around us like stream water rounding rocks.

"I thought you loved me," I said. It sounded stupid and rehearsed.

He took my arm. "It wasn't you I was married to." He turned me toward the subway and smiled, a big loose grin that for a moment changed everything.

At the game we got a couple of hot dogs and settled into our seats along the first-base line. The green turf spread out like long backyards I'd known as a kid. The two women behind us speculated on my status. "His girlfriend," one finally whispered, loud enough for my father to hear.

"Actually," he said, turning around, "this is my daughter."

One woman said that he must have a lovely wife. He didn't answer, just smiled coyly and turned back to the game. I'd never seen him so comfortable. He seemed to have forgotten about the letters now, and it occurred to me how hard it must have been for him to live so out of his element in our suburban house.

Already there were several birds that had found their way into the stadium, and they flew in disoriented figure-eights under the lights. The birds started me worrying about foul balls, and I asked him what would happen if one came my way. "Don't worry," he said. "I'll catch all the balls."

The game started and the innings went slow. We drank beers.

He flirted with the women, teasing them about their lack of baseball expertise. I was trying to pinpoint the first moment that I had known for certain he would leave us. We were drinking beers under the branches of this magnolia tree. The pale pink silky petals were long gone, and the big shiny leaves gave the tree a neolithic look. Sweat dripped from his nose into his beer can. "Sometimes being around here makes me feel like a bag of bones," he said, and looked up to the house and to my mother, sunning herself on the deck in a ribboned lawn chair.

During the third inning he stopped talking to the women, turned, and whispered that neither really was his type. It was just that he always thought about how much he hated being alone.

"You've never really been alone," I said. There was a piece of paper floating gracefully from the top tier. It moved horizontally and light shone through it.

At home my mother was probably sitting in the TV room with the deck door and windows open to the dark yard. No lights, just a cool flicker of screen showing her summer nightgown and heavy body underneath.

"You left us both."

"No," he said, shuffling the program with his big hands.

I waited for him to finish.

"Look," he said, "it has to be hard on you to have your father falling in love."

"You are always in love with one thing or another," I said, and as I spoke I realized how true it was and also how it was his most appealing quality. A bat cracked then and we stood to watch a home run arch above the grandstand lights into the blue night.

The Yankee runner tapped the bases and jogged home. The next batter did a scarecrow step up to the plate. I put a hand to his wrist. There was one last thing I needed to know. "Do you ever think about it, Mom or the house?"

"No," he said, as if reminded of a small humiliating incident that happened long ago. "I don't really think about it that much." He kept looking straight ahead to the outfield.

"Then what about me?" But before he could answer the bat sounded again and a foul ball headed for us. It landed a few rows up in a rustle of people reaching.

My father grabbed my hand and said quickly, "If one comes to you, let your hand drop. Nothing can hurt you if you give with it." And he showed me, his hand open and falling, how to absorb the force of an imaginary ball.

No One's a Mystery

ELIZABETH TALLENT

For my eighteenth birthday Jack gave me a five-year diary with a latch and a little key, light as a dime. I was sitting beside him scratching at the lock, which didn't seem to want to work, when he thought he saw his wife's Cadillac in the distance, coming toward us. He pushed me down onto the dirty floor of the pickup and kept one hand on my head while I inhaled the musk of his cigarettes in the dashboard ashtray and sang along with Rosanne Cash on the tape deck. We'd been drinking tequila and the bottle was between his legs, resting up against his crotch, where the seam of his Levi's was bleached linen-white, though the Levi's were nearly new. I don't know why his Levi's always bleached like that, along the seams and at the knees. In a curve of cloth his zipper glinted, gold.

"It's her," he said. "She keeps the lights on in the daytime. I can't think of a single habit in a woman that irritates me more than that." When he saw that I was going to stay still he took his hand from my head and ran it through his own dark hair.

"Why does she?" I said.

"She thinks it's safer. Why does she need to be safer? She's driving exactly fifty-five miles an hour. She believes in those signs SPEED MONITORED BY AIRCRAFT. It doesn't matter that you can look up and see the sky is empty."

"She'll see your lips move, Jack. She'll know you're talking to someone."

"She'll think I'm singing along with the radio."

He didn't lift his hand, just raised the fingers in salute while the pressure of his palm steadied the wheel, and I heard the Cadillac honk twice, musically; he was driving easily eighty miles an hour. I studied his boots. The elk heads stitched into the leather were bearded with frayed thread, the toes were scuffed, and there was a compact wedge of muddy manure between the heel and the sole—the same boots he'd been wearing for the two years I'd known him. On the tape deck Rosanne Cash sang, "Nobody's into me, no one's a mystery."

"Do you think she's getting famous because of who her daddy is or for herself?" Jack said.

"There are about a hundred pop-tops on the floor, did you know that? Some little kid could cut a bare foot on one of these, Jack."

"No little kids get into this truck except for you."

"How come you let it get so dirty?"

" 'How come,' " he mocked. "You even sound like a kid. You can get back into the seat now, if you want. She's not going to look over her shoulder and see you."

"How do you know?"

"I just know," he said. "Like I know I'm going to get meat loaf for supper. It's in the air. Like I know what you'll be writing in that diary."

"What will I be writing?" I knelt on my side of the seat and craned around to look at the butterfly of dust printed on my jeans. Outside the window Wyoming was dazzling in the heat. The wheat was fawn and yellow and parted smoothly by the thin dirty road. I could smell the water in the irrigation ditches hidden in the wheat.

"Tonight you'll write, 'I love Jack. This is my birthday present from him. I can't imagine anybody loving anybody more than I love Jack.' "

"I can't."

"In a year you'll write, 'I wonder what I ever really saw in Jack. I wonder why I spent so many days just riding around in his pickup. It's true he taught me something about sex. It's true there wasn't ever much else to do in Cheyenne.' "

"I won't write that."

"In two years you'll write, 'I wonder what that old guy's name was, the one with the curly hair and the filthy dirty pickup truck and time on his hands.' "

"I won't write that."

"No?"

"Tonight I'll write, 'I love Jack. This is my birthday present from him. I can't imagine anybody loving anybody more than I love Jack.' "

"No, you can't," he said. "You can't imagine it."

"In a year I'll write, 'Jack should be home any minute now. The table's set—my grandmother's linen and her old silver and the yellow candles left over from the wedding—but I don't know if I can wait until after the trout à la Navarra to make love to him.' "

"It must have been a fast divorce."

"In two years I'll write, 'Jack should be home by now. Little Jack is hungry for his supper. He said his first word today besides *Mama* and *Papa*. He said "kaka." ' "

Jack laughed. "He was probably trying to finger-paint with kaka on the bathroom wall when you heard him say it."

"In three years I'll write, 'My nipples are a little sore from nursing Eliza Rosamund.' "

"Rosamund. Every little girl should have a middle name she hates."

" 'Her breath smells like vanilla and her eyes are just Jack's color of blue.' "

"That's nice," Jack said.

"So, which one do you like?"

"I like yours," he said. "But I believe mine."

"It doesn't matter. I believe mine."

"Not in your heart of hearts, you don't."

"You're wrong."

"I'm not wrong," he said. "And her breath would smell like your milk, and it's kind of a bittersweet smell, if you want to know the truth."

The Football Factory

JOHN UPDIKE

The dignitary was surprised that the factory was located in farm country—a gently rolling plain hazy with pollen and tractor exhaust, not so different from the land where, a half century ago, he had been born. Corn had been the crop there, while here interminable dull-green rows of potatoes dominated, with some fields given over to the slightly broader and brighter stripes of pick-them-yourself strawberries, tidily mounded between weed-suppressing strips of black plastic.

The factory itself was low, its flat roof only one visual notch higher than its parking lot, and but for the garish glitter of the rows of parked cars would hardly have interrupted the landscape. The company president and the floor manager, both wearing shirts and ties but coatless, greeted them at the entrance, a small door to one side of a long concrete loading platform. Their escort, the local mayor, introduced the dignitary, his liaison man, and the reporter and the press photographer who would accompany their brief tour. The mayor, knowing the dignitary's tight schedule, emphasized the "brief." The company president, who wore conspicuous cuff links in the form of gold footballs, was pink with pleasure, whereas the floor manager, who was to conduct the tour, appeared relatively sallow and tense; he gave them all their protective goggles and red plastic safety hats without any of the playfulness, the sheepish sense of childish fun, that such a procedure usually elicits. To be polite and to lubricate the encounter, the dignitary asked the president if there had been any significant recent changes in their manufacture of footballs.

The question seemed to be an awkward one. The president's china-blue eyes slid around his office, from desktop to filing cabinet to industrial performance plaques to oversize display football to framed letter from former sports hero to the face of his floor manager, resting nowhere. "Well," he said, "there's always subtle changes—an eighth of an inch here, a degree or two of curvature there—but the last revolutionary step was the half circle on the end instead of the full circle. That was really the last major innovation. Before that, all I can think of is the clear plastic bladder, for the less quality models."

The dignitary became interested in spite of himself. "Who determines these changes? The league heads?"

"Supply and demand, like everything else," the president said, his pinkness intensifying but his appearance of pleasure ebbing. "Changes trickle down from the leagues, yes, but there's also a trickle-up effect, from the schools and colleges. You get pro players used to a certain style of pebbling on the leather, a certain specific amount the laces are spaced and raised up, they're going to be most comfortable with it all the way along, way into their careers. We don't make policy here, we just make footballs."

The president's palpable relief at having arrived at a joke of sorts, after so long a traversal of what seemed to be thin ice, communicated itself to the company and released them to their tour. The floor manager led the visitors down a long wooden hall, past a bulletin board and time clock and production charts and a pair of lavatory doors, and opened a steel door into bedlam. It was a controlled, steady bedlam of clanging, huffing, rattling, stitching, stamping, and breathing; a giant presiding set of lungs seemed to be inhaling and exhaling through the mechanical din, as if about to pronounce an anguished word. To the almost blinding richness of activity and noise was added the intermittent flash of the photographer's camera as he recorded the dignitary intently observing different aspects of football manufacture.

The group was led around to the far side of the huge room, through lanes of machines and workers who seemed no more conscious of the visitors than the machines were, to a corrugated wall where the hides were unloaded and stored. "We try to keep the inventory low," the floor manager explained, slapping a broad stack that came up to his chest. "Inventory ties up cash." In the din, his shouted words were precious and had to be strained after. Often, he merely gestured.

First, the hides (imported from Argentina, Florida, and Texas) went to a young woman at a machine that stamped big pumpkin-seed shapes from them. It was wonderful to see how quickly she placed the oval die, snatched back her hand, let the machine descend and lift with a hollow plucking sound, laid the punched piece of leather in a stack, and shifted the hide and die for another such quick subtraction. When all the pieces were stamped out, the waste remnant, minimal and tangled like a wet bikini, was tossed into a barrel. It somehow surprised the dignitary that the hides, whitish on their unpebbled side, still testified to the four-legged shape of the steer and bore organic irregularities that were taken into account by the deft worker: she did not put all the leather pieces into the same stack but sorted them into three or four grades as she worked. She had the pensive pale profile of a maiden rendered in Art Nouveau stained glass, and ringleted blond hair caught up into a tight red polka-dot kerchief, and long arms whose motions unfailingly glided in silent obedience to the rhythm of the machine; she formed, in her young and pensive beauty, a human island in the midst of clatter, and even through the mechanical furor the intensity in the dignitary's contemplation of her profile must have psychically tugged at her, for she glanced aside, risking in that moment's inattention severance of her fingers.

The floor manager, his initial tension expansively relaxing as he settled into his field of expertise, was describing the nuances of hide—the relative thicknesses and consistencies of the shoulders versus the flanks, and the problem of barbed-wire scratches and gorings acquired by the animal in its wandering, irresponsible prefootball condition. The men moved on, to terrible machines where whiningly revolving bands of steel shaved the ovoid leather pieces to a uniform thickness. The workers here were sitting down and with a certain insouciance flipped the pieces in and out and onward. Traveling belts transported square gray buckets of leather from one violent, efficient process to the next. Four pieces made a football, and soon the pieces met their fated companions and traveled in quartets, in two-pointed four-ply sandwiches, of which two pieces were punctured with lace holes and one with another hole to admit the bladder valve. At a kind of printing press fed with gold and black foil, one of the four pieces was branded with the company's name and logo. At rows of ferocious industrial sewing machines, pairs of sides were sewed together; huddled women peered into spots of light where their knobby tense hands guided the doubled leather along a single curved edge stitched by a chattering needle. Then the two halves, nested together, shaped like open pods, were sewn into a single unit, at machines even more powerful, by women and men even more highly trained, than at any previous stage. The floor manager shouted, "Takes four to six years' experience to be trusted with this procedure. Toughest part is the tips. See how they trim a little bit off? Otherwise there'd be too much to drive the needle through. You'd get a sort of lump on the end."

The dignitary stared at the brightly illuminated hands that with habituated sureness and strength perfectly pulled the doubled leather along its curve, around the acute corner, back up the other side, around the other corner, back to the patch for laces, cut the thread, and finally tossed the wadded, limp, hopeless-looking result into a waiting square gray bucket. A strange blue light kept bursting into the visiting dignitary's hypnotized gaze, and he realized it was the photographer, flashing away. No doubt his expression had been suitably fascinated. He asked, "Don't they ever get bored? I mean, do you ever get employee burnout?"

A hint of tension returned to the manager's sallow face. "Not at the prices we pay 'em," he said. "This is one of the top jobs. Like I say, four to six years of experience before they can handle it." Quite unexpectedly, he smiled. "Now I bet you're asking yourself the question everybody takes this tour asks themselves."

"What's that?"

"How do the footballs get turned right side out?"

Belatedly the dignitary realized that the hopeless-looking assemblages of leather were inside-out footballs. Amid the many impressive, implacable machines he had lost sight of basic objectives. He wondered if he were especially stupid or merely innocent regarding the rigorous, intricate, and yet basically blunt steps whereby things are made. His whole adult life had been spent in the realm of the immaterial—speaking, thinking, performing, conferring, making impressions on men's minds. His childhood acquaintance with matter and its earthy principles had been perfunctory and not pleasant enough to prolong. He had yearned for a life free of dirt and calluses, and his success was measured by how much time he now spent in airplanes. Only in airplanes, above the clouds, going somewhere at someone else's expense, did he feel fully himself: impervious, clean, transient, a lord of thin air.

"People always love the turners," the floor manager assured him, smiling as if an obscene treat were in store.

Before they could witness the turners at work the group had to admire the computerized assembly lines, whereby a laborer at any machine could with a touch signal for more units to stitch or punch, and a gray container would be sent on its programmed way. The lanky lad manning the multicolored computerized control panel slapped down a bucket of grayish ovoid liners, of what

looked like felt or cardboard; the dignitary had somehow missed
the part of the process where the leather was lined. And then
another slapped-down bucket, of half-moon-shaped reinforce-
ment patches for underneath the lace holes, skimmed on its zigzag
way. There was more to making a football than met the eye. The
flashbulbs went off with less regularity now, and the dignitary felt
his brain wearying. The mayor, too, who had been on this tour
many times, and the press reporter, his ballpoint pen tucked back
into his corduroy jacket, looked drowsy and overwhelmed, here
at the acoustical center of the din.

But the turners woke them up. A row of men, standing each at
a bench equipped with a knobbed upright metal post, writhed like
damned souls as, muscles bulging through their T-shirts, they
whacked the limp inverted footballs over their posts, pushing one
point in, and then with savage yet skilled tugging brought that
point out through the gap left for the lace holes and, twisting the
impaled, half-actualized football tenaciously about, with more
whacking and tugging, brought the other end through and tossed
the result, its thick seams turned inward, into a gray bucket, which
then moved along to a group entirely of women—because, the
floor manager shoutingly explained, their hands were small—who
inserted the bladders and gave each football a whiff of air. The
machines that provided air, tall shining canisters such as contain
milk in cafeterias, were what had initially struck the dignitary's
ears as the sound of lungs, of breathing, of intake on the verge of
speech, permeating the mechanical agitation. From the bladder
inserters the footballs passed on to the lacers: these, too, were all
men, because of the brute strength required, but their dance of
frantic effort was performed sitting down, with a length of thong
and a slender hook that became in their gauntleted, bandaged
hands a shuttle that with furious speed wove shut the football.

Little remained to complete the industrial process—complete
inflation, a computerized weighing to ascertain that the inflated
football was within a fraction of an ounce of the regulation weight,
a painting on of the white circles or half circles at the football tips,
a visual inspection and sorting into flawed and flawless, and the
packaging of the flawless balls into individual boxes decorated with
company slogans and colorful images of athletic heroics.

The dignitary was allowed to hold one. It felt good, weightless
and taut, with that remembered ballistic urgency. In his own high
school, thirty-five years ago, he had played second-string end. The
occasional fancy catch, but he couldn't stand up to the battering,

the blocking and being blocked. He felt something was expected of him. "Why is it called a pigskin?" he asked the floor manager.

The man's face was slightly plump, with a disagreeable deep dimple in the center of his chin and an asymmetry to the eyes that would have led an inspector to toss his head into the reject barrel. The rejects, it had been explained, were not thrown out as trash but marketed at a lesser price, to old-fashioned poor boys in patched knickers, the dignitary imagined, and to inner-city high schools on slashed budgets.

The floor manager smiled, as if the dignitary had once again lived up to predictions. "People always ask that," he said, "and, you know, I've never looked up the answer. They must have been made of pigskin once, but ever since I've been in this business it's been cowhide pure and simple. If you ever take a look at pigskin, it's not at all suitable. No grip on it."

The dignitary nodded politely, but his mind and eye kept wandering back to the turners, spotlighted at the center of the vast factory like a chorus line gone mad, the lack of synchronization in their precise, strenuous movements making it terrible, each man alone with his demon, his recalcitrant football, wrestling eternally with his individual sins. Each man wore a shirt aggressively stylized, like the costumes of criminals—one T-shirt bearing a big lavender-lidded Madonna, another the slogan *Born to Lose*, and a third a tie-dye of lichenlike circular overlappings. One man, the only black, had a shaved head, and the whites tended to have hair long in the fashions of the passé sixties, in a ponytail or straggling to the shoulders. Several had Pancho Villa mustaches, and others displayed blotchy purple tattoos. The strength of these men! How much evening beer must it take to drown these eight hours, to recharge these aching muscles! Not all were in their first youth, but as a group they were younger than the lacers, who bent into their own repetitive torment with a cagier power, a thrusting crouch, their right arms flailing.

"How much does an experienced worker earn?" the dignitary asked, feeling increasingly dreamlike. Lowering his eyes from the distant row of radiant, revolving turners, he discovered almost at his feet a pool of peace. Next to a painted I-beam pillar a coffee urn had been set up, with Styrofoam cups, and a few metal folding chairs were scattered about; here the workers could take a break. Several women were seated here, among them the lissome pale Art Nouveau beauty whom, a half hour ago, the dignitary had watched stamping hides into football fourths. Beneath him now she was wearily smoking a cigarette and brushing a wisp of her stubbornly curly blond hair back into her red polka-dot kerchief.

In his mind he bent down and asked her to marry him. She looked up, her greenish-blue eyes a bit faded and dull and cautious, and, with less surprise and gratitude than he had expected, consented. Her voice exposed the flat rural accent of the region; though not old, she had been knocked about enough to be guarded in her enthusiasm about anything.

They left the factory together, the inhuman clatter fading behind them, and found a split-level ranch house with aluminum siding painted a poisonous green, a kind of open combination living/dining room and a cozy basement den where they put the television set and had a fireplace. They were very happy. She returned to the factory after their honeymoon on a charter flight to Las Vegas, and he loved the way she would bring home on her body the smells not only of sweat and cigarettes and coffee and machine oil but of leather. The scent of cowhide, of vast sage-flavored grazing spaces, wafted permanently from her delicate hands; she kept her nails close-clipped so that her fingers had a grublike and guileless look; he never failed to be stirred under their indolent tired fragrant touch. They had two or three kids, to add to the child she had had at seventeen by that bastard of a first husband, and on Saturday nights would weave and shriek their way home bloated with beer and munchies in their battered pickup truck. Even into her middle age, when she got dressed up she had a smudgy-eyed, high-hipped glamour, in her satiny turquoise slacks with pegged ankles and slingback spikes, her kinky long hair careless down her touchingly thin back.

Their first years, he sat home with the babies, and now and then went off to fulfill a speaking engagement that had been contracted for in his old life; but as the invitations and his savings dried up, he succumbed to her offhand but repeated suggestion that he might find work at the factory too. He became—one of the oldest men ever successfully to do so—a turner. The work itself was curiously rejuvenating, and after those first nightmare weeks, when it seemed every evening as though he might die of weariness and shoulder pain, his body developed the muscles and his brain the peculiar furious torpor that the job required. His upper body became lumpy with ugly muscle, and he woke each day to the bliss of knowing he didn't have to be polite to anyone. His tattoos spread; he lost his front teeth in a bar fight. His dreams as he lay beside her pale, lightly sweating slenderness were of strenuously turning things inside out and revealing the glory hidden within every pebbled, scarred, tough exterior.

"Strictly piecework," the floor manager was explaining to him, in answer to his question. "If they want to take a break for coffee, they do it at their own expense."

"And how much, at those rates, can a skilled worker earn?"

These were not questions the man enjoyed answering. He said grudgingly, "Oh, an experienced top-flight stitcher on one of the big machines, for example, after deductions for benefits and withholding, might take home upwards of three hundred a week."

The dignitary made a rapid calculation. He earned four months' worth of such work with a single speech at a big-city chamber of commerce.

The mayor had begun to glance at his watch, and the press photographer had sealed his cameras up in their black plastic jackets. The group gave only cursory attention to the machine, a tall vertical metal cabinet somewhat like a French pissoir, wherein the footballs were masked and automatically received, with a sharp hiss, their spray-painted circular or semicircular stripes.

Back in the president's office, the silence seemed eerie. One's head felt light without the helmet and the goggles. The president had put on his suit coat for the little ceremony of saying goodbye. Pink with pleasure, he presented the dignitary with a pair of cuff links in the shape of footballs—bronze, however, not gold like his own. "Was it what you expected?" he asked.

"Not at all. It was much more"—the dignitary searched, trying to find the exact word; for what made him so good (he thought) at these ceremonious occasions was that extra particle of courteous attention he brought, that focused willingness to make a small gem of the most transient event—"*divertissant.*"

The word seemed wasted on the president. "We've pretty well trimmed all the fat out of the operation," the portly man stated. "That's what we're proudest of."

"He loved the turners," the floor manager said, with a chortle on the verge, the dignitary thought, of presumptuousness.

"Most folks do. A lot of them, they can't get over it."

"And the ferocious stitchers," the dignitary said. "And the girl stamping out the big raw hides."

"Everybody plays their part," the president said. "We try to make them feel that. Anybody has an idea how to make the operation more efficient, we encourage that person to speak up."

The mayor felt constrained to interrupt. "Mr."—he had forgotten the dignitary's name, but covered nicely—"Mister here has to catch a plane."

The handshaking began. "It was a pleasure."

"A pleasure for us."

"No, truly. I wouldn't have missed it."

"Well, shows there's a little more than potato fields out in this part of the world."

"Indeed. Much more. And thank *you*. A great tour. You really know your football manufacture. And thank you, Mr. Mayor. For working this into your busy schedule."

"My pleasure. Learn something new every time I'm taken through."

"No, no. *My* pleasure." The dignitary found himself shaking the press reporter's hand now, and smiling, and then the photographer's, and then that of an underling who had wandered in with a big square bucket of special souvenir footballs with one side of white vellum for whole teams to sign. "Thank you, a real treat, a *real* treat, thank *you*," he heard himself saying, deftly stamping them out.

Grandfather, Heart of the Fields

WILL WEAVER

The hunters were all Hansens. They were all dressed in red and stood in the snow near their pickups. Benny's father said again, "You're sure there was nothing."

"Nothing," Benny said.

"Goddammitanyway," his father said in a rush; his breath smoked in the December air and a clear droplet spun from his nose.

Benny turned away. He leaned on his rifle and tried to get his breath without taking the frozen air too deeply into his lungs. Beside Benny, three of his cousins lay back on the snow, their coats open at the throat and steaming. Benny and they had just finished driving the big timber where the snow was hip deep in places. Benny's father, his uncles, and his grandfather had been on stands waiting for the deer to break out. But there had been no deer.

Benny looked down the field to his grandfather. The grandfather's gray Ford sat parked in the northeast corner of the hayfield, alongside a low patch of brush. The brush broke the outline of the Ford, shielded it from the timber and from the eyes of any deer that might try to come east across the open snow. A yard-wide oval of carbon blackened the snow beneath the Ford's tailpipe. To keep warm, his grandfather ran the motor all day. And by its constancy, the Ford's dull, thumping idle was a part of the landscape of pines and snow and fields, a sound that, like a steady breeze, went unnoticed until it died. But during deer season, the Ford's pumping rhythm never ceased.

Benny wondered if his grandfather got lonely, there in the car all day. He knew his grandfather took with him only a cold egg sandwich, a thermos of Sanka, and the old twelve-gauge shotgun with a single slug—"In case one tries to come east," as the old man said every year.

The grandfather no longer carried his own deer rifle, the silvery Winchester Model 94, because Benny had it. Benny's father and uncles decided those things. They awarded the rifle to Benny because they believed the grandfather's eyes too dim to make good use of the rifle, and because, at age sixteen, Benny was the oldest grandchild.

Benny felt of the rifle, drew his glove along the worn walnut stock. He thought of walking on to the Ford to talk with his grandfather, but his burning lungs and thighs said no to the snowy road ahead. Today, however, was the last day of deer season. They would not have to hunt tomorrow, and Benny would visit him then. He would make lunch, scrambled eggs and toast and cranberry jelly and Sanka, for his grandfather. And then they would sit together by the oil burner and listen to the radio.

"Well, that's it for this year," Benny's father said, and cursed again.

Benny turned. Across the bluing snow, two fluorescent orange hunting caps swam out from the timber's shadow. Drawing light from air, the hats bobbed toward Benny and the others in separate rhythms. They were the last of the drivers. There was now no chance for the deer.

"Weren't nothing in there," one of the cousins muttered from the snow.

"Hell," Benny's father said quickly. "There's deer tracks goin' into that timber but none comin' out. What does that tell you? It tells me you drivers got too spread out and the deer got back through you."

None of the drivers said anything because Benny's father was mostly right. Some of the cousins had gotten disoriented by the gray, sunless sky and had wandered in and out of the drive line. Other cousins, tired of the deep snow, walked the higher ridge trails instead of working through the bottom brush in the draws and holes. The deer, a great buck along with some does, had not stirred.

Maybe the deer weren't in the timber in the first place, Benny thought. Though he had seen the buck's tracks earlier in the day, had seen the buck himself in the alfalfa and cornfields all that fall, by now Benny barely believed in the gray-brown ghosts.

A hundred yards away, the orange caps rode bodies now: Benny's Uncle Karl and another cousin. "So where'd they go?" Karl called across the snow as if to get in the first word.

Benny's father spit.

"They didn't cross south," Karl continued, waving his rifle. "They didn't go west because of the lake. And they didn't come north because you were there. Unless you didn't see 'em."

"They didn't come north," Benny's father said, a tic of anger working his forehead.

The cousins were all standing now.

"Hell, I don't know," Karl muttered. "Maybe they're hiding under these goddam pickups." His boot thudded against the fender, and snow fell over the tire.

"Maybe they came east, through here," one of the cousins said.

"Then Grandpa would have seen them," Benny answered immediately.

The hunters all looked, first to Benny, and then down the field to the grandfather's Ford. But Karl turned his back on the grandfather.

"Hell, the way his eyes are these days, he couldn't see a deer if it jumped over his car."

Benny turned quickly to his father, who only looked down and kicked snow from his boots as he nodded in agreement.

"Honk the horn for him," Karl said, jerking his head toward the Ford, "and let's go home."

"I will—I will—" Two of the youngest cousins scrambled to be first into the pickups. The horns blared across the fields and their echoes wavered back from the timberline. The others began to case their rifles but Benny remained standing, angered at his father and uncle. He waited for the Ford's brake lights to blink on red, for the race of the engine and the black blossom of exhaust.

But the Ford's idle pulsed evenly on. There was no blink of light, no black smoke, nothing. From the side of his eye Benny saw his father, gun half cased, look up and freeze. The others straightened and stared downfield to the Ford. White-faced and wide-eyed, the cousins at the pickup horns now looked about as if they had done some terrible wrong.

"Honk again," Benny's father said with an odd slowness.

The horns blared and the timber honked back the faded replies.

"Again," Karl said quickly.

At the third honking there was motion by the Ford, brown motion from the brush alongside the car. Three deer uncoiled from the bushes, their white tails flagged up and bouncing. Behind Benny someone scrambled for a rifle. "No!" Benny's father shouted.

The big buck and two does leaped a car's length in front of the Ford and then ran straight away north. The buck's antlers flashed through a last slant of sunlight, and then all three deer disappeared into the shadow of the timber.

"Holy Christ—" someone began, but stopped. In the silence, the Ford's thumping idle beat in the air like the heart of the fields.

"Grandpa!" Benny cried. He ran toward the Ford, tearing off his coat for speed, outdistancing the others. As he neared the car he saw his grandfather slumped in the front seat. Benny tore open the door.

"What? Whoa!" his grandfather exclaimed with a start. "You scared me there, Benny!"

"Grandpa! Are you—didn't you hear us honk?"

The grandfather blinked. The white wisps of his eyebrows moved as he thought. "I don't rightly know," he finally said. "I guess I heard, but then I thought I was dreaming. Or something like that. I wasn't sleeping, nosir. But I was dreaming, somehow...." His voice trailed off. The others were there now, crowding around the car. Benny held onto his grandfather; he buried his face in the roughness and the woody smell of the old wool coat and held his grandfather tight.

"Here now, Benny," the old man said, "where's your coat? It ain't July, you know."

One of the cousins had retrieved Benny's coat, and he stood up to put it on. His grandfather looked around at the hunters. "Any luck today, boys?"

No one said anything. Then Benny's father answered. "No, no luck today, Dad."

The grandfather shook his head. "Guess we'll have to eat track soup this year. And that's thin eating, I always said."

Benny's father nodded.

"Everybody out?" the grandfather asked, squinting across to the timber.

"Everybody's out," Karl answered.

"Well, guess I'll drive on home, then, and get myself a hot cup of Sanka."

The Ford's engine raced, the car lurched forward from its melted bed of snow and then moved evenly away from the hunters. They all stood silently as the Ford receded up the snowy field road toward the yellow yard light and the buildings.

"Sanka," Benny's father said quietly, to no one in particular. "That's not even real coffee."

"How does he drink that stuff, anyway," Karl said softly, he too expecting no reply.

Then they all inspected the deer beds. They pointed here and there in the snow, shaking their heads all the while. Finally, they finished loading the pickups and then drove in the grandfather's tracks that led up to his house and then beyond, to the county road that forked away to their own farms and homes. But tonight the chain of headlights behind Benny and his father did not pass through the grandfather's yard. One by one the trucks turned in and parked. Doors thudded. Laughter hung in the frosty air as the Hansens, all of them, converged on the yellow lights of the grandfather's house.

Cloud

JOY WILLIAMS

It was spring break, it was Easter week. Rusty's parents were giving a party but she was going downtown with her friend Caroline. Her sister, Steffie, was helping with the party. This was in Key West where everyone came for the spring, but Rusty and Steffie's parents lived there.

"You look nice, Steffie," Rusty said.

Steffie's shoulders were sunburnt like a child's. There was a thin line of sweat above her lip, and that was childish and dear, too, to Rusty. Steffie had thick, short blond hair, beautiful hair that was almost white, and she was wearing new black and white shoes and a sundress with little black polka dots on it.

Steffie's eyes wandered behind her thick glasses. She patted Rusty's hand.

"Buster and David are coming, Alexander and Joan, John and Lucy...."

"Everyone's coming, that's right," Rusty said.

"I like Buster and David. I liked it out there on the boat."

Buster and his friend David had gotten married just the week before on a boat, and all their friends had been on the boat with them. They sailed out to just where the clear turquoise tropical Atlantic meets the inky dark waters of the Gulf Stream. A lot of homosexual people liked getting married out there, along that line. The great Gulf Stream was rough and deep and almost black; it was strange. And then there was the bright clear water.

"Can only men get married out there?"

"No, no, anybody can get married out there if they want."

"I'll never get married," Steffie said. "I don't want to."

Out in the garden, their mother was saying, "Oh, my God, Eric, look at *this*!" Eric was their father. He was tall and bald and wearing a seersucker suit. He was not their real father, who had left when Steffie was three. The man in the seersucker suit was often described as being a saint. Their real father was far from being a saint. He lived up the Keys on a boat named *Sloop du Jour*. Rusty was embarrassed for him because he was such a jerk. When Steffie was three, he had just bailed out.

Everyone was looking up at the telephone line that led into the house.

"That is so disgusting," Caroline said.

A hawk on the line was tearing apart a pigeon. The pigeon's eyes were shut and it fit neatly between the hawk's shaggy legs. Feathers drifted down to the capped cistern upon which the bar was set.

Eric waved his arms. He threw an ice cube. He threw another ice cube, and the hawk rose and flew grandly off into a nearby sapodilla tree.

"Oh, honestly," their mother said.

It was Caroline's birthday and she was taking Rusty out to dinner. Then they were going to hit all the bars and cafés but they had to be back by midnight. Rusty thought her parents let her get away with a lot because of Steffie, but she didn't actually want to get away with that much. Caroline was visiting her from school. They went to boarding school together and both had one more year to go. Rusty had already chosen her courses for next year: Art History, The Vietnam War, Aesthetics of Music, and Spanish. It all seemed a little vague. Most of her friends were going to be in Conspiracy Theories, with particular emphasis on the Kennedy assassinations, but she hadn't been able to get into that course. Too many people had signed up for it, so they had chosen the class by lottery. So there she was. A lot of people had been disappointed. One of her best friends was stuck taking Plants Useful to Man, which was the most odious and maddening course of all, particularly if, like your friend, you were not much of a humanist and would spend most of your time trying to find plants useless to man, plants that just existed in their own way, for other purposes, which apparently, according to the creepy woman with chin hairs who taught the course, were very few. This friend wasn't going to be able to visit her, which was too bad, but there were other friends who were going to come down: Lucy and Leslie and Lauren. Her mother couldn't keep them straight. Rusty's favorite course was one she was taking this semester in Beliefs. She was reading *The Cloud of Unknowing*, which was a fourteenth-century English mystical text propounding the *via negativa* approach to the incomprehensibility of God. Rusty felt dumb using foreign phrases, so she almost always said "the negative way" instead of *vía negativa.* It was a nice little book. It was hard getting into it, but that was only right.

Caroline wanted to go to Coc'Cola's but when they got there she didn't like it because the lounge was decorated with big black-and-white photographs of good-looking young men holding infants, which Caroline thought was antifeminist. So they went to the Kraals, which was fun.

"Do you know that Mr. Wheatley has a set of 'A Day in the Life of Bobby Kennedy' bubble gum cards?" Caroline said. "I didn't even know they existed." Mr. Wheatley was teaching Conspiracy Theories, and Caroline had gotten in the course.

"Ask me if I care," Rusty said. Everybody said that.

Caroline wanted to go to Louie's, but Rusty was sure they'd get carded there so they went to The Captain's instead. As they were walking down Duval, a boy on the other side of the street yelled, "She's got those pants!" and fell down on his knees as though in awe. It was true Caroline did have the pants; they were the only thing she got for her birthday, practically. They were the most famous, stylish pants. Caroline had almost had a heart attack when her luggage didn't arrive with her on the connection from Miami, though nobody's luggage ever did. It all came in ten or twelve hours later. But Caroline had said that was it, she was never going to check a bag through with those pants in them again.

They were drinking beer. It was Corona that year. Everyone was drinking it. Still, it was good beer. After a while, they went to another place, the Club Exile, and sat at a table overlooking the street. The streets were full of people. A man with an iguana on his shoulder strolled by.

"The Keys are so great," Caroline said.

Some boys sat down at the table with them. They were drinking something they called a Fuzzy Navel, but that couldn't be the right name, Rusty thought; who would name a drink that? Later in the night, most people switched to Kamikazes or Margaritas or gin and grapefruit, which she had heard called Greyhounds, but other people said no, that was a Salty Dog, though she had always thought a Salty Dog was vodka and grapefruit juice.

"So where are you from?" Caroline asked one of the boys. When he told her, she was delighted. "That's where my fake ID is from," she said. He had five driver's licenses from different states. The other boy was talking to Rusty. He was from out west and he was talking about lightning and rocks and driving around. When you were from out west that's what you talked about. He was asking her if she wanted to see sunrise. Sunrise was better than sunset, he said, not so many people. Rusty looked at her watch. "It's eleven-thirty," she said, and they all laughed, but she and Caroline got up to go home then and they said goodbye. The one boy said to the other boy, "So what do you want to do?" "I suggest we hang out," the other boy said.

Caroline and Rusty were quiet walking back, even tired; they didn't want to admit it. Rusty was thinking about her little book. She really was reading it. *Work hard and with all speed in this nothing and this nowhere.* She liked that. She liked, too, how whoever wrote *The Cloud* talked about time. How it was very precious and you knew it was precious because we are never given two moments of time side by side, but only in succession. It was a weird little book. No one knew who wrote it. What was nice about it was that you couldn't talk about it really; that was the whole point.

"I'm going up and say good night to Steffie," Rusty said when they got home.

"Say good night to her for me," Caroline said.

Steffie's room was in the eyebrow of the house, beneath the eaves. It was the best room, Rusty thought. It was full of toy animals and had a rose Chinese rug. When Steffie was little, it wasn't difficult for her really, but now it was getting hard.

"Don't you want to get undressed for bed now, Steffie?" Rusty said. "It's late. Do you want me to help you?"

"I like these shoes an awful lot. I hate to take them off yet." Steffie was sitting on her bed, turning her feet this way and that.

"How was the party?"

"It was a nice party," Steffie said. "I served the shrimp and the green stuff made with alligator pears. I met the man who was formerly the handsomest man in town, and I met a woman who had almost forfeited her life while bathing." Steffie talked this way sometimes. People thought it was delightful. "Do you remember the lady we waved to from the car, the one who waved at us?"

"When was this?" Rusty said.

"Last year, I think it was. Well, I wonder who that lady is."

"I don't know. Just a nice lady."

"Do you think she knew we thought her house was pretty, and the flowers, or do you think she thought we were someone she knew?"

"I think she knew we thought her house was pretty."

"I think of other places," Steffie said. "When I'm there, I think of here. I wish I didn't do that."

"What are you thinking of now? We've been here a long time."

"You haven't been here, Rusty. You've been at school in that snowy place. But I'm not thinking of anyplace right now."

"We're going snorkeling tomorrow, Steffie. It's going to be a beautiful day."

Steffie swung her head back and forth. "I'm too big to go snorkeling."

Rusty's heart lurched. "Steffie, you love snorkeling. Nobody gets too big for that. What happened at the party? Nothing happened at the party, did it?"

"People are kind to me, Rusty," Steffie said. She took off her new shoes and carefully put them side by side next to the bed.

It would get harder for Steffie, everyone knew, even Steffie. There wasn't anything to do about this. Outside, a breeze made the palm fronds rustle. It was one of the prettiest sounds there was.

Every time Rusty came back, Steffie was stopping one more thing.

"You love lying on the water and looking down at the reef. It makes you happy," Rusty said. "Can't you remember?"

"I haven't forgotten it, I just can't remember it," Steffie said. "It's better not to have forgotten it maybe."

Rusty didn't want her stopping one more thing, but nothing she could say would make the difference. Rusty looked at the shoes, then back at Steffie. But the shoes were still there at the corner of her eye.

"Don't be scared," Steffie said. That was what she said to them when she went into the hospital the last time. She had said it the first time too: Don't be scared, to them.

Downstairs, Caroline was still awake. She told Rusty she'd been thinking about the boy with the five driver's licenses. She wondered if she would see him again. She told Rusty she remembered this from the last year she visited. If you liked somebody you'd better make some plans because people didn't stay around this place forever.

NOTES ON CONTRIBUTORS

Alan Cheuse, the author of two short story collections, three novels, and a memoir, serves as book commentator for National Public Radio's *All Things Considered* as well as host and Producer of the NPR/PEN Syndicated Fiction Project co-production, *The Sound of Writing*. He teaches in the writing program at George Mason University in Fairfax, Virginia. The memoir *Fall Out of Heaven*, the story collection *The Tennessee Waltz*, and the novel *The Light Possessed* are his most recent books. A native of New Jersey, he now lives in Washington, D.C.

Caroline Marshall was raised in Minnesota, where she worked as a newspaper reporter, foundation administrator, and poet-in-the-schools before migrating to Washington, D.C., where she continued to teach and served as poet-in-residence at Children's Hospital for eight years. She has held several fellowships in poetry and is the author of *Fugitive Grace*, a collection of poems. In 1987 she became Director of the PEN Syndicated Fiction Project and Executive Producer of *The Sound of Writing*.

Richard Bausch's stories appear regularly in *The Atlantic, Esquire*, and *The New Yorker*, and frequently in *Best American Short Stories* as well. He is the author of four novels and two collections of stories, his latest being *The Fireman's Wife and Other Stories*. His novel *Take Me Back* and his story collection *Spirits* were both nominated for the PEN Faulkner Award for Fiction. He lives in Virginia and teaches at George Mason University.

Edward Abbey lived most of his life in the Southwest, where he worked for many years, part-time, as a ranger with the National Park Service and as a firefighter with the U.S. Forest Service, until his untimely death in 1989. The author of numerous novels, he is perhaps best known for *Desert Solitaire* and *The Monkey Wrench Gang*. Among his recent books are a collection, *One Life at a Time, Please*, and a novel, *Fool's Progress*, both of which appeared in 1988.

Steve Amick's work has appeared in *Phoebe, ACM* (Another Chicago Magazine), and the *Laurentian*. A native of Michigan, he now lives in northern Virginia, where he has his own rock band, "Steve Amick & His Own Worst Enemies."

Rick Bass is originally from the South but currently makes his home on a ranch in Montana. His stories have been anthologized in both *Best American Short Stories* and *Prize Stories 1989: The O. Henry Awards*. His first collection, *The Watch*, appeared in 1989, followed by *Oil Notes*, an essay and memoir about oil prospecting, and *Winter, Notes from Montana*.

Charles Baxter is the author of three short story collections, *Harmony of the World, Through the Safety Net*, and *A Relative Stranger*, as well as a novel, *First Light*, and a book of poetry titled *Imaginary Paintings*. He teaches at the University of Michigan in Ann Arbor, where he also makes his home.

Madison Smartt Bell is a native of Nashville who now lives in Baltimore, where he teaches at Goucher College. He is the author of six novels, the most recent being *Doctor Sleep*. In 1987 he published his first story collection, *Zero db*. His second, *Barking Man*, appeared in 1990. His novel *Soldier's Joy* won the Lillian Smith Award in 1989.

Gina Berriault was born in California, where she has continued to live, writing short stories, novels, and film scripts. The recipient of numerous fellowships, she has also taught at the University of Iowa and at San Francisco State. Her most recent books are *The Lights of the Earth*, a novel, and *The Infinite Passion of Expectation*, a collection of stories.

Lucienne S. Bloch received the American Academy of Poets Prize while a student at Wellesley College. Her novels include *On the Great-Circle Route*, which was published in 1979, and *Finders Keepers*, which came out in 1982. Her most recent is *Sightings*. In 1979 she also contributed to the "Hers" column for the *New York Times*. Born in Belgium, she now lives in New York City.

Roy Blount, Jr.'s collections include *One Fell Soup: or I'm Just a Bug on the Windshield of Life, Not Exactly What I Had in Mind*, and *Now Where Were We?* A book about the Pittsburgh Steelers, *About*

Three Bricks Shy . . . and the Load Filled Up, appeared in 1989, and *First Hubby*, a novel, in 1990. He lives in New York City.

T. Coraghessan Boyle is a native of Peekskill, New York, who now lives in Los Angeles. He is the author of six works of fiction, including *Budding Prospects, Greasy Lake, World's End*, which won the PEN Faulkner Award in 1987, and *East Is East*. His most recent collection of stories, *If the River Was Whiskey*, came out in 1989. Boyle teaches at U.S.C.

Ethan Canin grew up in California, where he returned briefly after studying medicine in Massachusetts. While still in medical school, he began publishing stories in *The Atlantic, Esquire*, and *Ploughshares*. His first collection, *The Emperor of the Air*, won the Houghton Mifflin Literary Fellowship. He lives in San Francisco.

Elizabeth Cox lives and writes in Durham, North Carolina, where she also teaches at Duke University. Her stories have appeared in *Antaeus, American Short Fiction*, and other magazines. Her novels are *Familiar Ground* and the recently published *The Ragged Way People Fall Out of Love*.

Nicholas Delbanco is the author of nearly a dozen novels, including *The Sherbrookes Trilogy*, two story collections, and several books of nonfiction. The co-founder, with the late John Gardner, of the Bennington Writing Workshops, Delbanco now serves as Director of the University of Michigan's Writing Program and the prestigious Hopwood Awards. His latest book, a collection of stories called *The Writers' Trade*, appeared in 1990. He lives in Ann Arbor.

Robert Dunn lives in New York City, where he teaches fiction writing at The New School for Social Research. His work has appeared in the *New York Times, The New Yorker*, and *The Atlantic* as well as numerous other magazines and *Prize Stories 1980: The O. Henry Awards*.

Louise Erdrich became widely known for her first novel, *Love Medicine*, which won the Book Critics Circle Award for Fiction in 1985. *The Beet Queen* followed in 1987 and *Tracks* in 1988. With her husband and collaborator, Michael Dorris, she recently published the novel *The Crown of Columbus*. She is also the author of two volumes of poetry, *Jacklight* and *The Baptism of Desire*, the latter published in 1990. She lives in New Hampshire.

Rosario Ferré was born in Puerto Rico, where she returned after receiving her education on the U.S. mainland, to create the literary magazine *Zona de Carga y Descarga*. Both a novelist and a short story writer, she recently began translating her work into English. Her latest novel is *Sweet Diamond Dust*. A collection of stories, *The Youngest Doll*, was published in the spring of 1991. Ferré divides her year between Puerto Rico and Washington, D.C.

Laura Furman, a native of New York City, worked as an editor for several major publishing houses before she moved to Texas, where she now teaches at the University of Texas at Austin and edits the quarterly *American Short Fiction*. She has published two collections of stories, *The Glass House* and *Watch Time Fly*, as well as the novels *The Shadow Line* and *Tuxedo Park*.

George Garrett is the author of thirteen works of fiction, including *The Elizabethan Trilogy, Death of the Fox, The Succession*, and *Entered from the Sun*. Among his awards are the T. S. Eliot Prize for Creative Writing from the Ingersoll Foundation and the PEN Malamud Award for Excellence in the Art of the Short Story. A native of Florida, Garrett currently resides in Charlottesville, Virginia.

Allan Gurganus's best-selling first novel, *Oldest Living Confederate Widow Tells All*, appeared in 1989 and was awarded the Sue Kaufman Prize for First Fiction by the American Academy and Institute of Arts and Letters. Born in western North Carolina, he now lives in New York City. His latest book is the story collection *White People*.

David Michael Kaplan's fiction has appeared in *The Atlantic, Playboy,* and *Redbook*, as well as numerous other magazines. Several of them have also been published in *Best American Short Stories* and *Prize Stories 1990: The O. Henry Awards*. His first short story collection, *Comfort*, came out in 1987. His first novel, *Skating in the Dark*, will appear in the autumn of 1991. He lives in Chicago and teaches at Loyola University.

Janet Kauffman lives in rural Michigan. Her work has appeared in *The New Yorker, Vanity Fair,* and *The Paris Review.* Her novel *Collaborators* was nominated for the PEN Faulkner Award in 1987. She has also published a collection of poems, *The Weather Book,* and two collections of stories, *Places in the World a Woman Could Walk* and *Obscene Gestures for Women.*

James Howard Kunstler is an artist and journalist as well as a writer of fiction. His magazine articles appear frequently in such periodicals as the *New York Times Magazine* and *Adirondack.* His novels include *An Embarrassment of Riches, The Halloween Ball,* and *Thunder Island.* He lives in upstate New York.

Ursula K. Le Guin's many works include novels, stories, essays, and books for children. Among them are the novels *Always Coming Home, The Dispossessed,* and *The Left Hand of Darkness,* as well as the story collections *Buffalo Gals and Other Animal Presences* and *Catwings.* Her *Dreams Must Explain Themselves (Essays on Fantastic Literature)* and *Dancing at the Edge of the World: Thoughts on Words, Women, and Places,* came out in 1988 and 1989, respectively. She lives in Portland, Oregon.

Barry Lopez also makes his home in Oregon. *Of Wolves and Men,* which came out in 1979, *River Notes: The Dance of the Herons* (1980), and the short story collection *Winter Count* early established him as a preeminent writer with a broad range. His subsequent books include *Desert Notes: Reflections in the Eye of a Raven, Crossing Open Ground, Arctic Dreams,* and, with artist Tom Pohrt, *Crow and Weasel.*

Wright Morris is the author of more than twenty books, *The Territory Ahead: Critical Interpretations of American Literature* among them. His fiction includes *Love Among the Cannibals, What a Way to Go, In Orbit, Fire Sermon, A Life,* and *The Field of Vision,* which won the National Book Award in 1956. He was born in Nebraska, the setting of most of his best-known works. He lives in Mill Valley, California.

Lewis Nordan is a Mississippi native who now lives in Pittsburgh, where he teaches at the University of Pittsburgh. He has produced a novel, *The All-Girl Football Team,* which came out in 1989, and two collections of stories, *Welcome to the Arrow-Catcher Fair* and, most recently, *A Hank of Hair, a Piece of Bone*.

Joyce Carol Oates's publications include more than twenty novels and many volumes of short stories, poems, and essays, as well as plays. She lives in Princeton, New Jersey, where she is the Roger S. Berlind Distinguished Lecturer in Creative Writing at Princeton University. Her novel *Them* won the National Book Award in 1970. Her latest books are *Heat and Other Stories* and *Twelve Plays*.

Richard Panek grew up in Chicago, where he worked as a newspaper reporter and editor. A graduate of the Medill School of Journalism and the Iowa Writers Workshop, he now lives with his wife and son in New York City, where he writes both journalism and fiction.

Robert Pinsky is a native of the New Jersey shore who now lives in Newton Falls, Massachusetts, and teaches at Boston University. He is the author of four books of poems, *Sadness and Happiness*, *An Explanation of America*, *History of My Heart*, and *The Want Bone*, which came out in 1989. His collection of essays, *Poetry and the World*, was nominated for the National Book Critics Circle Award in Criticism in 1988.

Reynolds Price was born in North Carolina, where he has continued to spend much of his life, teaching at Duke University and writing stories, novels, essays, and plays, as well as a volume of translations from the Bible. His story collections include *Names and Faces of Heroes* and *Permanent Errors*. His latest novel, *Kate Vaiden*, won the National Book Critics Circle Award in 1987. A memoir of childhood and family, *Clear Pictures*, came out in 1989.

Jude Roy's short stories have appeared in *The Southern Review*, *The Best of Lafayette*, *American Short Fiction*, and *The Southwestern Review*. Roy now lives in South Carolina and teaches English at Clemson University.

Lore Segal was born in Austria and emigrated to the Dominican Republic when Hitler's troops invaded her homeland. She later moved to New York City. Her first book was a memoir, *Other People's Houses*. Among her subsequent books are the novel *Her First*

American and a translation of *Grimm's Fairy Tales*, illustrated by Maurice Sendak. Segal divides her time between New York City and Chicago, where she teaches at the University of Illinois, Chicago Circle.

Mary Lee Settle's many books include the five novels of the Beulah Quintet—*Prisons, O Beulah Land, Know Nothing, The Scapegoat,* and *The Killing Ground*—the award-winning *Blood Tie,* and, most recently, *Charley Bland.* She makes her home in Charlottesville, Virginia.

Susan Richards Shreve lives in Washington, D.C., teaches at George Mason University, and serves as an occasional essayist for the *MacNeil/Lehrer NewsHour.* She is the author, among other books, of the novels *A Fortunate Madness, A Woman Like That, Children of Power, Miracle Play, Dreaming of Heroes, Queen of Hearts, A Country of Strangers,* and the recent *Daughters of the New World.*

Darcey Steinke's first novel, *Up Through the Water,* appeared in 1989. A Virginia native, she now lives in Brooklyn, where she is at work on a new book.

Elizabeth Tallent lives in California, where she teaches at U.C. Davis. Her books include two collections of stories, *In Constant Flight* and *Time with Children,* and the novel *Museum Pieces.*

John Updike's most recent book is the Pulitzer Prize-winning novel *Rabbit at Rest,* the fourth in a series that includes *Rabbit Is Rich,* which won the Pulitzer Prize in 1981. Prolific as an essayist, poet, and critic as well as a short story writer and novelist, he has published dozens of books. His collections of stories include *Museums and Women and Other Stories, The Music School, Pigeon Feathers and Other Stories,* and *Problems and Other Stories.* He lives in Beverly Farms, Massachusetts.

Will Weaver lives in Minnesota, which provides the setting for much of his work. *Red Earth, White Earth,* a novel, appeared in 1986 and was subsequently adapted for television. A collection of stories, *A Gravestone Made of Wheat,* came out in 1989. He teaches at Bemidji State College.

Joy Williams writes both novels and short stories. The former include *Breaking and Entering, The Changeling,* and *State of Grace,* which came out in 1989. She has written two collections of stories, *Taking Care* and *Escapes.* She divides her time among the states of Arizona, Connecticut, and Florida.

ACKNOWLEDGMENTS

"Drunk in the Afternoon" © 1989 by Edward Abbey. Broadcast summer 1989. First published in the *Chicago Tribune Magazine* (June 25, 1989) and the *Oregonian* (July 30, 1989).

"Unnaturally Warm for October" © 1989 by Steve Amick. Broadcast fall 1989.

"Heartwood" © 1989 by Rick Bass. Broadcast fall 1989. Previously published in the *Chicago Tribune Magazine* (March 4, 1990) and *The Best of the West #3* (Gibbs Smith, 1990).

"Lake Stephen" © 1989 by Charles Baxter. Broadcast fall 1989. First published in the *Chicago Tribune Magazine* (November 5, 1989). Reprinted from *A Relative Stranger* (1990) by permission of W. W. Norton & Co.

"Mr. Potatohead in Love" © 1989 by Madison Smartt Bell. Broadcast summer 1989. Reprinted from *Barking Man* (1990) by permission of Ticknor & Fields.

"The Overcoat" © 1989 by Gina Berriault. Broadcast summer 1989. First published in *American Short Fiction* (Vol. 1, No. 2, Summer 1991), the University of Texas Press at Austin.

"Days of Oaks, Years of Salt" © 1986 by Lucienne S. Bloch. Broadcast summer 1989. Previously published in the *San Francisco Chronicle* (October 26, 1986), *State Magazine* (October 10, 1986), the *Village Advocate* (October 19, 1986), and the *Albuquerque Journal* (October 21, 1986).

"The Way Mama Tells It" © 1989 by Roy Blount, Jr. Broadcast summer 1989. First published, in a slightly longer version, in *The Atlantic* (July 1989).

"The Little Chill" © 1989 by T. Coraghessan Boyle. Broadcast summer 1989. Reprinted from *If the River Was Whiskey* (1989) by permission of Viking Penguin.

"Angel of Mercy, Angel of Death" © 1989 by Ethan Canin. Broadcast summer 1989.

"Old Court" © 1989 by Elizabeth Cox. Broadcast fall 1989. First published in *American Short Fiction* (Vol. 1, No. 1, Spring 1991), the University of Texas Press at Austin.

"Dying for Some Time" © 1989 by Nicholas Delbanco. Broadcast fall 1989.

"The River Song" © 1989 by Robert Dunn. Broadcast fall 1989.

"The Immaculate Conception of Carson DuPre" © 1983 by Louise Erdrich. First broadcast winter 1987. First published in the *Arizona Republic* (December 1983).

"The Dreamer's Portrait" © 1976 and 1989 by Rosario Ferré. Broadcast summer 1989. Reprinted from *The Youngest Doll* (1991) by permission of the University of Nebraska Press.

"That Boy" © 1989 by Laura Furman. Broadcast summer 1990.

"The Right Thing to Do at the Time" © 1989 by George Garrett. Broadcast summer 1989.

"Nativity, Caucasian" © 1987 by Allan Gurganus. Broadcast spring 1988. Previously published in the *Village Advocate* (November 22, 1987), the *Chicago Tribune Magazine* (December 6, 1987), the *St. Petersburg Times* (December 12, 1987), and *Harper's* (1990). Reprinted from *White People* (1991) by permission of Alfred A. Knopf.

"Piano Lessons" © 1989 by David Michael Kaplan. First published in *American Short Fiction* (Vol. 1, No. 2, Summer 1991), the University of Texas Press at Austin.

"The Shirt" © 1989 by Janet Kauffman. Broadcast fall 1989.

"Doom" © 1989 by James Howard Kunstler. Broadcast fall 1989.

"Texts" © 1990 by Ursula K. Le Guin. Broadcast summer 1990. First published in the *Oregonian* (May 27, 1990) and *American Short Fiction* (Vol. 1, No. 1, Spring 1991), the University of Texas Press at Austin.

"Remembering Orchards" © 1990 by Barry Lopez. Broadcast fall 1990. First published in the *Oregonian* (January 6, 1991) and *American Short Fiction* (Vol. 1, No. 3, Summer 1991), the University of Texas Press at Austin.

"What's New, Love?" © 1989 by Wright Morris. Broadcast summer 1989. First published in *American Short Fiction* (Vol. 1, No. 3, Fall 1991), the University of Texas Press at Austin.

"Owls" © 1991 by Lewis Nordan. Broadcast fall 1991.

"Where *Is* Here?" © 1989 by Joyce Carol Oates. Broadcast summer 1989. First published in the *Chicago Tribune Magazine* (April 1, 1990) and *American Short Fiction* (Vol. 1, No. 1, Spring 1991), the University of Texas Press at Austin.

"Something to Do with Baseball" © 1988 by Richard Panek. Broadcast spring 1988. First published in the *Chicago Tribune Magazine* (April 5, 1987), the *San Francisco Chronicle* (April 19, 1987), the *Sacramento Bee* (May, 1987), the *Village Advocate* (May 3, 1987), and *America Illustrated* (1990), a publication of the U.S. Information Agency.

"Salt Water Jews" © 1989 by Robert Pinsky. Broadcast fall 1989.

"A New Stretch of Woods" © 1989 by Reynolds Price. Broadcast fall 1989. First published in *The Leader* (August 31, 1989) and the *Chicago Tribune Magazine* (December 12, 1989).

"Le Traiteur" © 1989 by Jude Roy. First published in *American Short Fiction* (Vol. 1, No. 3, Fall 1991), the University of Texas Press at Austin.

"The Movie Murders, or the Killer in the Cast" © 1989 by Lore Segal. Broadcast fall 1989.

"Pineville" © 1990 by Mary Lee Settle. Broadcast summer 1990.

"The Locker Room" © 1989 by Susan Richards Shreve. Broadcast fall 1989.

"My Father's Girlfriends" © 1989 by Darcey Steinke. Broadcast fall 1989. First published in the *Chicago Tribune Magazine* (April 4, 1989).

"No One's a Mystery" © 1985 by Elizabeth Tallent. Broadcast spring 1988. First published in *Newsday* (January 27, 1985) and the *Cincinnati Enquirer* (January 13, 1985). Reprinted from *Time with Children* (1987) by permission of Alfred A. Knopf.

"The Football Factory" © 1989 by John Updike. Broadcast summer 1989.

"Grandfather, Heart of the Fields" © 1984 by Will Weaver. Broadcast fall 1989. First published in the *Chicago Tribune Magazine* (September 9, 1984), the *Hartford Courant* (October 14, 1984), the *San Francisco Chronicle* (October 21, 1984), and the *Kansas City Star* (December 9, 1984). Reprinted from *A Gravestone Made of Wheat* (1990) by permission of Graywolf Press.

"Cloud" © 1989 by Joy 'Williams. Broadcast summer 1989.